C000197936

Also by R.W Peake

Marching with Caesar-Conquest of Gaul

Marching with Caesar-Civil War

Marching with Caesar-Antony and Cleopatra, Parts I & II

Critical praise for the Marching with Caesar series:

"Fans of the author will be delighted that Peake's writing has gone from strength to strength in this, the second volume...Peake manages to portray Pullus and all his fellow soldiers with a marvelous feeling of reality quite apart from the star historical name... There's history here, and character, and action enough for three novels, and all of it can be enjoyed even if readers haven't seen the first volume yet. Very highly recommended."
~The Historical Novel Society

"The hinge of history pivoted on the career of Julius Caesar, as Rome's Republic became an Empire, but the muscle to swing that gateway came from soldiers like Titus Pullus. What an amazing story from a student now become the master of historical fiction at its best."
~Professor Frank Holt, University of Houston

Marching with Caesar

Rise of Augustus

Volume Six

By R.W. Peake

Marching with Caesar –Rise of Augustus by R.W. Peake

List of Maps

Foreword

As the career, and story, of Titus Pullus moves along towards its conclusion, it creates in me a unique mix of emotions. On the one hand, it's hugely gratifying to see so many readers take an interest in this story of a man from the ranks of the Legions of Rome, who, by an accident of birth finds himself living during the most tumultuous and impactful period of Roman history. Yet, on the other, it's probably no surprise that I've become extremely attached to Titus and all that he represents, but like all stories, we are nearing the end of his particular journey, so it will be hard to say goodbye nonetheless. And this, what will be the penultimate book in the Marching With Caesar that revolves around Titus, took me into largely uncharted territory, the nebulous world of what historians now call the Early Imperial period, at least as far as the Legions of Rome are concerned.

I have made a point in my earlier books, and I think it bears repeating here, that the biggest problem I found in researching this part of the story is the dearth of sources, at least those that go into any level of detail about what are now called the Augustan Reforms. While there is an abundance of material that give scholars, enthusiasts and authors a huge amount of details about the organization, training, and life in the Legions of Imperial Rome, starting later in the reign of Augustus, the same can't be said for the period of time when the reforms were taking shape. Just as the political landscape of Rome didn't change overnight, going through a long and gradual, albeit bloody, process, I believe that the same standard applies to the reforms that Augustus wrought on a Roman army that consisted of more than forty Legions, spread over the entire Republic.

This is why some of the purists among my readers might experience a head-scratching moment or two as they think, "But wait. Camp Prefects didn't do that!" or "Tribunes were responsible for this!" However, just as the powers of the political office that we now call the Emperor of Rome evolved over the course of Augustus' long reign, I would argue that the same process applies to these reforms. Perhaps they didn't; maybe these reforms just appeared from within Augustus' prodigious brain exactly as they are now known, but not only would that be extremely unlikely in my opinion, it would make for a more boring story as far as Titus is concerned!

That said, it's not strictly for narrative purposes that I meddle with Augustus' refinements to the Legions. Perhaps it's also because of my overall ambivalence towards the man himself that makes me loath to not have some trial and error when it comes to his changes with the Legions, because although I can't deny his overall brilliance, the more I learn of the man, the less I like him. My personal feelings aside, creating this atmosphere of a state of flux, where the men of every level of Roman society are feeling their way along in what was inarguably a new Rome is a crucial aspect of Titus' story, in both the macro sense of Roman sociopolitical landscape, and the micro of Titus' own struggle to improve his lot in life.

As far as I have been able to ascertain, there was no Army of Pannonia, at least not one with any formal name. And while Siscia (modern-day Sisak) was certainly a base for the Legions stationed in Pannonia, there's no source that I found that gives a definitive date for the creation of a depot there. It was used by the future emperor Tiberius as his base of operations in quelling the revolts that were a regular occurrence in the decades after the conquest of the province, so I took the liberty of establishing a Legion presence there perhaps earlier than actually happened. Also, the composition of this fictional Army of Pannonia is entirely my own invention; I have no idea which Legions were stationed in Siscia.

Finally, thanks again goes to my editor Beth Lynn of BZHercules, for helping me get Titus' story into a coherent form and catching my many mistakes. Marina Shipova's outstanding cover art again helps tell Titus' story by making the statue of Augustus that is in the Museo Nazionale Romano come alive; I particularly like the look he's giving Titus! Also, to my team of advance readers; Joe Corso, Margaret Courtney, Jim Zipko, Stu MacPherson and Ute St. Clair, a big thanks for their suggestions, comments and, most importantly, catching those mistakes that only true fans can spot! And as always, thanks to you, the readers for taking such an interest in Titus' story, and I hope you enjoy this part of his journey.

R.W. Peake
July, 2013

Prologue

Because of my status here in Arelate, my presence is expected on all major holidays and festivals, but very early on I disabused the duumviri of the idea of my participation in any of these that held religious connotations. I cannot say that it has not caused me some difficulties, but when I made a vow to stop asking the gods for their intercession and aid, very early in my tenure as Camp Prefect, I was serious about it.

Unfortunately, some men are too thick and the *duumviri* did not know me well enough at the time to take me at my word, leading to an incident about which I still have some regret, even if they got what they deserved.

It was for the festival of Quinquatrus, my first such since my arrival in Arelate. Despite Diocles' best attempts to convince the delegation of town elders that their mission was ill-conceived and doomed to failure, they insisted that they be led into my private study. This is my sanctuary, my refuge, and only Diocles and Agis, my longest-serving companions and servants, are allowed entry. This is where I have dictated the story of my life, and I spend most of my time indoors and awake in this room, reading, and reflecting. I am proud of my library, but I also know that should other Romans of Arelate who are of the upper classes see my extensive collection of books it would cause me more trouble than any boost to my pride is worth. There's Pullus, I am sure they would say, putting on airs and getting ideas above his station, thinking that just because he has been elevated to the equestrian order, he *is* an equestrian, like us. And as I have learned, to many, perhaps most, of the upper classes, this makes me dangerous.

Therefore, I was in a sour frame of mind, when Diocles returned after I had sent him to inform the delegation standing in the *triclinium* of my indisposition to visitors at that moment.

"Titus, they won't take no for an answer," he told me. "They insist that you give them some of your time. They say it's important."

"It better be," I grumbled, but rather than wear him out by sending him back and forth conducting an argument by proxy, I bade him to bring this group of pests to me.

There were three; two of them I recognized on sight and had actually spoken to both on more than one occasion, while the third was unknown to me. Two were members of at least the equestrian class, while the third man wore the iron ring that told me he was of the Senatorial class. They were also sleek, well-fed, and expensively oiled and barbered, and the fact that they all wore togas told me that this was indeed an official visit of some sort. Standing, I greeted them with as much courtesy as my stewing anger allowed, which latter state they either ignored or weren't aware of, although that would change in the next few moments.

"Salve, Prefect Titus Pullus, late of the Army of Pannonia," the man I assumed was the elected spokesman of the group greeted me.

"Salve, Marcus Glabro," I replied, "and to what do I owe this unexpected surprise?"

I was determined that while I would not be outright rude, I was not going to indulge these men by using words like 'pleasant'.

"I believe you remember Quintus Claudius Varro?" Without waiting for me to answer, I assume because he could see that I did, he indicated the last man, the one wearing the ring, although his toga did not have a purple stripe, which I found odd. "And this is Gaius Valerius Marcellus."

In something of a test, I ignored Glabro and Varro, but offered my hand to Marcellus first, and as I suspected he would, there was a brief hesitation on his part. It was just the barest fraction of an instant, but I am too old and experienced not to recognize the sign of a Roman who believes himself to be superior in any way, deigning to engage in a greeting where both men are equal. Also, as I suspected, when he did grasp my forearm, his arm was as smooth as the bottom of a baby, despite the fact that he was at least my age, if not a few years older.

"Prefect Pullus, it is a pleasure and an honor to finally meet you," he intoned, making it clear that it was anything but what he had just described.

Already tired of this banal dance, I was deliberately insulting, when I turned away and sat in the chair behind my desk, although I did not compound the affront by not asking them to take one of the stools on the opposite side. Diocles, who had been hovering in the background, caught my eye and when I glanced in his direction, he merely lifted an eyebrow in a silent question, to which I gave a brief nod. He disappeared to get wine, and I hoped that he would not bring back any of a decent vintage.

"So you're not here for a chat, I presume," I began, "so perhaps you can tell me the purpose of your visit."

I was somewhat surprised, when it was not the highest-ranking Roman who spoke first.

"As you undoubtedly know, we're just a couple of days away from Quinquatrus," Glabro replied.

When I said nothing, he seemed to get a bit flustered, but pressed on.

"Yes, well, as I was saying, Quinquatrus approaches. And we," he indicated his companions, "are here to persuade you to grace the festival with your presence."

"And why would you want me so badly?" I asked, although I suspected I knew the answer.

"As you know, you're the highest ranking man from the Legions here in Arelate," Glabro explained, unnecessarily. "So it reflects well, not just on the city as a whole, but especially on that segment of our citizens who are also retired from the Legions."

"And I'm sure you know why this is important," it was Varro who interjected this.

I did, very well. A large segment of the men retired from the Legion in and around Arelate had found the transition to civilian life to be difficult. They quickly became bored with the mundane existence that is the lot of their civilian counterparts, and bored men, particularly Legionaries, tend to fill their time in ways of which the upstanding citizens of Arelate would not approve. This was especially true, because a fair number of those activities brought the former Legionaries into direct conflict with their fellow citizens. It was a situation that, even in the short time I had been in Arelate at that point, I could see was not only bad, but was getting worse. When I reflect on it, I would liken it to the way, once a wolf stalks and kills a sheep, he has only a taste for mutton. Once my fellow Legionaries discovered how comparatively soft the other residents of Arelate were, there was a small segment of them that took full advantage of this, terrorizing and intimidating others, mainly for the simple reason that they could. Considering the attitude with which Legionaries, even before they run rampant and are still under the standard, are regarded by many civilians, there was already a built-up hostility on the part of many men. I cannot recount the number of conversations I either overheard or was part of where this attitude of civilians towards Legionaries was discussed, so there was a lot of simmering anger already present when a man settled down. However, unlike most of the men, I distinctly remember the long conversation with my then-Secundus Pilus Prior Sextus Scribonius, the man I also count as my best and most trusted friend even now, when I was the Primus Pilus of what was known as the 10th Equestris. This was during the period of what is now known as the second civil war, in that early period, when the two men who became bitter adversaries were uneasily sharing power. We had been parked on the Campus Martius outside Rome, when this topic of civilians' hostility toward Legionaries had been brought up by one of the other Pili Priores. And it had been my wise friend who, in his quiet but effective way, presented the other side of the argument: how, because of all that we had done in our conquest of Gaul, a situation was created, where the section of the Forum Boarium that sold slaves was glutted, putting so many of the men of our class out of work. As he pointed out, it was not very realistic to think that men who could no longer feed their families, because there is no competing against a service or labor that is essentially free, would view us as anything but the cause of their own misery. It had not surprised me at all that this argument had fallen on deaf ears among the other Centurions, but it was something I remembered, even if other men did not.

"I understand why you're concerned, but I'm not sure what this has to do with me," I countered.

"Because of your reputation," Glabro said quietly, "and if you're seen participating in events like Quinquatrus, it will send a message to others of your," he fumbled for the word, "status."

"Yes, it's as Glabro says," Varrus added, sitting forward on his stool to look at me with what I assume was his earnest expression. "If they see Titus Pullus, *Prefect* Titus Pullus, marching at the head of the procession, and participating in the rituals at the temple of Minerva, we think this would be a huge help in letting those men who are running wild right now know that they should be following your example."

"While I appreciate your faith in me, I can't say that I share it," I told them frankly. "In fact, I'm almost positive that it won't have any impact at all."

"But we must try," Glabro argued, and now there was no mistaking the pleading tone, which clearly disgusted Marcellus, who had been completely silent to this point.

"I agree that you need to try something," I shook my head, pretending that I was actually regretful, "but I don't believe that I'm the solution to your problem."

That was obviously too much for Marcellus, who, with a snort of angry contempt, jumped to his feet, careful to arrange the folds of his toga before he deigned to address me, as if he was about to orate in the Senate.

"I told these two this approach was a waste of time," Marcellus sneered down at the two, who looked suitably embarrassed, although I did not know if it was because of what he said or at Marcellus' outburst, in general. "I've dealt with you Legion types for too long to believe that such soft words would do anything but put you to sleep."

Well, you have that much right, I thought, but I remained silent, just looking steadily at the man, wondering just how much of an idiot he would be, and how angry I would get.

13

"Now, see here, Pullus," giving me the answer to at least the second question, "you need to be at this procession, that's true enough. But you also need to take a more active role in not just this festival, but all official holidays, as well. And," I suppose he was trying to intimidate me with his imperious stare, "you need to take matters into your own hands and get your Legionary...*scum* under control!"

I am not sure what else he was going to say, because I decided to put an end to this fruitless conversation, and I did so by standing up and merely taking a step in Marcellus' direction, confident that my height and bulk—as diminished by age as they were—and just my experience in intimidating men who were much, much harder than Marcellus would be enough to still his tongue. I was correct.

"I've listened to you, now you're going to listen to me," I spoke the words quietly, but I made sure they carried as much menace as I was capable of projecting, and I was pleased to see the color completely leave Marcellus' face, as he took a staggering step backward.

In doing so, he bumped into his stool, which caused him to plop down onto it, but his eyes never left mine. Thankfully, I was too angry to be amused at the comical sight of his sudden demotion, as it were.

"I. Will. Not. Be. In. Your. Festival." I bit each word off, staring down at Marcellus as I did.

I suppose that, since I was not looking in his direction, this emboldened Glabro to squeak a protest.

"But..." was as far as he got.

"*Tacete!*" I roared, and not only did all three men visibly jump from their stools, I was sure I heard some of the scrolls in their pigeonholes rattle, which made me feel a bit better that as old and enfeebled as I may have been, I was still capable of creating a blast of such volume. "I'm not through speaking!"

Out of the corner of my eye I saw that Diocles had just entered the room, carrying a tray with a small jug and four cups, but he immediately turned around and disappeared, without a word spoken. I had to fight a smile at the sight of him scurrying away, no doubt to warn the others that I was in full voice and that some item of furniture was in the last moments of remaining in an intact state, but I managed.

"Look around you," I finally spoke again, and while I was not yelling, I put the *vitus* into my voice—as we used to say— that I had used to such good effect for so many years. Turning slightly away from them, I pointed. "Specifically, look right there."

I was pointing to a small alcove in the far wall that is standard in every Roman villa, at least every one that I've been in. It was completely bare, and I could tell that at least one of the men understood its significance, because I heard him gasp, although he did so as my face was still turned away, so I do not know who it was.

"Tell me what you see," I said.

For a moment, none of them spoke, prompting me to raise my voice again in a demand that someone answer the question.

"Nothing," Varro finally found his tongue. "There's nothing there."

"That's right," I agreed. "And you know why?" Without waiting for an answer, I roared the words I had been longing to say, ever since this trio of fools trooped into my sanctuary, babbling about a religious festival. *"Because I piss on the gods!"*

All three of them immediately made the sign to ward off evil, but I was completely undeterred.

"I piss on the gods," I repeated, "I piss on their cruelty. I piss on their capriciousness and the way they use us mortals as their pets, for their own amusement. I want nothing to do with any beings who can be so cruel and uncaring!"

None of them said a word, and I suppose their silence compelled me to actually offer an explanation, one that had been bottled up inside me for many, many years.

"Let me tell you about my relationship with the gods," I began. "I prayed and made a sacrifice every day to Juno Lucina when I learned that my sister Livia was carrying her husband's child. Granted, the sacrifices weren't much; I was just a youngster, and we were very poor. But I did this every, single day. And yet, she died."

15

I held up one finger.

"I prayed and made sacrifices to both Concordia and Spes to find an answer and see the way to repairing my relationship with my best friend and longest companion, Vibius Domitius, who had been by my side since we were boys. We joined the Legions together; we fought together; we were part of the conquest of Gaul with Divus Julius, but in the first civil war our paths diverged. I can't count the number of sacrifices I made and the prayers I offered for the gods to hear my plea that we reconcile our differences before one or both of us passed into the shade. But Vibius is dead now, and it's too late. In this life anyway."

I held up another.

"I had a family once; a wife, or at least a wife in everything but name," I amended, "and two children, a boy, named for my then-best friend. When I was in Africa and learned of the plague in Brundisium, I spent a small fortune making supplications to Aesculapias, Carna, Febris and even to the god Olloudius, who's worshiped by my woman's tribe, so that my family would be spared. They weren't."

Holding up a third, I continued, "Every year, before a campaign, I would make offerings to Mars, Bellona, and Fortuna, asking them to spare as many of my men as possible. I knew that it was impossible to come out from a campaign unscathed. But in two of the last three campaigns as Primus Pilus of the 10th, I lost two entire Cohorts!"

At the thought of the twin tragedies of losing Nasica's Tenth Cohort in Parthia and Metellus' Third Cohort during the Actium campaign, I felt a sudden catch in my throat as, without warning, the three men began shimmering in front of me. But I refused to shame myself in this manner, no matter how painful this was turning out to be.

"Finally," I suddenly decided that my examples would stop there; there were, and are, other memories, but they are even now still too fresh and raw to touch upon. "I've watched you members of the upper class use the gods in your own way, as a method of controlling the lower classes, playing on their superstitions and fear. And while I've heard more patricians than I can easily recall tell the Head Count that what they do is for the good of Rome, I've only seen that to actually be the case with two men, and two men only." I shook my head. "No, I've earned the right to live the rest of my days as I see fit, and I want no congress with the gods. And," I finished quietly, "anyone, no matter their status or rank, who tries to force me to break my vow will find themselves with a kind of trouble that neither of us wants."

"Are you *threatening* me?" Marcellus gasped, while the other two men were trying to make themselves as small as possible and were examining the mosaic on my floor with great interest.

I did not blame them; it is an exceptionally fine mosaic, although I have a feeling that was not the true cause for their interest in what was under their feet.

"Call it what you like," I replied to Marcellus. "But that was your intent when you came here, wasn't it? As you said yourself, these two," I indicated Glabro and Varro, "were wasting their time trying to reason with me. So you came with the intention of convincing me with some sort of threat, I imagine." I pretended to think about it. "Let me guess; at some point you were going to say something like, 'Augustus will hear about this'?"

The startled look that flashed across his eyes told me what I needed to know, and I heaved a sigh, as I regarded him with a look that I suppose was equal parts contempt and pity.

"Marcellus," I said tiredly, "I've been threatened by not only men, but by Cleopatra herself, a woman who was more dangerous than you in every way imaginable. You're just another empty toga, and this conversation is over."

Looking down at the other two, I did feel some sympathy for them. In fact, I could not fault their motives. It was just that they had made a very poor choice in me.

Yes, I am a wealthy man; I am an equestrian, and I retired at the highest rank available to a boy born on a dirt-poor farm in Baetica. In fact, I have achieved everything I set out to achieve, and I have seen and experienced things, both good and bad, that very few men have. But looking down at these

17

men, with their expectations and demands, their petty jealousies and constant attempts to maneuver themselves into a better position in regard to one man, and one man only, it was impossible for me to think of all these positive things. Instead, I was consumed by disgust at and contempt for the idea of all the time spent, and, yes, all that I had lost fighting for men like these for forty-two years. In that moment, it was hard for me to even entertain the idea that all that I had accrued over the years — honors, status and riches — even came close to balancing against all that I lost.

"Get out," I said.

I do not know, if I did not say it loudly enough, but none of the men moved.

"Get out of my home!"

Now there was no mistaking that I was speaking loudly enough, as all three men literally jumped to their feet. I suppose they were helped by the distance I achieved when I kicked one of the empty stools across the room. The sight of them scurrying out of the room, in much the same way that Diocles had a few moments before, was quite gratifying. Watching them leave, I saw Marcellus pause at the doorway, turning about to give me a venomous look.

Before he could open his mouth, I spoke for him, "Yes, I know. Augustus will hear of this."

Snapping his mouth shut, he tried to make as dignified a retreat as a spineless, puffed-up, and self-important piece of *cac* can.

And I am still waiting to hear from Augustus.

(Note from Diocles: As I would learn later, Augustus obviously did hear about this, but fortunately, my master and friend Titus was never aware of this. But that is for later.)

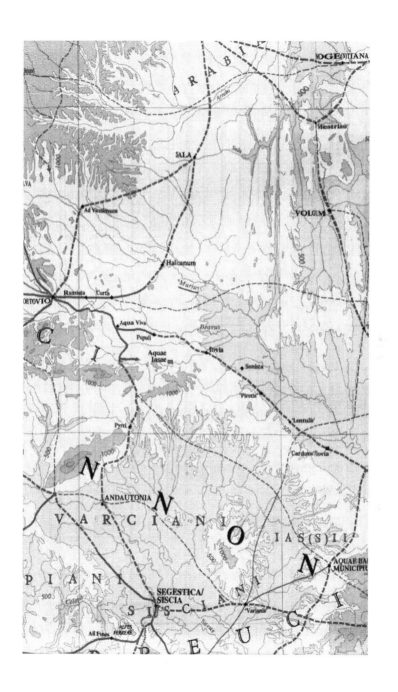

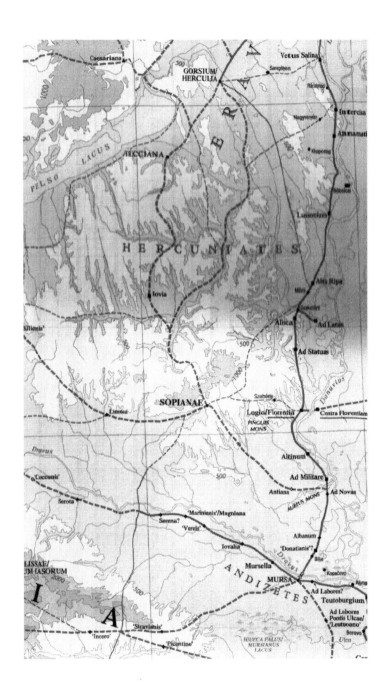

Chapter 1- Camp Prefect

Although getting Scribonius and Balbus into the Evocati had required the permission of Octavian, the transfer of a lowly Optio from one Legion to another is a relatively simple matter that was extremely unlikely to come to the attention of Caesar, Agrippa, or any man of Legate rank. I had done it the first time, getting Gaius transferred from the 14th to the 10th, and it would be accomplished again by the same means, except this time it would cost more. The simple fact was that Gaius was a veteran now, and an Optio at that, making him more valuable than a *tiro* or *gregarius*. However, I was prepared to pay whatever it cost, while Gaius offered to contribute from his meager savings. Although I suspected that his eagerness to come along was due as much to his feelings for Iras as any attachment he had to me, I was not about to take umbrage at that. All that mattered to me was that he would be where I could continue to keep an eye on him. The truth was that I had a bad feeling about the prospects of the men of the 10th who were being sent to Syria. Albinus had promised to remain in contact to let me know what happened, and with the bulk of the Legion now gone, those remaining were in the process of packing, making ready to ship to Syria.

I sent a message to Aulus Honorius Macrinus, the Primus Pilus of the 8th Legion, already in Pannonia, opening communication about securing Gaius a spot in the 8th. In my mind, the 8th was the best and only choice, being a Spanish Legion, despite the fact that it was unlikely that there would be many men left who had marched in Gaul. I knew of Macrinus by reputation, which was another reason I had thought of the 8th, since he was highly regarded by those who knew him. Agrippa did not spend much longer in camp, but I made no effort to see him again, and neither did he send for me. That was probably best for both of us, given that the last two times we had met, things had not gone well, particularly for me.

All that was left for me to do before Scribonius, Balbus, Gaius, and I left for Pannonia was to wait for the birth of my child. Therefore, with no more duties to attend to, I resolved to spend the time with Miriam, no matter what harm befell me. The part of the camp that had belonged to the 10th was deserted, and I found myself at a complete loss without the routine of daily duties. Unfortunately, this did not help my frame of mind, which in turn did not help Miriam. It took a week before we settled into a new routine where I was actually present for most of the day. Continuing my daily exercises, I was finding that I actually had more time to devote to them now. Fortunately, Miriam and I worked through the difficulties created by the combination of my sudden availability and her discomfort to the point where once again we started enjoying each other's company, if not in any physical way. We would spend full watches talking in much the same way that we had when we first met when I was looking for books in Damascus, and it was good to see her laugh again. Iras stopped glaring at me, meaning in turn that she and Gaius got along better, even if I was still not happy about their situation. I know that my actions and treatment of Miriam were very un-Roman, since most of the time the men separate themselves as much as is possible from a pregnant woman, but I was old enough and beyond caring what others like Scribonius and Balbus thought, at least about this.

"What if it's a girl?" Miriam asked me one evening, to which I answered with a shrug.

"I know that I'm supposed to want a boy, and I do, but I wouldn't mind if it's a girl child. As long as she looks like her mother and not her father."

Miriam blushed prettily, but I could tell that she was pleased. Speaking truthfully, a large part of me did not want a boy because of my fear that he would be as large as I was, and while Gisela had been a well-built woman, with the type of wide hips that midwives say are perfect for delivering babies, Miriam was much more slender through the body. I would find myself waking up at night to stare at her figure, the big lump of her belly sticking up, offering a prayer to every god I could think of that she would not suffer the same fate as my mother. The services of a midwife had already been purchased, but still not satisfied, I sent Iras to the forum on the market day to ask the inevitable gathering of women there for recommendations for the best midwife available. It was not so much that I did not have faith in the woman we had; she had come recommended, or so I had been told, it was just that Nicopolis was growing on an almost daily basis, and I knew that it was possible if not likely that another midwife would arrive that may have been more qualified before Miriam's time came. Of course, as with all things, there are rarely benefits without some corresponding disadvantage; Nicopolis' very newness also meant that people did not know each other very well, while relatively few babies had been born to that point. Iras returned only to inform me that it appeared that the woman we had was the best available, at least from what she had been told by the women she had asked. I briefly considered finding a physician, of which there were a fair number, since they are mostly Greek to begin with and we were in the area, but I almost as quickly dismissed the notion. Childbirth is a woman's affair and even in my limited experience with the matter, I could not ever remember seeing a male doctor attending a birth. With every option exhausted, I contented myself with continuing to send Iras to make daily offerings as the day approached.

Perhaps a week before the birth I received a reply from Macrinus, who said that while he would be happy to add young Gaius to his ranks, at the moment there were no openings for Optio in any of the upper Cohorts. The only slot he had open was in the Tenth Cohort, which under the reforms of Octavian meant that the lowest quality men were being shuffled from the other Cohorts. Reading his words, I could not tell if this was a statement of simple fact or if it was an oblique attempt at extorting more money from me. Deciding that it would be wise to check with Gaius first, since I could not dismiss the possibility that he would opt for staying where he was at, even if it was in Syria, I asked him what he wanted to do and he did not hesitate.

"I don't care if it's in the Tenth Cohort, as long as I can be where you're at," he said, a little too quickly.

I gave him a sidelong glance, not believing him. "You mean you want to be where Iras is," I said.

He blushed, giving a sheepish grin."Her too," he admitted.

"You understand that the Legions are being reorganized, so they're putting the weaker men in the Tenth Cohort," I warned him, which he just shrugged off.

"It just means that I'll have to be a better leader," was his reply, said with all the assurance that comes with youth, as if there was no doubt in his mind that he was up to the challenge.

That was half the battle, I had to acknowledge, but just hoped that he was not underestimating the difficulty while overestimating his abilities. With that question answered, I decided to send a reply, asking what it would take to find a place for Gaius in one of the upper Cohorts. If Macrinus was soliciting a bribe, I believed that this would flush him out, telling me one way or the other. There were also the other Legions in the Army of Pannonia, as it was being called, but I was not keen on sending Gaius to any of them, with the possible exception of the 11th or 15th. The 13th had a bad reputation for switching sides, depending on who was paying the most, while the 14th was still dogged by its ignominious fate when it had been wiped out not once, but twice. The 11th had been a solid, if unremarkable Legion in Gaul, except that had been long ago, and I did not know any men in the Centurionate, which held true for the 15th as well. Therefore, I decided to wait to see what kind of response I got from Macrinus before worrying about the next step. Everything had been done that could be done to that point, making everything else just waiting. Then, one day, when I was at the stakes with Scribonius and Balbus, Agis came sprinting up, his eyes wide with what I took to be equal parts excitement and fear.

Without waiting for permission, he gasped out, "Master, Iras sent me. It is time!"

I have said it many times. The gods are cruel, using mortal men as their playthings for their amusement. As much as they have given to me, they have also taken as much, if not more. For the second time in my life, they took from me that which was most dear. All of the prayers, all of the sacrifices meant nothing to them when compared to the opportunity to have a laugh at my expense. I do not know why in one way they have chosen to give me so much, while in another they have taken everything that makes life worthwhile. I do know that I plan on asking when I arrive in their world, but I will have a sword in my hand when I do. And from that day forward, I never uttered another prayer to the gods, nor did I make a sacrifice to them. I piss on the gods and their cruelty.

For the second time, I witnessed the most horrible fate a man can endure, the loss of his family. Miriam died because of a massive hemorrhage, and before the baby could be saved, it suffocated. As he had with Gisela and his first family, my master decreed that neither he nor anyone around him would speak of Miriam or the baby, so I am writing this while he sleeps, because I know he would be very angry with me for speaking of it. It was not just Miriam that died that day; something in my master died as well, and he has never been the same from that day forward. Whereas he had been in a deep depression when Gisela and his children died, he had eventually recovered, but it is now 14 years since Miriam and the babe's death, and he still has fits of melancholy where I fear that he will lose his mind, or his life. There have been moments where he seems to forget for an instant, and he will laugh, but as quickly as these moments happen, they are extinguished like a lamp snuffed out. It is as if he suddenly remembers the pain, and it chases all the joy from his soul. And he has been true to his word; he has never uttered the name of a god, nor has he made any offerings or sacrifices to them in all these years. At first, he forbade all the members of his household from worshiping their own gods, but after Scribonius talked to him, he relented. His only stipulation was that we not do so in his presence, so we keep the figures of our household gods out of his sight. The other change in my master was that he no longer talked of the desire to settle down. He became the Titus Pullus of old, a man with no softness in him, completely devoted to his career and to the army. I cannot say that he became cruel, but there was definitely a hardness about him that I had not seen in some time. It has been sad to watch a man who cut a part of himself away, but I know why he did so, for he would not have survived otherwise. As formidable a warrior as my master may have been, and still is, he is a mortal man, and we mortals are consigned to suffering through the travails of life. And in one respect, I will say that Titus Pullus, for as much as he was given, has suffered more than most men.

Now that there was no longer a reason to linger, I left for Pannonia, taking my household and my friends with me. I regret to say that for the others it was a somber journey, since I was in no mood for small talk, either by me or from others. In fact, I did not much want to hear the others talking among themselves either. Traveling north, we followed the coast, passing through Macedonia first, then Dalmatia. The country grew increasingly rugged and we rode with our hands on the hilts of our swords, spread out slightly in order to avoid being surprised. This was country perfectly suited for ambush, and the bandits of Dalmatia were well known. In fact, I hoped that some men would be stupid enough to try and attack our party, because I desperately needed the release of battle. Of all the people in our party, the one person I could not stand to be around was Iras, and I am afraid that I was very cruel to her, albeit only with words. I can look back now to see that she was as grief-stricken as I was, but at the time, I ignored the puffy and reddened eyes, the sudden bouts of weeping, and the rips in her clothing. Somehow, I convinced myself that she was secretly relieved that Miriam was gone and would escape at the first opportunity, so I ordered her legs shackled every night. This was not a popular order with anyone; even Agis made it clear that he did not believe she needed to be restrained, while Gaius thought to speak to me about it the first night before taking one look at my face and thinking better of it.

We made good progress, mainly because I was not interested in sightseeing, or in the feelings or condition of the others, and we reached Siscia less than four weeks after we left Nicopolis. We did stop at Salonae for a couple of days to rest the horses, giving me the opportunity to stock up on more wine, which I was drinking in large quantities every night when we stopped. It helped me sleep at night, but the next mornings were rough, in turn making the others' lives equally miserable. Our first sight of Siscia came after we crossed the Dinarics, the range of low mountains that cut the coastal area off from the interior of Pannonia. Located at the confluence of three rivers, Siscia was a Roman city in name only, at least at that point, being more Pannonian than Roman. The walls were wooden, yet they were very stout and more than 20 feet high, with the houses and buildings similarly constructed. Streets were churned mud and crowded with newly arrived settlers, many of whom I recognized as recent retirees from the Legion. Several of them saluted, out of force of habit, which I returned for the same reason, but for the most part I ignored their calls as I rode by, not wanting to engage in talk that would inevitably lead to a topic I had no wish to discuss. When they had last seen me I had been married and expecting a child. Seeing these men so soon was a bitter reminder that was no longer the case. Many of the native buildings either had been torn down or were in varying stages of destruction to be replaced with those of a more Roman style.

We did not linger in the town, taking a quick look around before pushing through to the gate on the eastern side, following the road for about a mile before we came to the camp, discovering that what we had been told about the camp being hard up against the town walls was incorrect. In fact, it was built on the site of the original camp when Octavian had first campaigned here, with more permanent buildings being added over time. It was now a fully operational base, with a *Praetorium* made of brick, along with the quarters of the senior officers like me. We presented our orders at the gate and, because we were expected, we were waved through. Leaving Diocles, Iras, and Agis behind with the baggage and other slaves, the rest of us entered the *Praetorium* to report our presence formally. There was a Tribune of the broad stripe present, another of the eager and ambitious young men that passed through the command of the Legion, most of them having no more impact on the performance of a Legion than the way sticking a finger in a cup of wine does when it's then pulled out. This young man seemed to be exceptionally haughty, which I was in no mood to endure, practically making it inevitable that there would be words exchanged.

"I see that your orders are dated more than a month ago," he sniffed. "I didn't realize that it took so long to travel from Nicopolis."

I heard Balbus mutter a curse behind me while I took a step closer to the Tribune, staring down at him, and he took an involuntary step back before he seemed to realize he was showing weakness. Tilting his chin up, his lips drew into a thin line as he mentally prepared himself to put me in my place. I do not believe that he was ready for what I said.

"Can you read, Tribune?" I asked him quietly, and his face flushed.

"Of course I can read, in Latin and Greek," he snapped.

"Then perhaps you would be so kind as to read those orders again." I switched to speaking Greek without a pause, clearly surprising him considerably.

Obviously reluctant, but unable to argue with what was a reasonable request, his eyes dropped to the scroll, scanning the text.

Pointing to a line, I said helpfully, "It's that section that I think you might want to review."

His brow furrowed as he tried to work the words out, which was understandable. Caesar's practice of putting a dot over the last word of every sentence had been picked up by a number of others, yet it had not become standard practice, and the clerk who had written out my orders had not bothered with such a convenience. The Tribune read, then reread the sentence I had pointed out, but he still did not understand.

"I'm the Camp Prefect for the Army of Pannonia. That means that I'm second in command of this entire army, which means that I'm your superior officer, Tribune."

"That's impossible," he protested. "I'm the senior Tribune, and on my return to Rome I'll be a member of the Senate. No man from the ranks, no matter how highly placed he is, outranks me."

"Not true," a new voice interrupted. "And if you would spend more time reading the orders that come into the *Praetorium* instead of worrying about who was spending more time with me than you, you'd know that, Claudius."

I turned to see a man not much older than the Tribune Claudius, but with an aura of ability and command that marked him as a natural leader. He was richly yet simply dressed, wearing a senatorial and a signet ring as his only jewelry. Without waiting, he strode over to me, offering his hand.

"And it's a great honor and privilege to welcome Titus Pullus as my second in command."

I said nothing, not because I wanted to be rude, but because I did not know who the man was; my orders had not named the Legate. Seeing my hesitation, he provided an answer to the mystery.

"I am Marcus Licinius Crassus, Legate of the Army of Pannonia."

That is how I met my new commanding officer, a man who very few have ever heard of despite his great deeds, and who always serves as a reminder of how dangerous it is to cross Octavian, even if it is unintended.

Marcus Crassus was the grandson of Caesar's old colleague, and the son of Publius, who had perished at Carrhae with his father when Marcus was just a babe. Young Crassus was one of the wealthiest men in Rome thanks to his grandfather's famous avarice, yet he carried the burden with ease. Our first meeting was suitably brief, since Crassus wanted me to settle in and rest before we talked army business. Tribune Claudius, who I learned was of a very minor branch of that famous family of the Claudii, had been suitably embarrassed, meaning for the next several days he made himself scarce whenever I was present. Scribonius and Balbus, as Evocati, were expected to find their own housing in town and as was always the case when the army settled into a spot, the rents were exorbitant for what was little better than a hovel, to hear the two tell it. Finally, I could endure their complaining no longer, offering them space in my quarters, which were spacious and even more luxurious than I had become accustomed to as Primus Pilus. I even had my own private bath in a small building just behind my living quarters. The villa had hypocaust heating, the first I had ever experienced as part of my living arrangements, but I was assured that the winters were suitably bitter to make it a requirement, not a luxury. While Scribonius and Balbus were settled, Gaius' status was a little bit trickier. I learned that the 8th was not actually stationed at Siscia, but was out on the frontier to the northeast, and while they were not under siege, the situation was tense.

"I'm afraid that if you were hoping for a peaceful assignment that you're going to be disappointed," was how Crassus put it.

"I want nothing of the sort," I replied.

He raised an eyebrow in surprise, looking at me intently, but I did not elaborate. I had no desire or intention of explaining my situation. After a moment, seeing that I was not going to say more, he continued.

"Are you familiar with the Bastarnae?" he asked me, and I shook my head.

"I've heard of them, but don't know more than that."

"Think of Scythians, but much meaner and wilder, and not as dependent on the horse as the Scythians. They're from the area north of Thrace, and until recently, they've not been a problem. But they got greedy and they took advantage of the fact that we were occupied with the Dacians, and first they crossed the Ister River. They conquered that part of Moesia, namely the Triballi and the Dardani tribes, which frankly we didn't care about. Looking back, I think that was a mistake, because they took our reaction, or lack of it, as a sign of

30

weakness. Recently, they crossed the Nisava. Are you familiar with that river?"

I thought for a moment, trying to recall what I had heard. I knew that it was important, that it formed some sort of boundary, but it was more of a guess when I ventured, "It's part of the border of Thrace, isn't it?"

He nodded in confirmation.

"Correct. Specifically that part of Thrace that belongs to the Dentheleti."

I shrugged, since the name of the tribe meant nothing to me.

"We have a treaty with Sitas, the king of the Dentheleti," he said meaningfully.

That was when I understood the significance. During the civil wars, many of the kingdoms and territories that had some sort of treaty of friendship with Rome had suffered depredations of one sort or another at the hands of their enemies, namely because we were too occupied with our own troubles to offer the help that we were bound to by treaty. Most of these offenses had yet to be punished; Armenia came to mind, but first the Republic itself had to be set to rights. However, Crassus apparently had decided that the place to start was here, with these Bastarnae.

"Sitas is blind, and old, and I've met him," Crassus said, like that explained why we were going to chastise the Bastarnae. "The 8th is the nearest to the area, and I've already sent orders for them to prepare to move into Moesia. I'll be joining them, and I'm hoping that you'll be at my side."

"Where else would I be?"

I did not understand the statement, and I saw him hesitate so I nodded to him, encouraging him to be honest with me.

"It's just that you've already had a full career, and you've seen more battle than almost any man left in not just this army, but any of the armies," he explained. "And nobody would blame you, and I certainly wouldn't, if you chose to remain behind with the bulk of the army. In fact, in some ways it would make more sense for my second in command to remain behind."

"General, I appreciate your concern," I said firmly, "but I didn't come here to sit in my office. If you want me to go with you, I'm more than happy to do so. And I'm more than happy to wield a sword for Rome, despite my advanced and decrepit age."

He chuckled at my heavy-handed attempt at humor, giving a small wave.

"Fair enough. I just wanted you to know that I wouldn't hold it against you if you chose to remain here."

"I appreciate it, but that won't be necessary. So, when are we leaving?"

Since we would be heading to meet the 8th, I decided to bring Gaius, while Scribonius and Balbus made it clear that they would not be left behind to molder in the camp. Diocles came along as well; only Iras and Agis were left behind to finish getting things settled in. Watching Gaius and Iras cling to each other saying their goodbyes was painful to watch, the scene reminding me of happier times, which seemed like years ago and not just weeks. Joining Crassus and his staff, we were accompanied by an *ala* of cavalry as bodyguards, along with some ex-gladiators that apparently belonged to Crassus. This was my first opportunity to see the country we would be operating in firsthand while we followed the Sava River east. The roads were not of a high quality, meaning the going was not nearly as swift as it would have been if we had been on a good Roman road, yet it gave me time to examine not just the land, but the people and where they lived. It was an obviously poor country, with small farms where the inhabitants were barely scratching out an existence. Their huts were made of whatever materials were available, usually logs or even sticks, with mud in between to chink the cracks.

The people were thin; they were also a hardy people, and it was easy to read the hatred and anger in their eyes when we passed by, although they would look away when we turned to face them. My first impression was that these people were far from conquered and that it would be some time before they began to come around to the benefits of being part of Rome.

The land itself was fertile, at least along the river valley, but it was clear that they did not have the same level of sophistication that we or even the Gauls possessed when it came to utilizing the land in the most efficient manner. Traffic on the road was light, composed mostly of men and women walking, carrying bundles of goods, although we did run into an occasional wagon. Interspersed every few miles were mean little villages, little better than a collection of huts and hovels, with small pens for pigs and goats attached and doorways cut into a wall for the animals to be brought into the house during the night. All in all, it was a depressing landscape and I did not understand why we considered this area to be a valuable addition to the lands of the Republic.

Because of the lack of civilization, we spent every night out in the open, and I have to say that I was impressed that Crassus did not insist on having his tent erected, since the weather was fair. I had noticed that he had traveled light for a man of his station, and the more time I spent with him, the more I liked him. We had yet to go into battle, which would be the real test, but to that point, I liked what I saw. He apparently felt the same about me, because we developed an easy rapport, talking about all manner of things. Since he had little memory of his grandfather, or his father for that matter, Crassus pumped me for information about them. There was not much I could tell him firsthand about his grandfather, but his father I was happy to talk about, remembering the popular young officer in Caesar's army in Gaul. While it had been with the 7th Legion that Crassus had his famous exploits in Aquitania, I relayed what I remembered from the events, and most importantly, what we in the ranks thought of his father. Crassus seemed to appreciate how fondly his father was remembered and on more than one occasion, I thought I detected the glint of a tear in his eye as he listened to what I had to say. Scribonius and Balbus added their own recollections as well, so he knew that I was not just trying to flatter him by talking so well of his dead father. This was the manner in which we passed the miles, reaching the largest town in the region, Sirmium, which was supposedly named for the first king of the Triballi. Word of our progress had reached the people; consequently, there was a line of supplicants who wanted Crassus' time to make a complaint or plea. I could not help noticing that when they thought it was to their advantage, the people were quick to avail themselves of our system of patronage and were eager to abide by our laws.

"I don't have time to hear your pleas at this time, but when I return I will be happy to do so," Crassus announced.

In an instant, the crowd, which had been docile to that point, turned ugly. They pressed in around us, making me thankful that we were still mounted, but in that moment we were cut off from both the cavalry and the gladiators, who had been too busy leering at the women to pay attention to their job. Men were shouting at us, some of them in heavily accented Latin, most in their own tongue, while others were shaking their fists at us. It was a confused mess and while I was not particularly worried, I saw that it was nevertheless a dangerous situation. Suddenly, one of the men reached out to grab Crassus' horse's bridle. Before I formed the conscious thought, I had drawn my sword and in one quick stroke, severed the arm of the man who had grabbed the bridle. Just as quickly, all movement and sound stopped, everyone frozen in astonishment at the sight of the man standing there, a puzzled look on his face as he stared down at his arm lying in the mud at his feet, all while the stump of his arm spurted blood into the face of the man standing next to him. Taking advantage of the momentary paralysis, I wheeled Ocelus around, calling to Crassus to follow while using my horse's big body to shove people aside. Crassus seemed every bit as astonished as the crowd, but knowing that the spell would not last, I called to Scribonius, who was nearest to Crassus.

"Get him out of there and follow me."

Scribonius did not hesitate, with Balbus moving as quickly, and between them, they turned Crassus' horse. This snapped him out of it; digging his heels into the sides of his horse, he leapt through the crowd, knocking people sprawling. Unfortunately, this roused the mob from their daze as well, and they roared their anger. Meanwhile, the man I had struck collapsed to the mud, completely unheeded by his supposed friends. Finally, the gladiators noticed that something was amiss, turning their mounts to meet us as I came trotting up.

"How about earning your fucking pay?" I snarled at their leader, a scarred brute named Prixus.

"Don't you worry about my job, soldier boy," he snapped back, moving back towards Crassus, who was still trying to push his way out of the crowd.

Without hesitating or slowing down, as Prixus drew abreast of me I stuck my left arm out straight, my forearm hitting the gladiator in the throat. My momentum in the opposite direction swept him from the saddle like he had been struck by a scorpion bolt, and he landed heavily on his back in the mud, the wind rushing from his lungs, his eyes rolling back in his head. His men wheeled to face me, ranging their own horses in a rough semicircle, but I still had my sword in my hand. Without their leader, they looked to one another, unsure of what to do. Hearing the sound of horses behind me, Scribonius called out that they were clear of the trouble.

Pointing to Prixus, who was struggling to his elbows, I said, "Unless you want your boss to get torn apart by this mob, I suggest you help him onto his horse. The rest of us are getting out of here."

Without waiting to see if the others were following, but knowing that Scribonius and Balbus would be there no matter what, I trotted out of town.

"I had been hoping to spend at least one night under a roof," Crassus said ruefully, looking back at the tops of the buildings of Sirmium.

"We can go back if you want," I told him.

He shook his head, giving me a grin.

"No, I'd rather sleep outside than be torn apart by a mob."

"Good. So would I. They turned ugly awfully quickly."

"It's like this throughout the province," he replied grimly. "It's true that we've held this place for the last five years, but the natives clearly haven't fully accepted the idea."

"At least it won't be boring," Scribonius observed.

"What happened back there with Prixus?" Crassus changed the subject, which I knew was coming at some point.

"He fell off his horse," I replied.

"I can see that," Crassus said with a touch of asperity. "I'm asking how it happened."

"I think his horse shied at the commotion and he wasn't paying attention."

Crassus said nothing for a moment. When he did speak, his tone was careful.

"Well, I did notice that neither he nor his men seemed to be paying much attention to what was happening. I suppose that makes as much sense as anything else."

He turned to look at me.

"Like you knocking him from his horse."

"Now why would I do that?" I asked innocently, trying to ignore Balbus as he smirked, riding on the opposite side of Crassus.

The Legate shook his head, clearly realizing that he would learn nothing more.

Instead, he said quietly, "Be careful, Pullus. Prixus is a bad man to have as an enemy."

I held out my hand, which he looked at curiously.

"See how my hand is trembling?"

He gave a short laugh, but did not press the matter any further. The bodyguards were riding towards the rear of the column and I could feel the eyes of Prixus boring into my back. I knew that Crassus was right, that I had made an enemy for life, yet I did not care. In fact, at that point, I did not care if I lived or died.

Pushing on, our ultimate goal was where the 8th was camped at the junction of the Savus (Sava) and Ister (Danube) River. The Ister is similar to the Rhenus, running in an easterly direction for hundreds of miles, and the 8th was camped on its southern bank, but west of the Sava, which turned south into Moesia at this point. Whoever had chosen the site had chosen well for defense, with essentially two rivers as a barrier to the Bastarnae. However, it would make offensive operations difficult because the Bastarnae were on the other side and, if they had their wits about them, they could make things very difficult for us when we began to move against them. I squinted, trying to see any sign of an enemy encampment on the other side, but the sky was clear of smoke that would signal the fires of an army.

Deciding to hold my suggestions about relocating the camp, I waited to see what Crassus would say and I was gratified when, about a mile further on he turned to me and said, "I think we need to move the camp to the other side of the river. What do you think?"

"I agree," I said instantly. "I think it's sending the wrong message to these Bastarnae for us to be in a defensive position. They're the ones who are the aggressors, and we shouldn't be seen as cowering behind a river."

He nodded in agreement, and with that decided, we approached the camp. The *bucina* call that signaled the approach of an unknown party sounded, and I saw helmeted heads appear above the palisade as the guard Cohort watched us approach. Turning to the standard bearer, Crassus ordered it unfurled so that we could be more easily identified, but even so, we were all a bit nervous. While the 8th was not a raw Legion, they could not be considered truly veteran and we had all been in the army long enough to have known someone or seen firsthand when a nervous sentry flung a javelin before being sure of the identity of his target. We saw a transverse crest appear, followed by a gravelly voice ordering us to halt when we were a couple hundred paces away.

"Who goes there?" came the standard query in such situations.

"General Crassus and Camp Prefect Pullus of the Army of Pannonia," Crassus called out in a loud voice.

He did not have to include me, but I appreciated the gesture.

"Advance, General and Prefect," the duty Centurion answered.

This was the dangerous part; if one of the sentries was twitchy and one of us had a sudden itch or something that might cause him to panic and hurl a javelin at us. Consequently, I kept a wary eye on the faces of the men lining the parapet. Fortunately, none of them looked nervous or alarmed and once we got within the prescribed distance, the Centurion told us to halt again. It was at this point that it was normal for the duty Centurion to give the signal to open the gate, but he did not give the signal.

More curious than angry, I called out, "What's the delay, Centurion?"

There was a pause before he answered, his tone apologetic.

"I'm sorry, Prefect, it's just that I've never seen either you or the General before and my Tribune has given strict instructions that we not allow anyone to enter unless they're recognized in person."

"What do you think we are; Bastarnae?" I asked irritably, chafing at the delay.

Crassus did not seem in the least put out, and he explained why.

"This is as much my fault as anyone's. I drilled it into Cornelius' head that he should not make assumptions about anyone since we don't know the Bastarnae well, and they could try something, posing as Thracians or Dacians."

"That's understandable, but I hardly think we could pass for barbarians."

"True," he granted, then grinned at me. "I never said Cornelius was particularly smart, but I can count on him to obey his orders to the letter."

"It's comforting to know that he's commanding a Legion," I observed sourly.

"First, he's in titular command, but you know better than anyone how that goes. Macrinus is really commanding, and he's a good man. Second, we're here now so it doesn't really matter."

During our conversation, a plumed helmet appeared, framing a young face that peered down at us. He was a handsome youth, with an aquiline nose and a mouth I had heard women describe as pouty, which I think made him look feminine, but I supposed it was popular with the women of the upper classes. His eyes widened at the sight of his commanding general sitting patiently on his horse, and he immediately turned to snap an order. A moment later, the gate swung open, and I turned to signal to the others to follow us into the camp.

"It's about time," I grumbled as we rode in.

To my eye, I was forced to admit grudgingly that the 8th was a tightly run, well-disciplined Legion. It was little things like the fact that the men were not allowed to hang their laundry from the guy ropes of their tents, or were wearing their belts and at least their daggers even when seated at the fire. Seeing these things made me feel better about having Gaius serve in the 8th; it also reminded me that I owed Macrinus a visit on the subject. I would not have to rely on letters going back and forth, trying to guess what he really meant, whether or not there really were no slots available in the higher Cohorts, or this was just an attempt to squeeze more money out of me.

Speaking of Gaius, he had been extremely quiet on this trip, which I assumed was because he was being parted from Iras, but I must confess I was not displeased when I learned that the 8th was not in Sisica. Recognizing that there would be time enough for this matter about Gaius' position, I concentrated on getting familiar with the situation. In the *Praetorium*, on the wall of what was now Crassus' office, was a vellum map of the region, where charcoal markings denoted the latest information on where the Bastarnae were located. Crassus, Cornelius, and a man I assumed was Macrinus were standing in front of the map talking when I arrived. My assumption was confirmed when Crassus introduced me to Macrinus. Despite being several inches shorter than I, his shoulders were as wide and his chest as heavily muscled as mine. He had iron gray hair, cut short in our manner, but there was a jagged scar that ran from just below his hairline on his forehead all the way back, almost to the base of his skull. He had another scar across his cheek, similar to the one I carried, while his face was tanned leather.

As Crassus made the introductions and we clasped arms, the general commented, "If Macrinus were a few inches taller, the two of you could be brothers."

"My mother was a Suburan whore, so I suppose it's possible, but somehow I doubt Prefect Pullus and I are related," he replied, gripping my forearm.

He had a strong grip and I felt him applying extra pressure, so I gave him a grin and squeezed back. We stood there for a moment, testing each other's strength, and I must say my arm was beginning to ache, when by unspoken consent we released our hold on the other. We simultaneously began rubbing our forearms, causing both of us to laugh.

"I'd call it a draw from appearances," Crassus remarked.

Now that the pleasantries were aside, he turned our attention to Cornelius, who as the ranking officer on the location, would give the briefing. Holding a wax tablet, he frowned at it as he began.

"Er, it seems that the Bastarnae are conducting more than a raid, since they have their families loaded into wagons with all their possessions."

This was a very important piece of information; I was surprised that this was the first we were hearing about it, and I said as much. Cornelius flushed, but instead of speaking, he shot a glance at Macrinus, who evidently was expecting this reaction.

"Our cavalry scouting parties either have disappeared, or have been pursued so heavily that they had to go a long way out of their way to get back to camp," Macrinus explained. "So we didn't learn of the wagons until just two days ago, when a patrol we sent out a week ago finally made it back. Or at least what was left of them," he amended.

"Has there been any other contact?" Crassus asked, to which both Cornelius and Macrinus shook their heads.

"The truth is that we haven't seen them from the camp and I wasn't comfortable sending out foot patrols without more of a cavalry screen," Macrinus said. "We've been basically running blind more than three or four miles out."

"We've seen some columns of smoke," Cornelius added. "And we've had people approaching the camp saying that their homes have been destroyed, but of course we didn't allow them in."

Crassus pursed his lips, thinking things over.

After a moment, he said, "The fact that they've brought their families means this is more than a raid. Does everyone agree?" We all nodded our heads, and he continued, "What numbers are we talking about? How many spears?"

Cornelius consulted his wax tablet.

"According to the scouts, they give an estimate of at least 20,000 warriors. Most of them are on foot, but there appear to be about 3,000 cavalry."

"Double that," I said, causing Crassus to raise an eyebrow.

"Just like we're doing, they're sending scouts out, especially if they're looking to relocate," I explained. "So it's likely that there's double the number that the scouts reported."

"Do you think the same goes for the foot?" Macrinus asked, but I shook my head.

"I doubt it. They'd keep the heavy infantry with their families, and besides, they can't cover as much territory. No, I'm confident that if our scouts can count, they saw everyone on foot that's there to see."

"So the question is, can we send these people back to where they came from with one Legion?" Crassus asked.

For once, I kept my mouth shut because I did not know enough about the quality of the 8th Legion to make an assessment that would be anything but guesswork. Instead, I looked to Macrinus for the answer.

"It all depends on how spread out they are." Macrinus rubbed his chin. "If they're in a couple different groups and a sufficient distance apart, then I'd say yes, absolutely. But if they're all together or even close enough to provide support to each other when we attack, it would be a tough job. My boys aren't the most experienced, but our ranks have a lot of veterans, and we've been blooded, so my gut says that we could take them."

I liked Macrinus' answer, because it was not a boastful response, but a clearly realistic assessment of his Legion's chances. In the few moments we had been together, my opinion of the man was rising considerably. I looked at Crassus, since ultimately it was his decision, and he wasted no time.

"We're going to go on a scouting patrol, but with the whole Legion," he announced.

He gave us all a wide grin.

"Let's see if we can't go find some trouble to get into."

Crassus gave the orders to break camp the next morning, then cross the river, the first step in chasing the Bastarnae back to where they came from. It was strange for me, because for the first time, I did not actually have any duties to attend to, other than walking around looking important, I suppose. Men were hustling about, the evening air filled with the sounds of a Legion breaking camp and I decided to take advantage of the fact I had nothing to do to go look up Macrinus to discuss Gaius' fate. Now that I had met the man, I did not believe that he was squeezing me, but I wanted to make sure. I found him in his quarters, finishing up a stack of reports that had to be sent to the *Praetorium* before everything was packed up, and I stood in the doorway watching for a moment before I cleared my throat to announce my presence. He looked up, clearly irritated at the interruption, his expression changing when he saw that it was me, rising to *intente*, which I quickly dismissed.

Waving me in, he said, "I bet you don't miss any of this."

"No, not a bit," I agreed.

Dropping a tablet on the stack of finished reports, Macrinus sat back, regarding me with an expression that I could not read.

"I suppose you're here to talk about your nephew, and to find out whether or not I was just trying to get more money out of you to move him to a better Cohort."

Rather than be offended, I appreciated his frankness, deciding to reward his honesty with my own.

"That's about the size of it."

"And? What do you think?" he asked me.

I considered for a moment, then relying on my gut, I shook my head.

"I think that it's exactly as you said in your letter, that there isn't a spot available in the upper Cohorts."

I could see that my answer pleased him. With that out of the way, he offered me a seat and a cup of wine, which I accepted. We sat, sipping from our cups for a moment, making small talk about the coming movement and the prospects for battle.

Then, Macrinus set his cup down, giving me a long look before he said carefully, "Since the last time we communicated on this subject, there has been a change in circumstances."

Ah, here it comes, I thought. I was wrong; he *is* going to squeeze me.

"There's now a vacancy in the Fifth of the Third for an Optio. The day before you and the general arrived, the Optio died of a rupture after a weapons drill. The doctor thinks that there was something else wrong with him because he wasn't struck that hard, and he'd been complaining of a pain in his right side. He didn't show up for evening formation and when his Centurion went looking for him, it was too late."

"That's convenient," I said, trying to sound like I believed Macrinus, but I clearly did not succeed, because his face flushed.

However, when he replied, his tone was even and did not show any offense at my rebuke.

"Actually, Prefect, it's not convenient at all. The reason I bring it up is that I know that sooner or later you'd hear that there had been a vacancy, but the fact is that I wouldn't recommend that your nephew fill that slot."

"I can assure you that he's more than qualified to handle a Century in one of the better Cohorts. The only reason he wasn't in the First of the 10th was because he's my nephew and I didn't want any charges of nepotism being leveled against him," I said stiffly, growing angry at Macrinus' presumption that Gaius was an Optio only because of his relationship to me, but Macrinus waved his hand in dismissal of my objection.

"Prefect, I can assure you that it has nothing to do with the qualifications of your nephew. In fact, I've been making the assumption all along that being your nephew meant that he was personally trained by you, and anyone trained by Titus Pullus of the 10th Legion is more than capable of handling the duties of Optio in any Cohort. No, my concern isn't that your nephew can handle the duties, it's the Centurion he'd be under that's the problem."

Now I was feeling a bit foolish, despite a part of me still being suspicious that Macrinus was making excuses to avoid putting Gaius in one of his better Cohorts. However, I was willing to listen, so I indicated he should continue. Macrinus hesitated for a moment, and I could see he was considering how much he should divulge.

To offer encouragement, I said, "Macrinus, remember that I was a Primus Pilus for a long time. I know that every Legion has its secrets, and that not everyone who's in the Centurionate is there because he belongs there. I give you my word that I won't be running to Crassus or betray your trust in any way."

My words seemed to be what he had been hoping for, as he nodded and continued.

"The Tertius Hastatus Prior's name is Glabius, and he's a flogger, among other things."

The fact that this Glabius liked to flog his men was not good, but would not necessarily affect his Optio, except perhaps by association, so I knew there had to be more. I waited as Macrinus seemed to struggle to find the right words to continue.

"Unfortunately, that's not the worst of it. Glabius is squeezing his men. The Fifth Century is the worst in the Legion for men on punishment and, as you might expect, their morale is horrible. The whole thing is a mess, and I wouldn't feel right putting your nephew into that situation. I don't know him, but I suspect that if he was trained by you, he'd have something to say to Glabius, and Glabius might be the best man with a sword in the entire Legion."

It sounded like Macrinus was a little afraid of this Glabius, but I knew better than to bring that up.

Instead, I asked, "Why can't you replace him?"

Macrinus gave me a long, searching look, saying nothing for several moments.

Finally, he spoke slowly. "I think you know why, Prefect. He is . . . connected. And he came with the Legion. He's been with the 8th for longer than I have."

Macrinus did not need to say any more than he had, because I knew exactly what he meant. Glabius was somehow connected to Octavian, or perhaps he was not, but had convinced Macrinus that he was, and Macrinus was understandably unwilling to test that fact.

Turning my attention to where it looked like Gaius would be headed, I asked, "Tell me about the Tenth. Which Century would he be going to?"

"Actually," Macrinus replied, "I do have a bit of good news on that. After thinking about it, I decided that I need to make some changes and move some men about. So I can offer your nephew a slot in the Seventh, in the Second Century. The Pilus Posterior is a good man, even if he is from Etruria. His name is Sextus Vettus, and he's one of my most dependable, and his Century is a good one, one of my best."

That sounded good, but I was struck by what he had said, prompting me to ask, "If the Century is so good, why is it in the Seventh? It seems like with this reorganization that Caesar has mandated, it would be good to move them up?"

He hesitated again, and I reminded him of my oath that everything would stay between us.

"I understand what Caesar is trying to do, and I applaud it," he said carefully. "But we're out here, about to face the Bastarnae. You know better than anyone that an upheaval the likes of what Caesar has mandated takes time to adjust to, for everyone, Centurions and Optios included. We've done as he ordered by doubling the size of the First Cohort and we took the opportunity to cut out the dead wood when we reduced the size of the Centuries, but frankly, Prefect, that's as far as I'm willing to go right now. Once we're through with the Bastarnae, then we'll finish making the changes that he's ordered. I hope that this isn't a problem for you."

"It's not. In fact, it makes perfect sense," I assured him, and I could see he was visibly relieved, while this was the first time that I got an idea of how powerful and influential others viewed this new post of Camp Prefect. "Does Crassus know about this?"

He nodded, then said, "The general is in complete agreement and as far as I know, has told the other Primi Pili of the Army of Pannonia to do as I'm doing until we're through putting down this invasion."

"Then that's all that matters," I said lightly, but Macrinus seemed worried.

"You don't think Caesar will take it like we're disobeying his orders?"

"No, I think he might," I was forced to admit. "But he's in Rome, and we're out here. And I give you my word that if he says anything against what we're doing, I'll speak up."

That seemed to soothe him considerably, and I stopped myself from adding that given my rocky relationship with Octavian, it was just as likely to condemn as it was to absolve us.

It took a matter of more than a watch to find a suitable fording spot for us to cross the river and if the Bastarnae had had their wits about them, or had been led by a somewhat competent general, they would have arrayed themselves to stop us when we crossed. The ford we used still forced the men to cross in water that was almost chest-deep, making

Crassus order the cavalry to line up above and below the ford like we had done so often in Gaul. We made it across, but with only a couple of watches of daylight left, Crassus gave the order to make camp just a mile from the river. We were headed in a roughly southeasterly direction, where we would be leaving the gentle terrain of the river valley, the line of hills in the distance promising harder marching to come. When it got dark, we could see a smudge of light on the horizon that experience told us was the fires of the Bastarnae.

The next morning, we broke camp, continuing our pursuit by moving steadily towards the spot where the fires had been the night before, with what remained of our cavalry providing a screen. It was our first full day on the march, subsequently making it the first day where I rode the whole time, and rode with the command group instead of my Legion. It was a new experience, but I must say that I did like being higher than the men of the Legion, amazed at the change in perspective it brought. Not having a Legion to lead was another matter; I found that I missed the banter and chattering that took place in the ranks. Even when I tried to walk with the men for a bit, I found that they were too intimidated by me, which I suppose was understandable. Even as Primus Pilus, the men knew me and were around me on a daily basis. Meanwhile, the men of the 8th barely knew me, and what they did know was that I was second only to Crassus, which put me on a level just below the gods. The result was wide eyes and tight lips when I tried to make conversation with the *Gregarii*. I did take a moment to stop to talk to Gaius, wanting his men to see that I knew him and thought highly of him, but he was clearly not pleased. Although I understood his desire to stand on his own two feet and be seen as his own man, I still felt very protective of him, while I knew how valuable the patronage of a higher ranking man was to my career. Since Gaius had made it clear that he wanted to stay in the army past his first enlistment, I saw no harm in doing what I could while I was still able to help him climb as high as he could. I saw the men of his Century giving him sidelong glances as I trotted Ocelus back to the command group, and I fancied that they were viewing him with newfound respect. Scribonius and Balbus were having similar struggles coping with their new status, and we rode together talking about it.

"I feel about as useful as tits on a man," Balbus grumbled.

Although his remark made me laugh, there was much truth in what he was saying.

"We're not accustomed to having nothing to do," Scribonius agreed, giving both of us a grin. "But I for one am getting used to it. I like not having to worry that Publius left his javelin behind at the last stop, or that Crito stole a chicken from the farm we just passed."

"Not me," Balbus said glumly. "That gave me an excuse to thump someone, and that made my day."

While it was true that Balbus was known for going through his share of *viti*, he talked more about thrashing his men than actually doing it, and he had been well loved by the men of his Century.

"I know what you mean," I admitted. "I'm at a loss just sitting here riding along without a care in the world."

"Well, all I can say is that we earned it," was Scribonius' reply, something that for once all three of us agreed on.

After passing by the range of hills that ran along a north-south axis, and behind which we had seen the reflected glow of the Bastarnae fires against the clouds the night before, we turned almost due south, where our scouts had reported their last sighting of the enemy. Making camp on the crest of a small hill some 15 miles south of the Ister, the men of the 8th worked quickly and efficiently, another sign that they were well-led. This had been the first full day on the march, always a tough day for a Legion, and I was pleased to see that despite their fatigue, the men responded well. I was also tired, but not nearly as much as I thought I would be, which I put down to the fact that I had spent most of the day on Ocelus. The gray stallion and I had definitely formed a bond and for the first time in my life, I actually looked forward to climbing onto his back to spend the day with him. I must confess that I spoiled him rotten, and I still do now that we are both in our dotage.

Our cavalry scouts returned with the news that the Bastarnae, evidently now alerted to our presence, had not stopped for the evening. We had begun to see signs of their predations, in the form of smoking farmhouse, around which were the bodies of men and women who had decided to fight for their homes. What was puzzling me was the intention of the Bastarnae; if they were migrating and looking for a new homeland, why were they still moving? The land we were in was about as fertile as the region provided, at least from what I had been told, so I did not understand their intent. I was not the only one that was puzzled. That night Crassus, Macrinus, and I discussed the matter.

"If they were just looking for plunder, why bring their families?" Macrinus asked, to which neither Crassus nor I could answer.

I thought about it, then ventured an idea.

"Maybe it's a custom of their people to take their families with them on any kind of raid."

Crassus considered this before shaking his head.

"Militarily, that doesn't make any sense," he said. "It just slows them down, and gives them more to worry about."

"It also gives them more to fight for," I pointed out, but I could see that neither man was convinced.

The fact was that we had no idea why they brought their families, and would only learn the answer when and if we captured some Bastarnae in a position to know. The next morning, we set out, heading south, this being the last direction we knew the Bastarnae had been located. Despite seeing signs that they had been there, we still saw no Bastarnae themselves. It was odd, since it would have been normal that a small detachment of the enemy would have been shadowing our movements, yet there was still no real sign of them. After questioning the few survivors that we came across, we learned that while few of the Bastarnae rode horses, their main weapon was supposedly a fearsome sword or something similar that could cleave a man in half, at least if the terrified people we met were to be believed. Naturally, this was instantly relayed through the ranks, and men began talking about the Bastarnae as if they were invincible, all of them standing my height or higher while carrying these great weapons dripping in blood. This weapon, called the falx, required the man wielding it to use two hands according to witnesses, which told me immediately that we would be able to make short work of them, since defending themselves with such a weapon would be difficult against the short Spanish sword.

Consequently, I took a turn walking about the fires that night and to hear the men, these Bastarnae were all Hercules incarnate, compelling me to do what I could to dispel such talk. Stopping at one fire, I listened to the men talk until they became aware of my presence, the conversation stopping as if their throats were cut with a knife. Taking advantage of the silence I asked the men if they minded if I took a seat, which of course they agreed to, scrambling to make room.

"You know," I began, "we thought the same thing about the Arverni, and the Suebi." I saw that I had their attention, so I continued, "In fact, when we faced Ariovistus, we were at Vesontio, and as I recall, there were some Tribunes and even some Centurions who were convinced that we were doomed." I chuckled at the memory, though it was contrived. "Some of the Tribunes suddenly remembered very pressing business they had at Rome. Something about having left a lamp lit in their villa," I joked, gratified to hear the men laugh. "Oh, it was quite a time. But then Caesar called his Centurions and Tribunes to a meeting in the forum, which of course he chose so that we could all linger about and hear what he said. He chewed their asses, I can tell you that. There was nothing but bloody ribbons left when he was through. 'What business is it of yours where we march?' he asked. 'Why don't you trust me to know exactly what I am doing?' They were all shamed, and so were the rest of us. But then Caesar told everyone that he would march with just us in the 10th because he knew he could count on us no matter what. And, well, you know the rest, don't you?" Heads nodded up and down, and I could see that the men felt better.

"Well, I've overstayed my welcome," I said, the men making a half-hearted protest, which I waved away. "I know it was long ago, before any of you were born, but I do remember what it was like to be a *Gregarius*, and I remember how I had the *cac* scared out of me whenever my Primus Pilus showed up at my fire, so I can imagine how you feel when someone like me shows up."

I turned to leave, then heard a voice tremulously call out, "Prefect? May I ask you a question, sir?"

Turning back to see a wide-eyed lad staring at me from across the fire, I was struck by how young and old he looked, all at the same time. He looked young because he was, but he looked so much like so many of my comrades of 30 years earlier that I felt a pang in my heart.

"Of course you can, son."

For a moment it looked like his nerve would fail him, then one of his comrades jabbed him in the ribs, and I heard him whisper, "Go ahead, ask him."

"Is it true that you were one of Caesar's Equestrians?" he blurted out, and I instantly saw that he was not the only man who wanted to know.

"What's your name?" I asked the youngster, who flushed with pleasure that I would bother to ask.

"Aulus Settius, sir."

"Well, Settius, to answer your question, yes I was."

"What was it like? Weren't you . . ." his voice dropped off, embarrassed that he had spoken before he thought the words through.

One never asks another man if he's scared; it is one of those unspoken things that we all know is there, that we all have fear, but it is not something that you talk about around the fire. However, I did not take offense, knowing that his question was innocent.

"I was scared *cac*less," I told him, causing looks of astonishment. "But not for the reason you think. The fact is that I had never sat on a horse before, and I was sure that I was going to fall off in front of Caesar and shame myself and my Cohort."

This drew an appreciative chuckle, so I told the whole story again, for perhaps the thousandth time, the words now coming as if they were second nature. I spoke of how I had been helped in picking out a horse by a sympathetic cavalry trooper, who had instantly seen my inexperience, and how I had clutched at the horse's mane with all my strength, bouncing uncomfortably while we trotted to the agreed upon spot to meet the chief of the Suebi. I recalled how I had been so focused on keeping my horse still that I barely paid attention to what was going on, until I had locked eyes with the yellow-haired man, and how we had exchanged insults. Of course, over the years, the things I said to him have become much cleverer, with his responses that much more slow-witted, but the men appreciated them, which was all that mattered. When I had finished, I was pleased to see that they were much more at ease, giving me hope that I had done some good and I bade them a good and restful night before making my way to another fire to repeat the process. There would be no need, nor would it be possible to visit every fire; just one per Cohort would be enough to have the story spreading throughout the 8th Legion. Once I was done, I retired for the night, feeling useful for the first time since I had become Prefect.

Continuing our search for the Bastarnae, they were proving to be as elusive as a wisp of smoke. Two days after I had gone around the fires, we finally found the swath of churned earth that is the telltale sign of a large group of people, animals, and wagons, except that it had rained so much it was impossible to tell which direction they were heading. The tracks ran in a north-south direction so, thinking they were headed deeper into Moesia, we turned in that direction. As we marched parallel to the track, it became clear after perhaps a half-day that we were headed in the wrong direction. Stopping for a quick conference, Crassus, the Tribunes, Macrinus, and I rode a short distance away from where the men rested to discuss matters.

"It doesn't make any sense," Crassus said. "They're headed back in the direction they came from? Why would they come all this way just to burn a few farms and villages?"

"I think they learned that we were marching after them, and they turned back," Macrinus said.

"That might be," I said doubtfully. "But we're just one Legion against 20,000 warriors? I don't see why they'd be scared of that."

"Maybe they don't know it's just one Legion," Cornelius spoke up, and we turned in some surprise to the young Tribune, who blushed mightily at the attention.

"I think the Tribune might be right," Macrinus said thoughtfully.

Crassus nodded in agreement, then said, "I believe he may be as well, but we're still going after those bastards. I plan on making them sorry they ever decided to leave their lands."

Turning a Legion on the march in the opposite direction is not nearly as easy as it probably seems it should be. If it were just a case of making the drag Legion the vanguard, with the vanguard Legion becoming the drag, it would be simple, but there is the baggage train that must be moved aside, and turning the wagons requires a good deal of room to maneuver. Complicating matters was the ruined earth of the Bastarnae track, which we had to avoid putting the wagons into or they would become bogged down in the soft earth. It took almost a quarter part of the day to get everything turned around before we were back on the march, this time heading north. The fear that the men had for the Bastarnae had disappeared, turning into irritation at the wild chase they were putting them through. We marched the rest of that day before making camp. It was that night that Prixus, the gladiator who was the chief of Crassus' bodyguards, decided it was time to get even with me.

I will say that he chose his time well. I had gone to Scribonius' and Balbus' tent, where we passed the evening drinking more than we should have, considering that we were on the march, but riding instead of walking convinced us that we could indulge ourselves. Consequently, I was weaving a bit when I left their tent, my mind elsewhere, thinking of a slim, brown woman with large eyes. On an impulse, I decided to go visit Ocelus. For some reason, being with my horse when I felt a bout of melancholy coming made me feel better. I heard him blowing as I approached his stable; like all the stallions, he was penned off separately to avoid the inevitable clashes that happen between males when there are females involved. When I called his name, he nickered softly in answer, his ears pricked forward. Looking back, I should have been on my guard because Ocelus was not acting in his normal fashion, nosing through my tunic looking for a hidden treat, instead tossing his head nervously, pawing the ground.

"What's the matter with you?" I asked him, reaching out to soothe him with a pat on the flank.

The blow, when it came, was completely unexpected, slamming into my kidney like a hammer, and it was just the first. The second blow was to the back of my head, my knees buckling immediately, stars exploding in my head as I reached out to grab the top rail of Ocelus' stall. A hand that felt like it was made of iron grabbed my arm, keeping me from steadying myself, while more blows rained down on me. Without the support of the stall, I fell to my knees, trying to cover my head with my arms, but they were grabbed by a pair of hands on each one, pulling them away from my body. To that point, nobody had stepped in front of me, so I could not see who was attacking me, nor had a word been spoken, the only sounds the harsh breathing of the men beating me, but it was hard to hear because of the roaring in my ears. Despite the fact that I was dazed and disoriented, I noticed that whoever was beating me was taking care only to strike me from behind, with most of the blows to my body. I felt and heard one of my ribs snap, a white-hot stab of pain lancing through my body and I opened my mouth to cry out, then something stopped me. Suddenly, I recognized that as much as they were trying to hurt me, they wanted to humiliate me by making me cry out and that mulishness that had dogged me from my first days came back as I clamped my mouth shut. This seemed to arouse my attackers to new heights of fury, making the next several moments some of the most painful of my life. Although I do not know why, I did not put up much of a struggle once my arms had been secured, despite the fact I could tell that if I had used all my strength I would have been able to pull free. It is hard to describe, but there was a part of me that accepted this beating, the first such experience of my life, here in my forty-eighth year. All I can ascribe it to is that I was relieved that for the first time since Miriam's death, I was feeling something, anything other than the numbness that seemed to soak through every fiber of my being. I do not know how long they continued; I suppose that somewhere along the way I lost consciousness, because my next memory is the smell of damp earth and manure, the feel of it pressing against my cheek. The next sensation I felt was the pressure of something against my foot, followed by a nickering as Ocelus nosed me. Thinking to reassure my horse, I tried to push myself up, but I was stopped by a rush of pain that for the first time forced a moan from my lips, and I fell back to the ground. I could not take a deep breath and, for a few moments, I had to fight a rising panic that I was going to suffocate there on the dirt floor of the stable. Finally calming down, I once again tried to push myself up, resolving to ignore the pain no matter how bad it was. Putting my hands flat on the dirt, I pushed upward with all my strength, hearing someone scream out in horrible pain. That is the last thing I remember of that night.

If there is a more unpleasant way of waking up than being bounced about in the back of a wagon being pulled over a rutted road, I do not know what it is, nor do I want to find out. Jolted back to consciousness by a particularly deep rut that felt like it was focused on beating me as badly as I had been the night before, I heard myself groan when I opened my eyes, sensing movement before seeing Diocles' face hovering above me, his eyes filled with concern.

"Am I dead?"

He gave me the kind of smile that one gives a badly injured man, shaking his head quickly.

"No, master, you're not dead, but you gave us quite a scare. You're in the back of one of the wagons now, and you're safe."

"I gathered that," I muttered, more intent on taking an inventory of my body than having a conversation.

Wiggling my toes, I flexed my leg muscles next, relieved that they were relatively pain free, but when I tried to turn my head, a sharp pain at the back of my skull stopped me. After that, I tried my arms and I was surprised to find them more or less intact, despite my forearms being sore where my attackers had grabbed my arms to pin them. The major source of my pain was in my back, explaining why I had been placed face down on a wooden board in the wagon. Seated next to Diocles was a bearded man I recognized as Crassus' personal physician, a man named Philipos. Seeing me look at him, he cleared his throat before speaking in heavily accented Latin that was barely understandable. I waved a hand at him to stop him.

"I speak and understand Greek, so tell me how bad off I am."

"You have at least one broken rib, and perhaps two. You've been passing blood for the last two days......"

"Two days?" I interrupted, looking over at Diocles, who nodded unhappily.

"As I said, master, you gave us quite a scare. You've been unconscious for two full days."

That got my attention, I can tell you. The only other time I had been out for that long had been when I was almost killed at Munda, so I immediately understood how badly I had been injured.

"Is there any permanent damage?"

Words could not express my relief when the physician shook his head.

"No, you'll heal in time, though at your age it will take longer than it would have in the past. Your back is heavily bruised, and it will take some time before they fully disappear."

"You don't have to remind me that I'm old," I snapped.

Turning back to Diocles, I saw that he was standing up, heading to the small door of the wagon.

"Where are you going?"

"The general ordered me to let him know the moment you regain consciousness."

He jumped out, while I endured the examination of the physician, who peeled back the poultices that had been placed on my back. Taking a jar from his bag, he began dabbing some vile-smelling concoction on my back, only stopping when I described in vivid detail what I would do to him and his family if he continued. Rather than be intimidated, he just shrugged, obviously accustomed to such threats from his patients.

"It's up to you if you want to take longer to heal," he sniffed. "This," he waved the jar, "is worth its weight in gold and it will help you heal much more quickly. But if you can't bear a little discomfort in order to be back on your feet more quickly, that's your affair."

"I wonder how much discomfort you'll feel when I shove that jar up your ass?" I growled, but he just laughed, showing even, white teeth.

"According to you Romans, I would enjoy it, being Greek. So perhaps you should think of something else to threaten me with."

Realizing that in this battle of wits I was overmatched, I very grudgingly said, "If you think it's going to do some good, go ahead and put that stuff on. But it smells like rank horse*cac*," I could not resist a Parthian shot of my own.

"Ah, you guessed the secret ingredient," he said as he resumed his ministrations.

Philipos was just finishing up when the door was thrown open, Crassus hopping inside.

"I heard a rumor that you were alive, but I had to come see for myself."

"Forgive me for not getting to my feet, sir. I'm alive, but I've felt better."

"I can imagine," he said dryly. "You gave us a scare, Prefect," echoing Diocles' words as he sat on the bench opposite.

He wrinkled his nose, looking over at the physician.

"I see you're using your famous concoction on the Prefect, and that it smells as bad as always."

"I didn't notice you complaining when it worked," the physician retorted, and Crassus grinned, turning to me.

"He's right. It smells like Pluto's asshole, but it does work." Turning serious, he asked me, "Prefect, did you see who did this to you?"

"No, I didn't."

I waited to see what Crassus would say next, since Prixus was his man, and while I had never told him the details of our encounter, he knew that something had happened between us.

"Well, I'm sure you have an idea who it was." He looked at me levelly, his eyes revealing nothing.

"Not really," I said, seeing what might have been a flicker of anger flash across his face.

"That's disappointing," he said after a moment. "Because I was hoping that you could identify the culprit, who we both know was Prixus."

I stared at him for a long time, trying to decide how much the man could be trusted. As far as I was concerned, I could hardly be blamed for being extremely leery of placing my faith in anyone of the upper classes, given all that I had experienced, yet to that moment I had seen nothing in Crassus' nature that suggested he was of the same breed as Lepidus. Or Octavian, for that matter, which I believe was one of the causes of what happened to Crassus later. Seeing that I was not going to say anything, he heaved a sigh.

"You see, the problem is that Prixus and his men were very careful. Normally a man administering a beating as severe as you endured would bear the marks of his handiwork, but apparently, they wrapped their hands in rags to avoid having skinned knuckles. Not just any rags, either, but lengths of linen cut into strips that just happen to be the width of a man's hand."

"That's a trick of the *pankratiostoi*," Philipos observed. "Something that a gladiator would know."

"How do you know they wrapped their hands?" Diocles asked curiously.

"We found them discarded by the stables, so they couldn't be connected to the beating of the Prefect."

"Have they been questioned?" I asked, despite being sure I knew the answer.

"They have," he sighed, "but they all took solemn oaths that they were together playing dice. It was quite elaborate, I must say. They described almost every throw that was made, who won how much, and so on. Which is how I know they're lying." He looked down at me as he said, "I was hoping that the Prefect got a glimpse of them, but since he didn't, I suppose I have to have them tortured."

"No," I said, sharply enough that the extra force caused me to wince in pain. "Don't do that." I saw his brow furrow, and I hurried to amend my words since he clearly did not appreciate me making it sound like an order. "I'm asking that you don't do that, sir. As I said, I didn't see them, and I'd hate to think that possibly innocent men would be tortured because of a minor misunderstanding."

I will say that the words tasted foul in my mouth, because I was lying through my teeth, and Crassus looked supremely unconvinced.

"So you're saying that you're worried about these men, even knowing that they beat you to a pulp?"

He gave a snorting laugh.

"I don't know that they're the ones who beat me, sir. It could have been someone else."

"Who? You haven't been with this army long enough to make an enemy who hates you enough to risk the consequences of assaulting a Camp Prefect."

"Maybe some Bastarnae sneaked into camp." Even as I said it, I knew how absurd the idea was.

Crassus gave another snort, this one of clear impatience.

"I know you don't expect me to believe that, Pullus. And there's more at stake here than your pride. I can't allow my second in command to be assaulted and let it go unpunished."

"I didn't say anything about it going unpunished," I replied.

"And that's another thing, Prefect. I can't worry about my bodyguards showing up with their throats cut while we're on the march. That's as unacceptable in its own way as letting them get away with it."

"Nobody's going to show up dead, sir. I give you my word that nothing will happen that would cause you embarrassment or disrupt our operations in the field."

I was lying, and we both knew it, but as far as I was concerned, this was the first major test in our relationship as Legate and Prefect and I was gambling on him trusting me. He said nothing for a very long time before he finally relented.

"Very well. I'm going to trust you on this, Pullus, but don't disappoint me."

He stood to leave, giving me an awkward pat on the shoulder as he did so.

"In the meantime, rest and recover. If we catch up to the Bastarnae, we're going to need you."

I spent another day in the wagon before I felt up to riding Ocelus, but I did not spend a full day in the saddle before I had to retire back to the wagon for the rest of the time. I could only move with difficulty, with sudden motion being out of the question, which meant that if we had caught up with the Bastarnae, I would have been sitting in the wagon for the fight. Scribonius and Balbus kept me company, but neither of them could stand the jolting ride for very long before they left to climb back on their mounts. The hardest part of the ordeal was not the pain, but enduring the smirks of Prixus and his men. However, I had learned the value of patience, albeit the hard way, so I ignored them. Continuing north, we closed in on the Bastarnae, who were clearly fleeing the country at our approach. Talking it over with Crassus and Macrinus, the only reason we could come up with was that they thought they were being chased by the whole army and not just one Legion.

"Although all they have to do is come ride up that hill over there and look down and see that it's just us," Macrinus commented.

"I don't think they have any real interest in fighting us," Crassus replied. "I believe they just thought that they'd take advantage of our absence, and now that we've shown up, they want to go home."

Despite the fact I could not discount what the two were saying, I was not so sure that the Bastarnae had no intention of facing us. There was just a nagging feeling that would not go away that something was happening that I could not identify, but had learned long before not to ignore.

"We'll see," was all I would say, and the Legion continued its pursuit.

After another day, our scouts returned to inform us that it appeared that the Bastarnae were intent on crossing back over the Ister River, because they were commandeering every boat they could find.

"If we hurry, we can catch them before they cross the river," Crassus said at our morning briefing.

"We can pin them there and finish them off."

Exchanging a glance with Macrinus, who gave me a slight shrug, I felt compelled to ask Crassus, "Why would we want to do that? Shouldn't we just be happy that they're heading back where they came from?"

"And only have them come back as soon as we leave?" Crassus shook his head. "No, we're going to make sure that they don't cross the border again."

Although I did not agree, I could not argue that the order made sense, and really all there was to do about it was salute, then carry out Crassus' orders. As it would turn out, the Bastarnae were given a reprieve, and if they had been smart, they would have used that opportunity to get away and never come back. On the next day, shortly after we started the march that would take us to the banks of the Ister to face and slaughter the Bastarnae, the cavalry contingent that acted as rearguard sent a man galloping up to us in the command group. Barely sketching out a salute, the rider said something to Crassus that none of us understood, then Crassus snapped at him to slow down and repeat himself.

"There's a large force of warriors to our rear, marching our way!"

Chapter 2-Runo

Crassus wasted no time.

Turning to me, he said quickly, "Pullus, I need to know what's going on in our rear. Take your Evocati friends and go take a look, then report back to me immediately."

Without waiting for my acknowledgment, he turned to Macrinus, who had come trotting up at the summons of the *bucina* call.

"What Cohort is marching drag?"

"Today, it's the Seventh."

"Good. Have Palma turn about and stand ready."

I did not hear the rest since I had already trotted off with Scribonius, Balbus, and the other Evocati following behind. There were only 20 Evocati attached to the 8th Legion, the rest being with the bulk of the army, not enough to engage a force of any size, yet large enough to deter an enemy scouting force from attacking us. Moving quickly until we reached the base of a ridge that we had just marched over, I stopped for a moment to give the others their orders.

Indicating Scribonius and Balbus, I said loudly enough for all to hear, "We're going to go up the ridge and see what's on the other side. I want the rest of you come halfway up and wait for us there."

Pointing to two other Evocati, I posted one on each flank, out perhaps a quarter mile to warn us if anyone tried to come up from a different direction.

"I don't remember volunteering for this," Balbus grumbled.

"You didn't," I said, giving him a grin. "But you're coming anyway."

Trotting up the hill until we neared the crest, we slowed to a walk so that just the top of our heads inched up over the rim of the hill. Once we reached a point where we could see, we stopped, searching the ground in front of us. At first, I saw nothing, then Scribonius pointed off to our right.

"There. See? That cloud of dust?"

As I turned to where he was pointing, my heart started beating more rapidly; there was indeed a smudge of dust hanging just over a line of trees. The ground was not exceptionally dry, so I knew that it would take quite a few feet to create even that size cloud, but at that moment, we still could not see anything.

I sighed and said, "I guess we have to get closer to see exactly what's headed for us."

"Whoever it is, there are a lot of them," Balbus replied.

Nevertheless, they both followed me without complaint when I crested the ridge. Before I crossed over, I turned to signal for the rest of the Evocati to follow me, then headed down the slope towards the line of trees. Drawing closer, we could see by the position of the dust that whatever was causing it was still on the far side of the trees, meaning that we would have to go into the forest, which I did not like at all. It could not be helped; Crassus had ordered me to find out what kind of threat was headed for us, and that was what I would do. Reaching the trees, I repeated my orders to the other Evocati, taking Scribonius and Balbus with me. Since we had skirted this small forest when we had marched by, I did not know what to expect, and I was dismayed to see that the space between the trees was choked with undergrowth. It was not anything that Ocelus and the other horses could not push through, but there was no way to do it silently, or at least so I thought. If this advancing force had scouts of their own, a practical certainty, there was no way to get close enough to get a good look at what was coming quietly with our horses crashing through the brush.

Leaning down, I whispered to Ocelus, "I need you to move as quietly as you can, boy. I know it's hard, but I know you can do it."

Twitching his ears and pawing at the ground in answer, Ocelus began moving forward. To my intense relief and surprise, he began weaving through the dense undergrowth, making hardly a whisper of sound. I turned to see that Scribonius and Balbus were following, their horses following Ocelus' lead, communicating in that way that horses seem to have that is beyond our understanding. All I could do was give a shrug while pointing at my horse, which was moving like a cat, albeit a big one, in the basic direction I had pointed him. I became so fascinated watching Ocelus navigate his way that I forgot to keep looking farther ahead than just a few feet. We were also approaching upwind, because Ocelus gave no indication that anyone was nearby. Making his way so quietly that when he picked his way through what looked like a solid wall of growth, we were no more than 20 paces away from a man on horseback, who had evidently just pulled up because his horse had alerted him to our presence. He was dressed in a manner similar to what I had seen of the Dacians, in a short tunic and a cloak of a muted brown tone. He was young, although by this point, everyone looked young to me, but he had a full beard of a reddish color, with very vivid blue eyes, opened wide in surprise. His mouth hung open, and in one of those strange moments of clarity that seem to happen in times like this, I noticed that he was missing one of his front upper teeth. For several long, slow heartbeats, we just sat staring at each other, before he roused himself from his trance to jerk the head of his horse around. The beast, as startled as its rider, reared a bit, then pivoted on its back legs, taking a giant leap away from me before I came to my senses.

Scribonius had just come up behind us and, looking over my shoulder and seeing the fleeing scout, shouted, "Titus, we can't let him escape!"

Without thinking about it, I jammed Ocelus in the ribs with my heels while slapping his rump hard with my left hand, the first time I had ever struck him in such a manner. It was a lucky thing that my tension at being surprised had caused me to grip the reins extra tightly, or I would have been thrown off when he made his first jump like he was shot from a ballista. Suddenly, in the space of time it takes to blink an eye, we were thundering at full speed, ripping through the thickets as if they were not there. In just a few bounds, we closed the distance that the scout had gained with his initial burst, but I quickly realized that I was more concerned with not falling off Ocelus' back than taking down another mounted rider. Instantly following that was the thought that I had never fought on horseback, and had no real idea how to do it.

Looking ahead, I could see the brighter light and thinning trees that signaled the end of the forest. Leaning forward, I shouted to Ocelus to go faster. He must have understood because I felt the bunching of his muscles between my thighs, and before I could take a full breath, we were pulling abreast of the Bastarnae. He had been down low over his horse's neck, making his own pleas to his mount to go faster, but then he sensed me next to him. In one fluid motion, he swung his spear, whipping it over his head in a backhand that I just managed to twist aside to avoid, hearing the tip whistle past my ear even above the roaring sound caused by the speed of my horse. My sudden movement almost unseated me, taking a heartbeat of time to regain my balance before I drew my own sword. Immediately, I let out a string of curses; as always, I had been carrying my Gallic blade, which is an infantry weapon, and for fighting on the ground there is no finer weapon in the world. But this was a cavalry fight, and while somehow Ocelus had known or sensed to draw abreast of the man on his left side, I needed a blade at least a foot longer to do any good. The scout had recovered from his first swing at me, making a second attempt, but I was ready for it this time, knocking the blow aside with my blade. Gritting my teeth, but refusing to offer up a prayer to the gods, I decided to rely on my skill and willingness to die, nudging Ocelus with my left knee, commanding him to move closer to the Bastarnae scout. Seeing his ears twitch backward, I could almost hear his thoughts, asking, "Are you mad?" yet he obeyed instantly.

We were now about a hundred paces away from the edge of the forest. I heard shouting off to the right, yet I could pay no attention, since I had pulled within arm's length of the Bastarnae. Moving Ocelus this close to the other horse was extremely dangerous because neither animal was running in a perfectly straight line, picking their way around obstacles, and my movement made the man panic. He took one last wild swing, his body twisting sideways, only the fact that he was a superb horseman keeping him from falling off. It did not save him from my blade as I thrust it into his unprotected side. I heard him grunt, except that he did not fall, stubbornly clinging to the saddle and I understood that since I had been unable to put my weight behind the thrust, using only the strength of my arm, it had not been a killing blow. In desperation, I reached out while still holding my sword, grabbing the neck of the man's tunic while pushing Ocelus in the side with my right knee, moving him to the left. Immediately veering away, it felt like my arm was going to come out of its socket, but I just managed to hang on so that the man was dragged from his saddle. Releasing my grip, I watched him slam into the ground at a full gallop and he let out a scream as his body tumbled through the underbrush, arms and legs flailing wildly. Panting for breath, my arm felt as if it were on fire, but I was also exultant, feeling the flush that comes with victory and vanquishing your foe. That feeling was short-lived, as I heard Scribonius behind me, shouting a warning.

"Don't let the horse get away! They'll know something is wrong when they see him come back without his rider!"

But it was too late; I caught just a glimpse of the hindquarters of the animal as it went bursting out of the woods, into the brighter light. Cursing, I turned Ocelus about, blowing hard but otherwise showing little fatigue, and trotted back to where Scribonius was just dismounting, sword in hand. He walked over to the fallen man, who was moaning in pain and bleeding heavily from the wound in his side. I reached the two, and it was then I noticed that Balbus was missing.

"Where's Balbus?"

Scribonius jerked his head in a direction indicating generally back in the direction where he had just come.

"This one's partner," he explained. "He was deeper in the woods and somehow we missed him. Balbus cut off his line of retreat, and he headed back that way."

That explained the shouting, and I could only hope that Balbus and the rest of the Evocati managed to stop this man's partner. Despite his obvious pain, our new captive was glaring up at us.

"He's a feisty one," Scribonius remarked, nudging the man with a toe, who responded by spitting at us.

Immediately, I took a step forward to put my foot directly on the man's wound, causing him to throw his head back, letting out a shriek of agony. All signs of defiance were gone, and he looked up at me with haunted eyes, seeing in me not a shred of pity.

"How many Bastarnae are in your party?" I asked him, speaking in Latin but very slowly, hoping that he knew enough of our words to understand me.

He cocked his head, then shook it.

"Pluto's cock," I muttered, switching to Greek and repeating the question.

I got the same reaction, and I turned to Scribonius.

"I thought these people spoke Greek, or at least understood it."

"They do, as far as I know, but let's face it, we don't know much about the Bastarnae."

Squatting down, Scribonius examined the man's wound, then asked him quietly, again in Greek, "You understand us, don't you?"

For a moment, the man did nothing, and I was sure that we were wasting our time. Finally, he nodded slowly.

"Good," Scribonius said, shooting me a look of satisfaction that he had been able to extract from the man with a kind tone what I had not with a boot to the side.

"Your wound isn't fatal. If it's treated, you'll live," Scribonius said meaningfully. "And I give you my word as an officer of the Roman army that it will be treated, but only if you cooperate. Do you understand?"

The man said nothing, just nodded his head. Scribonius was right; if treated, his wound was not fatal, except that he was losing blood rapidly, his eyes beginning to dim as he weakened.

"We know that the main Bastarnae army is trying to cross back over the Ister, but we also know that you're a scout of another Bastarnae force. How large is it, and did you get separated? Are you a war party, or do you have your families like the main group?"

The scout lay looking up at Scribonius, a strange expression coming over his face when my friend asked the question. When Scribonius was finished the man said nothing, looking from Scribonius to me, then back to Scribonius, still not speaking. Then, he gave an almost imperceptible shrug, and I began to get angry.

"This is a waste of time," I growled, taking a step forward and lifting my foot to kick him in his side again.

He let out a gasp, holding his hands up in supplication, shaking his head wildly.

"I . . . not Bastarnae."

My foot stopped, hovering just above his side as Scribonius and I looked at each other.

"What do you mean, you're not Bastarnae?" Scribonius asked. "What other tribe is marching with the Bastarnae?"

Again, the man shook his head.

"We not with the Bastarnae. We march against Rome on our own." Some of the defiance came back and he looked into my eyes, the hatred in them needing no translation. "This is our land, not Rome land. We will destroy your army, Roman. We will drive you out of our land and you will never come back."

"Where are we exactly?" I asked Scribonius.

He cocked his head, thinking for a moment.

"Moesia, I believe."

This got a reaction from the man, who nodded vigorously.

"Yes! I Moesian. My army is from Moesia. And we will kill all of you and Rome will never come back!"

Scribonius stood, and we moved a few paces away so the prisoner could not hear us.

"I think he's telling the truth," he said.

"So do I. It makes sense, I suppose. I know that the Moesians have been just as much of a handful as the Pannonians and all the other tribes in this gods-forsaken place.

I'm guessing they saw a chance to strike a blow at just one Legion."

Turning back to the man, I asked him, "How many are in your army?"

At first, he refused to answer, but all I had to do was lift my foot and he blurted out, "Many thousands! Many!"

I sighed, rolling my eyes at Scribonius. It was clear that this youth had little experience in his army.

"You need to be specific." I saw he did not understand the word, and I searched for a better way. "We need to know exactly how many thousands there are. Ten?"

He shook his head.

"Less? Six?"

Another shake of the head.

"More. Fifteen?"

That got a shrug, which I took to be a positive answer. I cursed again, turning back to Scribonius.

"What do you think?"

Scribonius frowned, considering the question.

"I don't think it's that many, but I think it's more than 10,000, just judging from that cloud of dust. Whatever, I think we've gotten all we're going to out of him."

"Not quite," I answered. Squatting back down, I asked the scout, "How many men like you? On horses?"

In answer, he first held up three, then four fingers, prompting another curse from me.

"Four thousand?"

He nodded. This was not a good situation to be in at all. We were essentially one Legion caught between two vastly superior forces, in numbers at least. If these two separate armies were in communication and realized our predicament, we were dead men, every one of us. I turned back to the scout, thinking to ask him if he knew whether or not some sort of pact or alliance had been enacted between the Bastarnae and Moesians, but realized he would have no idea.

When he saw my hesitation, I think he mistook it for fear, because he blurted out, "We will drive Rome from these lands!

70

Runo will kill all of you, and Rome will leave and never come back."

Scribonius and I exchanged a look; we had at least learned the name of the leader of this army. This Runo did not know it yet, but he had made the lives of his people very, very difficult. I knelt by the scout, who was little more than a boy, looking him in the eyes, and I was struck again by what a vivid color of blue they were, almost the color of Caesar's but a little darker.

"Even if your Runo does manage to kill all of us, boy, there's something you need to remember." I paused for a moment, then said, "Rome always comes back."

While I spoke these last words, I drew my dagger across his throat, cutting so deeply I could feel the blade grating against the bone, almost severing his head. His eyes opened wider in astonishment, a gurgling sound emanating from the hole, his back arching and heels digging into the ground, which began drumming with each spasm of his legs as the light left his eyes. Wiping the blade off on his tunic, I stood up, turning to see Scribonius standing there, open-mouthed in astonishment and anger.

"Titus, you killed that boy," he gasped. "After I gave him my word that he'd live!"

"You gave your word," I said shortly. "I didn't."

And without waiting for a response, I walked over to leap onto the back of Ocelus.

"We need to go tell Crassus about this. And find Balbus. Are you coming or not?"

I looked down at him standing there, and for a long, awful moment, I thought he might actually say no, but he closed his mouth, the muscles of his jaws clenching, then gave a curt nod. Climbing aboard his own mount, he followed me while we retraced our steps back in the direction we had come.

Balbus had indeed caught the other scout and was waiting for Scribonius and me with the rest of the Evocati at the edge of the forest. I briefly related what we had learned on our way back to the Legion at a fast trot. Passing the Seventh standing ready, nodding to Gaius, but not stopping to let him know what was happening, we made our way to the command group. I made my report to Crassus and Macrinus, who had remained with his general while we were gone, the rest of the Legion having halted and were resting easy.

"Moesians?" Crassus echoed when I told him what was headed our way. "It has to be that bastard Runo behind this," he said.

"That's who the scout said was leading this army," I told Crassus, impressed that he had instantly identified the leader of the Moesians without being told.

"He's been causing us trouble for years," he explained. "But I never thought he'd have the nerve to actually get an army of that size to march for him."

Crassus considered the situation for a moment, the rest of us remaining silent while he decided what to do. As second in command, I suppose I could have spoken my mind without waiting, but I was learning to trust the man.

Finally, he said, "We need to deal with this threat now. The Bastarnae can wait."

He turned to give Macrinus his orders, and I waited for him to address the one nagging thought that had occurred to me in the forest. After a moment when it became clear he was not, I spoke up.

"What if it's a trap?"

That stopped him, and he turned in his saddle, a concerned expression on his face.

"What are you talking about?"

"What if the Bastarnae and the Moesians are working together?"

"What makes you think that?"

"Thirty years of experience," I replied, but not unpleasantly. "It happened in Gaul more than once, where tribes worked together. Have you noticed that the Bastarnae line of march has drawn us deeper into Moesia? That might be an accident, but then again, it might not. Have we heard from our scouts? Have they made it back across the river?"

Crassus looked troubled, exchanging a glance with Macrinus.

"As a matter of fact, no. Silva just sent a man back to tell me that the Bastarnae have gathered enough boats but they haven't crossed yet. His report says that they're just camped on this side of the river, not moving."

"So we're essentially between two numerically superior forces, and we don't even have a river to protect us from one of them."

Crassus did not hesitate a moment, calling for a mounted trooper, who I assumed had been the man sent by Silva, the cavalry commander. While waiting for the rider to reach his side, Crassus took a wax tablet from an aide.

Using his stylus, he scrawled a quick note before pressing his signet into the wax.

Handing the tablet to the rider, he said, "Take this to Siscia quickly. Take a spare horse so that you can switch mounts. Tell Tribune Claudius that I expect him to be marching by daylight after he's received this order. Now go!"

The man did not hesitate, saluting as he wheeled his horse, going off in search of a spare mount. Crassus turned back to me, thanking me for bringing up the possibility, which I just shrugged off.

"I'm just doing my duty. And I don't know that they are working together."

"But I don't want to find out the hard way," Crassus agreed. "Regardless, these Moesians are closer than the Bastarnae, so if they are working together, they'll miss their chance. We're going to tackle the Moesians first, and hopefully they'll be finished before the Bastarnae show up."

With that, he issued the orders to turn the Legion around, form up in battle formation, then march back up the ridgeline that was between the 8th and the forest that the Moesians would be passing through. The Moesians had undoubtedly been alerted that something was amiss, with the return of a riderless horse and the disappearance of one other scout, yet that actually worked in our favor. If this Runo was even a somewhat competent commander, the disappearance of his scouts would slow his advance while he sent out either a larger scouting party, or a detachment of his infantry into the woods. Meanwhile, the 8th made the necessary movements to array themselves and I found myself with the rest of the Evocati and the command staff, waiting while Crassus cantered about making sure that things were going as he wanted. After a moment, I felt eyes burning a hole in my back, turning to see Scribonius glaring at me. Sighing, I nudged Ocelus to walk over to my best friend, who said nothing, just continued to stare at me.

"What?" I finally snapped, despite knowing exactly why he was upset.

"You know what," he said, his tone quiet, but I could hear the seething anger just underneath. "You killed that boy, Titus, after I had given him my word.'

"You didn't break your word," I insisted, the mulishness in me coming back to the surface.

A part of me knew that if I just apologized and admitted what I had done was wrong, things would be fine between us, but I was not in the mood to apologize or make peace in any way.

"Oh, I don't give a brass obol about that, and you know it," Scribonius snapped, his face turning red with anger. "There was no need to kill that boy. Don't you have enough blood on your hands to last you ten lifetimes?" He took a deep breath, clearly struggling to compose himself. "It's just that I've never seen you kill when it wasn't necessary, and killing that boy wasn't necessary."

I only shrugged, refusing to look at him, knowing that every word he spoke was true. Then he said something that only Sextus Scribonius could have said to me without being run through.

"Killing that boy won't bring Miriam back," he said quietly. "No matter how many people you kill, you'll still feel that loss."

I glared at him, yet I could not find any words to say. My silence must have encouraged him to continue, although I wished he hadn't.

"I know you've turned your back on the gods, but know that I pray every night to them, on your behalf."

"Don't," I interrupted him, my voice harsh. "I piss on the gods, every one of them. I don't want my name in your mouth when you beg the gods for favors."

He just looked at me sadly, shaking his head as he heaved a great sigh, looking at the men of the 8th, who had moved into position.

"Well, it looks like they're ready to move," he said, turning away from me to trot after the Legion, which was now marching up the hill.

I opened my mouth to call out to him, to say something, but no words came and I sat there for several moments before I followed.

Crassus positioned the first line just below the crest of the hill, yet with enough room for the second line to be on the same side. We would be hampered by the lack of cavalry, especially if the scout had been correct in his numbers, but Crassus called the Evocati together and, placing me in charge, ordered us to remain behind the Legion on the crest so we could move to a danger point if needed. Before he could leave, I called him to the side, somewhat embarrassed about what I had to tell him.

"General, I have a problem." I pointed to the sword at my side. "This blade is too short to fight from horseback, and I believe that the same goes for Scribonius and Balbus."

Our first day on the march, I recalled that I had noticed that the Evocati who had this status for a while all carried the *spatha*, the longer cavalry sword, but truth be told I had not thought much about it. Now I knew why they did so, and I was chagrined to admit to Crassus that I had not thought to change weapons.

"So it is," he remarked, then thought a moment. "No matter. I have a spare in my wagon. Go tell Crito that he's to give it to you for the duration, until we get back to a spot where you can purchase your own blade." I thanked him, then left to find his slave, and he called out after me, "Pullus, this is just a loan, remember. I want that blade back."

I was irritated that he would feel the need to make that comment, at least until I saw the blade.

"This is his spare?" I gasped when Crito handed it to me.

The scabbard alone must have cost a small fortune and I was tempted to refuse it, fearful that if something happened to it I would have to pay for it, but when I drew it, my hesitation vanished. I saw immediately that it was a Gallic blade like my own, though I was forced to admit that the workmanship was even better than mine, and I wondered how much this weapon cost. Reminding myself to thank Crassus, now understanding why he had said what he had, I was faced with a dilemma. I could not carry two swords at my side and while I could have put my own in my own wagon, I just could not bear to part with it. It had been my almost constant companion into battle for more than 20 years and Crito, seeing my hesitation, made a suggestion.

"Master, many men strap the scabbard to the saddle. In fact, Master Crassus has done so on many occasions."

My immediate thought was that in all the confusion and galloping about in a battle, that the scabbard would come loose and be lost.

"Have you ever fastened a scabbard in this manner?"

He shook his head, but said, "No, but I've seen it done many times. I know I could do it in the same way."

His manner was so certain that I decided to let him and I dismounted Ocelus to hold the reins while he worked. He used some leather thongs and when he was finished, I gave the scabbard several tugs in different directions, but it seemed very secure. Leaping back aboard Ocelus, I threw him a coin as a thank you, then went to find the rest of the Evocati. When I found them, I could see that Scribonius was still angry with me, while from the furtive glances between them, I surmised that he had been speaking to Balbus about what I had done. I wish I could say that I was feeling guilty about my actions, yet I did not. Truthfully, I did feel badly, but it was because Scribonius was angry with me, and I was now equally angry with him. Nevertheless, I forced myself to keep my tone professional when I told the two to go to the Legion quartermaster to draw two *spatha* for themselves. Balbus pointed to the one strapped to my saddle.

"I don't suppose that it will be like that one, will it?"

I laughed at that.

"Not likely."

"Good," he said as they trotted off. "Because if it was, you'd never see me again."

By the time the first Moesian scouts appeared out of the woods, the sun was hanging low in the sky. Runo had obviously stopped to send more scouts out, slowing his advance through the woods. Despite expecting it, the mounted still men pulled up short at the sight of a full Legion, waiting on the hill for them. The ridge ran for a few miles in either direction, meaning that if Runo chose to try to find a spot farther along than where we were, we would simply fall on his flank by traversing the length of the ridge. Peering up at us for several moments, the scouts wheeled their mounts to flee back into the forest. It was some time later that we could see the underbrush between the trees start to shake, followed by the appearance of the vanguard of the Moesian army. Calling it an army is being charitable; it was more of an armed mob, at least by the way they marched. Even from the distance we were at, it was clear to see that what they had going for them was in numbers alone. They came boiling out of the woods, flowing in our general direction until the front ranks came to a sudden halt still some distance away from the base of the hill.

"Where's their cavalry?" I heard someone ask.

That was a good question, since all that was in sight at this point was the Moesian infantry. The men of the Evocati began looking in other directions, until one of them shouted. Pointing east of our position, farther down the ridgeline, we could just make out a smudge of dust, under which was a dark line that experience told us was a body of men and from the speed they were moving, we knew they had to be mounted.

"They're trying to roll us up," Balbus commented.

"I guess this Runo isn't as stupid as we thought," I grunted before telling Balbus to hurry and find Crassus with this news.

Meanwhile, the rest of the Moesian army had emerged from the forest, moving in the direction of the men of the first line. The sound of their shouting finally began reaching us, a dull roar that came washing over us in a sound I had heard so many times before it was impossible to count. Scribonius was clearly thinking the same thing.

"By the gods, to think I would have missed out on this! This never gets old!"

I looked over at him as did he at me and we exchanged a grin, our anger with each other evaporating in the excitement of the moment. Despite being outnumbered, with a sizable force of cavalry on our flank, I could see that he was as unworried as I was, which I suppose came from the habit of victory, especially against native tribes such as what faced us here. Starting in Gaul, we had always prevailed against our enemies, even when we had suffered temporary setbacks like at Gergovia. The only real defeat we had ever suffered was in Parthia, but we put that down to the mistakes made by Antonius, who had proven to be unlucky and unfit to command such an enterprise. Otherwise, we had looked over our shields at every enemy that came at us, only to see the deaths and the backs of every one of them. What I took to be the Moesian officers were all mounted, while one of them, who I was sure had to be Runo, went galloping across the front of his mob, waving his sword in exhortation. I will say that they responded, raising their own arms to shake them in our direction.

"Why do they always do that?" Scribonius asked, and I turned to him in mock exasperation.

"Do you know how many times you've asked that question over the years?"

"It just never made any sense to me," he said, his tone defensive. Then, seeing I was teasing him, he laughed. "It's just that it never does them any good."

"They don't know that," I pointed out. "They don't know how many men we've faced who've done the same thing."

"True," he granted. "But they're going to find out soon enough."

Our conversation was interrupted by a commotion when Balbus came galloping back, while two Cohorts from the rear line detached themselves to begin moving back in our direction up the ridge.

"Crassus is sending those two Cohorts down the ridgeline to the east and he wants us to take up a position in between them and the rest of the Legion," Balbus told us.

"You heard the man," I called out.

As a group, we went trotting over to a spot equidistant between the two Cohorts that were now forming up facing east, and the rest of the Legion. The second line had shuffled over to cover up the gaps so that there was now roughly a Cohort in the second line directly behind the gaps between the Cohorts of the front line. The men were standing ready, waiting for the Moesians to begin their advance up the hill. Runo made one more pass in front of his men, dividing them into two lines of their own, but it was more just two mobs instead of ordered lines like ours. Taking my attention away from the sight in front of me, I looked to the east, trying to gauge how far away the Moesian cavalry was, except they were still too distant to make anything out more than just a dark smudge.

"Pluto's cock, that idiot is advancing now without waiting for his cavalry," Balbus laughed, pointing down the hill.

Surely enough, he was right; the men of the Moesian front rank, still shouting their individual battle cries, had begun shambling towards us. I heard the Centurions of the front rank Cohorts shouting orders to their men to hoist their shields, followed by the clattering sound of the men obeying. The Moesians hit the bottom of the slope before launching into a run, giving a great shout as they did so.

"Not only are they not waiting for their cavalry, they started their attack much too soon. They're going to be completely winded before they ever reach the front rank."

Scribonius looked over at Balbus and me as he finished, reaching down to heft his coin purse.

"I'll wager a hundred sesterces that our boys don't even have to draw their swords before the attack is broken."

Now, I knew as well as Balbus that taking that bet would be foolish, but given all that had happened between us, I thought that making what I knew to be a losing wager might make things a little smoother between us.

"I think these Moesians are tougher than that," I countered, hefting my own purse. "I'll take that wager."

"Ha! Your money is as good as mine," Scribonius hooted, clearly pleased.

I hope so, I thought, then turned my attention back to what was happening before us.

If Runo had waited for his cavalry, the outcome might have been different, but I highly doubt it. One thing is certain; if he had waited, they would have inflicted more casualties and we would have had to do more to save ourselves than we did. Scribonius, like I knew he would be, was right about the Moesian attack crumbling before our men even had to draw their swords. The combination of two volleys of javelins and the lung-searing effort of an uphill charge was more than enough to shatter the Moesians, who went streaming back down the hill, leaving a large number of bodies behind. The Moesian cavalry only got within a mile of our makeshift line of two Cohorts, then seeing their comrades on foot being repulsed, did not even try to make an assault. Helping our cause was the fact that their numbers were much smaller than the scout had told us, there being little more than a thousand men on horseback, and they followed the rest of the Moesian mob without throwing so much as a javelin in our direction. Our own losses were laughably light; no more than a dozen men had been wounded, some of them from their own comrades, whose grip on their javelin had slipped at the last moment and their missile had gone low into the front ranks. That was the official story anyway; the truth is that this happens quite often, and more often than not, it is men settling a score over a private feud. The evidence is that these wounds are almost never fatal, most of the time hitting men in their lower extremities and almost never in the torso where the wound would most likely kill them. It is also impossible to prove that a man had the intent of wounding a comrade, and even if another man witnessed it, he would not open his mouth. This was the sort of thing that happens in a Legion that is outside even the power of the Centurions, no matter how much none of us want to admit it. Otherwise, we were unscathed, the men flushed with their easy success and clamoring to be allowed to pursue the enemy into the woods, something that Crassus wisely forbade. He pacified them with the order to go among the Moesian dead and wounded to take what they could from the bodies. The air filled with the after-battle sounds of men moaning in their last moments, followed by short, high-pitched screams when a blade was thrust into their chests. There was also laughter, with a lot of good-natured exchanges about what pieces of loot had been discovered, along with a fair number of shouted arguments when men claimed a particular prize simultaneously. All in all, it was a normal after-battle scene, which the Evocati and I sat to watch while keeping an eye out on the off chance that Runo tried another attack.

Crassus came trotting up, a wide grin on his face, returning our salutes as he said, "Well, that was easy."

"That it was," I agreed. "But what do we do now?"

"We're going after them," he replied, looking at the woods and the country beyond. "We gave them a bloody nose, but we need to teach Runo and these Moesians a lesson once and for all."

"How far do you propose to chase them?" I asked.

"As far as it takes. As long as the Bastarnae stay where they are, or better yet, go back across the river."

"If Runo retreats farther south, that's going to encourage the Bastarnae to stay on this side of the river," I said doubtfully. "And we still don't know for sure that they aren't cooperating."

"If they are, they're doing a horrible job of it," Crassus said, his tone a bit short.

Understanding that he had made up his mind, I kept my mouth shut. Seeing that I was not going to argue, he wheeled his mount about to watch the men, who were finishing up their looting.

"We don't have much daylight left, but I don't want to make camp here because of the stink, even though this is a good spot."

He looked over at me and asked, "You were in those woods. How far to the other side? Did you get a chance to see what the ground looks like?"

I thought for a moment, trying to recall how wide the strip of forested land was, then replied, "It's not more than a mile. In fact, it's probably a bit less, but we never made it out of the woods, so I don't know. I imagine that it's not much different than where we're at now."

"Take the Sixth Cohort and using the Evocati as a screen, push through the woods and see what's on the other side," Crassus ordered.

Trotting over to the Sextus Pilus Prior, I relayed what Crassus wanted, and in moments, we were leading the Sixth down the slope into the trees. It was easy to follow the trail of the retreating Moesians that had gone crashing through the underbrush in their headlong flight from the battlefield, leaving behind trampled earth and torn-up bushes, along with a variety of debris that is always part of a scene where fighting has taken place. Pierced shields, studded with the shafts of our javelins were the most common, along with bloodstained garments. Farther along inside the relative shelter of the forest, we found the first of the men too badly wounded to keep up with their fleeing comrades. A good number of them had already succumbed to their wounds, but the ones who still lingered were quickly dispatched by the men of the Sixth marching just behind us. Giving the order to spread out, we rode with our hands on our swords. Despite the unlikelihood that Runo would have his wits about him enough to leave some men behind to ambush us on entering the forest, I had not survived this long by taking unnecessary risks, and my Evocati comrades were of a like mind. When we had been in the forest the first time, it had taken only a matter of a few moments before we were at the far edge, but we had been going at a full gallop then. Now the time dragged by as we moved slowly and carefully, still following the trail of the Moesians, which at least made the way easier. Finally reaching the far edge, I ordered a halt, both to give the Legionaries a rest and to decide what to do next. I did not like the idea of bursting out into the open without knowing what was facing us, but peering through the brush, even as trampled down as it was, only allowed us to see a few hundred paces ahead. To get a good idea of the lay of the land, and more importantly to ensure there was no ambush, there was nothing for it but to go out there.

Calling to Scribonius and Balbus, I said, "You may as well go with me."

"Why is it always us?" Balbus grumbled as he followed along.

"When did you become such an old woman?" I asked him.

"When I realized I actually had a chance to live to a ripe old age," he countered. "But you seem determined to keep that from happening."

"At least you're not bored."

"I could do with some boredom," Balbus replied, except by this point we were already out into the open.

After the gloom of the thick woods, I had to pause a moment to let my eyes adjust to the bright light before taking a good look. If there had been archers or other missile troops about, we would have made very tempting targets, especially since I was wearing the muscle cuirass I had been presented at my retirement, marking me as a high-ranking officer. I made a mental note to wear my old mail shirt the next time we went into battle, it being less conspicuous and more comfortable as well. With my eyes adjusted, I scanned the surrounding terrain, first nearby, looking for an immediate threat, then farther out. Following the scarred and battered earth with my eyes, I could just make out the tail end of the Moesian army on its continued retreat, except they had slowed to a walk. There was another ridge perhaps two miles away, and the leading edge of the Moesian army was just crossing over it as we watched. Balbus pointed to a spot on the ridge that looked flatter, like some giant had cut off the top of the hill.

"That looks like a good spot to camp. By the time we get there, the Moesians will be long gone."

Agreeing with him, we began to head back to the rest of the Legion. The Sextus Pilus Prior called my name and when I trotted Ocelus over to him, he asked if I wanted them to march back with the rest of the Evocati. Remembering what it was like to be marched back and forth by heedless officers, I told him to remain in place to wait for us to come back. I was rewarded with a smile and an enthusiastic salute, then I caught up with the others.

The engineering officers were sent forward to survey the spot that Balbus had found, while the Legion marched up. Fortunately, Balbus' eye for picking a spot was sharp, the engineers finding it suitable, with a stream flowing at the foot of the ridge on our side to provide water. Because we would not be staying more than a night, it did not need much more consideration, and the sun was hanging low, just above the horizon when the 8th began work on the camp. While the men worked, Crassus held an impromptu war council with Macrinus, Cornelius, and me to discuss our next move.

"As I told you earlier, I'm determined to chastise Runo in a manner that neither he nor the Moesians will ever forget. They'll be easy to follow, but we're going to be cautious. We hurt them today, but we didn't break them, and they're still dangerous."

He paused, waiting for comments, but I did not have anything to add to that, since he had addressed my major concern. Chasing a wounded enemy is always a dangerous business, because fear makes men desperate, and desperate men are unpredictable. As long as we were cautious, I was not too concerned.

84

"The biggest problem," Crassus continued, "is that we're almost blind without Silva and his squadron. But we have 20 Evocati, and they'll have to do." Looking at me, he said, "Prefect, I want you and the Evocati out scouting. Go in pairs or at most in a group of four, and take spare mounts with you. I want you out at least five miles in front of us at all times, and I'll need constant reports back."

This was the first scouting mission I had performed in many, many years, and the first time ever I had done it on horseback. Still, I knew there was no other answer than to say, "Yes sir." Which I did, thinking about the best way to accomplish what Crassus had tasked us with.

"What if they reach a town or city?" Macrinus asked this question, and Crassus did not hesitate.

"We take it. We have our artillery, which I believe is more than adequate for whatever we may run into."

His words immediately reminded me of Samosata, with its huge black stone walls that we had been completely unprepared for, but I kept my thoughts to myself.

"Along the way, we lay waste to everything we find," Crassus finished. "No farm, no village, nothing is to be left standing two miles on either side of our march. Prefect, I'm counting on you and your Evocati to let me know of anything worth destroying as well."

With our orders given, we retired to our respective men. Despite the fact that the Evocati were not formally under my command, it was turning out that Crassus viewed them as an extension of my post, and for the rest of the time I was with him, it was to be that way.

"I think the best way to proceed is with two groups of four and six pairs. The larger groups will ride parallel, on either side of the line of march of the Moesians," I explained. "The rest of you will be responsible for making sure that nobody suddenly shows up on our flanks, and spotting anything that's worth burning and looting. Crassus' orders are pretty clear on this. We burn everything that we can't take with us."

There are few orders more welcome than the one that gives men a license to run wild. Any pig, chicken, or item that had the smallest value was fair game, not to mention the women that were not smart or fortunate enough to make themselves scarce, so my words were met by wide grins all around. Because these men would be the first to find anything that met that description, it also meant that they would have the first choice of the most valuable loot, provided, of course, they could carry it with them on horseback. Nonetheless, as I had seen on more occasions than I could count, a woman fit across a man's saddle quite easily. Once the basic orders were given, the next task was to determine who would be in each group. My group was easy; selecting Scribonius and Balbus, we filled out the fourth with a grizzled veteran and former Secundus Pilus Prior of the 12th Legion, Aulus Novanus, a short, barrel-chested man originally from Cisalpine Gaul, whose Latin still carried the accent of the region. With these matters settled, we retired for the evening, ready to start out the next day in search of the Moesians.

Leaving behind the men breaking camp, we set out the next morning, heading southeast. As I have said many times before, there is no way for an army to hide its trail, especially one that is leaving behind men who have finally succumbed to their wounds. The trail was marked with a series of freshly dug graves as we went, rapidly reaching the five-mile mark that Crassus had set with no sight of the enemy. We could just see the other group of four horsemen, led by an Evocatus named Maxentius, at least when the terrain permitted. We were each leading an extra horse like Crassus had commanded, but I had no intention of using the spare, such was my confidence in Ocelus. He never seemed to tire, and was always eager to see what lay just on the other side of a hill. Now he was pulling at the reins, clearly chafing at the stop, but we were not going to move for a bit and he finally settled down to start chomping at tufts of grass while we scanned the horizon. Finally, I spotted a far off smudge hanging low in the sky, trailing off a bit farther south than the trail would indicate. Since none of us knew anything about Moesia, we had no way of knowing whether or not Runo was taking his army to a city or town. The fact that it appeared that the Moesians had changed course might mean any number of things, but there was only one way to find out. After waiting what I deemed sufficient time for the 8th to have closed the gap on the march, I sent Balbus back to Crassus with the news that the Moesians had turned.

"We're going to cut across, so come back to this spot and then head for that notch and you'll pick up our trail," I told Balbus, pointing to a spot in the hills that roughly intersected with the cloud of dust.

Climbing back aboard our mounts, we headed out, after signaling Maxentius' group of our change of direction. It quickly became apparent why the Moesians had not taken the most direct route; the ground becoming rougher, the terrain undulating even more. It was not bad for horses, but for men it would have been extremely wearing, especially for a mob as demoralized as this one. The good part of it was that it allowed us to close with the Moesians more quickly, despite putting us in danger more quickly as well, since it was highly likely we would run into Moesian cavalry patrols. While it was certainly harder going than the track we had been on, I was confident that the men of the 8th were fit enough to traverse this terrain without much difficulty. It was about midday when we stopped again, the cloud of dust much closer now while the Moesians kept moving on their new course. Just when we were about to start out again, Scribonius called out, pointing back in the direction we had just come, and I turned to see Balbus trotting up.

"Did you have any trouble finding us?"

"A little," he admitted. "But I marked the spot where we turned off from the Moesian trail, so they should find it with no problems."

Thinking about it for a moment, I decided it was time for a conference between my group and that of Maxentius, and I cantered Ocelus to the top of the small hill that we had stopped on. Pulling up, I looked in the direction where I had last seen Maxentius and the other men, yet there was no sign of them anywhere. Cursing, I scanned the area, looking down into the nooks and crannies of the surrounding ground. Still I saw nothing, not a wisp of dust or a sign of disturbed earth that would give a hint of what had happened to them. I seriously doubted they had been ambushed; the air was quiet that day, making the sounds of fighting carry even the distance between us. Deciding to press on in the hope that Maxentius and his men had just chosen to go in a direction that took them out of my range of vision, I rode back down the hill, whereupon we resumed our journey. Shortly after we did so, Novanus, who was riding in the lead at that moment, suddenly pulled up short on the crest of a small hill. We all immediately stopped, while he signaled for me to join him, and I trotted Ocelus up.

"What is it?"

In answer, he simply asked, "Notice anything?" while pointing to the last spot that we had seen the dust cloud.

Following his finger, I saw immediately what he was referring to; there was no longer a dust cloud.

"They've stopped," I muttered, looking at the sun in the sky.

"They're either stopping early, or they've arrived where they were headed," Novanus replied.

"There's only one way to find out."

I signaled to Scribonius and Balbus to join us, informing them of the new development.

"Should one of us go back and alert Crassus?" Scribonius asked, but after considering for a moment, I shook my head.

"Not until we know for sure. I just wish Maxentius and his bunch would show up somewhere. Now that we're getting close, it's going to be more dangerous."

"Remember what we're supposed to be doing," Scribonius warned. "If we get caught, then we've failed."

"If we get caught, we're not going to give a brass obol if we failed, because we'll be dead," Balbus interjected sourly.

With that cheerful thought, we began closing the distance to where the Moesians had stopped.

Not long after we resumed, we reached a river. Wide, but fortunately not deep, it was nonetheless nerve-wracking to cross, since there is not a more vulnerable target than a man crossing a river. Consequently, we crossed one at a time, fortunately without any incident. The river made a gentle curve that ran through a narrow defile where it had cut through the softer rock of a ridge, which we traversed, the slope so steep that it required us to switch back and forth. Nearing the top, we slowed, repeating the process of inching up so that just our eyes were able to see over, until the country beyond lay in our view. What we saw was not heartening, to say the least. Beyond this ridge was a narrow valley, where the river left the defile and flowed through it. Rising steeply from the opposite bank of the river was a flat-topped hill, on which sat a good-sized fortified position, though at that moment we were too far away to tell if it was just a hillfort or a complete town. Although we were unable to tell what the walls were made of, we could see that they were very tall; how much was wall and how much was part of the hill we would not know until we got closer. While we watched, we could see tiny figures rounding around the base of the hill out of sight, and I guessed that these were the stragglers from the Moesian army, meaning that whatever entrance there was to the place was on the far side. Because of its location, there was no way we could effectively sneak around to do a thorough scouting of the place without being seen. First, we would have to cross back over the river, which did not look possible to do up in the defile, the terrain simply too rugged. Descending the ridge to cross the valley floor, we would be spotted immediately if we were to try to circle around on the opposite side. We sat in silence for several moments before Balbus finally said what we were all thinking.

"That is going to be a right bastard of a job."

"That it is," I agreed.

"Maybe Crassus will change his mind once he sees this place," Scribonius suggested.

"He might," I said, but I was doubtful.

He had seemed adamant to teach Runo and the Moesian people a sharp lesson. Taking this place would surely do it. The only question in my mind was whether or not he would wait for the rest of the army before trying to assault this place.

"We haven't seen the other side," Novanus said. "It might not be as strong as this side looks."

"Let's hope so."

Knowing that we had seen all we could at that point, I told the others it was time to head back to Crassus and the Legion. We were about to descend back down the ridge when suddenly Balbus, who was taking the lead, pulled up short, causing a shower of rocks to cascade down the slope, making the horses nervous.

"Pluto's cock," he swore, pointing across the river to our right.

It took a moment before I caught movement and once I was able to focus, I saw that it was a small group of horsemen, riding hard across our front on the far side of the river. They had just become visible because a clump of trees along the riverbank had obscured my view, which had also hidden their pursuers for a brief span. My mind was just starting to register that the small group consisted of four men when a much larger group burst into view from behind the trees.

"That's Maxentius!" Novanus exclaimed.

After watching a moment, I saw that he was right. Maxentius had been riding as his main horse a chestnut-colored mare, his spare horse a jet black, and it was this black horse that Maxentius was frantically whipping as he and his comrades tried to outrun their pursuers. None of them were leading their spare horses, and I assumed that they had been abandoned once the chase started. Their pursuers were clearly Moesian, and also were clearly better horsemen than the men they were after.

"Why are they headed in that direction?" Scribonius wondered.

I thought I knew.

"I think they wanted to run into us and double their numbers."

"Lot of good that would do. There must be 40 or 50 men after them!"

Scribonius looked at me, dismay plainly written on his face.

"What do we do?"

Thinking quickly, I made a decision that I was sure would be met with protests.

"We're going to attack."

I was not a little surprised when none of the others demurred or made any complaint, instead just pointing the noses of their horses down the slope, which we descended much more quickly than we had gone up. It was also noisier and more dangerous, at least for Balbus and Novanus, who had to worry about dodging rocks that the hooves of Scribonius, his spare horse, and my mount dislodged, yet we made it down safely. We put our horses into a gallop, slowing only to splash across the river before pounding up the steep bank, veering to the left in pursuit of the Moesians.

What I was counting on was the element of surprise, aided by my rock-solid belief in our superior skill in combat. Perhaps conveniently, I was forgetting that this would be a fight on horseback, but I have no doubt that we would not have done anything differently even if each of us had stopped to think about it. Maxentius had been leading his men on a weaving, erratic course, partly because he was unfamiliar with the terrain, but I knew that eventually he would have to turn back in a northerly direction, because that was where Crassus and the 8th were located. Armed with that knowledge, I led the men on an almost directly northern course, at least where the ground permitted, keeping an eye on the low-hanging cloud of dust that marked the path of the pursuers. If there had been any time to think about what to do, perhaps we would have come up with a better plan. Yet with every passing moment, it became more likely that the Moesians would run Maxentius down, and I am not sure what we could have done differently. Also working in our favor was that our horses were still fresh, while the Moesians had been after Maxentius for some time, although we did not know exactly how long. Ocelus ate up ground with every stride; for a moment, I forgot that we were headed for a fight, instead just reveling in the feeling of power and speed that emanated from my animal. His nostrils were fully dilated, but he had not even begun to work up a sweat, the drumming of his hooves competing with the shrieking of the wind in my ears as we raced along. I was clinging to the reins for all that I was worth, feeling like a boy again, exhilarated and afraid all at the same time, watching for any holes or other obstacles that would be gone before my eye could register it enough to make an adjustment to his track. The others were following closely behind, their spare mounts trailing behind them, the gap steadily closing. Bursting through a gap in some trees, I saw the Moesians perhaps 200 paces away as we came up on their right flank. So intent were they on running down Maxentius, not one of them even glanced in our direction. I did not need to urge Ocelus on; seeing the Moesians, he seemed to sense what I wanted and opened his stride even more, stretching his neck out, almost literally flying over the ground. Taking the risk, I loosened my grip on the reins with my right hand to draw the *spatha* that Crassus had loaned me.

"Titus, wait!" I heard Scribonius yell.

Turning in the saddle, I saw him waving at me frantically. Sawing on the reins, I slowed Ocelus, who clearly did not like being curbed like this. The Moesians were now pulling away, but as yet, none of them had seen us approaching, though we could not count on that lasting.

"What is it?" I snapped, angry that Scribonius had slowed us down.

As usual, he had a reason, and a good one at that.

"Let's use the spare horses as a diversion," he said, quickly explaining what he was thinking. Seeing immediately that it could only help, I agreed. Taking his spare, he tied one end of the bridle to the second spare horse, and that of the second to the third. Once that was done, he wasted no time, reaching out to grab the bridle of one of the horses, then spurring his own, resumed his pursuit of the Moesians. Back at the gallop, he pointed the leading spare horse in a slightly different direction, meaning that if they remained on a straight course, they would run across the front of the Moesians, between the enemy and Maxentius and his men. Releasing the animal's bridle, he smacked the nearest horse on the rump, which not being burdened with riders, pulled away quickly. There was no guarantee that they would run in the direction we hoped, but horses are herd animals, and the lure of other horses was too strong to ignore. They pounded along straight and true, cutting across the front of the Moesian cavalry. The enemy was no longer at a full gallop, their horses having grown tired, yet neither was Maxentius. On the other hand, we were going full speed very quickly, while as I expected, Ocelus immediately opened a gap on the others. If I was still praying to the gods, or believed that they had not turned their back on me I would say that they had a hand in our attack, because it could not have been timed more perfectly. Just as the spare horses went galloping by, drawing the attention of every Moesian in the group, I held my arm out rigid, aiming for a rider about a third of the way from the rear of the Moesian column.

"Caesar!"

Bellowing the name of our old general at the top of my lungs, I was thinking of him and not Octavian, which the others quickly picked up. Just glimpsing the face of my target when he whirled around at the sound of my voice, I could see it was white with shock and surprise as the point of my blade slammed right under his right rib cage. I had never hit a man with my blade going so fast in relation to him, the impact nearly tearing the sword from my gasp and I felt myself slide backwards over the rear of the saddle, flailing to grab the front of it before I flew off my horse. Somehow, I managed to latch on, staying in the saddle and wrenching the blade free before Ocelus and I passed. The other three had each slammed into a man and, in the time it takes to blink, things became a mass of confusion, fear, and anger. Men began shouting in alarm in their tongue, turning their horses to meet this new threat, the momentum of our horses taking us into their very midst.

Suddenly surrounded on all sides, I realized that for the first time in my career, this was the time where the edge beat the point. All of our training with the Spanish sword focused on the thrust instead of the slash, but I recognized that trying to skewer men from horseback when they were on the defensive was not an easy task. Instead, I began swinging my blade, slashing left and right, the Moesians jabbing at me with their spears in answer. Twisting and turning, I was just managing to avoid the thrusts of their longer weapons, the thought striking me that we should have been carrying shields. Risking a glance, I saw that Scribonius was in much the same predicament I was in, swinging wildly with the unaccustomed sword, but I was pleased to see that there were men reeling in their saddle or already fallen to the ground around him. Meanwhile, I had scored several blows, and the surprise initially counterbalanced the disparity in numbers, yet that advantage was dissipating with every beat of our heart. It was becoming clear that the Moesian commander had not kept his head about him, dividing his forces to send part of them to take care of the four of us, while continuing his pursuit of Maxentius. Instead, we were now essentially surrounded by the entire force, our only hope now that Maxentius had heard or seen what was happening, turned around, and taken the initiative by making his own attack. Someone struck me a glancing blow from behind, knocking the breath from me, but on this day, I was wearing my old mail shirt so it absorbed most of the blow, yet I knew from experience that some links would need to be replaced. Twisting about just in time, I saw a Moesian with hair and beard the same color as the boy's who I had killed in the woods, lips twisted in a grimace of fear and hatred, pull his arm back to land another thrust to my unprotected back. Without thinking, I swept my *spatha* in a backwards stroke, just as he made his thrust. Again, it was either a matter of dumb luck or the gods favor; whatever the case, my blade struck the man's spear shaft just behind the head of the spear, slicing through it as if it were a twig. I barely felt the impact of my blade striking the shaft of his spear; in fact I had been expecting to meet some resistance and so put my body weight into the stroke, which twisted me almost all the way around until I was lying almost flat on Ocelus' hindquarters. Before I could pull myself upright, another spear came whistling into the space that I had just occupied. Knocking the shaft upward with my *spatha*, I sat upright, then jerked Ocelus around, kicking him in the ribs as I spotted an opening, needing to get out from where I was in the middle of all the Moesians. However, seeing what I intended, one of them jumped his horse into the spot before I could take advantage. Scribonius and Balbus had managed to get side by side, facing in opposite directions so they could watch each other's backs. Novanus was surrounded in the same manner as I was, except he was too far away for me to get to him to pair up the way Scribonius and Balbus had.

My arm was growing tired from my continual slashes at any threat, then one of the bolder men pushed closer, trying to grab Ocelus' bridle. Ocelus, seeing a strange hand come into his field of view, suddenly reared, front hooves flailing out, one of them catching the man square in the forehead, caving in his skull. Flung backward by Ocelus' sudden movement, it was only at the last instant that I grabbed a handful of his mane to keep from being thrown. The dead man was still upright in his saddle, while his horse, smelling blood, suddenly bolted, riding past me and throwing the man's body from his back. Using my knees, I pushed Ocelus around to follow the fleeing horse, and we managed to push past the Moesians trying to block our path, albeit because I cut one man's face in two. With a bit of breathing room, I wheeled about, looking for Scribonius and Balbus. Just then, I heard another shout, but this one was a welcome one.

"Magnus!"

I did not know what had taken them so long, but when Maxentius and his men finally did attack, it was with devastating effect. Drawn by the sound of their battle cry, I watched them hurtle into the mass of Moesian horsemen on the opposite side from where we had made our own attack. Men and horses screamed in panic and pain when Maxentius and the others slammed into their midst, slashing and cutting their way towards us. Renewing my own attack, I kicked Ocelus in the ribs. Having drawn blood on his own account, he needed no urging. This time, I headed to help Novanus, who had just been struck a blow that caused him to reel in the saddle, arriving just in time to keep him from falling, using my free hand to steady him. There was blood running down his face from a cut to his forehead, and he pawed at his eyes to clear them.

"I'm all right," he muttered, pulling away from me to charge at the man who I assumed had been the one to strike him.

Determined not to let him get cut off again, I followed him, choosing a large man wearing a fine suit of armor for my next target. He was intent on closing with Novanus, but at the last moment, either saw or sensed me coming, and with a reflex that would have done a cat proud, managed to wheel his horse, bringing his shield up just in time to meet my blow. I had straightened my arm to make a thrust, using Ocelus' momentum to drive the blade home, except instead of punching into flesh, the tip hit the shield instead, glancing upward. The force of the blow drove my arm upward, exposing my side; my opponent did not hesitate, except Ocelus chose that moment to rear again, flailing with his hooves and knocking the man's spear to the side. Coming down, the hard surface of his hoof gouged the shoulder of the Moesian's mount, in turn causing the other horse to let out a shriek of pain and twist away. The movement was so sudden that it almost unseated his rider and left him exposed, giving me an opportunity to strike the man a blow at the base of his neck. The blade cut deep, almost severing his head, sending a spray of blood into the air, with his head flopping to the side. My last sight of horse and rider was the beast fleeing with his rider slumped over in the saddle, head bouncing grotesquely with the stump of his neck still spurting blood.

Giving Ocelus a pat on the shoulder, I said, "I don't know if you did that on purpose, but thank you, boy. You saved my life."

In answer, Ocelus tossed his head while I looked for another target. However, the attack by Maxentius had shattered the Moesian cohesion, their men turning to flee instead of fighting. There were a few diehards left, still engaging with Scribonius and Balbus, and Novanus and I rode over. In a few heartbeats, we put a couple in the dirt and the rest to flight. As quickly as it had happened, the fight was over, leaving us panting, with our horses blowing, pawing the earth and hopping about as their nerves settled down from the action. While gathering our wits and catching our breath, Maxentius and his men trotted over. It was only then that I saw that there were six men instead of four. I instantly recognized the extra pair as two of the Evocati that had been sent out together, Libo and Messala their names. Seeing my questioning gaze, Libo explained.

"We saw Maxentius and the rest being chased by the Moesians, but we didn't know what to do, so we kept pace with them, waiting to see what happened. When you attacked and they stopped chasing, we joined up with them."

While that explained Libo and Messala's presence, it did not explain what had taken Maxentius so long to make his own attack, but his reason was a valid one.

"Our horses were blown," he said, his tone apologetic. "We would have attacked sooner, except our mounts would have foundered. We had to let our spares go during the chase, but it would have taken us just as long to switch out mounts as it did to let the horses rest a bit."

That made sense, so I did not hold it against him. Checking on the others, I was relieved to see that there were only minor wounds, the most serious being Novanus, who had taken a spear to his lower left side, just above the hip. The wound was not deep, but it was a nasty gash and we helped him remove his mail shirt, which I examined closely, looking for missing links. There is always a danger, even with a minor wound, that pieces of a man's tunic or links from his mail shirt are driven into the wound. If that happens and they are not removed, that man is in for an ugly, lingering death. To my dismay, I saw that there was a section of links missing, but we did not have time to try to fish about in his wound to find them or search the ground to see if they had fallen.

"We have to get moving. Those Moesians are likely to be coming back, either to get their dead or to have another go at us."

There were now ten of us and we had inflicted more than a dozen casualties on the Moesians, making the odds much better, but that was no reason to tarry. Once Novanus was bound up, we headed north, back to the safety of the Legion, and to report to Crassus on what we had found.

As we rode, I asked Maxentius, "Magnus?"

He instantly knew what I was talking about, giving a short laugh.

"It was all I could think of, and Plautus and I started with Pompey's 1st. I heard you use Caesar's name when you charged, so I decided to use that of Magnus."

"I was thinking of young Caesar when I did it," I said.

"No you weren't," he replied genially. "You were calling on Divus Julius. That's all right. Pompey Magnus would have been a god too, but he lost, so he isn't."

"Just be careful using his name when we're around the rest of the Legion," I warned.

"Don't worry. I've lived a long time by using my head. I won't do anything stupid."

And he did not; I never heard him mention Pompey's name again.

We did not reach the Legion until after dark, only finding the camp because we spotted the torches on the ramparts from a distance. Novanus was reeling in the saddle, but he was a tough bastard and made no complaints, although I know every mile we traveled, he must have been in agony. We gave the watchword when we got within hailing distance, and only then were we permitted into the camp, where I immediately headed to the *Praetorium* while the rest of the men headed to their quarters except Novanus, who went to the hospital tent. Crassus was still awake, and I was relieved to hear from him that all of the other Evocati had made it back safely. I told him briefly what we had learned and showed him on the crude map the relative position of the stronghold we had found.

"And you think that Runo's entire army is there?" he asked.

"The place is big enough to hold that many," I told him. "But we didn't actually see them all enter the place."

"We'll just have to find out," he said confidently. "Can we reach this by tomorrow, given the terrain we have to cross?"

I thought for a moment.

"Since it's too late to try and head them off, we can take the same route they did and be there by late afternoon. If you want to take the shorter route, we might get there earlier, but it will be harder on the men and they will need time to recover."

He listened, then made a decision.

"We'll take the short route. The men need a good, hard march, and if we show up sooner than they expect, it will hurt their morale."

I did not argue, since there was sense in what he said, despite knowing that the men would not feel the same way, but such is the nature of the army. Decisions are made every day that the men do not like, which they obey nonetheless, and in the long run, it is better for them. Hard marching makes hard men, and it is men of iron that make up the Legions, as the Moesians were about to discover. We talked a bit more about what I had seen of the defenses and the nature of the fort, but I made it clear that my examination had been anything but thorough.

"Once we make camp tomorrow, we'll do an inspection and find a weak point. We always do."

With these matters settled, I took my leave to head for a bath and a scraping to get the sweat and grime of battle off of me. Diocles had taken Ocelus to be rubbed down, fed, and watered, but before I took care of myself, I stopped by his stable with an apple to thank him for saving me.

"You did well today," I murmured to him as he munched on his treat. "I never thought I'd go into battle on horseback, but I'm glad that it's you carrying me."

He nickered softly in answer, then I bade him good night. With my bath done, I felt almost as good as new, except that I was extremely sore, with a huge bruise on my back where the blow had struck but not penetrated my mail. I wondered idly whether my new cuirass would have stopped the thrust, even if I had no real intention of finding out. Thinking about this reminded me that I needed to get my mail shirt repaired, so before I went to my tent I took it to the armorer, rousing the duty *immunes* from his cot to drop it off. I gave him a gold *denarius* to ensure that it would be ready for me to pick up before we went into battle again, which meant I would use the cuirass in the meantime. My last task was to check on Novatus, but the physicians were still working on him so I could not see him, though I could hear him yelling plainly enough. Finally, I retired to my quarters, only to find Scribonius and Balbus waiting for me, along with a cup of wine.

"That was close," Balbus said after I informed them of my talk with Crassus. "We have no business fighting on the back of a horse."

"It's harder than it looks, isn't it?" I agreed.

"The next time we're going to be used as cavalry, we need to have shields," Balbus grumbled, but his comment made sense, and I agreed that we needed to draw some from Legion stores, except I had no idea if the Legion carried them as part of their inventory.

The cavalry shield is much different than the one the Legionary carries. To begin with, it is flat instead of concave like the Legionary shield so that it can be lashed to the saddle, although it is oval instead like the shields were before their recent redesign. It also uses two loops to attach to the arm, which is passed through the loops. This is important because it leaves the hand free to grasp the reins of one's horse, except that it does limit its use as an offensive weapon. With a handle behind the boss, the way the Legionary shield is designed, the shield becomes an extension of the hand, meaning that when a man throws a punch, he does so with devastating effect. Not so with the cavalry shield, but that could not be helped.

"What do you think Crassus is going to have us do tomorrow?"

I shrugged. "I'd imagine that he'll use us for security like today, then to serve as his bodyguard when he makes his inspection of the stronghold."

"Why are we wasting our time on this?"

I must say that I was surprised at Scribonius' question, his pensive expression unsettling me even more.

"What do you mean?" I made no effort to hide my surprise. "We can't let the Moesians rise up in revolt whenever the mood strikes them, and from everything Crassus says, this Runo is a troublemaker. If we don't stop him now, we'll just be here some other time."

It made sense to me, and I could see that Balbus agreed, yet Scribonius was not so easily swayed.

"Moesia isn't even a province."

"Yet," I interrupted, but what he said was true. "It's one in everything but name, and it's just a matter of time before Octavian annexes the place, though the gods only know why he wants it."

I had disciplined myself to refer to Octavian as Caesar in front of everyone except for my two closest friends, while in my head, he would always be Octavian. There was only one Caesar in my heart, and even now that has not changed.

"So let someone else bother with it then," Scribonius said with some asperity. "This just seems to be a way for Crassus to win honors."

"So what's wrong with that?" I retorted, a bit stung because by this point I liked Crassus quite a bit.

"Do you really think that Octavian will let someone win glory after all that's happened?" he asked quietly. I confess that had not even crossed my mind, at least until Scribonius spoke out loud. I did not answer, and he continued, "With all that's transpired, after fighting with Antonius for more than ten years to see who'd become First Man, I really don't see him letting anyone challenge that."

"Then why would he allow Crassus to pursue such an aggressive campaign?"

"Who says that he did? We don't know what Crassus' orders are. For all we know, he may be expressly forbidden from going on any military adventures like this, but he's taking the risk that if he wins a great victory that the mob will support him."

While I could not argue that this was a possibility, it seemed to be pointless to speculate.

"Then that's on his head, not ours. We're just following orders."

"That didn't help with Octavian when we were with Antonius, did it?" Scribonius pointed out. "Or have you forgotten that warning that Agrippa gave us when the Legion was retired?"

I had not forgotten it at all, and Scribonius' words struck home, but I could not see what could be done about it.

"So what are we supposed to do? Refuse to do what Crassus orders?"

"No," Scribonius said reluctantly, heaving a sigh. "I don't know exactly what we should do about it, to be honest. But just know that you shouldn't expect Octavian to welcome Crassus with open arms when he returns to Rome. Should we be successful, that is."

"We will be," Balbus interrupted. "The 8th may be a bit green, but they're good boys, and they're well led. We'll make short work of these bastards."

We retired for the evening, yet I found it hard to sleep. Scribonius had given me much to think about.

As expected, we reached the ridge overlooking the stronghold fairly early in the day. Despite the men being tired, Crassus wasted no time in having them make camp in the valley just across the river from the fort. We could see the parapet lined with people watching us while the camp was erected with the usual speed and efficiency of a Legion of Rome. With the men at work, Crassus and his engineering officers, escorted by the Evocati, crossed the river to perform a thorough scouting of the site, looking for weak points. The road, little more than a wide dirt track, curved around to the east and when we followed it, we saw that another, smaller river fed into the larger one so that the fort was located in the notch formed by the junction of the two.

"That complicates matters," Crassus commented, but he did not sound disheartened about the new development.

The road ran along the banks of the large river before turning up the hill and running straight to the fort, where a large wooden gate secured the entrance. Our inspection showed that it was indeed more than a fort, and was a small town, which Crassus immediately seized on.

"We'll cut off their access to water by diverting the river."

I stared at him, unsure that I had heard correctly.

"With one Legion?" I asked incredulously, to which he shook his head.

"I received a message yesterday from Claudius. The rest of the army should be here in no more than three days. I'm going to send a messenger with our exact location."

That made me feel better; however, it was still a very ambitious endeavor, reminding me of Scribonius' warning the night before. How would Octavian react to a feat like the reduction of a town, especially in such spectacular fashion? Continuing our inspection, we saw that while the slopes of the hill were steep, they were not exceptionally high, meaning that the spoil that we dug to divert the river could be used to make a ramp. The nearby hills had sufficient timber to make several siege towers, although we would only need two or perhaps three. Once we came a little too close, and immediately arrows started flying through the air from the ramparts.

Fortunately, the Evocati had been keeping their eyes open for such a move, enabling us to trot out of range before they could do any damage. Otherwise, the Moesians made no attempt to harass us in any way. Our inspection done, we returned to find the camp completed and retired immediately to the *Praetorium* to discuss the plan in detail. Using the drawings made by the engineers, we sketched out our plan of attack. It would be straightforward, and after discussing it further, it was decided that we would not divert the river except as a last resort if our assault was repulsed, but Crassus,

Macrinus, and I were confident, especially with the reinforcements from the rest of the army, that would not be necessary.

"Once the rest of the army is here, it shouldn't take more than a week to build the ramps we need," the chief engineer, Galerius Paperius, told us after making some calculations on how much timber we would need and how much earth needed to be moved. That meant a week of hard, brutal work for the men, but it was not anything I had not done myself, thinking back to those times in Gaul when we would end the day filthy and exhausted from shoveling and hacking all day. With our initial plans in place, there was nothing more to be done in the *Praetorium*, and I went to retrieve my mail shirt, which had been repaired with new links before going to check on Novanus. The moment I arrived in the hospital tent, I knew that things had not gone well with him, since the *medici* on duty, seeing me, hurried to intercept me before I reached him.

"The doctor wants to speak with you before you see your friend," he said, which is never a good sign, and I waited for the orderly to fetch him.

A few moments later, Crassus' physician, Philipos, appeared, his face grim as he approached me.

"How are the ribs?" he asked, surprising me a bit.

"A bit sore, but they're fine. What's going on?"

He hesitated a moment, evidently trying to gather his thoughts. "His wound is suppurating," he began.

"Isn't that good?" I interrupted, but if he were offended, he made no sign.

"Not this early it's not," he replied, shaking his head. "We tried for some time to probe the wound and make sure that we removed all foreign debris. We retrieved some links of mail, and a bit of cloth from his tunic, but apparently we missed something."

"Then go back in and get the rest of it out." I did not understand why it was so difficult.

"If we do, we will probably do more harm than good."

"How? If you say his wound is going to corrupt, then he's a dead man. What is there to lose?"

"First, men do not always die, and Novanus is a strong man. Second, probing into the wound will probably drive the foreign matter deeper into his body, and the surgery alone will probably kill him."

"How many men survive their wounds turning corrupt?"

He hesitated, then said softly, "Perhaps one in ten."

"How about we ask Novanus what he wants? It's his life, after all."

"Very well." He turned to walk over to where Novanus was lying, in a far corner of the tent.

It was not in Charon's Boat, but if Philipos was unable to get whatever was still in his body out, that would be his next stop, and his last. I followed Philipos, and the moment I saw him, I knew that it was serious. His eyes were bright with fever, two red spots on his cheeks showing the fire raging in his body. Beads of sweat dotted his forehead and he watched us approach with a look mixed of equal parts hope and desperation.

"One in ten isn't very good odds," he said, causing both of us to stop and exchange a glance. "You can't whisper to save your life, Pullus," he explained, "and this Greek fake isn't any better. I heard everything you said."

"Then you know what we want to ask you," Philipos replied. "Do you want to think about it? But I must warn you, every moment that passes, the infection is spreading."

"I don't need to think about it." Novanus' jaw was set. "Do what you need to do to get whatever is in me out."

"Very well." The physician turned to an orderly, telling him to bring his instruments, along with a jar of wine.

"Can't you give him poppy syrup?" I asked.

"No, it would disrupt his breathing too much. It would likely kill him."

The orderly held Novanus' head while he let him gulp down as much wine as he could. Not wanting to watch, I turned to leave, but Novanus grabbed my arm with surprising strength.

"Pullus, don't leave," he begged. "Stay here and help me through this."

I did not know Novanus that well, yet I knew how ashamed I would feel if I left him, so I agreed. The physician gently removed the dressing from Novanus' side, causing Novanus to gasp in pain when he did so. The wound, despite not being that old, had already turned a bright red around the edges, with a mixture of blood and pus oozing from the gaping hole in his side. I did not remember it being that wide when we first examined it.

Seeing my gaze, the physician explained, "We had to widen the wound in order to get to the foreign matter."

"So are you going to have to cut me open even more?" Novanus asked, and it was easy to hear the fear in his voice.

"Yes, I am afraid so."

"Pluto's cock," Novanus swore bitterly, then drank another cup of wine.

Handing it to the orderly, he took the leather-wrapped stick that was scarred from the gods only knew how many sets of jaws clamping down on it, putting it in his own mouth.

"Ready." His voice was muffled by the bit.

The physician selected an extremely sharp-looking blade, Novanus' eyes following every movement.

"Maybe you shouldn't look," I suggested.

Novanus said something unintelligible, then grabbed my hand, but I did not pull away. Bending over Novanus, Philipos first pressed around the edges of the wound, forcing a groan from the injured man. More fluid leaked out of the hole, which the physician had the orderly swab away before making a small cut at the edge of the wound. Novanus' grip on my hand tightened, which was beginning to get uncomfortable, but I did not complain, knowing that what I was feeling was nothing compared to him. Philipos then took a long slender probe with a hooked end, inserting it into the wound, while an orderly held a lamp just above his head to allow the Greek to peer into the gaping hole in Novanus' side. Novanus gave a sudden jerk, which in turn caused the probe to go more deeply into his side, and he let out a choked scream, almost breaking my knuckles in the process.

"Strap him down," the physician snapped.

The *medici* quickly had him secured before the operation continued. Resuming his probing, Philipos, sweat now running freely from his forehead to drip down onto Novanus' body, made delicate motions with the probe, staring intently into the cavity. Suddenly, I felt Novanus' grip go limp; when I glanced down, I saw that he had finally fainted, which was a blessing for everyone. I do not know how long the Greek worked, but it seemed like a full watch before I heard him mutter something.

"What? Did you find it?"

He nodded, slowly removing the probe. Hanging on the hook was a single link of mail, dripping blood. Dropping it into a bowl, he stepped back to take a deep breath.

"Is that everything?"

He did not answer at first; instead, he busily checked Novanus' pulse and breathing, putting his ear to the man's chest.

Finally, he said, "I hope so. Because I do not believe he can take much more. Now we will wait and see."

Novanus was still out cold, which was good for him, since the *medici* were not very gentle as they swabbed up the oozing matter before redressing the wound. Seeing that there was nothing left for me to do, I thanked the physician, offering him a gold denarius as a token of appreciation.

He refused it, saying stiffly, "Prefect, I do not need to be paid to do a job for which I am already rewarded."

"Fair enough," I replied, though I was secretly impressed. "Then take it as a retainer for future services that I may be needing."

He gave a laugh, yet took the coin, a bit reluctantly perhaps.

"Very well. I will keep this as a deposit for supplies I might need the next time you show up battered and bruised."

His words reminded me of Prixus and the debt I owed him. I just hoped that taking this stronghold would give me the opportunity to even the score between us.

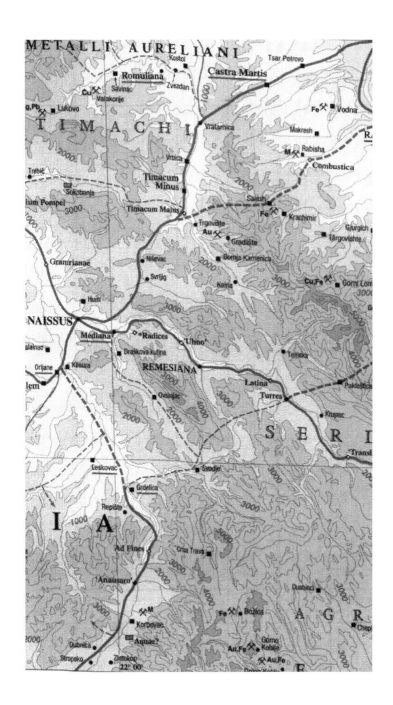

108

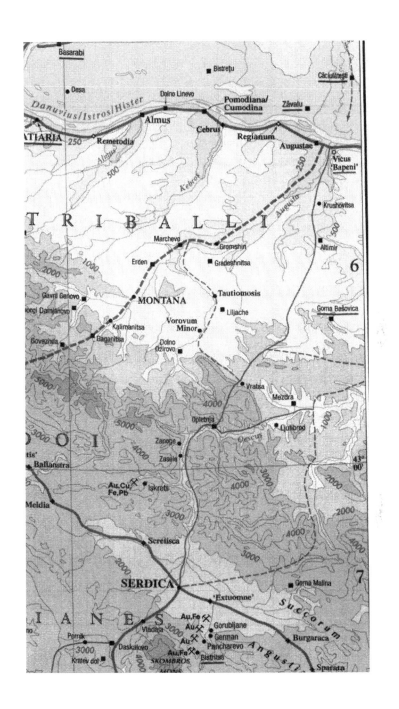

Chapter 3- Naissus

Work began the next morning, first with the digging of a ditch that provided a covered approach to the foot of the hill that the town was perched on. The ditch then turned so that it ran parallel to the walls, curving around until it came within 50 paces of the second river. The other end did the same, except it terminated the same distance from the first river, effectively cutting the town off from reinforcements on three sides. While half the men worked on this project, the other half worked to fell trees to use for the various pieces that would be used for the siege. There were two siege towers to be built, along with protective turrets to house our artillery within range of the town walls. At first, the Moesians lined the walls to watch us work and to jeer at the men, firing an occasional arrow or sling bullet when they thought someone came close enough to strike. However, conducting a siege is boring work, not only to perform but to watch, and before the end of the first day, the only Moesians left on the rampart were those on guard duty. In all reality, there was nothing much for me or the Evocati to do, although Scribonius and Balbus went with me to inspect the men at work. This was just an excuse to go find the Seventh to check on Gaius, who seemed to be happy to see me. His depression at leaving Iras behind appeared to have been lifted, but it could have been he was just acting that way in front of me. His men were working well, and I could see that they responded to him without the use of the *vitus*. Stopping to talk to Pilus Posterior Vettus, I asked him how Gaius was doing in his duties. I was happy to see that he did not hesitate.

"He's doing well. Much better than I thought he would," he admitted.

I said nothing, just lifting an eyebrow in response because I was fairly sure I knew why he felt that way. Seeing my face, he turned red, but did not shrink from what he wanted to say, for which I respected him.

"You know how it is, Prefect. Most of the time when someone is thrust on us, it's a bad fit. But Porcinus is a good leader, although he's a bit soft for my tastes. The men seem to respond, though, and that's the important thing."

"Thank you for your honesty, Vettus," I told him. "And yes, I do know how it is. But I also assure you that I'll never put a man in the position to lead Legionaries who isn't qualified to do so, no matter who he's connected to."

"Thank you, Prefect, that's good to know."

Our business with the Seventh concluded, we continued our inspection and I was pleased to see that there was very little shirking going on. Some is inevitable; men lifting less than a spadeful of dirt, for example, or carrying wicker baskets that are not completely full. Or men who did more leaning on their axe or turfcutter than actually using it, although the few times I saw that happening, it was only a matter of a few heartbeats before a Centurion or Optio descended on the hapless man with their *vitus* swinging. Even with one Legion, the work was progressing rapidly. Then, with the arrival of the rest of the army three days later, just as Crassus had predicted, it was only a matter of a full watch before the Moesians sent a delegation under a flag of truce.

My presence was demanded by Crassus, while the senior Tribunes were left in the outer office; Claudius seething with anger at the slight, with Cornelius just looked relieved. Ignoring the poisonous stare of the senior Tribune, I joined Crassus, who was seated behind his desk. He motioned to me to stand behind him before telling his clerk to let the Moesians, who had been held outside the gates, to enter and come to the *Praetorium* under escort.

"Now we'll see how much power Runo has," Crassus commented while we waited.

I wondered what he had in mind, deciding to wait and see rather than ask. A few moments later, we heard a commotion outside, followed by the clerk slapping the leather flap that served as a door. Crassus turned to give me a grin, then sat and did nothing for several moments.

The clerk obviously had been let in on what Crassus wanted to do because he did not knock again, meaning that the delegation was kept waiting for some time before Crassus finally barked, "Enter."

Pretending to read a scroll on his desk that only I could see was blank, he ignored the men as they filed in. They were dressed in a manner that marked them as men of the upper classes of their society, with richly embroidered tunics, covered by cloaks of a variety of colors. They were all bearded, while some had their hair bound up in a knot that reminded me of the Suebi. Others simply had their hair greased to hang loosely over their shoulders. Some were warriors, others were clearly merchants, and they were all nervous approaching Crassus at his desk. Crassus did not look up, continuing to study the blank scroll, making it hard for me to keep a straight face, but I did my best to look imposing, glaring at the Moesians. Some of them dared to meet my gaze, but most looked away immediately. I wondered if any of them knew that I had slain a few of their number just a couple days before. One Moesian in particular stared at me with undisguised hatred, furthering my suspicion that he had been present the other day. Neither of us broke our gaze until the Moesian that had apparently been designated to be the spokesman cleared his throat.

"Yes? What is it that you want?" Crassus did not bother looking up, his tone abrupt.

"Governor," the man began, but Crassus cut him off.

"I am Legate Proconsul Marcus Licinius Crassus, and you will address me by my proper title."

The man's face reddened, though I could not tell if it was from anger or embarrassment. The man I had locked eyes with made no attempt to hide his anger at Crassus' words, his lips curling back from his teeth, making a hissing sound as he did so. One of the others elbowed him in the ribs, while the spokesman ignored what was happening behind him.

"My apologies, Legate Proconsul Crassus." I was somewhat surprised that the man's Latin was so good. "My name is Charax, and I am the elder of Naissus, which your troops are in the process of besieging. I have been elected to speak on the behalf of my people in the hopes that we can come to some sort of agreement. We regret that the action of one of our nobles has led us to this moment….."

Before Charax could continue, Crassus interrupted him again.

"Let us not waste each other's time, shall we? You come to me asking what it will take for me to call off the siege of your town. It is simple. Surrender Runo to face justice…"

"We will do that," Charax answered immediately, to which Crassus held up a hand.

"I was not finished." His tone was icy. "Surrender Runo, and disarm the men who marched for him immediately."

"It will be done," Charax said, although his mouth tightened a bit, while the others were clearly unhappy.

"Again, I was not finished," Crassus snapped, and I could not tell if his anger was feigned or not. "And for the damages incurred to Rome, you will make a payment of two thousand talents."

"Two *thousand*?"

Charax gasped, but the sound was drowned out by the cries of the other men. In truth, it was an outrageous sum. In that moment, I knew that Crassus was not interested in coming to terms; he just wanted the pretext to continue the siege.

"We could not possibly produce that sum, Legate, and I believe you know that," Charax said through clenched teeth.

"Your financial woes are of no concern to Rome. All that matters to us is that you pay what you owe us for Runo's predations."

"And who is it that decides what we owe to Rome?"

This came from the man who had been glaring at me, except he spoke in Greek and not Latin.

"*I* decide," Crassus said coldly, answering him in flawless Greek. "For out here, as far as you are concerned, I am Rome, and what I decide is Roman law. That is what it means to have Proconsular authority."

"Then you will die beneath our walls," the hotheaded Moesian shot back, drawing horrified looks and protests from his comrades.

"Aderbal does not speak for the rest of us," Charax said quickly, shooting the man a poisonous glance.

"Then you should not have brought him to this meeting," Crassus replied. "My conditions stand. Surrender Runo," he held out a finger, "disarm his men, under our supervision," holding up a second, then the third, "and a payment of three thousand talents."

"Three? But you said two!" Charax wailed.

"It's another thousand because of the threat your man Aderbal here made towards me," Crassus said, making it sound like the most reasonable thing in the world.

Charax's shoulders slumped in defeat, at last understanding that this meeting had been a waste.

"If we don't have two thousand, then we are hardly likely to have three," he said dully, but Crassus was unmoved.

"Then we have nothing more to discuss."

They turned to the clerk who had shown them in, and he nodded at the door. For a moment, I thought that they would refuse, while Aderbal looked like he was seriously considering making an attempt to jump across the desk. I realized then the real reason Crassus had wanted me there, and I put my hand on the hilt of my sword, looking the man in the eye as I did so, daring him to make a try. His jaws clenched, clearly furious, but after glaring at me a moment, he turned to stalk out with the others. The clerk shut the door, and I felt the tension slowly drain from my body.

"I think that went well." Crassus grinned up at me, but I did not share his happiness.

"Was there anything they could have done to keep us from taking this town?"

He looked at me for a moment, studying my face before he replied.

"No," he said slowly. "Why? Is that a problem?"

"Not really. I just would have liked to have known that beforehand."

He inclined his head in recognition of what I had said.

"You're right. I should have told you. I apologize."

"No need to apologize, General," I said. "I just ask that I be kept informed of your decisions so that we present a united front to the men."

"Of course," he agreed.

With that, I was dismissed, and I left more troubled than when I had walked in. Despite the fact I did not particularly care whether Marcus Crassus took this town or not, I was afraid that there were others, or at least one other man in Rome, who would care, and would not like it one bit.

With the question of the Moesian surrender out of the way, work continued on reducing Naissus. Once the trenches were completed, turrets were built along the trenches that ran parallel to the walls, with *ballistae* and scorpions placed in them. Now that the other Legions were present, not only was the original camp expanded, but two Legions were sent to the other side of the river to cut off the road leading to the town. Naissus was effectively encircled and cut off, making their end inevitable, which meant that the Moesians began to try to break the stranglehold. Their major deficiency was that they were poorly led; Runo showed little imagination, simply sending out sorties of varying strength, with seemingly unclear orders. Rather than try to affect a breakout where mounted men could be sent for help, all of their efforts seemed to be focused on destroying one of the two ramps at any given time. The only thing they accomplished was whittling down their force a few dozen men at a time, along with giving our men some good experience. The Moesians themselves were brave enough, except they were poorly disciplined, fighting as individuals rather than as a unit. The damage they did to the ramps was minor, usually being repaired by midday of the day after the attack. I do not know for sure, but I suspect that Paperius, the engineering officer, had studied Caesar's account of our time in Gaul, because the ramps were built precisely in the same manner as at Avaricum, with a layer of logs covered in earth, followed by another layer running in the opposite direction. And like Avaricum, the Moesians attempted to fire the ramp, though they did not try it by

115

tunneling underneath the way the Gauls had. In fact, the Moesians seemed averse to doing any sort of digging at all, making no sorties by tunneling, choosing every time to come out of the only gate into the town.

Having only one entrance into the town certainly made it easier to defend, but it also meant that we only had to watch one spot, especially since the Moesians did not try to open up another exit. A week after the rest of the army arrived, as Paperius had predicted, the work was essentially completed. Two ramps, one on each side, along with two siege towers, had been built and were ready to be rolled up each ramp. All that remained was filling in the last section nearest the wall with earth and rock, while the mantlets that the men would use to carry the materials under cover were lined up the ramp. The assault was set for the next day and in both camps the men went through their pre-battle rituals, while I circulated among the Legions in both as well, telling jokes and relating stories of the times I had done the same as they were doing now. Crassus had not informed me of what role I was going to play the next day, but I planned on being somewhere in the fighting. That evening, Crassus held a command briefing for the Tribunes, Primi Pili, and Priores, where he gave the details of his plan of attack.

"It will be a simple assault," he began, while I thought to myself that I had yet to see an assault go simply, but I held my tongue. "We'll bombard the walls with *ballistae* and scorpions until the last possible moment, while we're rolling the towers into place, to keep the Moesians busy. The Legion that will be conducting the assault on the far side will have the job of not only clearing the parapet, but of opening the main gate. I want the two other Legions ready to enter the town, though I only plan on using one and keeping one in reserve."

There was a bit of grumbling by the Primi Pili at this, since Crassus had not announced his decision on who would lead the assault. The Legion in reserve would miss out on the looting of the town, which would make the men of the unlucky Legion extremely unhappy. However, Crassus had thought of that and held up a hand, smiling at the Primi Pili.

"You don't have to say anything, I already know what your objection is, and I've thought of that. The town will be divided into four parts, and each Legion will get one part to loot."

Not surprisingly, this cheered up the Primi Pili, and they settled down to wait for Crassus to announce who would be conducting the assault.

I had already been told, and I watched the faces of the Primi Pili as Crassus said, "I've decided that the 8th, because they've already faced the Moesians and know what to expect from them, and the 13th will be the Legions leading the assault. The 8th will be on the far side, and will have the job of opening the gate."

He turned to Macrinus. "Primus Pilus Macrinus, I'm counting on you."

Macrinus saluted, promising that the 8th would perform well.

Crassus then looked over at me to say, "Prefect, since we don't have the cavalry here, we're going to have to use a scratch force made up of the Evocati, the Tribunes, and my bodyguards. We'll be the first in the gates once they're opened. I know that I can count on you and the Evocati."

I nodded my head, not feeling the need to salute him.

"We'll begin the bombardment a third of a watch before dawn," Crassus announced. "And the assault will begin a third after that."

"Do we have enough ammunition for a bombardment that long?" asked the Primus Pilus of the 14th, Gnaeus Saenus his name.

Crassus assured him that we did, and I knew that he had ordered men to comb the banks of the river for stones that were of a sufficient size and smoothness to use in the *ballistae*. Meanwhile, he had the armory *immunes* working into the night to make more scorpion bolts. With those matters decided, we were dismissed, but Crassus held me back, the rest of the men filing out. For perhaps the tenth time, I saw the senior Tribune Claudius shoot me a poisonous glance; again I ignored it, long used to the envy of men like him.

"I'll be happy that you'll be with me tomorrow," Crassus began.

I was not sure what his point was, yet I sensed that he was more nervous about the coming attack than he had let on.

"There's no place I'd rather be," I assured him, which was true enough. Perhaps if Miriam had lived, it would have been a lie, but she had not, meaning nothing else really mattered. "And I assure you that the Evocati will do well tomorrow. Most of us haven't done much fighting on horseback, but we'll hold up our end."

He seemed relieved to hear me say that, then paused a moment, as if trying to decide whether to say more.

Finally, he said in a low voice, "I'll have Prixus and his men with us as well. But tomorrow I'm sure that things will be extremely confused, and there's no telling what might happen."

He stared at me meaningfully, but I was confused. Was he giving me his tacit approval for killing Prixus? Why would he do such a thing, I wondered? He had hired Prixus, after all; why would he want me to kill him?

As if in answer to my thoughts, he whispered, "The worst mistake I ever made was hiring him and his men. They've caused me nothing but trouble, and I don't know how to get rid of them."

I stared at him, hardly believing what I had just heard. Here was the grandson of one of the most powerful, and definitely the richest Roman of our time, admitting that he was not as powerful as I had thought. There was a desperation in his voice that was impossible to ignore.

I stared down at him for a moment before I said, "I understand your dilemma, and I'll do what I can."

His shoulders slumped in obvious relief and he closed his eyes.

"Thank you," he whispered.

"I promise you that I'll do what I can," I repeated, not wanting there to be any misunderstanding, "should the opportunity present itself. That's the best I can promise."

He nodded his head in understanding before he suddenly turned to his desk.

"I'm afraid I have quite a bit of work to do, Prefect, so if you will excuse me."

Knowing that I was being dismissed, I said nothing, and left the office. Now, in addition to surviving the assault, I had more to worry about with trying to remove Prixus from the employ of Marcus Crassus. There was a part of me that did not like the idea that I was a hired blade, yet the truth was that I had my own score to settle with Prixus. Besides, I decided that it would not hurt to win Crassus' favor while removing a man who was a threat to me personally at the same time.

The next morning started early; in fact, I do not believe many of the men got much sleep at all. The camp was a hive of activity, men hurrying about and performing their last-minute tasks. The 8th would be crossing the river on the bridge that had been built a half-mile down from Naissus, and they were leaving the camp early to get into position. Before they left, I found Gaius with his men, and while he exuded the confidence of a true professional, I knew him well enough to see how nervous he was.

"Don't do anything stupid," I warned him, but he barely seemed to be listening.

"I won't," he answered, his eyes roving over each of his men.

Stepping away from me, he called to one of them.

"Placus, I told you to leave the sack behind. I don't want it flopping about when you're going over the wall."

He looked at me apologetically.

"I'm sorry, Uncle, but I really need to see to the men."

"Go ahead," I replied, a little hurt but understanding nonetheless. "Just remember what I said."

"Yes, I remember," he said absently, his mind already elsewhere. "Don't do anything stupid. I won't."

With Gaius returning to his men, I was left standing with Ocelus' reins in my hands. Sighing, I was happy that I did not need help to mount my horse like so many men did, meaning that there was no witness to my dismissal by my nephew. Guiding Ocelus through the men who were going about their tasks, I returned to find the Evocati ready to mount their own horses. Leading them out of the camp, we crossed the bridge. I had Crassus' *spatha* still strapped to my saddle, choosing to wear my own blade at my side, and I saw that most of the others had done the same. We would be going in on horseback, but I did not expect that we would stay that way, dismounting at some point when we had gotten inside the walls. That was when the Spanish sword would be the most useful, when we were in the streets and alleys of Naissus.

On the other side of the bridge, we waited for the 8th to march across, followed by the other Legion. As we were waiting, the artillery began their firing at the walls, first with blazing balls of pitch, both to start fires and to illuminate the targets for the men manning the weapons. The scorpions held their fire, waiting for there to be more light, real or artificial, enabling them to pick their targets. The sounds of the fireballs striking the wood of the walls punctuated the air with a noise only slightly less substantial than if the missiles had been stone. Each one flared more brilliantly than the last when they splattered against the wood, but none of them caught fire. Still, some of the missiles struck other targets and we could hear the men screaming as first their clothes, then their flesh caught on fire. A couple men toppled over the edge, their screams cut short when they hit the ground at the base of the wall, tumbling and cartwheeling down the slope of the hill. By this lurid light, I caught a glimpse of the men of the front ranks of the 8th, their faces clearly on edge and nervous, and I remembered how it felt to be waiting to go up and over a wall.

It finally became light enough for the scorpions to open fire. Within a matter of moments, they swept men off the parapet, the bolts sometimes passing through one man to pierce another. Not much time passed before the Moesians realized that their best hope was to keep their heads below the edge of the parapet, the sign for which Crassus had been waiting. He gave the signal for his *cornicen* to sound the call to begin the advance, whereupon the men assigned to push and pull the tower began straining at the ropes. Neither tower was near the size of those we had built at Avaricum but they were still very heavy, and it took a moment before the tower began to move. Meanwhile, a courier had galloped off to cross the bridge to ensure that the Legion on the other side had begun their own advance as well. Slowly, the tower began to move, rocking over the ground, despite our best efforts to smooth the path that it would travel over beforehand. The hard work began when they hit the ramp and there was a scary moment when part of it collapsed under the weight, the tower suddenly leaning over at a dangerous angle. For several moments, the tower was stuck, so two more Cohorts were dispatched to help heave it out of the rut.

This delay caused another problem; the commander of the artillery sent a runner, who came dashing up to Crassus to gasp out, "We're running low on scorpion bolts. If the tower doesn't get to the walls immediately, we won't have enough left to keep the Moesians' heads down. They'll be able to fire on our men!"

I must commend Marcus Crassus, for he did not panic, or even look all that perturbed.

Without moving his head, he snapped to Cornelius, "Get up there and find out how much longer before they get the tower moving again."

Cornelius saluted, then jabbed his mount in the ribs, galloping off.

"This is not good," Crassus muttered, but I was not sure if he meant this for my ears or not.

"No, it's not. But we'll get through it."

I saw him swallow hard, then give a curt nod.

"Yes, we will. I just hope that it doesn't cost too many lives."

With the extra men, the tower began moving again, righting itself, much to the relief of our side and the dismay of the Moesians. However, when it was still about 20 paces short of the walls, we heard one last twanging sound of a scorpion bolt, followed by a long silence.

"Cerberus' balls, we're out of ammunition," I heard Balbus growl.

I turned to glare at him, not thinking we needed someone to point out the obvious.

"Can we use *ballistae*?" Crassus asked nobody in particular.

"We can, but it would be dangerous. In fact, I think it would cause more harm than good," Macrinus replied from where he was standing, watching his men make the final push of the tower against the wall.

"I agree," I put in.

Crassus did not look surprised; neither did he argue.

While a scorpion can be aimed with some precision, a *ballista* is another matter entirely. Between the missile used and the nature of the weapon itself, placing a *ballista* shot is largely a matter of luck, the variance of where it can land so wide that I had seen it cause almost as much damage to our own ranks as to the enemy, just because of one misfire or errant shot. Turning our attention back to the tower, we watched it move the last few feet into place. It was not hard up against the wall; the ramp that would drop, with two large iron spikes affixed to what would be the bottom, would give the men the ability to dash the last few feet to make a running leap onto the parapet. What had been just shadowy shapes had now become distinct and visible, the gray light of dawn turning red with the promise of a bloody day. Visibility worked both ways and now that the Moesians were not forced to keep their heads down, there was enough light for them to see the men of the 8th pushing forward to take their spot. I do not know what prompted me to ask because I had assumed that, especially given its size and composition since the reorganization, the First Cohort would lead the assault, but I did anyway, probably as much out of boredom as curiosity.

"Who's the lead Cohort?"

There was no answer and since my eyes were on the tower, I did not see what reaction Macrinus had, if any, to my question. But the silence got my attention and I turned to look his direction. My stomach lurched when I saw that he was looking in every direction but mine, and I nudged Ocelus forward to stand next to him. Staring down at Macrinus, who still refused to meet my gaze, I asked again, my tone cold this time.

"Which Cohort is leading the assault?"

"The Seventh," he said after a moment.

"The Seventh?"

I could feel my jaw drop, my stomach tightening even more. I turned my attention to the tower, but while I could see men climbing the ladders to ascend to the top level, I could not make out individual faces. I did see that the Moesians were now trying to fire the tower, slinging jars of pitch and oil that had been set alight onto the roof and sides. Fortunately, the green hides that had been nailed to the surface of the tower did their job, so that while the flames burned for the time it took to exhaust the supply of flammable material, they did not catch to the wood.

"Why the Seventh?" I demanded, not caring about how it appeared to be questioning a Primus Pilus.

Macrinus' face flushed, but his tone was calm as he replied, "Because Pilus Prior Palma requested the honor of leading the assault, and I saw no reason to refuse him."

"Ah, so he paid you a bribe," I said caustically, and he shot me an angry look.

"I assure you, Prefect, that it isn't like that."

He seemed about to say something else, then his mouth snapped shut.

"So you say," I sneered.

Seeing he was not going to say anything more, I wheeled Ocelus about and went trotting past Crassus, who looked stunned. I felt Scribonius' eyes on me, and knew that he did not approve of my behavior.

I refused to meet his gaze when I reined Ocelus in, muttering as I did so, "Save your breath."

He looked at me in mock surprise.

"Why would I say anything? I think you handled that very well. After all, you wouldn't have objected if someone came and told you how to run your Legion, even if it was because their nephew might be in danger."

"I thought I told you to save your breath," I grumbled, knowing that he was absolutely right, and that I owed Macrinus an apology.

Balbus did not help matters when he pointed at the top level of the tower, where several sections of men were gathered, waiting for the moment when the rope holding the ramp would be cut and it would fall.

"Isn't that Gaius there?"

My heart stopped in my throat, following his pointing finger to see a tall, lean figure with a white strip on his shoulder, standing next to the ramp. Despite being unable to see his face, I knew the way he held himself and the shape of his body very well. It was indeed Gaius, and it looked very much like he intended to be the first onto the ramparts.

There is no way to adequately describe the feeling of helplessness as I sat watching the ramp drop, then Vettus, Gaius and their men go surging up and onto the ramp. Their roar reached our ears a moment later, just before they dropped from sight, followed shortly by the sounds of a furious fight. I clutched Ocelus' reins tightly. Clearly feeling my tension, he started to paw the ground nervously, tossing his head and blowing. Feeling a hand on my arm, I turned my head to see Scribonius looking at me, trying to look reassuring.

"Titus, it will be all right. Gaius can handle himself. You trained him; I helped. He'll be fine."

"He better be, because I plan on killing him," I said, turning my attention back to the fight.

Crassus' attention was also fixed on the action on the walls, where men had stopped climbing onto the ramp. This was not unusual; after the first surge, it is common that things stall when the enemy on the rampart stops the first men over the ramp, but the fact that it happened much of the time made it no less nerve-wracking. For several moments, the men in the tower could only stand there, calling encouragement to their comrades just out of sight fighting on the ramparts. Then, I do not know if they were ordered to do so or thought of it on their own, a few men clambered up onto the ramp to begin hurling javelins in both directions down into the Moesians, who were evidently massed together as they fought our men on the rampart. Calling down to their comrades who were still in the tower, who passed them their own javelins, they continued hurling missiles at the Moesians. Whether or not it was the rain of javelins that broke the Moesians, we could not tell, but suddenly the men on the ramp leapt down into the fray, clearing the logjam in the tower.

Men resumed their progress, and Crassus, seeing this, turned to us and warned, "Get ready to move. The gate will be opening shortly."

I tied the chin thong of my helmet, still unaccustomed to the feeling of the lack of the transverse crest since it changed the balance of the thing, my neck tickled by the feathers in the plume. I was not helped when Balbus took one look at me, then shook his head.

"You look ridiculous."

"I didn't choose this," I protested.

"I don't care who chose it, you don't look like a Legate, or a Tribune, for that matter."

"All I care about is that it keeps my head from getting split open."

The rest of the Evocati had also donned their helmets and otherwise made ready before Crassus led us to a spot closer to the gate, but still out of range of any Moesian missiles. The shouting and sounds of fighting became more muffled, a sign that some of our men had made it off the wall and were now on the streets of the town next to it, fighting their way to the gate. My stomach was in knots, not because of the thought of the coming fight, either with the Moesians or with Prixus, but because I did not know what was happening with Gaius. Crassus' chief bodyguard, along with his four men, was sitting next to the Legate, all of their backs turned as they watched the gate. I stared at Prixus' bulk, covered in a leather cuirass of the style favored by gladiators, at least those who now worked as bodyguards. While it did not provide the same level of protection as a mail shirt, it is much lighter and gives the wearer more freedom of movement, and for a gladiator, movement is life. His forearms were covered in scars, the muscles of his arms like ropes of iron, and I knew that he was a very, very dangerous man. If Miriam had been alive, I probably would not have considered taking him on, especially with his other men around, but she was not and I thirsted for vengeance. I had never been beaten before; even with the circumstances of how it happened my pride had been hurt, meaning the idea of taking my revenge had never been far from my mind. Now that Crassus had given his tacit approval, I was determined that I would settle accounts with Prixus. It was not something I had breathed a word about to anybody, not even Scribonius, Balbus, or Diocles, though I imagine they knew me well enough to know I was thinking about it. Still, I had enough of dragging men into my disputes and I was determined to do this by myself. Suddenly, there was a screeching noise over and above the din of the fighting, tearing my attention from Prixus and back to the gate, which was opening very, very slowly.

"Get ready!"

Crassus kicked his horse, moving to the front of the group of horsemen. I was struck by how small our numbers were, particularly since we did not really know what lay beyond the gates, but we would have to make up for that lack with ferocity. Drawing the *spatha*, I heard the rasping sound as the others did the same, and Ocelus made a little hop, quivering with excitement or fear. It seemed to take an eternity for the gates to open; when they were about halfway, Crassus gave the order to begin heading for the entrance, starting out at a trot. Ocelus took a bounding leap and I had to rein him in so he would not go headlong up the road. Positioning myself to Crassus' left, just off his horse's hindquarter, Prixus was on the other side in the same spot. The rest of the men trailed behind us in a wedge, modified to be as wide as the gates would allow. I knew that he was trying to time our approach

126

so that we would hit the entrance just as the gates opened up, and it almost worked.

We had just gone from the trot to the canter, Crassus pointing his sword at the gates, which were about three-quarters open and still slowly swinging open, crying out, "For Rome!"

With his call, he slapped his horse on the rump with the flat of his sword, and it leapt forward into the gallop. We were perhaps a hundred paces away, and Ocelus needed no urging to follow Crassus' mount's lead, nor did the others. Thundering up the road, the wind began roaring in my ears, almost drowning out all the other noise, my focus narrowed to just the gateway. While it would be close, I saw that we would hit the entrance at precisely the moment the gates finished opening. I do not know exactly what happened, but suddenly the gates stopped moving. While the gates were open enough to allow Crassus, Prixus, and me, unless the others pulled up to fall in directly behind us, they would not be able to make it past them. I waited for Crassus to give the order for them to do so, but instead he pulled up, his horse skidding to a halt not more than 50 paces away from the gate. All of the momentum of our charge had just been killed, in one of those happenings in battle that can turn the tide one way or the other. The other men did the same, except for some of them who had either not been paying close attention or their horses were too skittish, because they did not stop in time, and I heard the thudding sound of flesh smashing into flesh as one man's horse slammed into another. The animals whinnied in fear and anger; the air was filled with the curses of men. I turned just in time to see a figure tumble to the ground when his horse bounced off another beast, which in reflex lashed out with its rear hooves, sending the first horse rolling over the rider, who let out a sharp scream. Our charge was in a shambles before we had even really started it, and I thought for a moment that Crassus would pull us back to regroup. Instead, the gates began reopening, finally making it the rest of the way and without waiting, Crassus urged his horse forward again. Cursing, I followed, as did Prixus, who looked over at me, giving a sneering smile.

"Let's see if you can actually use that thing, soldier boy. You just stay behind old Prixus and he'll keep you safe."

I did not answer him, just stared straight ahead, my attention fixed on the entrance and what lay beyond.

Restarting, we reached a full gallop in just a few paces, Crassus leading us with his shout, "For Rome!" over and over.

My mind's eye barely had time to take in the scene before us as we thundered up the road, the horses laboring up the sloping grade that led into the town. Finally reaching a point where we could see more than just the gateway, we were greeted by the sight of a mass of densely packed Moesians, facing a rough semicircle of our own men just two ranks deep, backs to us while they tried to push the enemy away from the gate.

"Stand clear," Crassus began shouting over and over to the Legionaries who were facing the Moesians directly opposite the gate.

While I personally would have turned and tried to push the Moesians down the street next to the wall instead of driving deeper into the town at that point, I followed Crassus nonetheless. Giving the man opposite them a huge heave with their shields, just as if they were performing a change in relief during battle, the Legionaries scrambled out of the way when we came through just before we slammed into the front rank of Moesians. Already staggering backwards from the push they had been given, that first rank of Moesians bounced off the bulk of Crassus' mount, as well as Ocelus and Prixus' horse. Leaning to the side, I thrust hard at a man who had stumbled, dropping his shield in the process, yet his luck was with him that day because his fall threw my aim off. I barely had time to recover before I had to dodge a thrust from a spear, catching the point on the cavalry shield that I had fastened to my arm. Despite doing some practicing with the unfamiliar shield, it was still very awkward, but I managed to ward off the blow. I felt more than saw Balbus pushing up next to me on my left, offering me more protection, allowing me to concentrate on a man on my right who had tried to wedge himself in between Crassus' horse and Ocelus, in an obvious attempt to get underneath Crassus' horse to gut him. My blade thrust down into his back before his own blade could strike up into Crassus' mount, eliciting a high-pitched scream, with frothy blood spewing from his mouth, telling me that I had punctured one of his lungs. Twisting the blade free, I felt Ocelus taking a step forward, kicking the man in the head in the process, suddenly stopping his screams.

Men were shouting, while Crassus was wielding his blade well, clearly accustomed to fighting from horseback. Glancing over, I saw that Prixus, with one of his own men now beside him to the right, was flailing away with his blade, drawing blood with almost every stroke. We had pushed our way several feet forward from where the men of the 8th had been and since I could not afford to look behind me, I could only hope that they had kept their heads and were following behind us. Moesians were still clearly eager to fight, since they continued to press against us, and Ocelus reared several times, lashing out with hooves when men came too close or made a jab at him with a spear. From my vantage point above the fray, I could see that the Moesian line still ran more than ten men deep, but there did not seem to be anyone in clear command. There were several men who were wearing better armor than those around them, while one in particular was surrounded by warriors who seemed intent only on protecting him, and Crassus headed right for the man. The Legate cut his way through the packed mass of Moesians, with Prixus following close behind. Because the noble Moesian was slightly off to the right, when Crassus moved, he opened up a larger gap between him and me, except I was too heavily engaged to close it. Seeing this, a pair of alert Moesians jumped into the space immediately, before one of Crassus' bodyguards could move up to fill the spot. The bodyguard was dressed similarly to Prixus, but instead of a *spatha,* he carried a curved Thracian sword, very similar to the weapons wielded by the Moesians. He clearly knew what he was doing with it, so I do not know if it was overconfidence or just bad luck, but he pushed his horse more deeply than was wise, pulling ahead of me and even slightly ahead of Crassus to his right. Again, the Moesians wasted no time, a man leaping into the space behind the gladiator's horse, dagger in hand. At first, I was more amused than anything; bringing a dagger into a fight like this seemed to be worse than pointless, seeming downright suicidal, but he had something else in mind. With one deft motion, he slashed the blade across the large tendon just above the ankle of the bodyguard's horse, eliciting an almost human shriek of pain from the animal, before immediately going crashing down with his rider, who tumbled down into the midst of the Moesians. I saw the flash of blades rising up then thrust downward, the gladiator giving one short cry of pain and despair. The horse, meanwhile, was now thrashing about, struggling to get to its feet, its blood spraying onto the paving stones of the street while Moesians thrust their spears into the poor beast.

Somehow, I do not know how, Ocelus managed to avoid being struck by a flailing hoof, but he gave a snort of terror at the smell of his fellow creature's blood, once again rearing to lash out with his hooves. I had become, if not accustomed, at least prepared for the idea that Ocelus would act in such a manner, suddenly rearing up with no warning, ensuring that I kept hold of the reins at all times. This made using the shield somewhat more difficult, but I knew that to lose the saddle would mean certain death. Between gripping him with my thighs and my hold on the reins, I was never in real danger of being unseated. Finally, the downed horse's struggles slowed, finally stopping altogether, while Crassus continued his attempt to close with the Moesian, whose bodyguards had mostly been eliminated. I sensed another horse and rider coming up to the spot vacated by the gladiator and his mount; fortunately, the horse's body kept the Moesians from flowing into the space themselves. I was slashing and thrusting, trying to best a man who had considerable skill, because he was parrying my thrusts with what seemed to be almost contemptuous ease. The thought flashed through my mind that perhaps I had at last met my match, but while his defense was superb, his offense was only mediocre at best. Finally, it was Ocelus who broke the deadlock by reaching out, stretching his long neck out to grab the man's arm in his big teeth. It was completely unexpected, both by the Moesian and by me, the man giving a surprised yelp of pain when his shield arm was clamped in Ocelus' jaws. That was the only opening I needed, making a quick thrust to the man's neck, which was now exposed, the blade punching through the other side. He dropped his sword immediately, though his body remained semi-upright because Ocelus had not released him.

"Let go of him, Ocelus," I yelled, several times in fact, before my horse opened his mouth, the man dropping like a sack of grain.

I saw several men gaping in astonishment, while I was no less surprised than they were, but I could not stop to give my horse a pat on the neck. Pushing forward, I continued thrusting and slashing at every Moesian I could reach. Balbus followed me closely, and when the Moesians suddenly took an unforced backward step, I risked a glance behind me. We had moved the Moesians about 50 paces backward, the men of the 8th filling in the gaps we had made immediately. The rest of the Evocati seemed to be in good shape, each fighting their own battles with Moesians ringed around the periphery of the bulge that we had created. Crassus had finally reached the Moesian, after he and Prixus had cut down the remaining bodyguards, with Crassus slashing down at the man, who fended off the blow with his shield. Prixus moved in, but Crassus gave him a sharp command to leave the Moesian alone, then I was too absorbed in my own fight to notice what was taking place. There was another attempt by a Moesian to try to get under Ocelus' belly and I leaned down, still holding my shield high enough to ward off any blows from others, then chopped down with my blade. I was only able to strike a glancing blow, but it was enough to partially sever the man's arm before he fell under Ocelus' hooves, then rolled to safety, holding his spurting limb.

About then, I realized that it was Scribonius who had moved up next to me, and having my two oldest and best friends on either side of me gave me confidence to push forward even farther. The noise was almost deafening, with men shouting to and at each other, others screaming when they were struck, some mortally. Punctuating the noise was the clanging of metal on metal, and underlying that was the sound of metal striking the wood of a shield, or flesh. We were now almost even with the next cross street, giving the Moesians a way to escape the pressure we were putting on, and the men of the rear ranks began slipping away. It did not take long for the men closest to the fighting to feel the absence of their comrades behind them, prompting one of them to take that step backwards. In a matter of a few moments, all organized resistance crumbled, the man I was engaging making the fatal error of letting his fear overcome him and turning to run. Ending his life with a thrust between the shoulder blades before pausing to catch my breath, it gave me the chance to see how the others were faring. Spinning Ocelus around, I watched Crassus finishing off the Moesian noble with a lightning-quick thrust to the chest, after he had knocked the man's shield aside by using his horse's body. With our job essentially done, the Legionaries of the 8th went streaming past us, pursuing the Moesians, their Centurions and Optios bellowing at them to keep up the pressure and not let them regroup. I looked all about trying to find Gaius, but I did not see him, and I tried to tell myself that this meant nothing, except the knot in my stomach was impossible to ignore. Balbus and Scribonius pulled alongside me, Scribonius grinning at me as he wiped the blood off his blade.

"That was fun. Maybe I should have joined the cavalry after all."

"We're not through yet," I warned.

"I don't know about you, but I plan on getting off this beast for the rest of it," Balbus said. "I don't think going house to house on horseback is a good idea."

I realized that Balbus was right; it was time to finish this on foot. The streets of Naissus were narrow, and the one thing that being on horseback robs a man of is his mobility in tight spaces, as well as presenting a bigger target should some Moesian get up on the roofs of the buildings lining the streets. Granted, most of the buildings were squat wooden structures where one could see enough of the roof, that sneaking up that way would be next to impossible. However, there were a fair number of larger structures that would give an enemy a vantage point from where they could drop a rock or other heavy object down on us, causing grave damage. On horseback, it would be extremely hard to dodge something thrown our way, so I dismounted as a signal to the others that it was time to do the rest of this on foot. Wiping down the blade of the *spatha*, I sheathed it on the saddle of Ocelus, then seeing a Legionary tending to his wounded friend, I called him over.

"Watch our horses while you wait for the *medici* to come help your friend."

The man looked apprehensive, glancing around, and I knew he was looking for his Centurion or Optio.

I explained patiently, "Son, I'm the Camp Prefect, second in command of this army. If your Centurion has a problem, tell him to come see me after this is over."

He saluted, taking Ocelus' reins, who clearly did not like a stranger watching him and he tossed his head several times, trying to yank the reins out of the man's hands. Finally, I grabbed his bridle, speaking soothingly to him for a moment, which seemed to calm him down. With that taken care of, I drew my Gallic blade, liking the comforting and familiar feel of the handle, worn to fit my hand perfectly.

"Let's go finish this," I told the others, then began walking down the street.

Crassus was calling out commands to a couple of Centurions when we approached. He looked surprised to see us on foot, but when I explained why, he thought about it for a moment before nodding his agreement, although he did not dismount himself.

"I need to be able to see what's going on," he explained, which was true enough, except that I could have told him even that would not help.

Taking a town is one of the most confusing operations a Legion can perform, especially once all organized resistance is done and the men start to see opportunities to loot and run wild. However, I could look down the street we were on to see that the Moesians were starting to form back up several blocks away. At the same time, I could hear fighting still going on farther down both directions along the wall, with the men of the 14th taking over from the 8th, who continued to push past us to confront the Moesians down the street. Deciding that it would be good to head down the nearest side street running perpendicular to the main road leading from the gate, I called to the rest of the Evocati, then began to move. Farther down that street, I saw another group of Moesians, but between them and us was what looked like a Century of Legionaries. Deciding that they did not need our help, I turned to head in the opposite direction, stopping when Crassus called my name. Turning to look up at him, I saw that he was pointing in the original direction we had started.

"Prixus went that way," he said quietly.

I instantly understood what he was telling me, and what he wanted me to do.

I looked over to Scribonius, telling him, "Take the Evocati down that street. I need to talk to Crassus for a moment. I'll join you."

He gave me a long, searching look and I could tell that he did not believe me, but I had no intention of drawing Scribonius or Balbus into my troubles again. That had happened often enough in the past that I was unwilling to let it happen again. But he gave a curt nod of his head, then without saying a word to me, called to the others and they headed off in the opposite direction. Waiting a moment, I watched them move quickly down the street, then turned about, heading for Prixus.

Now on my own, I approached the rear of the Century that was facing a relatively small group of Moesians who, despite the disparity in numbers, were putting up a fierce fight. The Century was handling them with relative ease; the Centurion in command blowing the whistle frequently, meaning that the shifts were kept short so the men would not tire. Seeing the Optio in his spot at the rear of the Century, I made my way over. If he was surprised to see such a high-ranking officer in such a place, he covered it well, giving me a perfect salute.

"Have you seen four gladiators come this direction?" I asked the man, who knew exactly who I was asking about.

"You mean Prixus? Yes, sir. I saw him and his bunch head down that alley there," he replied, pointing down an alley where I could see a section of Legionaries already kicking in doors in search of loot.

"Are they yours?" I asked the Optio, who quickly shook his head, but would not meet my gaze.

I was sure he was lying. However, I was not in a position or even in the mood to do anything about it. What was happening was not uncommon; if the situation was under control, the Centurion often would send a section of men into nearby buildings to see what they could scavenge, before the official period of looting began. I was after Prixus, not some Legionaries trying to grab a few baubles and coins.

"Any idea why he headed that way?"

The Optio shrugged, only saying, "I thought I saw a woman head down that way right as we came up here to face these bastards."

That sounded like Prixus; I had heard him brag on many occasions about his appetite for the pleasures a woman can provide, making it clear he was not picky about whether those pleasures were given willingly or not. Following where the Optio had pointed, I headed down the alley, ignoring the men who were either dragging or carrying bits of plunder out and dumping them in a pile, under the eye of one of their comrades. Trusting that I would be able to find Prixus and his men, I listened carefully as I passed by a door or window of

135

each building, hoping to hear a voice I recognized. I had almost reached the end of the alley, where it emptied out into the next street that ran perpendicular to the gate road. Risking a glance around the corner in each direction, it was clear that our men had not yet reached this deep into the town, seeing Moesians in both directions I looked. Some were townspeople, but an equal number or even more were warriors, and I ducked my head back quickly before I was spotted. It appeared that Prixus and his men had managed to get into the town somehow without being spotted.

Turning around to walk back up the alley, I heard a low moan from a building I had walked by without hearing anything the first time. It was a woman's voice, moaning with something other than pleasure, the fear and pain clear even out here in the alley. Freezing in mid-stride, I strained to listen; after a moment, I heard a grunt, followed by a smacking sound, followed by the woman crying out in clear and obvious distress. Despite not knowing for sure that it was Prixus and his men inside, I decided to go in to find out, except when I examined the building more closely, I could not readily find a door. Walking about, I noticed a small recess that looked like a gap between the buildings, into which I barely fit, having to turn sideways to do so. As I sidestepped my way deeper into the recess, the light grew dimmer with every step, and I barely saw the doorway that led into the building. I could see why the woman had thought she might be safe inside, because the entrance on this side of the building was extremely hard to find. The structure itself was made of rough-cut stone, and it was dark inside, the only light coming from a window or other door in what I assumed to be the front of the building at the opposite end.

I unsheathed my sword very slowly before stepping into the building, since I could now hear men talking in low tones. One of them laughed and I immediately recognized it as belonging to one of Prixus' men, telling me I was in the right place. Lifting my foot, I slowly put it down across the threshold, then taking a deep breath, stepped inside. While my eyes adjusted to the dim light, I saw that I was standing in what appeared to be the main room. Immediately to my left was a wooden wall made of rough-hewn planks, running the length of the room, with an opening at the far end that clearly led to the back room, nearest to the alley. There was a counter to the right, also running almost the entire length of the front room, arrayed on which appeared to be bolts of cloth, along with sundry other supplies that told me that this was a weaver's shop. The windows were shuttered, but there were slats missing, and the front door was slightly ajar, which was what provided the light. I surmised that the girl had run in here, or perhaps she worked in the shop, and somehow Prixus and his men had found her. Moving carefully, I crept along behind the counter, trying to control my breathing, although I doubted that the gladiators were paying attention to anything other than the girl, or woman. Nearing the opening into the back room, I tried to place the approximate positions of each man by the sounds of their voices or breathing, yet it was impossible to tell. The woman was still moaning, a low continuous sound, which was clearly starting to irritate Prixus, who snarled at her to shut up. When she did not, there was the sodden sound of a fist smashing into flesh, but unsurprisingly that did not stop her crying; it only made it worse.

"If you don't shut your mouth, you *cunnus*, I'll cut your throat from ear to ear while I'm fucking you in your ass." Prixus' voice throbbed with fury and the promise that he was not only capable, but would enjoy doing that very thing.

Realizing that I could not waste any more time, I took a couple quick steps, and in my haste, my foot came down on a shard of pottery or something of that nature.

The cracking sound was probably not as loud in reality as I thought, but it was loud enough to cause the gladiator who had laughed earlier to say, "Did anyone else hear that?"

I did not wait for an answer, closing the remaining distance in two quick strides, turning into the entryway to come face to face with the gladiator who was coming to check on the noise. In the gloom, I could not clearly make out his features, yet I saw enough to know that he was caught completely by surprise. Before he could open his mouth to shout, I made a hard overhand thrust at shoulder level, and since he was shorter than I was, I had to angle the point slightly downward so that it punched into his mouth. I was taking a calculated risk, because as long as I aimed the thrust perfectly, the point of the blade would pierce through the back of his neck, keeping him from crying out. However, the blade would be harder to dislodge once it was stuck in bone, and could cause a fatal delay. What I was counting on was that because of the dim light, the reactions of Prixus and his surviving men would be delayed since the first man did not have a chance to raise a warning. Even as dark as it was, I could see the whites of his eyes opening wide in shock as his life ended in less time than it takes for one heartbeat. The muscles of his body went suddenly slack, the life fleeing from his body, despite his eyes staying fixed on mine. My arm was suddenly being pulled down by his now dead weight, threatening to wrest the sword from my grasp. Lifting one leg, I kicked the man hard in the chest, at the same time twisting the blade, which made a sucking sound as his flesh gave way to release it. Without waiting for the body to hit the floor, I moved quickly, but these were men trained for the arena, and their reflexes were nothing to be sneered at.

In those fleeting moments that it took for me to step farther into the back room, I sensed the relative positions of Prixus and his men, and I headed for the man nearest to me. In a perfect world, I would have preferred to go after Prixus first, but he was farthest away from me, standing over the body of the woman, who was lying on a set of crates. She was moving, but I could not see if he had actually cut her throat yet. My next target had catlike reflexes, taking a nimble hop backwards when I gave a hard thrust, my arm jarring when it extended and hit nothing but air. If I had been an inexperienced man, a missed thrust like that would likely be fatal, the natural reaction being to stumble forward a bit, but I had my feet solidly under me, which was a good thing. I do not know if it was the sudden movement of the air or just some extra sense that told me there was a threat to my right, where the third man had been standing, yet I twisted to the right just enough to avoid the thrust he aimed at me. I felt and heard the blade sliding across the front of my mail shirt, then before he could withdraw his blade, I reached over with my left hand, taking a guess where his wrist would be. It turned out I was wrong; instead of his wrist, I grabbed the blade next to the hilt. We both instantly realized my mistake and he gave a hard yank as my hand closed around the blade. I should have let go but I did not, choosing to tighten my grip with all of my strength. The pain was excruciating, the blade cutting deeply into my fingers, but I had taken a gamble and it was one that paid off. When a man sharpens his blade, very few spend much time working on the part of the blade next to the hilt, since it rarely if ever is actually used in combat, meaning that part of the gladiator's blade was relatively dull. Also, when I had grabbed hold, I felt that it was not a Spanish sword, which is double-edged its entire length, but a Thracian curved sword, which only is double-edged from the tip to perhaps a foot down the blade. Finally, I once again counted on being stronger than the gladiator, so that as far as he was concerned, the blade might as well have been embedded in stone, it not moving an inch from my grip. He should have let go but he did not, a mistake for which he paid with his life as I ignored the pain to make a quick thrust that took him high in the chest, just under his collarbone. He let out a shriek, falling backwards off of my blade while I dropped his sword, which clattered to the floor.

"Kill that fucking soldier boy," Prixus snarled to the remaining man, who had dodged my first thrust.

My left hand felt like I had thrust it into flames, and it was wet and sticky, but I could not think about that. None of us could see very well, just the dull glint of our blades, and I only sensed Prixus coming across the room, hearing the rasp from his scabbard as he drew his sword. His weapon made a whistling sound as he gave a downward stroke. More by reflex than by sight, I threw my sword up, meeting his blade with mine, jarring my arm up to the shoulder. There was a good deal of strength behind the blow, but my more immediate problem was the other gladiator, who took the opportunity to make a thrust of his own. Because of the darkness, or so I suppose, he aimed poorly, the blade striking me at an angle. Nevertheless, it did puncture the chain mail, the blade sliding along the left side of my ribcage, cutting deeply into my flesh. I heard someone hiss in pain and I suppose it was me, but I could not pay attention to that. Balling up my left fist, I punched out at the gladiator and it was more luck than anything that I managed to strike the man square on the point of his chin, or at least that is how it felt. He flew backwards, but my attention was on Prixus now, who was preparing for another attack.

"Come on, soldier boy, let's see if you're as good as everyone says. Come to Prixus, and I'll gut you like a fish."

I could just make out the point of his sword, weaving back and forth and for the first time I felt a sense of unease. I was fighting his kind of fight, and I was outnumbered; it occurred to me that I might have finally let my pride get me into a spot from which I could not extricate. In those moments, no longer than a few heartbeats, all that had happened to bring me to this point flashed through my mind. If Miriam had not died, I would undoubtedly not have pursued vengeance against Prixus. Somehow I convinced myself that if Miriam had lived, I would not have even had my dispute with Prixus. Like a flood bursting forth, I felt the anger surge through me. It was the same anger I first felt all those years before on that hilltop in Hispania and I welcomed it now like an old friend, a friend that I needed desperately. Suddenly, I did not care about anything other than killing Prixus, or anyone else who stood before me when it came down to it. Completely ignoring the other man, who had just regained his feet, I threw myself at Prixus, knocking his blade aside with my own as I did so. He had clearly not been expecting this, letting out a surprised gasp when I smashed into his body, my left hand grabbing for his throat while I used the pommel of my sword to bash him in the face. My left hand was too slippery with blood to get a good hold on his throat, and he had instantly tucked his chin down so it would not have mattered anyway. In turn, he tried to bring his sword up, but feeling the movement, I reached out, this time making sure to grab his wrist. Again, the pain in my hand was excruciating, yet it had to be overcome and ignored, or I would die here in this dirty back room. My closing with Prixus had one benefit; the other gladiator could not use his sword on me, because Prixus and I were moving violently about and in the dark, he would be as likely to stab Prixus as he would me. That did not stop him from joining the fray however, and he threw himself in our general direction, swinging a fist that either by luck or design hit me where his blade had landed moments before. Lights exploded in my head, but we were too close for me to bring my blade up, besides which Prixus had gripped my wrist with his left hand, locking us together. It felt like the bones would be crushed and ground into dust by Prixus' hand, both of us exerting every bit of strength into maintaining our hold on the other. Our faces were inches from each other and as we gasped for air, I could smell the wine and garum on his breath. Most importantly, I could smell the fear, rank and running deep in the gladiator. Shifting my weight onto my right leg, I lashed out with my left foot, catching the other gladiator on the kneecap, who gave a yelp before hopping back out of range. It was not a debilitating blow; I just hoped it would be enough to keep him from hitting me again for a moment. Prixus, sensing my momentary vulnerability, suddenly gave a violent heave, twisting and pulling me more to my right, leaving my left leg dangling in the air. I could feel myself starting to fall as Prixus suddenly released his grip on my right arm, which I flailed about, trying to maintain my balance. The only thing keeping me upright was my own hold on Prixus' sword arm, and now that Prixus had a hand free, he used his ham-sized fist to beat on my left hand. When that did not work, I watched in horror, unable to stop him as he bent down, sinking his teeth into my wrist. The roar of pain that came from my lungs deafened even me as I released my grip on his arm, falling to the floor. The natural reflex when falling to one side or the other is to use that hand to break the fall, which Prixus undoubtedly was counting on, since that would be my sword hand. Somehow, I do not know how, I ignored that natural reaction, twisting my body instead to land on my back and while doing so I lashed out wildly with my sword, swinging it in a wide arc at about ankle level. My reward was the feeling of contact with the tip of my sword, followed by a bellowed curse and Prixus falling to the floor himself.

The impact with the floor had knocked the breath from my lungs, but I thought I had a moment to gather myself since Prixus was down as well. However, I had completely forgotten the other man for a moment. Stars exploded in my head when he landed on top of me, his hands grabbing for my throat, clamping on my windpipe with a grip only slightly weaker than that of Prixus. There is nothing more panic-inducing than the feeling of suffocating and I bucked my body with all my strength, trying to throw him, but he was much too experienced for that, wrapping his legs behind mine for leverage. In a reflex action, I reached up with my left hand, trying to claw for his eyes. Instead, as usually happens, my hand landed in the vicinity of his mouth. For the second time I felt a pair of jaws clamping down, this time on my little finger, somehow in the exact same spot where I had been cut moments earlier. I suppose that made it easier for him to take one convulsive bite, completely severing the finger, the combination of the pain and the sound of the bone being bitten through causing my stomach to lurch. I felt the hot bile rising in my throat, except that it was unable to get out because of the hands clamped around my neck. Almost out of my mind with pain, I moved my right hand between our bodies, then after a moment of fumbling, grabbed hold of the gladiator's testicles. Wasting no time, I began squeezing with every bit of my strength, gratified to hear his shrieks of pain added to mine. The room was beginning to dim and I could feel my strength draining with every passing heartbeat, but still I continued to squeeze. Finally, I felt his grip loosen, allowing me to suck air in through my bruised throat, though it was not much. This gave me a bit more strength and with the last bit, I clenched my fist, feeling his balls rupture in my hand. The shriek that emanated from him as he completely released my throat, falling off me, hands clutching his groin, would have done a Gorgon proud. Gasping for every bit of air I could get, I lay panting for breath while holding my ruined hand up and away from me. In the shadows, a darker shape suddenly came into my field of vision, causing me to make a reflexive roll to the side, just as Prixus' sword came whistling down to bury itself in the dirt floor where my head had been. Somehow, I rolled to my feet before he could make another lunge, except I had left my sword on the floor, dropped when I had grabbed the other gladiator's balls. Too dark to see where it lay, I circled away from Prixus, who made another thrust, which I managed to dodge, just barely. He was limping from where I had nicked him with my sword, yet was clearly mobile enough.

"I'm going to enjoy this," Prixus said, the tip of his sword waving back and forth while he shuffled closer to me.

Instantly, I recognized that he was cutting me off, slowly but surely backing me into a spot where I would have no room to maneuver. Also knowing that he would not allow himself to be surprised by trying to close with him a second time, my mind raced desperately for a way to beat the man. One thing in my favor was that the rest of his men were out of action, with two dead and one wishing that he was, but without a weapon, I stood little chance against Prixus. The gladiator, beaded sweat on his shaved head picking up the stray beams of light, seemed content to take his time and I saw his remaining teeth gleaming dully in the light as he gave me a grin that held nothing good.

"You think you're so much better than me and my men," Prixus sneered. "But you're just like us. You're low-born scum, just like us. Just because you sucked Caesar's cock and killed a few Gauls and other barbarians that don't know which end of the sword to hold, you suddenly think you're one of them, some high-born *cunnus* whose *cac* doesn't stink."

Despite the darkness, I could see that he was truly angry. It was then I realized that this ran much deeper than my humiliation of him, giving me an idea.

143

"You're right," I said suddenly, seeing him frown in confusion. "I am low-born, but at least my mother wasn't a whore, and I knew who my father was. And the men I killed in Gaul were warriors, not some scared convict pissing himself."

"I am Prixus," he suddenly roared. "And I've had 72 bouts in the arena, and I won my freedom! The man hasn't been born who can defeat me."

"Yes he has," I said calmly, knowing that my lack of temper would just fuel his own rage. "I put you on your ass in the mud like a child. In fact, I've met children who were harder to beat than you were. I beat you once, and I'm about to beat you again. Except this time, I'm going to kill you."

"You lie! The only way you knocked me off my horse was by sneaking up on me. And you paid for it, didn't you?"

"You were facing me on that horse, weren't you? And who came after me like a fucking woman, with help in the bargain? In the dark, from behind. You're a gutless coward."

Letting out a roar of rage, Prixus leapt forward, making a hard thrust in the same movement and I dived to the side, for the second time violating the first rule of never leaving your feet. This time, however, I was doing so for a purpose, my hand sweeping along the floor, fumbling for my sword. Prixus pivoted about, aiming a kick at my head that missed his intended target, but struck me hard on the shoulder, knocking my arm in such a direction that my hand closed directly on the hilt of my sword. Wasting no time, I gave an upward swing, meeting Prixus' blade on its downward stroke, jarring my arm even more. I was now on one knee, but Prixus was not about to let me regain my feet and he pressed close, raining blows down on me that I sensed more than saw, somehow managing to parry all of them. Inevitably, he paused to take a breath, while I pushed to my feet and in one motion began my own attack, starting with a low, hard thrust, which he managed to knock to the side. Withdrawing quickly, I tried a combination move, both of which he parried. Neither of us was speaking now, both panting for breath, the air seeming especially close in the dank, dark room. There was a smell of blood, thick and coppery, along with the stench of death and *cac*, after one or both dead men's bowels released.

Prixus made another lunge, following it up with a sweeping backhand that whistled past my face, missing by less than the width of a hand. The darkness made it hard to judge distances and when I countered Prixus' attack, I aimed for a point farther back than I normally would have. I was rewarded with the feeling of the point of my sword striking something solid, followed immediately by a gasp of pain from Prixus, who recoiled backward from the blow. It was not mortal or even that damaging a blow, yet it was enough to shake Prixus' confidence, his posture suddenly changing to that of a man on the defensive. My left arm from the elbow down was virtually useless, the pain extremely distracting, but now I had given Prixus something to think about as well, and we continued circling each other in the small space between the walls and the bodies. I was vaguely aware that the woman had pulled herself to a sitting position and seemed to be watching Prixus and me, while the lone surviving gladiator was against the far wall, rolling about and moaning while he held his testicles.

"I'm going to feed you your balls, Prixus," I goaded the gladiator. "By the time I'm through with you, you'll be begging me to kill you. You gladiators wouldn't last a day in the Legions, and the worst man I ever commanded would chew you up and spit you out. But you know that, don't you? You know that you're a worthless piece of *cac*, that your mother was a brass obol whore, and your father was a poxed slave."

With another roar of rage, Prixus came at me, his blade slashing through the air as he tried to slice me into pieces. Shuffling backwards, I either parried or dodged his blows, letting him expend his energy while I waited for another opening. By this point, I had taken in enough of Prixus' style to have an idea of what to expect in his attack. He favored a higher thrust, along with a wider slash, which undoubtedly played well for the crowds at the arena. However, in a small, dark room, against a man like me, it left him vulnerable,

145

provided I was fast enough. I could also feel his strength fading, except I did not know whether it was from fatigue, or the wound I had inflicted earlier. My own energy was wavering as well, yet I understood that it would be the case that the man who walked out of this building was the one who somehow managed to summon his last reserves of strength at the right time. Prixus paused to take a breath, but I knew that he was expecting me to attack and he still had the strength to fend my attacks off, so I waited. This clearly puzzled him, though after a moment, he resumed his attack. This time, I saw that his waning strength had not been a figment of my imagination, it being significantly easier to parry his blows, each coming slower than before. He was gasping for breath now; while I was breathing hard, I had been able to conserve more energy simply by being on the defensive. Judging that this was the time, I launched my own attack and in a moment Prixus' face was a picture of desperation as I continually assailed him with a variety of thrusts and slashes. He was extremely skilled, but I had gained the advantage, which I had no intention of relinquishing now. We moved together, and I pressed against him so that now it was Prixus who was in danger of being cut off. Sensing this, he made a sudden move to try to gain some room. If he had not already been wounded, or was not as tired, in all probability it would have worked, but the combination of fatigue and darkness meant that his feet crossed over themselves so that he went down in a heap, falling backward away from me. Leaping across the space, I thrust down at his body, which he just managed to parry, lying on his back with his sword held above him. Lashing out with a foot, he caught me on the shin, but it was a glancing blow without much power behind it. With his other foot, he tried to scrabble backward, still holding his sword up and across his body. Suddenly shifting my aim, instead of trying to stab down into his body I flicked the blade in a slashing move downward, the edge striking the bone of his forearm, cutting through one bone and breaking the second, partially severing his hand. Prixus let out a scream of agony, dropping the sword, blood spraying out of a severed artery, his arm flopping grotesquely to the side in a direction that it was not meant to go. He clutched his ruined arm with his good hand, his torso and face covered with blood that shone in the dim light, looking black to my eyes. Even in the gloom, his panic and fear were clear to see while I stood there, my sword dripping, savoring the moment, and for that instant, the pain in my hand and side was nonexistent. I said nothing, vaguely realizing that I was weaving on my feet, but I put it down to the inevitable letdown that comes after a fight.

"Well?" Prixus' voice was hoarse with pain, and the defeat easily heard. "What are you waiting for? Go ahead and finish me, you bastard."

"You really don't think it's going to be that easy, do you?" I asked Prixus, and at the moment, I meant to do truly horrible and painful things to the man, but when I took a step toward him, my knee almost buckled. It was then I realized that I needed to finish this quickly or I would pass out myself. "I know you don't think so, Prixus, but this is the luckiest day of your life," I said, then thrust down hard with my Gallic sword, plunging the blade deeply into Prixus' chest.

He stiffened, arching his back and letting out a horrific groan, his heels kicking the dirt floor when I twisted the blade to pull it free. He gave a last rattling gurgle before his *animus* fled his body, leaving me standing, trembling from head to toe.

I am not sure how long I stood there before I became aware of a scuffling sound. Whirling about while bringing my sword up, I saw the woman, who had come to her feet, my movement causing her to let out a terrified gasp, while trying to pull her ruined clothing about her.

"I'm not going to hurt you, girl," I said wearily, but I did remember to speak in Greek.

Still, if she understood me, she gave no sign. Instead, she took a step backward, shaking her head but not speaking, still clutching what was little better than rags around her body. Suddenly needing to sit down, I staggered in her general direction, planning to use one of the crates. Letting out a horrified shriek, she ran to the corner of the room to cower there, whimpering as she crouched there. Ignoring her, I sat down heavily, trying to examine my wounds in the dim light. I had been in the room long enough for my eyes to adjust to what little light there was, but it was probably a good thing that I could not clearly see the wreckage of my hand at that moment. The little finger was now just a stump, throbbing with every beat of my heart, still leaking blood, along with the deep cuts on every other finger. With my good hand, I removed my neckerchief to wrap the wounded one as tightly as I could stand it, letting out a groan of pain. Perhaps it was that sound that drew the girl, but I felt a light touch on my shoulder, almost making me jump out of my skin, which in turn caused her to leap back. After seeing that she was not going to try and cut my throat, I relaxed a bit, and she took a timid step back in my direction.

"What do you want, girl?" I asked her, to which she shook her head, pointing instead at first my hand, then my side, which I had yet to examine. Realizing that she was offering me help, I told her, "I'm all right. I'll be going to the hospital tent to get patched up, so there's no need to worry."

She did not seem to understand or accept what I said, instead leaning down to peer at the wound along my side, which was visible through the rent in my mail shirt. Moving my arm out of the way, she gently probed the edges of the wound. Despite her soft touch, I winced, letting out a grunt of pain.

"Careful, girl, I'm not a side of beef that you're trying to tenderize," I complained. She shot me an amused look, shaking her head as she did so. "So you do understand me," I said, while she took a strip of what I supposed had been part of her dress, ripping it into narrower lengths. She still said nothing, but the look she gave me was answer enough. "I told you, I'm not going to hurt you," I said gently.

She refused to look at me, instead wrapping a strip around my chest. Seeing that my chest was larger than she had thought, she was forced to tie two pieces together.

Finally, she said with an accent I could not readily identify, "I know you won't."

Now it was my turn to be amused.

"And how do you know that?" I asked.

"Because you would have done so already and now you're too weak."

I was tempted to show her how wrong she was, but the truth was that she was right. Even if I had been inclined, it was highly doubtful that I could have done anything with her. With the wound on my side tightly bound, she stepped away, eyes going back to the floor.

"Thank you," I said awkwardly, not sure what else to do.

"What about him?" she asked suddenly, pointing to the man with the ruined testicles, who appeared to have passed out.

I looked at him, then gave her a shrug.

"What about him?" I repeated. "He won't be doing that anymore. To you or to anyone."

"He deserves to die," she spat with surprising vehemence.

"Then kill him," I replied carelessly, not thinking that such a timid young girl would have it in her.

She surprised me, though, taking a few steps over to where the man was lying, then bending down to pick up his sword. It was clearly too heavy for her to wield effectively, because she was barely able to get the tip off the ground, yet that did not stop her from stabbing down awkwardly into the man's body. It was not a fatal blow, but it clearly hurt, causing the man to let go of his testicles, screaming horribly. She was not through, however, stabbing him several more times until he stopped screaming, and moving. Nonetheless she kept going, her breath coming in ragged gasps while she continued thrusting the sword into his body. Finally, I reached out, gently taking the sword from her.

"He's dead, girl."

She began sobbing, her shoulders shaking as she bowed her head, her hair hiding her face. I stood there, not knowing exactly what to do, other than that I needed to get out of there and get to Philipos. The bleeding had been stopped by the makeshift bandages, but I suspected I needed to have the wound in my side cleaned out and stitched up. I also knew that something needed to be done with my hand. I was woozy, the room seeming to shift in front of me, yet something kept me rooted to the spot. It was as if this girl and I had shared something, except I did not know her. She was not very pretty; in fact, she was quite plain, yet there was something about her that sparked some sort of protective urge in me. Despite that, I was not sure what I could do for her, and the rest of this day would be dangerous enough without worrying about her, so I turned to leave.

"You might want to keep that sword with you," I said, knowing how awkward I sounded, but I thought it was good advice nonetheless. "The next few watches are going to be very dangerous. If you know a good place to hide . . ."

"I thought this was a good place," she said bitterly. "But I was wrong. I don't know a better one."

"That's why you should keep that sword with you. In case . . ." I did not finish, realizing that she knew better than I did what faced her, because Prixus and his men had just shown her.

"And if there is more than one? What good will this do?" she tried to wave the sword about, but again could barely lift it, starting a fresh round of tears. "I might as well kill myself now," she said miserably, then looked me directly in the face.

Even in the darkness, I could see the anguish and fear, making my decision for me.

"Come with me," I commanded her, heading for the door.

I was so accustomed to being obeyed that I did not even look to see if she was following. It was not until I was at the side doorway that led back out into the alley that I realized she was not behind me. I returned to find her still standing there, and I forced myself to be patient.

"Girl, I told you, I'm not going to hurt you. Now, you can stay here, and I promise you'll regret it. But if you come with me, I'll make sure that you're safe, at least until things calm down. You can believe me or not, I don't really care. I won't make this offer again."

Again, I did not wait to see if she followed me, just headed for the door, but I heard a scuffling step behind me as I reached the doorway. When I stepped out into the alleyway, pausing for a moment to let my eyes adjust to the light, I saw out of the corner of my eye that she was standing next to me. Without saying a word, I headed into the alley.

The fighting, at least in this part of the town, was over. The bodies of the Moesian dead that had made their stand in the alley had already been searched and looted, while the Legions had moved on. Heading back toward the gate road, I could hear the sounds of the fighting deeper in the town and I knew from experience that with an assault from both sides, those Moesians who had elected to fight were now caught in the jaws of a grinding, relentless beast, from which there was little chance of escape. Some Legionaries were either limping or being helped back out of the town to where the *medici* had set up the field hospital, and I turned to follow them.

"Follow me," I told the girl, who seemed hesitant to leave the town, but after one of the men helping the wounded called to her, making a lurid gesture, she hurried after me.

Crassus was nowhere in sight so I assumed he had gone deeper into the town, following the 8th. I wondered about Gaius and when we reached the area where the wounded had been laid out on the ground, I took the time to walk among the wounded, searching for his familiar face. Not finding him among the wounded, I felt a huge sense of relief, but I reminded myself that he could have been among the dead that had yet to be recovered. The girl had stopped at the edge of the area where the wounded had gathered, clearly distressed at the sight of suffering men, so that we were separated by several paces, which I suppose encouraged a group of men who had just carried two seriously wounded men to safety to believe that she was fair game.

"Hey there, little chicken," one of them called to the girl, reaching out to grab her by the arm. She shrank away, causing him to laugh and turn to his friends. "She's shy, boys. Let's see if we can't loosen her up some."

151

"She's with me," I spoke up.

They looked at me, clearly irritated at the interruption, but then they saw that it was their Camp Prefect. Their expressions turned sullen and I heard one of them mutter something, though I could not make out the words. My words had stopped the man from grabbing her, yet they did not move along, and I felt my anger starting to rise.

"Why aren't you men up where the fighting is?" I asked them, and they shifted nervously about in response.

The man who had reached for the girl apparently decided to brazen it out, saying with a touch of defiance in his tone, "We were bringing our wounded back to the aid station, Prefect. You wouldn't want us to let them lie there and bleed to death, would you?"

"Of course not," I replied reasonably. "But your duty is done, so you can return to the fighting. I know you wouldn't want to have it on your conscience that one of your comrades was struck down because you were trying to grab a piece of ass and weren't there to relieve him when the whistle blew."

This did not sit well with any of them, but neither could they argue. Giving me a perfunctory salute, they turned to walk back in the direction of the center of the town. I watched them to make sure they kept walking before continuing to the makeshift tent where the physicians were working. It would have been easy to find, both by the sounds of men screaming and the smells of burning flesh as wounds were cauterized. The girl shrank back, clearly not wanting to go into the tent, but my patience was wearing thin.

"If you want to stay out here by yourself, fine," I snapped. "But don't expect me to come rescue you from the next bunch bringing wounded back. They're going to be upset enough that they're missing out on the chance to loot that I won't guarantee they aren't as rough on you as Prixus and his bunch were."

That got her moving, and she scurried into the tent behind me. I was working on my last reserves of strength, the thought of fainting in front of men already wounded and suffering mortifying me to no end. The interior of the tent was lit by

152

several lamps, making the air stuffy and close, which did not help me, so I began looking for a place to sit down when I spotted Crassus' physician bent over a man lying on a cot facedown. I wobbled over in his direction, but before I could get to him, the interior of the tent began to spin and I staggered, sure that I was going to fall. An arm grabbed me around the waist, and I saw with some surprise that it was the girl, straining with all of her might as she grabbed my right arm, putting it across her shoulders for support. Huffing and puffing, we made it the last few paces to where Philipos, now aware of my presence, stood pointing to an empty cot. Collapsing onto it, I muttered a thank you to the girl, despite not being very happy that she had been the one to keep me from shaming myself.

"I will be with you in a moment," the physician called to me, and I waved at him, telling him to take his time.

I wanted to lie back on the cot, but my side ached too much, while my hand hurt even worse. My neckerchief had soaked through with blood and the slightest movement of my fingers was excruciating, but I forced myself to move them just to make sure that they still worked. A wave of sheer exhaustion came over me, yet I managed to remain sitting upright, knowing that to lie back would be too painful. To occupy myself, I watched the physician working on the supine man, and it took a moment to realize that it was none other than the Tribune Claudius. It took another moment for it to register that the physician was hard at work on the buttock region of the haughty Tribune, the sight making me burst out laughing.

Shooting me a glance of equal parts shared amusement and irritation, the physician said loudly, "The Tribune here has suffered a very painful and serious wound that requires my attention. He took an arrow in . . ."

He did not finish, instead just pointed down at the Tribune's ass.

"He got shot in the ass with an arrow?" I asked, again loud enough for everyone in the tent to hear, even the less seriously wounded snickering.

153

The Tribune's face was turned away, but even from where I was seated, I could see his ear turn bright red, although he said nothing.

"As I said, it's a serious wound. It penetrated both, er, sides, so to speak."

Now Philipos was struggling to keep his composure and I could not resist the temptation for some mischief. I attribute it to my almost delirious condition from my own wounds.

"How did you get shot in the ass, Tribune?" I called out to him. "You're supposed to be facing the enemy, not the other way around."

Snickers turned into open laughter, prompting Claudius to turn his head to face me, and the look he gave me was one of pure hatred.

"We were ambushed," he said stiffly. "One of the Centurions was too eager and led his Century into an ambush."

I should have just let it go, except that his inference that it was a Centurion's fault irritated me immensely.

"But, Tribune, I thought you outranked a mere Centurion. After all, you thought you outranked me when we first met and I'm second in command of this army. Shouldn't you have been in command and kept the Centurion from making such a basic mistake? I mean, since you obviously saw that he was making an error."

Claudius looked like he had been slapped, and there was an intake of breath by many of the men. Thankfully, none of them laughed. I knew I was behaving badly; senior officers should never show their petty quarrels in front of the rankers, but I considered this just payback for all of his slights to me.

"You will pay for that," Claudius said quietly, staring into my eyes to make sure I knew he meant it, I suppose.

"Tribune," I said, suddenly weary. "I've heard men tell me that for a long time. And they were men a lot better than you, and yet I'm still here. I'll try not to lose any sleep tonight."

His lips tightened but he made no reply, instead turning his face back away from me, while the physician gave me a reproving shake of his head. Titus, I thought, you just got rid of one enemy, and now you're making another one. And this is one of those upper-class bastards like Lepidus, and look at the mess he got you into. You deserve what happens to you. The girl had been standing there, not understanding a word, yet somehow knowing that Claudius wished me no good, and I was amused to see her scowling at the back of his head while the physician finished dressing his wound.

"You will have to lie on your stomach for the next few days," I overheard Philipos say to Claudius, who mumbled something in response.

His work with the Tribune done, the Greek walked over to me, sighing as he surveyed the damage.

"What happened to you this time?"

I was dreading this question, not from the physician as much as from my friends. Crassus I was not worried about; unless I had completely misread him, he would accept whatever lie I told him as long as he knew that Prixus was no longer a problem. It was Scribonius and Balbus that concerned me, Scribonius in particular, because I had never lied to them before.

"I was surprised by a couple of Moesians when I was looking for my nephew's Century," I answered with the first thing that popped into my head.

"And her?"

He inclined his head toward the girl, who was standing next to my cot. I had completely forgotten to account for her.

"I found her," I said weakly, knowing that it sounded more like a question than an answer.

One eyebrow lifted, but he said no more about it, taking hold of my bandaged hand while I tried not to wince. Carefully unwrapping the makeshift bandage, he revealed my bloody, ravaged appendage. It was the first I had seen it in full light and I could not contain a gasp on seeing the damage. My little finger was gone, bitten off between the first and middle knuckle, and I could clearly see the splintered bone protruding from the torn flesh. Each of my other fingers had a deep gash just above the palm, where I had grasped the Thracian sword of one of Prixus' men. I was just thankful that it had not been sharp, or I would have had nothing but a stump to wave around. Even so, I could see the gleam of bone showing through the caked blood, and I noticed that my hand seemed to be curled almost in a fist. Despite his gentle touch, the pain was very intense when the physician slowly straightened my fingers. Bending down, he examined the wounds carefully, before turning his attention to my little finger.

Shaking his head after a moment, he told me, "Prefect, I am afraid that we are going to have to operate on your finger."

"Why? What more can be done to it? It's cut off already."

Pointing to the splintered white mass sticking out, he replied, "The bone cannot protrude in that way. You'll be in constant pain, and every slightest bump you give it will cause you agony even greater. Also, it would never heal properly, and would likely become corrupt. I am about as certain as it is possible to be that you would end up losing your hand, if not more."

"What do you have to do?"

"We have to cut the bone down to the point where I can fold the skin over and cauterize it to allow it to heal."

"That sounds extremely painful." I tried to make a joke of it, but he did not smile.

"Yes, it will be, but it is the only thing to do."

I knew he was right, but my stomach was churning at the thought nonetheless. Turning his attention to my side, he unwrapped that bandage.

"How did you get this around yourself and tied off?" he asked curiously, and I pointed to the girl.

"She did it," I told him.

"You did a very good job of bandaging this wound," the physician told her in Greek.

She did not say anything, but it was easy to see that she was pleased at the compliment.

"It's a lucky thing you found her," he said dryly, probing the wound.

I could not reply because my teeth were clenched together so tightly, this being only slightly less painful than my hand.

"The good news is that your chest cavity was not penetrated," he told me. "But the bone is showing, and it needs to be stitched closed."

Using a pair of tweezers, he gently removed a piece of tunic from the wound, then after finding nothing else, pronounced the wound clean and ready to be closed.

"We will do that first, before we work on the finger," he told me, signaling to an orderly. "Pindarus will stitch your wound closed while I look at other men. When he is finished, I will return and we will get to work."

Before he walked away, he beckoned to the girl, who shot me a frightened glance. I nodded to her, encouraging her to follow him, which she did, albeit reluctantly. The *medici* came to begin the work of cleaning and stitching the wound on my side. He also brought a jug of wine, along with a smaller stoppered bottle. Before he began, he poured me a cup of wine, which I accepted gratefully, draining it in a gulp.

"What's in the bottle?" I asked as he worked.

"Poppy syrup," was his answer.

"Poppy syrup? For me?"

He nodded.

"But I thought he didn't use poppy syrup because it hinders your breathing," I protested, but he just shrugged.

"It's the orders of the physician. I don't know anything about breathing. I just know that what he's going to do to your finger is going to hurt like nothing you've ever felt."

With that cheery thought, he finished his work to leave me staring at the bottle, wondering how much I was going to be given.

The orderly had been right; even with a spoonful of poppy syrup, which made me feel deliciously drowsy and relaxed, making me understand why some men were as drawn to either smoking or taking syrup as much as wine, the work the physician did was excruciating. I was given a leather covered wooden gag and I almost broke a tooth from biting it so hard, trying not to watch him use a tiny saw to cut through the bone of my little finger. My hand was strapped down to a

157

board held out to the side, and coming from his tent where he was still recuperating from his own wound, Novanus showed up to provide comfort, or at least that is what he said. I think he just wanted to see me suffer the way he had, but I was happy to see him nonetheless.

The girl had been put to work cleaning up as more men were brought into the tent. The high-ranking men such as myself and Claudius were segregated, with a leather partition to screen us from the rankers, but it did not block out the sounds of agony and fear of the men brought into the hospital. The physician had to make a deep cut down the flesh of my finger to peel back the skin and muscle in order to expose more of the bone. Somehow, I managed to stay awake and quiet through that. It was the sawing that elicited a groan from me, but I refused to cry out, the sweat pouring down my face. About that time, Novanus reached out to offer me his hand, which I had done for him during his trial, and I took it gratefully, despite a part of me being ashamed of my weakness. Fortunately, the work of sawing through a small bone like my little finger did not take much time; I could not imagine what it was like for a man whose leg had to be amputated at mid-thigh. Once he was done, he tossed the fragment of bone into a bowl set aside for that purpose, or so I supposed. I do not know why, but it was the sound of the bone hitting the bowl that caused me to faint, although I was unfortunately not out very long. When I awakened, Novanus was still clasping my hand while the surgeon took the skin that had been left behind by the shortening of the bone, folding it over the end of the remaining stump. A brazier had been set next to my cot and I could see the wavy air above it that told me that it was burning fiercely. Using a cloth, he grabbed the end of an iron rod that had been placed in the brazier. I caught just the glimpse of the smoking, red-hot end before he grasped my hand firmly, pinning it to the board with surprising strength.

Looking over at me, he asked me quietly, "Are you ready?"

I tried to swallow so that I could speak, thinking I would say something to show my contempt for what was about to happen, but my mouth was too dry, forcing me to content myself with just a nod. Without any more delay, I watched the hot end of the iron moving down to my hand. I experienced the briefest sensation of an agony that made all the pain I had suffered to that point seem like it had been nothing more than stubbing my toe or cutting myself shaving before I fainted again. When I came around this time, Novanus had gone, and I could tell by the light from outside that it was late afternoon. The sounds of fighting had been barely discernible before, but they were totally gone now, and I was happy to see that the hospital tent had about the same number of occupants as when I had first been brought in. I could vaguely hear the sounds of shouting, noting that they did not hold the kind of urgency or fear of battle. Instead, the shouting I heard sounded happy, telling me that Naissus had fallen, the men having been released to sack the town. That thought made me look around and my heart sank because at first I could not see the girl. Then I heard a quiet cough; looking the other direction, I saw her seated a couple paces away, watching me intently. Seeing I was awake, she stood to come to my side.

"Good. You're awake finally," she said, and for the first time I noticed that her voice had a pleasant, melodic lilt to it.

Now that all the excitement had died down, it was also the first opportunity to examine her more closely. She was young, perhaps in her late teens, and my early impression of plainness was confirmed, the girl possessing an oval face with wide set brown eyes and a nose that reminded me a bit of a pig, upturned at the end. Her lips were full and she did have all of her teeth, which were surprisingly white and even. She had long brown hair that I imagined would have been shiny and quite pretty, but now it was matted and stringy, while her face was dirty from all that had happened that day. She had managed to put something that resembled a dress back together enough that she was covered, but I could see by the quality of cloth and cut that she had been a poor girl before this day. Now she was worse than poor, since I understood that whatever family she may have had before this were now either dead, or being rounded up to be sold as slaves. But her eyes were kind as she looked down at me, reaching out to give me an awkward pat on the shoulder.

"Thank you," she said hesitantly. "I do not know what would have happened if you had not come along."

"Yes you do, and so do I," I replied, my tone more harsh than I meant it, but the pain in my hand and to a lesser extent, my side, was distracting to say the least.

Her eyes turned downward, and she answered with a slow nod.

Feeling badly that I had spoken so harshly to her, I asked, "Have you had anything to eat?"

"No, but I am not hungry," she replied.

Then there was nothing to say, and she sat there while I dozed for a bit. I was awakened by a commotion, a moment later looking up into the faces of Scribonius, Balbus, and Diocles, their expressions various studies in concern.

"We've been looking all over for you," Diocles scolded me, but the relief was plain to see in his eyes.

"Well, you found me."

Scribonius surveyed my hand, heavily wrapped in a linen bandage, his face giving no hint of what he was thinking.

"What happened?" he asked, and I braced myself to lie to my best friend.

I repeated the story that I had told the physician. When I had finished, Scribonius and Balbus exchanged a glance, then Scribonius looked back at me, his eyes boring into mine. They held an expression that took me a moment to interpret. Finally, I recognized it as sadness, and I felt ashamed of myself. There was an awkward silence, the three of them standing next to my cot, while I tried to avoid their eyes. Then Diocles looked over to see the girl sitting there, taking it all in.

"Who's this?"

I opened my mouth, realizing that I did not know the girl's name.

"What's your name, girl?" I asked her.

"Egina," she said shyly.

160

"Her name's Egina," I told Diocles.

"Thank you, master. I never would have known if you had not interpreted for me," he said tartly.

"Hello, Egina. My name is Diocles, and I belong to Prefect Pullus," Diocles addressed her in his native Greek.

She looked at him in surprise.

"You are a slave?" she asked, and when he nodded, her confusion only seemed to deepen.

"But you don't talk to him like you are a slave."

"That's because I'm lying on this cot and can't beat him for his impertinence," I broke in, glad that the subject had shifted to something else.

"So you will beat him later?" This seemed to be very important to her for some reason.

"If I remember, but I must confess I usually forget." I said it as a joke, but I think she took me seriously, or else she had her own deadpan sense of humor.

"Then I will remind you," she said with a completely straight face. "A slave should not talk to his master in such a tone."

She turned to give Diocles a withering glare.

"And you obviously have forgotten your place."

With that, she gave him a dismissive toss of her head, leaving him staring at her completely flummoxed. Scribonius and Balbus began laughing, and despite the pain it caused my side, I joined in.

Suddenly, I remembered something that stilled the laughter in me, and I asked, "Where's Gaius?"

Neither spoke for a moment and my heart felt as if a hand was squeezing it, but their hesitation was because each was waiting for the other to speak.

Seeing my distress, and evidently forgetting for the moment his disappointment with me, Scribonius put a hand on my shoulder, saying quickly, "He's fine. Not a scratch."

The relief that washed through me was so intense that I let out a gasp.

"In fact, he's outside the tent, waiting for one of us to go get him. He knew you'd be angry with him, and he asked us to see you first."

"Go get him," I told Diocles, who seemed more than happy to escape from the wrathful stare of Egina.

"So where did you find her?" Balbus asked me, and I knew that just saying I found her would not be enough for Balbus or Scribonius.

"I stopped some of our men from carrying her off." Since I was speaking in Latin, I did not worry about Egina contradicting or reacting to my lie in a way that would alert my friends.

"Why would you do something like that?" Balbus demanded. "What do you care about some Moesian girl? Besides, the men deserve some fun for taking the town."

He was absolutely right; under normal circumstances I would not have given a second thought to allowing a group of Legionaries having their way with a woman belonging to the enemy, and I had to think fast to cover my tracks.

"Because they were doing it when there was still fighting left to be done," I explained.

Balbus said nothing for a moment, then gave a shrug.

"Then that's different." I tried to hide my relief at his acceptance.

A sneaking glance at Scribonius told me that he was not convinced in the slightest, but he still said nothing. Fortunately, Diocles returned with Gaius, who had managed to clean himself up a bit, but I could see his mail was still spattered with blood. After a quick examination, I saw that my friends had been right, that he was essentially unmarked, other than a nice bruise on his forearm.

"Uncle," he began to speak, but I cut him off immediately.

Despite the pain, I swung myself to a sitting position, glaring up at my nephew, who looked at the ground.

"What by Cerberus' hairy balls do you think you were doing?"

He refused to look up at me, but I could see the tops of his ears turning red, and he did not answer.

"I asked you a question, Gaius," I was getting angry now, yet when he lifted his head to look me in the face, I could see he was not in the least apologetic.

"My job," he replied evenly. "I was doing what you trained me to do."

"I didn't train you to take foolish risks," I countered, but he was not budging.

"So says the man who's won two Corona Muralis," he retorted, and my stomach tightened.

"Is that what this is about?" I asked incredulously. "You're trying to match me in some way?"

He did not answer and I felt the despair wrap around my heart, suddenly realizing why he had done what he had.

"Gaius," I forced my voice to be calm. "I'm honored that you're trying to emulate me, I truly am. And there's a part of me that's extremely proud of you for leading your men in such a valiant manner." I could see that he was pleased, which was not my intent, so I pressed on. "But there's a larger part of me that, as your uncle, and as someone who's deathly afraid of your mother, is absolutely horrified that you'd risk yourself in such a reckless manner."

"Yet I'm not the one who's sitting on a cot covered in bandages," Gaius replied coolly, and now it was my turn to feel the blood rushing to my face.

"This isn't about me," I snapped. "This is about you and you're taking needless risks."

"Uncle, I don't think leading my men and sharing the dangers with them is a needless risk. You taught me that, and now you're angry because I'm doing what you taught me."

What made this so infuriating was that he was absolutely right; I had stressed to him the importance of leading from the front. How could I impress upon him the reason I was so worried?

Looking over at Scribonius, Balbus, and Diocles, I told them, "Leave us for a bit."

The girl, Egina, seeing the others leaving, rose to join them, but I waved her down. Since Gaius and I were talking in Latin, I did not worry about her listening to what I had to say.

163

After they had left, I looked at Gaius, trying to form the words.

Finally, I said, "The reason I'm worried about you taking these risks is because I've made a decision."

I paused, but he said nothing, just waited for me to continue with a raised eyebrow. Fine, he was not going make this easy on me, so I plunged on.

"I've decided that I'm going to adopt you, and make you my sole heir. When I die, you'll receive most of what I have, and I can promise you, I've done very, very well in the army. Most importantly, once I finish my term as Prefect, I'll be made an equestrian, and as my heir, you'll be an equestrian as well. Along with your children."

Frankly, I had assumed that he had been expecting this, but judging from the way his jaw dropped, it appeared to be a complete surprise.

He did not speak for what seemed to be a long time, then finally stammered, "I....I don't know what to say, Uncle."

"There's not much to say," I said lightly. "I've made my decision. I'm sure your mother and father will approve."

"Oh, I don't doubt that," he answered instantly, yet there was a hesitation that made me wary.

"Then, what's the problem? You don't seem to be as happy as I thought you'd be."

"Uncle, I'm extremely honored, and I'm touched."

He paused, then closed his eyes and shook his head sadly.

"But I'm afraid I can't accept."

For a moment, I was sure I had not heard him correctly.

"What do you mean, you can't accept? Why in Hades would you turn down such an offer?"

"Because I plan on marrying Iras, and I know that you don't approve," he said gently. "But I love her more than anything, even this great honor you do me."

I sat on the edge of the cot, my head spinning, except I did not know if it was from my wounds or from what Gaius had just said. I had been sure that when presented with this opportunity, all thoughts of Iras would fly from his head immediately. Only at that moment did I see how wrong I had been. Sitting there on the cot, thinking of all the things that I had lost and how there was nobody really to share it with, I made my decision.

"I don't care about that," I said, and I do not know who was more surprised, me or Gaius. "Marry Iras, marry whoever you want. I want you to be my heir."

Gaius' face creased into a wide smile, then he bent down to hug me and kiss me on both cheeks.

"Uncle, you've made me the happiest I've ever been," he cried, and I saw the glint of tears in his eyes.

"Don't get carried away. I'm not dead yet," I joked.

He waved my jest away.

"I don't care about that. I'm just happy that you finally accepted that I love Iras."

If it had been anyone other than Gaius who had told me this, I would not have believed him, but I was sure that he was telling the truth.

"But, now that you're my heir, I don't want you taking the kinds of risks you took today," I warned him.

"Uncle, I'm going to do my job, the way you and Scribonius trained me to do it," he told me firmly and, despite my worry, I was proud of him for not wavering.

"Then you're going to have to endure me chewing your ass when you do," I grumbled, and he laughed that boyish laugh he had.

"Fair enough," he conceded.

With that settled, I told him to help me gather my gear, then beckoning to the girl, I walked stiffly out of the tent. Philipos, his eyes red-rimmed with fatigue from the long day he had put in, saw me leaving and hurried to intercept me.

"Where do you think you are going?" he demanded.

"To my tent," I told him.

"You need to rest."

I brushed his protest aside, saying, "I can rest in my tent just as easily as I can rest here. And you can use my cot for someone more seriously wounded."

Seeing that I was not going to change my mind, he told me to keep my hand elevated to reduce the swelling, and gave me a small bottle of poppy syrup.

"I don't need that."

"You will," he countered. "Take no more than one spoonful at a time."

I took it, albeit grudgingly, and with Gaius and Egina in tow, I left the hospital. Diocles, Scribonius, and Balbus walked with us to my tent and, as we did, Gaius told me about the assault.

"We took the rampart without any problem," he explained. "But when we went to open the gate, the Moesians put up a hard fight. I lost three men trying to get to the gate, but we got it open."

He went on to talk about his part of the fight, and from Scribonius and Balbus I learned the rest. Confirming what I had seen with my own eyes, the Moesians were individually brave, but they were poorly led. Instead of consolidating their forces by falling back earlier, small groups continued to fight, oblivious to the larger picture, so that they were surrounded and cut down group by group. The town was taken by late afternoon, the men now enjoying the fruits of the town as we returned to camp.

"And Runo?" I asked.

"Captured," Scribonius replied. "He's to be executed in the morning, in front of an assembly of the surviving nobles of the town."

"And the prisoners?"

"They're going to be sold," Balbus said, shooting a glance at the girl, who fortunately did not understand what was being said.

She was looking about wide-eyed, clearly awed by the sight of our camp.

"Where's Ocelus?"

"In his stable, eating his oats," Diocles assured me, which was just as well, because there was no way I could have ridden him.

By the time we arrived at my tent, I was exhausted, making it hard to keep from staggering. I headed immediately to my cot, where I collapsed, and almost as soon as my head hit, I was sound asleep.

I was awakened some time later by Diocles, who informed me that Marcus Crassus had come to check on me. I was struggling to my feet when he came into my private quarters without waiting for Diocles to show him in, waving me back down when I tried to stand and salute.

"You need your rest, Prefect. I just came to check on you the first chance I got."

"Thank you, sir," I replied.

Despite knowing the real reason for his visit, I also knew that he had to go through the formalities of appearing to care what happened to me.

"You had me worried when I talked to Philipos. He told me that you were gravely injured. In fact, I didn't know what to expect."

I pointed to my hand, which per Philipos' orders I was keeping upright.

"This is the most serious, but I just lost my little finger, and he says that I'll regain the use of the other fingers just fine."

I do not know if his relief was feigned or real, but it seemed genuine.

"That is good news." He smiled.

"I understand that the town fell with few problems."

"That it did," he agreed. "The men performed magnificently. And now they're enjoying their reward. It will probably take us two or three days before they're fit to march again." He grinned. "Apparently there was a lot of wine in Naissus."

This was one of those times that I was happy that I was not responsible for a Legion, because it would take quite an effort to get the men in hand again.

"I received a report from Pilus Prior Palma and from Pilus Posterior Vettus. They both said that your nephew Porcinus performed magnificently and with great bravery."

Despite being angry with him, the pride I felt at Crassus' words filled my heart; finding that words would not come, I just nodded. Crassus seemed to understand, favoring me with a smile, then pursed his lips.

"There is one item that concerns me," he began, and I braced myself. "It appears that Prixus and his men have gone missing."

"Really? That's surprising," I said blandly.

"Yes, it is."

His eyes searched my face for several moments before he continued.

"The last they were seen was shortly after we entered the town, when they headed down the first street branching off the gate road. The Optio for the Century responsible for that sector said that he thought they took off down an alley, apparently chasing a girl, which sounds like Prixus, I must say."

I nodded but said nothing.

"Wasn't that about the same area where you were ambushed?" he asked, his tone hesitant.

I pretended to think about it, then slowly nodded.

"I believe it is, sir."

"But you didn't see them?"

"Not that I can recall. Of course, as you see, I was in a bit of a scrap myself, so I don't really remember much."

Crassus watched me carefully, then said lightly, "Well, no matter. I'm sure they'll turn up somewhere, safe and sound."

"I'm sure they will, but I wouldn't bet on them being safe," I said quietly.

He let out a long breath, his relief plain to see, finally giving a brief nod.

Slapping his hands against his thighs, he stood. "Well, as I said, I just wanted to check on you and let you know how well your nephew performed. Get back on your feet as soon as you can. The army needs you, as do I."

Thanking him for his visit, I watched him turn to leave my quarters.

Just before he reached the leather curtain, he turned to say, "By the way, I'm recommending your nephew for the Corona Muralis. According to his Pilus Posterior, and seconded by his Pilus Prior, he was the first over the wall of the town."

So that was the payoff for getting rid of Prixus, I thought.

"Thank you, sir. Do you want to tell him, or should I?"

"I think it would mean more coming from Titus Pullus, don't you think?"

Favoring me with another brilliant smile, this time accompanied by a wink, Marcus Crassus left my quarters, looking for all the world like a man with a huge weight lifted off his shoulders.

It was not until late the next day that the bodies of Prixus and his men were found. It was Scribonius who came to tell me. He described how their bodies had been found in one room of the building, with signs of a fierce struggle. His face was composed, his tone emotionless while he talked, but it felt like his eyes were boring into my skull, able to see my darkest secrets.

"They obviously ran into a group of Moesians that weren't impressed with how skilled they were in the arena," I said when he had finished.

"That's the funny thing," he said, giving me his frown. "I saw the bodies myself. Their wounds weren't inflicted by anything that the Moesians carry. It was a Spanish sword that killed them, and from the looks of it, the same one."

"Meaning?"

I knew exactly what it meant and so did he, but I could not think of anything else to say.

"Meaning that one man managed to kill Prixus and his three remaining men," he said irritably. "Do you have any idea how many men there are in the army that could take on that number of trained, veteran gladiators and come out alive?"

"Not many," I admitted.

"That's an understatement," he shot back. "In fact, I can only think of one man who has the ability, and he just happens to also have a good reason to want Prixus and his men dead."

"You don't mean me, do you?" I was determined to keep maintaining my innocence, despite knowing that Scribonius was not going to be fooled.

"Of course I mean you." He was growing angry now, beginning to pace around my cot, something he often did when he was worried. "And here you are, bandaged up, with some pathetic excuse of a story that anyone with a bit of intelligence knows is nonsense. Titus, I've always known you are reckless, but how could you be so stupid? Don't you think that Crassus will be forced to do something about men in his employ being murdered?"

So that is what this is about, I realized. Scribonius was not angry with me for lying to him, or excluding him from my plan, although I am sure that was part of it. His displeasure with me was based in his ignorance that it was Crassus himself who had given his approval to go after Prixus. I relaxed somewhat, trying to decide how forthcoming to be with Scribonius.

"Actually, I don't think Crassus is all that upset about what happened to Prixus," I said carefully, his eyes narrowing at my choice of words.

"What do you mean?"

I bit back a curse; as smart as Scribonius was, he could be remarkably dense at times. I suppose that it was because his own mind did not have that deviousness that mine does.

"I mean," I said distinctly, staring hard at Scribonius, "that nothing is going to come of Prixus' death from Marcus Crassus. I can assure you of that."

Realization of my meaning slowly dawned in his eyes, causing him to take a seat on a nearby stool, landing heavily.

"But why?" he asked, clearly mystified. "I don't know how much Crassus was paying Prixus and his bunch, but it had to be a fair amount. Why would he be willing to just throw that away?"

"Maybe Prixus was proving to be more trouble than he was worth, and Crassus needed a way to cut his ties to Prixus, but couldn't because...well, because he was scared. Not that I know that for sure," I added hastily. "That's just my guess."

"Ah, I see." He thought for a moment. "It makes sense, I suppose, this guess of yours."

His mouth twitched, but I could not tell if he was fighting a grimace or a smile.

"The army is better off without Prixus, and so is Crassus," I said quietly.

"That I can't argue."

Scribonius stood to take his leave.

"Titus." His expression was serious. "You can't continue to act as if you're in your twenties. You were lucky this time, but even luck as famous as yours is bound to run out some time."

There was a time I would have argued with Sextus Scribonius, when I would have told him that the man had not been born who could defeat Titus Pullus, but I knew he was right. I had come very close to death, fighting Prixus and his men; it was equally as much luck as it was skill that I had managed to walk out of the building victorious.

"Hopefully there's nobody left for me to fight," I said jokingly.

"Not likely," Scribonius retorted, finally favoring me with a grin. "With your personality, I have no doubt that someone will want to kill you again." The smile vanished. "Next time," he said quietly, "don't keep me in the dark. You need someone to watch your back. And never lie to me again."

He did not wait for an answer before he left.

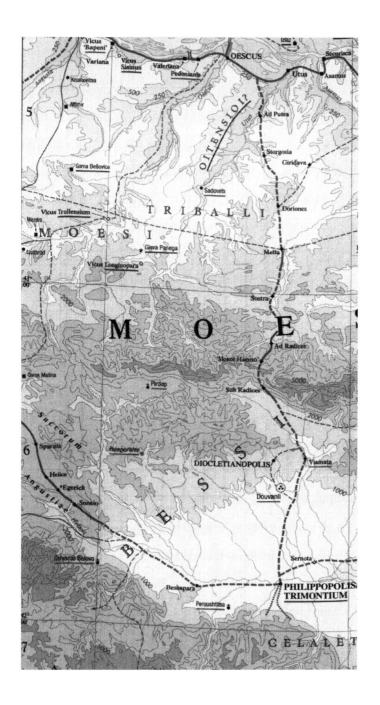

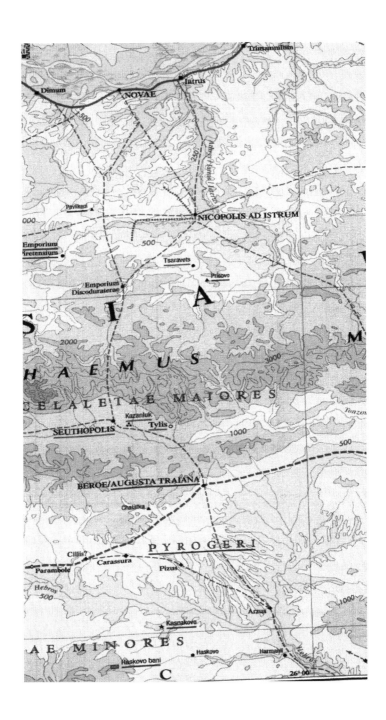

173

Chapter 4-Bastarnae

Like Crassus had predicted, it took two days to get the men fully in hand from their sacking of Naissus. The army smiths were kept busy forging chains with which to secure all the prisoners taken, more than 25,000 in all, between the remaining warriors, their families, and the occupants of Naissus. Crassus decreed that not everyone was to be sold into slavery, leaving about a third part of the population behind to remain in the town to keep it going. I did not know if Egina's family had been one of the lucky ones, yet it did not appear to matter, because she disappeared the day after the town fell. Our losses had been relatively light, but there still needed to be some shuffling done with Centurions and Optios, taking another day, thereby making our time at Naissus almost a month. Our cavalry was still north, watching the Bastarnae, who had apparently decided to sit and wait on further developments. My fears that they were working in concert with the Moesians proved to be unfounded, which I believe encouraged Crassus to make the decision to resume our pursuit of the Bastarnae. Despite being extremely stiff, with sudden movements impossible without terrible pain, I was determined that I would not ride in one of those bouncing wagons. My hand proved to be the biggest problem, since I usually held the reins in my left hand, meaning that now Ocelus and I had to become accustomed to using my right hand, which as we both learned was heavier on the bit than my left. The first day was the worst, with him almost bucking me off twice because of my heavy-handedness. As one can imagine, the slightest jerk was extremely painful, and the second time he opened the wound on my side, soaking the bandage through.

Regardless of my personal trials, the army marched north and it was clear to see that the assault on Naissus had done quite a bit of good for the men. They had been fully blooded now, performing what was usually the bitterest kind of operation, the assault and carrying of a fortified town or city, and their new confidence was clear to anyone with eyes. They sang their songs with more gusto, their banter now focused on those funny moments that happen in battle instead of just on the drunken revels of their off duty time. I was forced to admit that perhaps Crassus knew what he was about, having understood how much this army needed a sharp but relatively easy action to prepare it for whatever might lie ahead. By the end of the first day on the march, my hand was in agony, despite riding for a good part of the day holding it upright. I was seeing Philipos at the end of each day to have the bandages changed, but after seeing my hand the first time he did so, with every finger turning purple, I refused to look. He assured me that this was normal and he made me move my fingers about every day, which was painful to say the least. The strange thing was that with my hand wrapped up it felt like my little finger was still there, which he also said was normal.

Crassus never mentioned Prixus' name in my presence again, and as far as I know, not in front of others either. After a couple of days of some tension between Scribonius and me, things smoothed out, getting back to normal, where we passed the day joking and laughing like we always had. Marching northward, we received daily reports from the cavalry commander Silva about the activities of the Bastarnae, who had settled into a semi-permanent position next to the Cedrus (Lom) River where it emptied into the Ister, with their warriors conducting foraging raids to keep their people supplied. There had been some clashes between our cavalry and theirs, with mixed results; some skirmishes we took the honors, some they won. The country we marched through had been stripped clean, and supply might have been a problem but Crassus had the foresight to raid the granaries of Naissus to fill our own stores. This was a good move on his part and it was not like there were many people left behind to worry about. Fortunately, the weather held as well, only giving us brief showers in the afternoon, enough to cut the dust but not so much that the wagons bogged down in the mud. When we were no more than four or five days from the Cedrus River and it became clear to the Bastarnae that we were coming after them, they packed up. Using the boats they had commandeered, now months before, they crossed the back across the Ister river, then burned them to prevent our using the same craft to pursue. With this news, for a brief period of time, we thought that we would be returning to Pannonia, since the Bastarnae were now in their own lands. However, Crassus was not through chasing glory; at the morning briefing, after we learned of this latest development, he announced that we would continue to pursue the Bastarnae. My heart sank when I heard his words, because I had grown to like young Crassus immensely and I feared that he was playing with fire. Scribonius had convinced me that Octavian would not appreciate Crassus' thirst for personal honors, not after all that had happened the last several years. The last thing he would want was someone who attracted the affection of the lower classes, and I thought seriously about trying to talk to Crassus to warn him. After thinking it over, however, I decided against it; my experience with dealing with the upper classes definitely played a role in my decision. While I liked Crassus and thought he could be trusted, I was not sure enough of the man to take the risk. The others were not shy about voicing their opinions.

"How do we justify crossing into territory that belongs to people that we're not at war with, nor do we have a treaty?" Macrinus asked, although his tone was respectful.

Crassus was unperturbed by the question and in fact seemed to have a ready answer, which led me to believe that he and Macrinus had arranged this beforehand.

"This is a region that has been hard to pacify. We need to send a message to all of the tribes that any incursion they make, even if they leave before we're able to meet them in battle, will be punished severely. The Bastarnae have been living off land that doesn't belong to them. You've seen yourselves the extent of their depredation. That can't go unpunished."

These were fine words, and on the surface, they made sense. The reality was that if the Bastarnae had not stripped the land, we would have done it ourselves, but I suppose it

176

could be argued that we would not have been there if the Bastarnae had stayed put in the first place. Nevertheless, I knew that Crassus would have found a reason to wage war on some tribe out here, whether it was the Bastarnae or Moesians, so I said nothing, going along with the pretense.

Arriving at the river a few days later, we saw that while it was wide and the current fairly swift, it was nowhere near the challenge that crossing the Rhenus had been. The only major problem was that the Bastarnae had already denuded the forest, so rather than haul the logs for the bridge we would build for a number of miles, Crassus marched us downstream to find another suitable crossing spot. Fortunately, less than ten miles away, a site was found where the bottom was gravel and the river narrowed a bit, whereupon the men were set immediately to work. Crassus pushed them hard, not wanting to let the Bastarnae gain too much of a march on us, but they worked well, with no more than the normal amount of complaining. On the fourth day after the work began, the cavalry vanguard clattered across the bridge, followed by the rest of the army. Fortunately for our pursuit, the Bastarnae's own progress was slow; the scouts we had sent across the river when the work began returned with their position, reporting them to be about two days march ahead.

"We're going to push the men," Crassus told the Primi Pili. "I want a minimum of 30 miles a day out of them. Be sure to remind them of all the plunder that waits for them once we catch the Bastarnae."

He knew that was all the incentive they needed, and the men did not disappoint him. The first day they covered more than 30 miles, although they were all done in by the end of the day after camp was made. That day also marked the occasion of having my stitches removed from my fingers, with my heavy bandages replaced by lighter ones, while my finger still remained wrapped. Philipos suggested that I have a leather harness made for it that would protect the stump for the first few months. I had seen other men do as much, so I went to the leather-working *immunes* who stitched together a rawhide harness. It could not be worn immediately; my finger was still

177

too tender to be in contact with the rawhide that they used for the material, but a week or so later I was able to wear it. With the stitches out, Philipos gave me a series of exercises to do in order to restore movement to my left hand, and the pain was every bit as excruciating as the injury itself. During the march, I would concentrate on flexing my fingers over and over, then after a couple of days, I forced myself to use my left hand for holding the reins of Ocelus. He seemed to sense my discomfort, because he kept his antics to a minimum. Before, he liked to toss his head suddenly, trying to yank the reins from my hand in a sort of game, but while I was on the mend, he did not do it one time. I was still a long way off from being whole again, and I knew that it would be unwise to try to participate in whatever lay ahead. However, I also knew that when the moment of battle came, I was still likely to do something foolish.

On the third day after we crossed the Ister, our vanguard spotted the dust cloud of the retreating Bastarnae, putting us less than a day's march behind. The Bastarnae were as aware of our presence as we were of theirs, and we began to spot small groups of mounted men hovering about our flanks. Crassus did not bother trying to chase them off, knowing that the only thing that would be accomplished was wearing out our own horses, and besides, we were doing the same thing to their column. At the end of that day, we made camp, with Crassus setting the watch at quarter-strength, meaning that the equivalent of one full Legion was on duty manning the ramparts at any given time. Otherwise, it was a normal day on the march when we met to discuss our plans for the next day or two. Crassus had every intention of closing with the Bastarnae immediately, despite not all of the Primi Pili being as eager. Aulus Natalis, the Primus Pilus of the 13th in particular urged a more cautious approach.

"I think we should harry them first, wear them down like a pack of wolves does with a herd of elk," he suggested. "Not only will it wear them out being constantly on guard, they're more likely to make a mistake that we can take advantage of."

I saw at least one head nod; Vibius Aelianus of the 15th clearly thought this was a good idea as well. Crassus considered this for a moment, or at least appeared to before he shook his head.

"While that's certainly an idea with merit, I don't want to take the time that it would cost to do what you propose. No, we're going to close with these Bastarnae at the first opportunity."

Before the briefing was concluded, a runner sent by the duty Centurion at the main gate arrived to inform Crassus that a delegation of Bastarnae had approached under a flag of truce, wishing to speak to our general.

Smiling broadly, Crassus clapped his hands together. "Let's see what these barbarians have to say, shall we?"

Telling us to remain, we sat waiting in Crassus' office in the *Praetorium* for the Bastarnae delegates to be brought to us. While we waited, Crassus ordered his slaves to bring several amphorae of wine, which I found curious.

When I asked him why he was having so much brought, he explained, "These people are of Scythian stock. They're notorious for their weak head and greed when it comes to wine. I plan on giving them as much as they can drink to see what we can learn."

It was a cunning thing to do, and I for one looked forward to watching it happen. The Bastarnae were announced and unlike when Crassus had met with the Moesians, he did not keep them waiting. There were five of them, wearing their best attire, which seemed to be a combination of woolen tunics, cloaks of mostly greens and browns, and leather *bracae*, which I could see suited them for riding. They were all bearded, with their hair either plaited or hanging loosely about their shoulders. Three of the men appeared to be about my age or a little older, while two were younger, carrying themselves with all the arrogance of the highly born warrior. After the initial introductions, the first few moments were spent in measuring each other, with the younger men glaring at us as if their looks alone could strike us dead. I had remained seated the whole time and one of the young men chose to lock eyes with me,

179

transporting me back to the day with Ariovistus and the yellow-haired warrior. I had not had the opportunity to face that man in combat and I wondered if I would have the chance this time around. We stared at each other for the span of several heartbeats before the spell was broken by one of the other Bastarnae, who spoke in heavily accented Greek.

"Marcus Crassus, we have come on behalf of our people, who you call Bastarnae, to ask with all the respect due a great nation like Rome, to desist in your pursuit."

"Why would we do that?" Crassus asked, while offering the Bastarnae the first of what would be many cups of wine. "You have trespassed into the lands of people with whom Rome has a treaty of friendship. You and your people have caused great hardship to those people."

The spokesman bowed his head in acknowledgement of Crassus' words.

"You are right, Marcus Crassus. But we have caused Rome no harm, and we have seen the error of our ways, and have departed those lands of which you speak. We are now back in our territory, and now it is you who are trespassing."

"We would not be here if you had not made your incursion first," Crassus pointed out, but I myself was not so sure this was the truth, believing then and now that Marcus Crassus would have found an excuse one way or the other.

"Our people were starving," the spokesman replied. "We suffered a horrible drought two straight years, so we were forced to do something to feed them. Surely you can understand that."

"That does not justify you preying on others, and taking food from others. Now people who are our friends are starving."

"Surely Rome has more than enough to provide for them," the Bastarnae countered.

"Whether we do or not is none of your business. What is our business is making sure that our friends are allowed to live in peace."

Nothing was said for a few moments, each side only glaring at the other. Finally, Crassus favored the Bastarnae with a smile, holding up his hands in a placating gesture.

"Let's not allow things to become so contentious so quickly. Please, have some more wine. It is Falernian, which is one of our best vintages."

As Crassus had hoped, the Bastarnae did not refuse his offer, all of them eagerly holding their cups out.

"Tell me more about your people. We know very little about the Bastarnae." Crassus laid back on his couch, the tacit signal that, for the moment, the negotiations were suspended and it was now more of a social occasion.

For the next little while, we listened to the Bastarnae tell us about their history, their customs, then after a few more cups of wine, their prowess in battle. They boasted about this with seemingly no thought given to the fact that they were talking to men who were their enemies. As we had been told, the Bastarnae were originally Scythians, a branch of that tribe that had been forced to migrate south and west because of some long-forgotten troubles with other Scythian tribes. The lands they lived in now were more heavily forested, without the rolling, open plains that are the main feature of the Scythian lands. One result of this move was that their people relied on the horse less than their cousins to the east. That explained why there was a preponderance of infantry among their warriors. They went on to explain the origin of their heavy weapon that I have mentioned before, the falx. It is a multi-purpose tool, used for harvesting the thick stalks of flax, which they claimed was how the name was derived. They boasted that in the hands of a skilled warrior, a falx could split a man in two lengthwise, something that we found hard to believe, but they insisted was true.

"Hopefully, none of you Romans will ever find out," said the leader of the delegation, a man named Timonax, though he was smiling as he said it.

"I am sure we won't," Crassus said smoothly, while signaling for a slave to refill Timonax's cup, along with those of his companions.

The young man who had been glaring at me was the only one who did not participate much in the conversation; the only time he became animated was when talk turned to war and the Bastarnae prowess at it. His name, as I remember, was Scylax, and there apparently was some sort of blood tie between him and Timonax, but I could not determine what it was. With the evening progressing, the Bastarnae became increasingly drunk, while we Romans only pretended to drink from our cups, surreptitiously pouring out our wine when the Bastarnae were not looking so that it appeared that we were refilling at least as much as they were.

"So, Timonax, if we were to withdraw, what would we have to show for it?" Crassus asked this question out of nowhere.

Timonax looked at him in drunken surprise.

"Why, your lives," he replied merrily, lifting his cup in salute. "None of your men would be cut in two by a falx. Isn't that enough?"

Crassus appeared to actually take the response seriously, saying nothing for a bit, like he was thinking about it.

"It might be," he said cautiously, leaning forward as if he were about to impart a precious secret.

Timonax did likewise, clearly eager to be taken into Crassus' confidence. I sat there slightly stunned that these Bastarnae were seemingly falling for Crassus' act so easily.

"If we were to withdraw, would we do so without interference?" Crassus asked Timonax.

Holding up his hand, palm outward, then placing it over his heart, Timonax said, "I give you my solemn oath, Marcus Crassus, that should you choose to withdraw, you will do so in peace."

Scylax and the other younger man, whose name was Meton, both leapt to their feet, Scylax saying something in his native tongue to Timonax, the younger man's face red from wine and anger, or so it seemed. This engendered a heated conversation, with the two sides clearly arguing their viewpoints, Scylax and Meton on one side, the three older men on the other.

"I think you've poked a stick into a hornet's nest," I murmured to Crassus.

"It would certainly seem that way," Crassus agreed, but did nothing to stop the argument.

"Do you understand what they're saying?" I whispered to Crassus, who shook his head.

"But I think the meaning is clear. The two young men don't like the idea of allowing us to depart without teaching us a lesson of some sort. The other three clearly don't agree."

That had been my sense of the conversation and it was quite extraordinary watching the Bastarnae bicker among themselves like we were not even there. It was only after Crassus cleared his throat several times that Timonax seemed to come to his senses, making an awkward bow to Crassus.

"Please forgive us, Marcus Crassus. We were having a...er... discussion about this matter. Young Scylax and Meton obviously have a strong opinion, but as they are not in command of this delegation, I assure you that my word is what matters here."

"So it would appear," Crassus commented dryly. "And it is good to know that your wise counsel holds sway here."

Timonax was clearly flattered and was apparently inspired by Crassus' words to propose a toast to his hosts, saying that he hoped that this meeting marked the beginning of a new era of friendship between the Bastarnae and Rome. For a moment, it appeared that Scylax would refuse to drink from his cup, but Timonax gave him a warning glare, and he finally drained his cup in one swallow.

"I think that this would be a good time to adjourn this meeting," Crassus announced, and his guests were clearly disappointed that the drinking was over. "I would consider it a great honor if you were to stay here tonight as my guests," he told Timonax, favoring him with a knowing grin. "Especially given how much you have enjoyed our Falernian. I would hate to feel responsible for one of you falling from your horse in the dark and injuring yourself."

Scylax gave a drunken snort to show his contempt for this idea, while even Timonax seemed to be a bit affronted by the idea that they had no head for wine.

"I assure you, Marcus Crassus, the Bastarnae has not been born that cannot ride a horse, even when he is fast asleep, let alone slightly out of our head from wine right now as we are."

"Be that as it may," Crassus replied lightly. "I would feel responsible if something were to happen. Besides, your camp is a fair distance away, and we have not finished our business. It seems a waste to have to ride there, just to turn around, and then come back in just a short while."

That argument seemed to clinch it for Timonax, who beamed with pleasure at the thought of being the honored guest of a Legate Proconsul like Marcus Crassus, and he quickly agreed.

"Wonderful!" Crassus clapped his hands together, seeming to be genuinely happy that they had agreed. "I will see to it that you have accommodations, which I apologize for in advance. We are, after all, an army on the march."

"I am sure that whatever you choose for us will be more than suitable." Timonax seemed to enjoy the idea that he could be in a position to soothe Crassus' concerns.

Crassus turned to Claudius, who had been largely ignored, as had Cornelius, saying, "Tribune, you will surrender your quarters to Timonax and his deputies immediately. Is that understood?"

Claudius, who was still forced to sit on a soft pillow because of his wound, much to our amusement, looked as if a pig had come and taken a huge *cac* on his boots, but he was smart enough to know better than to argue with his general in front of the Bastarnae.

"Yes, sir," he said stiffly, then opened his mouth to ask, "Where will I sleep tonight?"

"With Cornelius, of course," Crassus said, and now Claudius looked very much as if he had been forced to eat that pig's *cac*.

The two Tribunes hated each other; Claudius making it clear that his family bloodline was far superior to that of

Cornelius, who despised Claudius for being the humorless prig that he was. I had come to rather like young Cornelius and I suppose his hatred of Claudius recommended him to me. He was not very smart, but he was brave and he tried hard, with a cheerful disposition that made him popular with the men, which was the exact opposite of Claudius. I concealed a smirk at the thought of Claudius being forced to share space with Cornelius, who it must be said did not look any happier at the prospect. With the sleeping arrangements settled, Crassus announced that he would usher the Bastarnae to their quarters himself, but before he left, he had a quiet word with me.

"Stay here, and keep the Primi Pili here. I have something in mind."

When Crassus returned, he wasted no time.

"We're going to steal a march on the Bastarnae. I want the Legions ready to march in a third of a watch, minus one Cohort from each to stay behind and guard the camp."

The Primi Pili all began talking at once, but for once, Crassus was not willing to let them voice their opinions or objections.

"This isn't open for discussion," he told them with a hint of iron in his voice, stilling the men's tongues immediately.

I was as surprised as the rest of them, but I was willing to hear him out before I said a word.

"My plan is simple. Our scouts have informed me that there's a large forest about three miles north of here, about the same distance south of the Bastarnae camp. We're going to march tonight, and move into the forest and take up positions with the Legions. Then, the cavalry is going to move into their position so that at first light, they're going to launch a raid on the Bastarnae." Crassus paused to let his words sink in, giving me time to think about what his intent most likely was, and I had to stop myself from smiling. "The Bastarnae, as we've seen tonight, are impetuous. And I believe that Scylax and his friend Meton are representative of a good number of the Bastarnae who are spoiling for a fight to punish us for following them into their lands. I'm counting on those hotheads to overrule the more cautious among them, and I think that seeing just our cavalry will encourage them as well. I want them to pursue our cavalry, who will put up enough of a fight to get their blood boiling and howling for their scalps. You can figure out the rest if you haven't already."

"They'll pursue our cavalry, and run headlong into our ambush," Macrinus said slowly, to which Crassus nodded.

"Exactly."

"But what about the delegation?" Aelianus asked. "Isn't it a violation of our own law to attack a party that we're in negotiations with?"

"Primus Pilus, that's something you need not concern yourself with." Crassus' tone was stiff, and I could see that he was not happy that the question had been raised. "What I need to know from you is if the 15th Legion will be ready to march within a third of a watch."

Aelianus plainly did not like the rebuke, but his tone was professional as he assured Crassus that the 15th would indeed be ready.

"Very well," Crassus said as he dismissed us. "Prepare the army to march."

I returned to my tent, assuring Crassus before I did that I was fit enough to accompany the army, to which he relented, but only after extracting a promise that I would not get involved in any fighting. Making the promise readily, I knew that it would be impossible to enforce should things go badly. Entering my tent, I tried to move quietly, since the only lamp that was alive was the one on Diocles' desk that we kept lit at night until we had both retired, telling me that Diocles was done for the evening. Having long before this point in time allowed him to create a private space for himself by using some wooden framed leather partitions that gave him his own small room, I could not see whether he was sleeping or not, but I assumed that he was. That was why, when I heard what I thought was a giggle, I was sure I was hearing things. When it happened again, I froze in mid-stride, holding my breath as I listened intently. After a moment, I heard it a third time, confirming what I thought I had heard; it was definitely, without a doubt, a female giggle. Completely unsure what to do, I stood there motionless, my mind struggling to understand what I had just heard. Finally, my curiosity overcame me and I tiptoed over to stand just on the other side of the partition, where I stood with my ear cocked. There was another noise, except this was no giggle, and I could stand it no longer. Crossing to the desk, I picked up the lamp, then returned to Diocles' sleeping cubicle, pulling the partition aside. In the flickering light, my eye sensed more than saw a flurry of movement as his blanket flew up above his pallet before settling back down, only his face showing. Blinking rapidly, Diocles feigned a yawn, throwing his arms out in an exaggerated stretch.

"Master?" I know he was trying to sound sleepy, but he was doing a poor job of it. "What is it? Did you need something?"

"No, no. I just thought I'd come and check on you. I thought I heard something," I said innocently.

He frowned, like he was mystified by what I could have heard.

"I didn't realize I was making any noise while I slept."

"Maybe you were having a bad dream." I must confess I was being cruel at this point, but I had to bite my lip to keep from laughing when he grabbed at this like a drowning man grabs a spar.

"Yes! That must be it," he said enthusiastically. "In fact, I recall now that I was having a very vivid dream that was quite frightening."

"Really?" I pretended to be fascinated. "What was it about?"

"About? Er, it was about . . . well, it was about this huge beast that was chasing me through the woods." Poor Diocles was struggling now, making it up on the fly like he was.

Finally, I could take it no longer, cutting him off in mid-sentence.

"Very well, as long as you're all right," I told him, bidding him good night. I turned as if to go, then I asked him, "Diocles, have you suddenly gained weight?"

"No, Master. Why do you ask?"

Without answering, I walked over and bent down, grabbing a corner of the blanket. Before he could stop me, I whipped it off him to expose the naked body of what appeared to be a young girl, who gave a shriek of fright. Even in the dim light of the lamp, I could see Diocles blushing furiously, almost as much as he is blushing now while I dictate this. But I must confess my eyes were drawn to the sight of the girl, although it was not for the reasons you might think, gentle reader. At first, I was sure that my eyes were playing tricks on me, and I wondered why I would be seeing that face of all faces.

"Egina?"

I was not even sure that it was the girl's name, but she turned her face to me, and I saw that it was indeed her.

"Pluto's cock!" I exclaimed. "What are you doing here?"

She said nothing and I realized that I had addressed her in Latin, so I repeated the question in Greek.

"What does it look like?" she said with more than a little fire.

"I know what it looks like," I replied, wondering why I was feeling so defensive after I had caught the two of them. "You know that it's against regulations to have women in camp," I said severely to Diocles, and this time I was not joking.

"I can explain," he told me, but I held up a hand to cut him off.

"There's really nothing you can say that would help you right now. But what I want to know more than what you're thinking bringing a woman into camp is where in Hades have you been hiding this girl?"

That is when the story came out. Egina had in fact left the camp that night after the fall of Naissus, but to keep her safe, Diocles had gone with her during a period when I was still unconscious and Scribonius was watching over me. When she returned to the city, she learned that her family had been one of those sold into slavery. With nowhere to go, her only real prospect for survival was to become a whore, or to hope that some man took pity on her and did not treat her like a dog or a farm animal. Diocles, seeing her despair, took pity on her, offering to let her come back to camp to stay for a night while she tried to decide what to do. Poor Diocles never had a chance after that and he had been hiding her, if that is the right term, with all the other camp followers that tailed behind the army wherever we marched. Legion wives took pity on her as well, and she had found a place among them. Apparently, he had been sneaking her into camp after I retired for the evening so they could spend time together. While I do not know who snared who, by the time I discovered the truth, they were both smitten with each other. Nevertheless, I drew the line at her coming into camp. Instead, I began writing Diocles a pass so that he could spend the night outside the camp, as long as he was back in time to attend to me in the morning and did not leave until he was through with his clerical duties. That was how I added another member to my household, at least for a time.

Putting a guard on Claudius' tent, the army, minus four Cohorts left behind to guard the camp, marched out of the Porta Praetoria in the dark. Aided by a full moon while guided by Silva's cavalry scouts carrying torches, we made good progress. We reached the edge of the forest still well before dawn, which was good, since moving through the thick undergrowth was quite a chore, requiring the leading Legion to chop a path. Riding with the command group, I told Scribonius and Balbus about my earlier discovery of the affair between Diocles and Egina, both of whom almost fell off their horses.

"I never thought he had it in him." Scribonius' teeth gleamed in the moonlight as he laughed.

"I thought he was a pederast like every other Greek," Balbus put in, loudly enough for Philipos, who was riding just ahead of us, to hear, but he ignored us with a shake of his head.

That reminded us of the joke that we had played on Balbus years before when Diocles had intimated that he was that very thing, which Scribonius and I still thought hilarious, while Balbus still did not. Our cavalry forged ahead, leaving the forest then continuing north, while the Legions were put to work throwing up a hasty breastworks about 50 paces into the forest, just far enough that we would not be easily spotted when the Bastarnae came in pursuit of our cavalry.

The work was finished shortly before dawn, giving the men the opportunity to roll up in their cloaks to catch some sleep while we waited. The command group and Evocati dismounted, sitting on the ground or on logs, talking in low tones. Our job would be to help contain any possible breakthroughs, although these were highly unlikely, then to help in the pursuit once the Bastarnae broke.

"What if they don't take the bait?" Scribonius wondered.

"Then we lost a lot of sleep for nothing," Balbus replied, but Scribonius shook his head, clearly thinking in larger terms.

"That's not what I'm talking about. Crassus can get away with keeping the envoys under guard as long as we have a fight. He can make up anything he wants as long as we have a fight with the Bastarnae and destroy them. But if they don't fall for this ruse, then what's he going to do with them?"

"Kill them, of course."

As usual, Balbus saw things in the simplest terms. In his view, most problems could be solved by killing someone.

"If he does that, Caesar will destroy him," I whispered, not wanting our conversation to be overheard now that it had entered into this dangerous territory. "He'll have murdered a diplomatic mission under flag of truce. They're protected under the rules of war, and have been for as long as men have been fighting. Killing them would be a huge mistake."

"But he can't just let them go," Balbus objected, and for once Scribonius agreed.

"That's why the Bastarnae have to attack, or else Crassus is finished."

He glanced about before he continued, dropping his voice even further.

"Although he might be finished no matter what he does."

"What makes you say that?" Balbus asked curiously.

Scribonius opened his mouth, but I caught his eye to give him a warning shake of the head.

"No reason," he managed to say, then gave a shrug as if it did not matter. "I'm just talking."

But Balbus was not so easily thrown off, his eyes narrowing in suspicion, glancing at me, then back to Scribonius.

"Then that's a first," he retorted. "I've never known you to talk just to hear your voice."

"Well, there's a first time for everything."

Seeing that he was saying no more, Balbus subsided, muttering under his breath about secrets being kept from him. Things were quiet then and I must have dozed off, because when I opened my eyes, the sky was already bright in the early morning. Standing stiffly, I felt every one of my years after a night on the cold hard ground, pulling a loaf of bread from my pack that Diocles had packed for me. Tearing off a chunk, I handed the rest to Scribonius and Balbus. We were standing there chewing on our breakfast when there was a commotion up at the breastworks. Beyond them, I could dimly make out the shape of a man on horseback come galloping up, yelling something. It was the watchword for the day, which he had begun shouting on his approach in order to avoid being riddled with javelins. Once past the breastworks, he quickly trotted up to our group to find Crassus. Our general was also having breakfast, standing with the Tribunes, returning the salute of the courier.

We were close enough to hear him tell Crassus, "The Bastarnae have roused themselves. They're engaging with our cavalry now."

Getting the Bastarnae to come after the cavalry was only half the battle, so to speak. It was essential that the actions of our cavalry be sufficient to incense the Bastarnae to the point that the entire Bastarnae army, or the largest part, came after them. To achieve that, Silva had been given orders to target the wagons, where the women and children normally slept, flinging torches onto them to set them ablaze. Once that was done, they were to withdraw slowly instead of fleeing immediately, engaging the Bastarnae briefly before falling back, luring them in our direction. To my mind, this was the weakest part of the plan; putting myself in the Bastarnae commander's place, I did not see how he could fail to recognize that this was a trap. But it appeared that Silva's raid had so enraged the Bastarnae that their passions blinded them to what would appear to be obvious if they had kept their collective heads.

Couriers came and went with updates, the sun rising higher in the sky with the promise of a hot day in every sense of the word. Shortly after dawn, Crassus had ordered our auxiliary force, some 5,000 strong, forward a mile from the edge of the forest. Their job was to act as more bait, acting as if they were coming to the rescue of the cavalry and putting up enough of a fight to give Silva's men the chance to disengage and slip back to the edge of the forest. Crassus believed that the thought of Silva and his men escaping would fuel the Bastarnae, who would probably be flagging in their pursuit by this point. The auxiliaries had been ordered to break off immediately upon Silva's men making it near the trees, then if possible, to appear like they had panicked and were fleeing. Crassus hoped that this would entice the Bastarnae into a headlong pursuit into the woods, where we were waiting. To me, it was an overly complicated plan and while I did not care for auxiliaries all that much, I still did not like the idea of ordering men to put themselves into the most vulnerable position one can assume in battle, with their backs turned, fleeing for their lives. That is when slaughter in battles usually occurs, when men turn and run. I did not envy the auxiliary commander, yet orders are orders and I expected him to obey. We were able to follow the progress of the fighting before they came into view by the sight of the dust cloud hanging above the combatants, rising above the low hill that was a mile away from our position, where the auxiliaries were placed. At least the auxiliary commander had placed them on the hilltop, giving them a downhill head start, I thought, watching the ranks of the auxiliaries momentarily open up to allow Silva's troopers to pass through.

"It won't be long now," Scribonius commented as we watched the auxiliaries close back up.

Just a few moments later, we saw the dark mass of the rolling tide of Bastarnae warriors crashing into the auxiliary lines, followed a few heartbeats later by the sounds of the clash. The rear ranks of the auxiliaries suddenly turned about to begin fleeing down the hill, leaving their comrades in the first two or three ranks alone to hold off the enraged Bastarnae warriors.

"I don't think they were supposed to do that," Balbus said dryly as we watched the fleeing men churning down the hill, arms and legs flying, discarding their shields, helmets, and weapons, ridding themselves of anything that slowed down their flight.

They caught up with Silva and his troopers, who had paused at the edge of the forest, giving the appearance of resting their animals, pushing through and past the horses, ignoring the jeers of the men of the Legions while they clambered over the breastworks to move to the rear. As they went filing past, they kept their eyes cast downward, clearly ashamed of their actions. We sat on our horses, watching them go, and I felt nothing but contempt for men who would leave their comrades behind to die, even if they were just auxiliaries. Turning my attention back to the hill, I was just in time to watch the rest of the auxiliary formation disintegrate under the Bastarnae onslaught. Men turned to run and, as I had feared, many of them were cut down before they could take more than a couple of steps. The Bastarnae came flowing over the hill, a mass of men in no visibly coherent order, just a thicket of weapons waving in the air as they roared their anger. Silva and his men were still in their spot a couple hundred paces from the edge of the forest, their horses beginning to toss their heads nervously, pawing at the ground while the Bastarnae paused to catch their collective breaths. A moment passed, then on some unseen signal, with a great shout, the Bastarnae began running down the hill. That was the signal for Silva to give the order to turn his men to head into the forest, but he did not do so. Along with the rest of the Evocati, Scribonius, Balbus and I moved farther back into the forest from where we had been watching so that we would not be spotted. Once we were back in our spot with the command group, we could only see Silva and his men, yet they still did not move.

"What's he doing?" Scribonius wondered, but I did not know the answer.

Ocelus, like the other horses, was disturbed by the sound and the vibration of the ground from the pounding of thousands of Bastarnae feet, and began hopping about nervously, snorting and tossing his head. Their tension was shared by every living being on this side of the breastwork, as men said their last-minute prayers, clutched their amulets, or checked the edge of their blades for the thousandth time. Finally, Silva's *bucinator* sounded the recall, his men needing no urging to wheel their mounts to move at the gallop into the forest. That was when I understood what Silva had been doing; if he had moved his men sooner, suddenly going to the gallop would have been suspicious, since they would have had more than enough time to escape. By waiting, he furthered the illusion of panic, while also giving his men the ability to get up the momentum needed for them to clear the breastworks and the line of men crouched behind them. The space in front of us was filled with the sight of leaping horses, men crouched over their necks as they jumped to safety, while a couple did not make it, causing horse and rider to tumble over the breastworks, onto the unlucky men crouched beneath. Horses and men shrieked with pain and I held my breath, sure that this would tip the Bastarnae off that something was afoot, but they were either committed or oblivious to the trap. All but one of the horses struggled to their feet to trot off, where it thrashed on the ground, one leg askew where it had broken, its cries of agony disturbing our mounts enormously.

"Someone kill that horse," Crassus snapped, the tension in his voice finally starting to show, and a man with the presence of mind to keep from standing erect crawled over to cut the horse's throat with a quick slash.

Its hooves flailed a moment longer, then were still, and without thinking, I reached down to pat Ocelus' neck. The Bastarnae were now in our field of view again, their individual faces distinct, and we could see their mouths open as they continued shouting their war cries, the sound deafening. I worried that the men would not be able to hear the commands, but when the *cornu* call came, all the men stood up, javelins in hand, ready to rain death on the Bastarnae.

"Release!"

The leading Bastarnae had seen a line of Legionaries suddenly seem to materialize a few dozen paces deep in the forest and they tried to come to a halt or bring their shields up, but they were doomed either way. Those who did stop were immediately trampled by their onrushing comrades behind them, and over the roar could be heard shrill, sharp screams as men were crushed. The rest were swept onward, unable to bring their shields up in time to block the hail of javelins that sliced down into their bodies. Like a giant invisible scythe, men in the front ranks were mowed down like stalks of wheat, one or more javelin shaft protruding from their bodies as they fell. Even men who were not mortally wounded by a javelin were killed by their comrades behind them continuing forward, crushed underfoot. A collective cry went up from both sides, one with the exultation of scoring a hit, the other with the despair of knowing one's death was at hand. However, the momentum of the Bastarnae was such that they did not appreciably slow, continuing forward while the Centurions gave the command to prepare the next and final javelin.

"Release!"

Again, our missiles knifed into the Bastarnae ranks, felling hundreds more Bastarnae warriors, yet still they came on.

"They're brave bastards, I'll give them that," Balbus shouted over the din, and I had to agree.

We were out of javelins now, the order then given to draw swords, but the Bastarnae were still shouting so loudly that we could not hear the distinctive sound of thousands of swords being drawn from scabbards. Waving their vaunted falxes above their heads, the surviving Bastarnae of the front ranks closed the remaining distance to the breastworks, their comrades behind them clambering over the piled bodies of their dead and wounded. Reaching the breastworks, I saw for the first time how the Bastarnae wielded their weapons. Like our cavalrymen, they carried their shields strapped to their left arm, making their left hand free to use for the falx. Chopping downward with it like an axe, they came at an angle that our men were unaccustomed to and I saw several of our men reel backwards, their helmets split in half, along with their skulls. I saw men have their arms severed in a single stroke, and while I did not see a man cleaved in two like Timonax had bragged, I did see one man struck on the shoulder next to the neck then watched the falx blade pass down through his chest almost to his waist. For the first few moments, it looked as if the Bastarnae would overwhelm our men, clawing and slashing through the breastwork, throwing themselves in a howling rage at the Romans standing behind. We had never fought men who used this weapon or fought in this overhand style, which looked extremely awkward, but was clearly devastatingly effective. Sitting on our horses watching, our nerves were growing increasingly on edge and I looked over to Crassus to see how he was reacting to what was happening. Instead of showing any fear or trepidation, he was sitting calmly, one leg hooked over the front of his saddle, munching on an apple while talking to Cornelius like they were watching a gladiatorial contest rather than a desperate battle. Every so often, he would snap out an order to one of his runners, who would dash off to carry the instructions to some part of the line. We were on a front of four Legions; he had left nothing in reserve, which I thought was another mistake, and for a short while, I thought that we would pay for that mistake with defeat.

Somehow, the men gathered themselves after the initial onslaught and seemed to be figuring out how to fight the falx effectively. Stepping underneath the overhand swing, holding their shield almost parallel to the ground above their head and giving an underhand thrust appeared to be the best way to defeat a Bastarnae. With the shield strapped to the Bastarnae's arm, the target area for such a thrust was dramatically smaller, but because that exposed area was in the region held most dear by men everywhere, the results were devastating, at least if you were a Bastarnae warrior. Most of the enemy warriors were being struck in the groin, eliciting the most horrific shrieks of pain and terror and scaring the horses, including Ocelus. As would be expected, the fighting was fiercest just in front of the command group, with the Bastarnae seeking to overwhelm our defenses at that point to either capture or kill Marcus Crassus. He was no longer quite so placid, having drawn his sword, exhorting the men to fight with everything they had. The men listened, the whistles sounding up and down the line for the relief, with the Legions beginning to fight the way they had been trained. This was my first real action where I did not actually participate in commanding a Legion or do any fighting, which allowed me to observe things in a way that I had not before. On an impulse, I signaled to Scribonius and Balbus, then without asking permission, went trotting farther down the line to watch each Legion in action. The 8th had been placed as the last Legion on the left, at the far end of the line and well before we drew even with them we could see that they were being pressed hard, yet were holding the line well. Macrinus had placed the men of the third line, the last three Cohorts, at a right angle to the left flank of the 8th, because the Bastarnae had attempted to move around it. Silva and his troopers were gathered in a clearing about 200 paces away, the cavalry commander having clearly seen that this was a danger spot, and they were watching the 8th pushing the Bastarnae back. The second line had not been committed yet, but we could see that the men of the first line, having gone through several shifts already, were tiring rapidly. The Tribune Claudius had been sent over here, ostensibly to command the Legion, but almost every Tribune knew that when the fighting started the most good they could do was keep their mouths shut, let the Centurions do their jobs, then take the credit afterward. However, Claudius gave every appearance of not being content to do that, and he trotted off to address Silva. When he reached the cavalry commander, he pointed in the general direction farther off our left flank, then we saw Silva shake his head.

"What do you think that idiot is doing?" Balbus muttered, but I was as mystified as he, and we sat watching an obviously heated exchange taking place between the two men.

Claudius shouted something, but we could not make out what he was saying, whereupon Silva gave a very stiff salute, snapped a command to his *bucinator*, then before the notes had died away they were trotting off in the direction that Claudius had indicated.

"You better do something about this," Scribonius told me and I stifled a groan, but kicked Ocelus forward to intercept Silva.

Calling his name several times before he heard me over the din, he halted his men readily enough, saluting as I rode up.

"What did he tell you to do?" I demanded.

"The Tribune has ordered us to move out on the left flank, and launch an attack on the Bastarnae right."

At first, I was not sure I had heard correctly. If Claudius had ordered Silva to engage with the Bastarnae cavalry, which was skulking about roughly in the rear of the center part of the enemy formation, that would have actually made sense.

"He didn't say the cavalry?"

Even with my low opinion of Claudius, I was willing to give him the benefit of the doubt, but Silva was emphatic.

"No, Prefect, he was very specific. He thinks something should be done to relieve the pressure on the 8th. He's sure they're about to crack."

"Pluto's cock, he would have gotten you slaughtered! Stand fast," I ordered Silva, who looked relieved at the reprieve.

Claudius had given an order that would essentially annihilate Silva and his men. By ordering them to attack the Bastarnae infantry, they would have had their backs turned to the real threat on the field at that moment, the Bastarnae cavalry. No matter how much of a dullard the Bastarnae cavalry commander may have been, there would be no way he could pass up the opportunity to slam into Silva's rear once they engaged with the Bastarnae foot. Claudius, seeing that I had intervened, came galloping up, his face contorted with rage.

I believe that his fury overrode his sense of caution, because he shouted at me, "What do you think you're doing?"

"My job in protecting this army," I replied, forcing myself to keep my tone calm, which seemed to drive him to new heights of anger.

"Well, you've just ensured the destruction of this entire army! Don't you see that the 8th is on the verge of collapse? I tried to prevent it, but you've brought disaster down on our heads, and don't think that Caesar won't know it! I will ruin you!"

Instead of answering, I merely pointed back over his shoulder, since his back was turned to where the second line of the 8th had moved forward and was even now pushing the Bastarnae back. They had thrown their best at us, we had weathered the storm, and now it was the Bastarnae who were taking those steps backward. Claudius turned to watch the men of the middle Cohorts, including Gaius, wade into the Bastarnae, picking up where the first line had left off. Bastarnae were now falling in two's and three's, cut down screaming and clutching their groins. Moving Ocelus closer to Claudius so that Silva and his troopers could not hear, I looked him in the eye.

"If you ever show that kind of disrespect to a superior officer again, I'll gut you like a fish," I told him calmly. "I don't care who your family is, boy. I don't care who you know. Out here, all that matters is competence and you're anything but. Cross me again and you'll suffer the consequences. Do you understand me?"

Claudius stared at the 8th wading into the Bastarnae, refusing to meet my gaze or answer. Since he had genuinely aroused my ire, I was not willing to let it go.

"I believe that when a senior officer asks you a question, an answer is expected, Tribune."

Slowly, he turned his head towards me, his gaze as malevolent as it is possible to be, but he answered.

"Yes, Prefect," he replied tonelessly. "I understand you very well."

"Good." I turned to go, but he was not through.

"Know this, Prefect. By Dis, I swear you will rue the day you speak to me as if you're my superior. You are a lowborn, insolent brute and why Caesar deemed you fit to hold such a high rank, I will never understand. But you've made an enemy for life, know that."

"Sonny," I could not hide my amusement, "the last person to call me a lowborn insolent brute was Cleopatra. And we both know what happened to her. She's in her tomb now."

Without waiting for a reply, I trotted Ocelus over to where Scribonius and Balbus were waiting for me.

"That looked like it went well," was Balbus' only comment.

"You know Titus, making friends wherever he goes," Scribonius could not resist adding.

I ignored them, and we trotted back to the command group.

When we reached Crassus, I reported to him that the 8th was carrying their part of the battle. In response, he pointed to our front.

"So is the 13th," he commented.

We watched the Bastarnae on our right continuing to fight, but their energy and enthusiasm was clearly flagging. Suddenly, Crassus pointed to a group of horsemen on the opposite side, where one mounted man, richly dressed and armored, was waving his sword in exhortation to his troops. Unlike the men on foot, he did not carry a falx, armed instead with a sword that looked very similar to our *spatha*. He was surrounded by men dressed in armor, all carrying weapons of only marginally lesser quality than his, and they were watching the fighting in front of them intensely.

"He must be their king," Crassus said suddenly. "Keep your eye on him. If we get the chance, we're going to go after him and I intend to kill that bastard."

What happened to not wanting me to fight, I thought, though I kept it to myself. Crassus began trotting his horse closer to the rear ranks of our line, shouting at the men, urging them to make one last effort. They responded, fighting even harder and as we watched, the Bastarnae crumbled. Like I had seen so many times before, it did not seem to take longer than it takes to blink; one moment men are fighting, then most or all of them immediately turn to run for their lives, on some unseen and unheard signal. Our men were ready, plunging blades into men's backs the instant they tried to turn and run. What saved even more Bastarnae from dying when they suddenly fled was the moment it took for the Legionaries to clamber over the makeshift breastworks. Despite it being little more than piled brush and fallen logs, it was enough to give the Bastarnae two or three steps. An additional obstacle was the Bastarnae bodies that were piled up at the foot of the breastworks, many of them still moving. The Centurions led their men over the breastworks, the men giving a great shout as they went off in pursuit. With the Bastarnae left giving way, it was just a matter of a few moments more before the Bastarnae center, now outflanked, had to decide whether to fight or run like their comrades. I was pleased to see that Natalis used his third line to swing down onto the Bastarnae center, essentially making their decision for them. What had been a hard-fought, bitter battle was now a rout, and the Bastarnae leader and his bodyguard quickly saw that all was lost. Rather than turn about in an attempt to outrun his men, the rear ranks of whom had already reached the spot where they were standing, they instead turned to begin galloping parallel to the two lines. Crassus understood their intent immediately; before they could flee they had to disentangle themselves from their own men, and that small delay in making their escape gave Crassus the opportunity he was looking for.

"Evocati, follow me!" He pointed his sword in the direction of the fleeing horsemen, then without looking back to see if we were following, kicked his horse into motion.

"We better go with him," Balbus said to me as he rode by, already at a canter.

"You should stay here," came from Scribonius, close behind Balbus.

The rest of the Evocati thundered by while I sat, trying to decide what to do. I had a legitimate reason not to become involved in any fighting; my hand was still practically useless, and I noticed that my side ached a great deal, which would make it awkward holding my cavalry shield. On the other hand, I thought, there's nothing wrong with my right arm, and I don't have to actually do any fighting. I gave Ocelus a hard slap on his rump, galloping after Crassus and the Evocati.

Ocelus closed the gap in a few powerful strides; as I pulled even with Scribonius, he looked over at me and rolled his eyes.

"I knew you wouldn't stay behind," he shouted while we went thundering after Crassus, who had opened his horse into a full gallop.

I saw one of the rearmost bodyguards turn; seeing Crassus and the rest of us in hot pursuit, he shouted a warning to the others. Without hesitation, they immediately began whipping their mounts, who responded with a burst of speed. Now that the Bastarnae were at a full gallop, I no longer had to hold Ocelus back, letting the slack out of the reins and giving him his head. Stretching his neck out, Ocelus' long legs ate up the ground while I clung to his back, laying my head down along his mane, gritting my teeth from the jarring impact that threatened to open my wounds. Crassus was still ahead of us, but Ocelus began closing the gap quickly. For a moment, I forgot what we were racing for and was just caught up in the thrill of seeing my horse outrun everything around it. Crassus' mount was a magnificent animal in its own right, a black stallion, and I could see his eyes rolling backward as we came into his vision.

The Bastarnae were in full flight, taking us away from the battlefield, and I had a fleeting thought about pulling up to go back to ensure that Claudius did not snatch defeat from the jaws of victory by doing something stupid. Deciding that not even a dolt like Claudius could ruin this triumph, I continued following Crassus, though we were almost even now. Turning his head briefly when he sensed the presence of another rider, our eyes met briefly, his eyes alight with the thrill of the chase. He gave me a wide grin before turning back to our pursuit, and we slowly but surely closed the gap. The rearmost bodyguards were now no more than five or six lengths away, their faces desperate as they kept glancing backward at us. Approaching a stretch of rough and rocky ground, the Bastarnae tried to veer away to choose a course that kept them away from the hazards, but the momentum of the leading riders, the nobleman among them, was too great. Going no more than a dozen strides over this ground, the nobleman's horse either tripped over a rock or stepped into an animal hole, because it came to an abrupt halt, and even from where we were we could hear one of its legs snap. The nobleman was thrown over the horse's head, flying through the air. Nevertheless, he made an extremely good recovery, tucking a shoulder then rolling several times before coming to a stop. The bodyguards reacted immediately, but our own impetus was such that we were on them before they could fully prepare themselves. Marcus Crassus held his *spatha* straight out and slightly to the side, catching one of the bodyguards just beneath the armpit when he was turning. It was at that very moment, as I continued sweeping past on Ocelus, heading for another bodyguard, that I realized I had not drawn my own *spatha*. Consequently, I was closing with a Bastarnae cavalryman unarmed, and it was little more than the span of a few heartbeats before I was on him. The man I had headed for was a well-built man a few years younger than me, with a tough, competent look about him. Fortunately, he looked as surprised to see me closing with him empty-handed as I felt, meaning that for the briefest shadow of a moment, he hesitated as if unsure what to do. That hesitation saved my life, and it was by pure impulse that I reached out with my right hand to grab the edge of the rider's shield before he could bring his sword up to stop me. Passing by with no more than a hand's breadth between our legs, Ocelus was still at the gallop and I squeezed my thighs together with all of my strength, grabbing onto the front of the saddle with my left hand at the same time. The impact was terrific; despite being unable to jerk the shield from his grasp because it was looped on his arm, I almost unseated him before my momentum forced me to release the shield or come off the back of Ocelus myself. The shock of pain that shot through my left hand when the stump of my little finger jarred against the edge of the saddle took my breath away. However, it did give me the chance to unsheathe my own *spatha* while I jerked Ocelus to a skidding stop, wheeling him quickly about to face my adversary. Since the Evocati outnumbered the Bastarnae bodyguard by almost three to one, men worked in teams to cut down one of the enemy cavalrymen. We were a good distance away from the battle now, the woods where we had been hidden just a green line, the pursuit and slaughter of the Bastarnae infantry obscured by dust. Jabbing Ocelus with my heels, he leapt towards my chosen enemy with a great snort, except this time I was prepared to face him. All thoughts of my injuries were suddenly gone from my mind; in fact I do not remember feeling them at all in that instant, despite just moments before being worried that they would open again. Just as eager to meet me, the Bastarnae came pounding across the ground for me, both of us with our arms straight out, meaning to stab each other. Out of the corner of my eye, I saw a blur of movement, coming from the opposite side of the Bastarnae, heading directly for him. He obviously sensed the same thing, so he brought his shield up tightly against his body to absorb the impact, which kept him from being able to swing it about to use it against me. All I had to do was dodge his own thrust, which I did easily, the impact of the point of my *spatha* punching into the man's chest and jarring me all the way to the shoulder. Twisting the blade free, as I rode past, I saw him reeling in the saddle, but somehow he managed to stay upright, and I saw frothy blood on his lips. Now able to see who had come to my aid I was a bit surprised that it was not Scribonius nor Balbus, but Novatus, now fully healed. The Bastarnae, with his strength rapidly waning, was parrying Novatus' repeated thrusts, until he could no longer hold his sword up. Even then, he used his shield effectively, thwarting Novatus' attempts to land a killing blow. I admired the man's courage and skill a great deal, so I could not bring myself to kill him myself with a thrust from behind. If he had been able to act offensively, using his sword, I would not have hesitated, but it had slipped from his grasp to fall to the ground. Finally, the Bastarnae was unable even to lift his shield, the blood streaming down his chin and bubbling from the wound in his chest, and Novatus gave him a final thrust. The man toppled from the saddle at last, while Novatus and I looked about for any other threat. Seeing that the rest of the Evocatus either had subdued the other bodyguards or they were in the process of doing so, we trotted our horses toward each other. Novatus gave me a huge grin.

"Now we're even," he cried, and I gave him a mock frown.

"How do you figure that?" I demanded. "That man was dead in the saddle before you ever struck a blow."

Novatus' mouth dropped, and he spluttered his protest.

"That's not so! He was still putting up a fight when I ended him!"

"You call that a fight?" I asked scornfully, then having had my fun, I smiled at him to let him know I had been joking, which he took with good humor.

Turning our attention to the scene around us, we witnessed the very end of the fight between Crassus and the Bastarnae noble. They had separated themselves a short distance from the main action and apparently had been engaging each other vigorously, both men red-faced and panting for breath. Crassus had dismounted, I suppose to make things fair, the two men now circling each other, their sword points weaving back and forth, each waiting for an opening. Crassus had a long cut running down the length of his sword arm, while the Bastarnae appeared to be unmarked. The other Evocati, seeing the same thing, probably assumed like I did that Crassus had been taking the worst of it, since several of them, Balbus included, began moving their horses towards Crassus to offer help.

Seeing them coming, Crassus, while not taking his eyes from the other man shouted, "If anyone tries to strike this man, I'll have him up on charges and I'll ruin him! He's mine!"

So instead of helping, we sat watching like we were at the games, some men even cheering Crassus on as if he were their favorite gladiator. Sitting there watching, I could see some of Prixus' teachings in young Crassus' style, and I was grimly amused at the sight.

"I just hope you do better fighting like that than he did," I muttered under my breath.

I thought I had spoken softly enough, though Novatus obviously heard.

"You hope he does better than who?" he asked, but I was not willing to divulge that tale to Novatus.

"Nobody," I replied. "I was thinking about something else."

He clearly did not believe me, yet to my relief, he did not press the issue, preferring to keep his attention on the fight happening in front of us. Suddenly, the Bastarnae made a lightning-fast slash, the tip of his sword a blur as it swept at Crassus. I do not know how he did so, but Crassus managed to dodge the slash, then almost as quickly lashed out with a quick thrust of his own, over the still outstretched arm of the Bastarnae. The noble was wearing a flowing cloak, and while Crassus had evened things by dismounting, he had not been willing to let the noble remove his cloak. The garment billowed about him, not only hindering his movement but also making it impossible to tell if Crassus' blow struck. The

Bastarnae had made a grunting noise, except that it all happened so quickly it was not clear if he had been wounded or if he had just exerted himself trying to strike his own blow. It was not until a moment later that Novatus pointed at the Bastarnae.

"Look at his side. Crassus got him."

The Bastarnae had made a half-turn in answer to Crassus' own move, a breeze blowing the cloak aside briefly, long enough for me to see that Novatus was right. The man's armor, a finely wrought cuirass, was slick and red with blood from the mid-chest, streaming down his front. I began watching the man more carefully and saw how labored his breathing had become. He was still clearly dangerous, and as if in answer to my thoughts, he made a lunging attack, combining a series of thrusts and slashes furiously, forcing Crassus to shuffle backward, desperately working to parry each blow. Despite Crassus managing to catch most of them on his shield, he was forced to sweep his blade across his body when one of the Bastarnae's blows slipped past his first line of defense. The sweat was pouring freely down Crassus' face, but it showed no sign of panic, instead set in a look of concentration and purpose. His attack spent, the Bastarnae stood panting for breath, waiting for Crassus' onslaught, while our general appeared in no hurry. I thought this was a mistake and I said as much to Novatus.

"He can't let him catch his breath," I said.

"I don't think there's much chance of that," Novatus replied, again pointing at the man. "See how his head is drooping? He's almost done for."

"Or he's hoping that Crassus thinks the same thing and is waiting for him to get sloppy," I countered, but Novatus was clearly unconvinced.

At last, Crassus raised his sword in salute to the Bastarnae, which I thought was the kind of gesture that only a member of the upper classes would make, before starting his own, presumably final attack. Crouching low while weaving side to side, he shuffled forward, his *spatha* held in a slightly modified first position; still parallel to the ground, but angled slightly upward and held higher. With a speed that was impressive, his blade flicked out in a thrust that I knew was more of a probe to see if the Bastarnae's reflexes were still intact and I saw that his block was a little late, the point of Crassus' blade actually making it past the edge of the shield. Crassus then feinted an overhand blow, drawing the Bastarnae's shield up to block a thrust that never came. Meanwhile, Crassus instantly recovered; instead delivering a thrust that began at waist level, he drove upward. Crassus had stepped into the thrust as perfectly as it could be done, the blade sliding under the edge of the Bastarnae's own round shield to punch through the cuirass, driving deep into the Bastarnae's gut. The Bastarnae was at the right angle for me to see his face, his eyes widening in shock. However, to his eternal credit, he did not cry out, despite the fact that a belly wound is the most painful of any except to the groin. Crassus twisted the blade to free it, which of course also caused more damage to the man's insides, and this did force a groan from his lips. Ripping the blade free, Crassus had to jump back in order to avoid the fount of blood that spurted from the wound. Thankfully, the cuirass worked to keep the man's intestines intact, although I do not suppose at that moment he cared much. Falling to his knees, the Bastarnae mouthed some words that I assumed was a prayer to his gods, before toppling slowly over, dead at Marcus Crassus' feet. Crassus had been true to his word; he had conquered the Bastarnae leader. Crassus knelt, head bowed in a silent prayer, then began stripping the armor and weapons from the dead man. He held his trophies aloft, with the men of the Evocati giving a great cheer of pride at the victory of our commander. Intermingled among the cries of joy, however, were some cries of despair from the surviving Bastarnae, most of them lying wounded on the ground. Balbus, sword in hand, stood over one such man, who was weeping unashamedly. He looked at me in consternation.

"I barely touched the man, and he's crying like a baby." He seemed indignant at the man shaming himself.

I walked Ocelus over to look down at the man. He had a wound in the thigh, but it did not seem to me to be sufficient to cause enough pain to have him weeping in such a manner.

"Why are you crying?" I asked the man in Greek.

He looked up at me, his face twisted in grief.

"Your commander has slain my lord," the man said bitterly.

He must have been important, I thought, and out of curiosity, I asked the man who he had been. The man looked at me as if I had gone mad.

"That is Deldo, king of what you Roman bastards call the Bastarnae."

The battle was over, the Bastarnae routed and in complete disarray, leaving well more than half their men dead on the field. Returning to the army, we found the Legions scattered about; some men were busy looting the dead, while others were still fighting small pockets of survivors who had formed rudimentary *orbium* and were still resisting. *Medici*, Diocles and other slaves among them providing labor, were busy assessing the wounded, having those with serious injuries carried on litters farther back into the woods, where Philipos had directed the erection of a hospital tent in a clearing. Drawing closer, it became clear that not all of the men were present, and when we reached the breastworks, I saw that it appeared to be the entire 8th Legion that was missing. Crassus, carrying the armor of Deldo, saw the same thing that I did and called to the small group of Tribunes gathered in a knot, no doubt congratulating each other on their heroism and exploits, despite it being doubtful that any of them had blood on their sword. The Tribune who turned to address Crassus was Claudius, and ignoring me, he pointedly saluted Crassus. He did not fail to notice the bloodstained armor strapped to Crassus' horse, and he complimented Crassus on his victory.

Crassus brushed the flattery aside, asking Claudius peremptorily, "Where did the 8th go?"

Claudius, ever prideful, stiffened at the brusqueness of Crassus, but he answered with a neutral tone. "Oh, Cornelius took them to go chasing after the remnants of the Bastarnae army," he said carelessly, giving a shrug that implied how unimportant anything Cornelius was involved in really was.

"And you didn't think it was a good idea to send another Legion with him?" Crassus demanded.

"For what?" Claudius scoffed. "There are less than 4,000 of these barbarians left. Surely one Legion is more than enough."

Crassus pointed to the low hill, which blocked the view of the other side, and over which the 8th had gone.

"Do you know what's on the other side of that hill?"

Now Claudius showed the first glimmering of doubt.

"No, but surely they used every man for this attack."

"And left their families and possessions unguarded?" Crassus' asked acidly. "I hope you're right."

Beckoning to us to follow, he went trotting in the direction of the hill. We fell in behind him, but we were barely to the base when a man came trotting over the crest, headed in our direction. Meeting him halfway up the hill, he saluted, gasping that he had been sent by Cornelius.

"We found the wagons of the Bastarnae, sir. And Tribune Cornelius says that he's isolated a part of the survivors from the battle in a grove and surrounded it, but that he doesn't have enough men to keep them contained and attack the wagons at the same time. He requests that at least one other Legion be sent up to support him."

Looking at me, Crassus said, "Prefect, would you be so kind as to fetch Primus Pilus Saenus and his Legion and bring them to join the 8th please?"

Saluting, I assured him that I would. Crassus continued on his way while I went and fetched the 14th. Marching with them over the hill, we saw the circle of wagons in the distance, with the charred remnants of those that Silva had burned showing as black spots. Only when I squinted could I make out tiny figures moving about, but we were too far to tell whether they were warriors or their families. Off to our left, perhaps a mile from the top of the hill, was a grove of trees standing by itself, while ringed around it were the men of the

8th Legion. Leaving Saenus and the 14th to make their own way to the wagons, I headed Ocelus down to where Crassus and the Evocati were gathered, Macrinus and Cornelius with them.

"Cornelius says they have about a thousand Bastarnae trapped in the grove," Scribonius explained. "He's tried to get them to surrender, but they refuse to come out."

While we watched, Crassus rode closer to the edge of the grove, where we could see Bastarnae crouched, waiting for what came next. Despite being unable to make out what Crassus was saying, I imagine that it was along the same lines as what Cornelius had said. I heard the Bastarnae shout a response, and just from the tone, it did not sound promising. After a short exchange, Crassus turned his horse to come trotting back to where we were gathered.

Shrugging, he said, "They don't want to come out, no matter what I promised."

Beckoning to Macrinus, he gave the Primus Pilus an order that chilled my blood.

"Set fire to the grove," he told the Primus Pilus.

Macrinus did not move immediately, as if he did not understand Crassus.

"Did you not hear me, Primus Pilus?"

"I heard you, sir. You want us to set fire to the forest."

"Exactly. If they don't want to come out on their own, then we'll burn them out."

Macrinus saluted, going off to make preparations. Each Cohort was arranged in a rough circle around the grove, and he ordered that they make fires. Once the fires were blazing well, he ordered some of the men to surrender their neckerchiefs, which were wrapped around the remaining javelins. There were not enough javelins for every man, but there were more than enough for the purposes Macrinus had in mind. Once the javelins were prepared, they were set alight, then the men designated to throw them ran forward to get within range of the forest. Flinging the javelins, hundreds of them went streaking into the grove, the Bastarnae working desperately to stamp them out, but there were just too many of the flaming missiles. In moments, smoky flames started licking up, catching in the underbrush first, and we could hear men crying out in terror at the thought of being consumed by fire. With the light from the fires growing brighter, we could see the figures of men dashing about among the trees, moving to avoid the rapidly expanding flames. The underbrush now fully alight and beginning to make a dull, roaring noise, it was not long before men came darting out in a desperate dash for freedom. Since we were out of javelins, these Bastarnae had to be dispatched with the sword, the men working in teams to surround an enemy and cut them down. Those Bastarnaes' cries of anguish and despair, along with the sight of them being slaughtered obviously convinced other men to stay in the grove, but personally, I would have much preferred the relatively quick end by a blade rather than burn to death. Perhaps it was the shame of being little better than an animal led to slaughter that kept most of the men in the grove, even as it burned down around them. Soon enough, the first of what would be many horrific screams began issuing from inside the grove when men caught fire. Not much longer after that, the first man came streaking from the woods, hair and clothing alight, shrieking in pain and fear. These men presented a problem; there was no way to get close to them to put them out of their misery without the risk of being burned and, as we soon saw, it became apparent that for most of these men, this was their last act of defiance. Running directly for our own men, these human torches were doing their best to try and take a Roman with them, sending our men scattering in all directions trying to dodge out of the way. Quickly blinded by the flames consuming first their hair, then their face, the Bastarnaes ran in an increasingly aimless fashion before collapsing, many of them still screaming with a pain that is impossible to imagine. It was extremely nerve-wracking, and it was not long before Marcus Crassus announced to us that he needed to see how the 14th was faring. By the look on his face, I thought that he just wanted to be anywhere other than at that place, and I must say that I was not happy that he chose to leave. As far as I was concerned, he had been the one who so callously ordered the men of the 8th to torch those poor bastards, and I thought he should at least have seen it all the way through. Before he had gone very far, Crassus called my name, motioning me to follow him.

"Lucky bastard," Balbus muttered, his eyes fixed on the blazing forest.

The heat, by this point, had become so intense that we had been forced to move a few dozen paces backward, yet we were still close enough to hear the agony of brave men burning to death. Catching up to Crassus, I said nothing, riding alongside him but not looking his way.

"That was a mistake," Crassus said in a shaken voice. I looked over at him in some surprise; his distress seemed genuine. "I just didn't think about what it would be like to watch all those men burn to death." He turned to look at me, his eyes haunted and I fancied I could still see the dancing flames in them looking back at me. "It was just a means to an end," he explained. "And I didn't stop to think how horrible it would really be. I'm sorry I made the men see that, Pullus."

My irritation with Marcus Crassus dissolved and I do not know what moved me to do so, but I placed a hand on his shoulder, giving him an awkward pat.

"What's important, sir, is that you don't repeat the mistake," I told him.

"That's the thing," he sighed. "There might come a time when I actually have no other choice, and I don't know if I could do it."

"You could," I assured him, and I was sure that he could.

Changing the subject, Crassus said, "Let's go see what kind of trouble the 14th is in."

Reaching the spot where the wagons of the Bastarnae had been, another scene of devastation laid before us, with the hulks of burned wagons spread about, blackened earth in a circle around each one. Interspersed among them were the stripped bodies of those Bastarnae that had been caught in Silva's raid, most of them appearing to be women and children. I frowned at the sight of the bodies, stark white against the dark earth, except it was not in distress.

"Silva wouldn't have had time to loot and strip those bodies," I pointed out to Crassus, who had apparently not noticed.

"Maybe the 14th," he suggested.

Somehow, I doubted it, since they would have not had enough time to be so thorough. Looking around, I saw no immediate sign of the 14th, save for what looked like a Cohort, spread about on the far side of the Bastarnae camp, which extended almost a mile across. Pushing on, we could see the circles of the Bastarnae campfires, with the wheel ruts of their heavily loaded wagons beside each one, except there were precious few intact wagons. Most of those that remained looked like they had sustained some sort of damage from Silva's raid, and the majority of those were partially burned. A few had more bodies about them, also stripped naked. Drawing closer to where the men of the 14th were gathered, we could see a double line of men laid out in a row. At one end of one line a number of *medici* were bent over, each of them working on a man, while at the second, there were none. This informed both Crassus and me that the 14th had been in some sort of fight, and had taken casualties. Seeing us approach, a Centurion parted from the small group of Centurions and Optios that had been talking, giving us a salute. It was the Decimus Pilus Prior, who gave his report to Crassus.

"We came up on the Bastarnae just as their wagon train was leaving, and their rearguard put up a stiff fight," he said.

I frowned, not liking what I was hearing.

"This many dead from a skirmish?" I asked the Pilus Prior, who averted his gaze as he answered.

"I wouldn't call what just happened a skirmish, Prefect. There were a lot more Bastarnae warriors than we expected."

I thought there was an implied rebuke in his statement, but Crassus appeared unperturbed.

"How many?" he asked the Pilus Prior, who rubbed his forehead in thought.

"At least 4,000 foot, and at least 2,000 cavalry," he answered.

Crassus and I exchanged a glance. What we had thought was a total victory had in fact only been a partial one, since a significant number of Bastarnae had obviously stayed behind with the women and children. It also explained the relative lack of cavalry present during our ambush, while according to our scouts, there were still a fair number of enemy cavalry unaccounted for.

"Who stripped these bodies?" I asked the Pilus Prior.

"Not us," he confirmed my suspicions. "They were like that when we got here."

"They must have stripped their own dead," Crassus mused, looking about at the pale bodies before returning his attention to the Pilus Prior. "Where's the rest of the 14th now?"

"They've marched after the wagons, keeping the pressure on the Bastarnae."

"They should be easy to find," Crassus said, beckoning me to follow.

Moving at a quick trot, we followed the churned earth as it pointed to a low notch between two tree-covered hills. They were not high, just enough to block our view of what lay beyond, except there was a plume of dust that told us that some sort of movement was still taking place. Climbing the notch, we looked down onto a valley that widened out as it went farther away from our position. At the far end, we could just make out the tail end of the 14th, still marching in column, telling us that they had not encountered the Bastarnae. Breaking into a canter, we quickly closed the distance, catching the last of the 14th just as they were leaving the valley. The sloping shoulder of one of the hills had obstructed our view of the country beyond and once we maneuvered between the marching men and the hill, we finally saw where the Bastarnae were headed. About three miles distant was yet another hill, with steeply sloping sides, perched on top of which sat something that we could not immediately identify, but was clearly man-made. Because the ground sloped slightly downward all the way to the base of the far hill, we could see the situation laid out before us, and Crassus pulled up for a moment to study things. The vanguard of the 14th was less

215

than a half-mile behind a dark clump that I took to be the infantry rearguard, with the line of wagons moving slowly away from them. It was plain to see that the wagons were heading for this hilltop, the head of the column less than a half-mile from the base of the hill.

"How in Hades do they think they're going to get those wagons up there?" Crassus wondered, something I was thinking as well.

"There must be a road that leads up to the top that we can't see," was all I could think of.

Satisfied that he had seen enough, Crassus and I resumed our progress, now moving at the canter past the rest of the 14th. Reaching the First Cohort, we arrived in time to hear Primus Pilus Saenus give his *cornicen* the order to shake out into battle formation. Now that we had closed the distance, we could see that it had indeed been Bastarnae infantry we had seen, and we were close enough to see that they numbered perhaps a thousand strong. Certainly not enough to defeat the 14th, yet I do not believe that was their intent, and in that they were already being successful. All they had to do was to delay us long enough to allow the wagons to ascend that road, which I was sure existed even if we could not see it. Looking beyond the rearguard, I saw the head of the wagon column snaking around the base of the hill, almost out of sight. We were also close enough to see that what lay on top of the hill was a large fortification, with a number of stone buildings within. Unlike Naissus, these walls were made of stone, large blocks of native rock that looked well made and solidly put together, the buildings made of the same material. This would be a much tougher nut to crack than Naissus had been, at least from the perspective of breaching the fortifications. I wondered how the Bastarnae were going to squeeze all of their wagons inside the fortifications, but that was their problem, and I turned my attention back to our immediate difficulty. When each Cohort marched up, they were put into position, facing the Bastarnae warriors who stood waiting for our advance. Crassus took over from Saenus in directing the men where he wanted them, putting the Cohort into double

216

line. We outnumbered the rearguard by more than three to one, so I doubted that the men of the second line would even be called forward. However, I also knew that the Bastarnae were fighting for their families, or what remained of them. They were perhaps a third of their original numbers, but that was still well more than 200 wagons. The rest were lying on the ground a couple miles behind us, their bodies now stiff and cold. Seeing how close they had been to the relative safety of this hilltop fortress, I could imagine how anguished and frustrated they must have felt. Obviously, the decision had been made, probably by Deldo, that it was safer to stop just a few miles short for the night than try to risk moving in the dark. It was easy to second-guess that decision, given how things had turned out, yet I do not know I would have made a different one at the moment. I had nothing against the Bastarnae; I did not hate them the way I did the Parthians, or the Egyptians, for that matter, making it relatively easy for me to feel some sympathy for them, although it would not stop me from sticking my sword into their guts when the moment came. That is the essence of what it means to be a professional soldier, I think; killing someone you don't hate, or in fact have some admiration for, and doing it without hesitation. The sad fact is that men of my experience and longevity in the Legions had plenty of practice in killing men we respected, and in some cases even knew and liked, during the civil wars, so my feelings about the Bastarnae and their plight would not impede me in the slightest. Nor would it impede any of the men in Marcus Crassus' army, and I watched the 14th making themselves ready to launch their assault. They had not had time to replenish their supply of javelins, other than what men scrounged from the first battlefield, meaning there would be little chance to soften up the Bastarnae before going to the sword. However, Saenus had the men pass what javelins they had to the center of the front rank, in order to concentrate their fire.

"We're going to try and punch a hole in their middle, and push through it," he explained to Crassus and me, a move that

I heartily approved of, thinking that it was a wise husbanding of resources.

Crassus was not so sure, however, but he did not overrule Saenus, which pleased both of us.

"Time is our biggest enemy right now, Saenus," Crassus told the Primus Pilus. "We have to sweep this rearguard aside if we're going to have any chance of stopping those wagons from getting into that fort."

Looking over the heads of the Bastarnae to where the wagons were still plodding along, I could see that the first few wagons of the column had already disappeared around the back of the hill, so I felt sure that no matter how swift a victory, we would miss our chance, although I kept my thoughts to myself. Calling one of his couriers, who had accompanied us from the main body, Crassus gave him orders by wax tablet, sending for the rest of the army to march to this location. Now that we knew where the enemy was and what they were trying to do, Crassus sent me to retrieve the 8th, their grisly task presumably having been finished by this time. The sun was less than a hand's breadth away from the western horizon, meaning the men would have to hurry if they wanted to get here to make camp before it was completely dark. Without waiting to watch the 14th, I turned Ocelus to canter back in the direction from which we had come to recall the 8th and guide them back.

The 8th and I arrived just as the sun was setting, where I could immediately see two things; the 14th had brushed aside the Bastarnae with few casualties and, judging from Crassus' face, they had been too late to stop the wagons.

"We didn't get a single wagon," he fumed.

We were watching the men working on the camp, sited on almost the exact spot where they had formed up to attack the rearguard. Not knowing how long we would be in place, Crassus ordered a detail of the 8th to dig a mass grave to throw the dead Bastarnae of the rearguard in, and I was amused to see that Gaius' Seventh was part of that detail. Despite not having to dig himself, he would have to endure the moaning

218

and complaining of his men about the foul job, which aside from filling in latrine ditches is the worst duty a man can pull. The rest of the army arrived a short time later, minus a Cohort and Silva's cavalry left behind to guard the wounded. We were now five Cohorts short, minus the other casualties, of course, including the four that had been left behind at the main camp. A manpower shortage was not the only problem; all of the palisade stakes, our baggage, and our tents were back at the main camp, along with most of the pack animals, now separated from us by a distance of several miles. Most importantly, for our purposes, all of the artillery, with the exception of some scorpions we had brought along, along with the engineering tools were also back there. Without this equipment, we could not conduct a proper siege. The four Cohorts would not be enough men to pack all that equipment, even with the help of the slaves and orderlies that had been left behind. Diocles and the higher-ranking clerks, who doubled as medical orderlies in battle, were back with the wounded. In short, our army was scattered to Hades and back, and before we could think of conducting the serious business of dislodging the Bastarnae, we had to consolidate. To that end, Crassus called a command meeting to discuss the best way to make this happen.

"I think we'll be safe tonight with just a ditch between us and whatever's left of the Bastarnae," was Crassus' judgment.

I agreed, although I was not so sure about after that.

"Once they see that we don't have a proper camp they might be desperate enough to throw everything at us to try and inflict enough damage that we'll withdraw."

"Good," Crassus said belligerently, smacking a fist into his palm. "Then we can crush them once and for all."

"That's a big risk, especially given that we still don't know where the rest of their cavalry is," I pointed out, reminded of what had happened at Alesia, when enough of the Gallic cavalry had escaped to flee to the various tribes to organize a relief effort.

In fact, I was worried enough about the similarity that I felt compelled to remind everyone about that very thing. This had a sobering effect, at least on the Primi Pili, which in turn brought Crassus back down to earth from his dreams of total victory in one stroke.

"Very well," he said after a moment. "I see what you're saying, and I agree that the prudent course would be to send at least one Legion back to strike the camp and bring all of our gear back to our present location. The 15th will be the Legion to go back and retrieve everything."

With that decided, I felt compelled to ask, "What about Timonax, Scylax, and that bunch? What do you want to do about them?"

Crassus thought for a moment.

"Bring them along," he said finally. "I think they still have some use for us."

Watches were set, along with the watchword, and with that we retired to spend the night wrapped up in our cloaks, trying to get what sleep we could in the chilly night.

The 15th left shortly before dawn the next morning, and immediately after first light Crassus and the command group mounted our horses to conduct a thorough inspection of the hill. Keeping a safe distance from the ramparts of the fortress, we circled the base of the hill, stopping every furlong or so while sketches were made and notes taken. Once we were on the opposite side of the hill, we could see that there was indeed a roadway cut through the rock, circling up the hill to the gate, allowing the wagons entrance. However, there were a number of wagons, minus the livestock, which appeared to have been at least partially emptied, parked end to end in a row down the roadway.

"That answers the question of whether they have enough room," Crassus remarked.

I could only imagine how crowded it must be inside that fortress, thinking that this would be a factor in our favor when conducting the siege. In such cramped conditions it is almost a given that disease will strike, something I thought particularly likely to happen in this case, due to a curiosity of the fortress and its position.

"There's no river or stream," I observed as we were finishing our circuit. "So where do they get their water from?"

"There must be springs on that hill," Crassus mused, gazing up at the walls as if he could somehow see them.

"Even if there are, how do they get rid of their waste?" I pointed out. "And whatever springs there may be there, I'm willing to bet that they've never been tasked the way they will with that many people to support."

Obviously pleased at the idea, Crassus rubbed his hands together and smiled.

"That means this shouldn't take long," he enthused. "Now we just need to get the army back together."

"And find the rest of the Bastarnae cavalry," I reminded him, a prospect that did not please him nearly as much as the thought of the siege.

When we returned to our semi-completed camp, the engineers immediately began making their plans for the siege and assault, and the men were allowed to rest while they waited for the 15th and the baggage. Since they had been ordered to stop to pick up the wounded on the way back, they were not expected until close to sundown, meaning that the men would be constructing the rest of camp in the dark. That was a minor inconvenience; by this point, most of the men could have constructed a camp, even a fortified camp in the face of the enemy, in the dark. After midday, the men were roused to go fell the trees and dress them for use in the towers and other fortifications that would be needed for our stay. The 15th arrived almost exactly when they were expected, the work stopping so all the men could help with constructing the camp. The palisades were thrown up first, then the tents were erected, and finally the personal baggage was distributed. The wounded were unloaded from the wagons to be placed in the main hospital tent. The dead from the main battle had been burned, their ashes placed in their urns back at the battle site, that duty performed by the guard Cohort while blessed by the priests who had remained behind. In other words, everything moved with the speed and efficiency that makes the Roman army the most unique, and most feared in the world. With all

221

this done, the men finally had their first hot meal in two days, relaxing around their fires and talking about the battle and its aftermath. The next morning, the real work of the siege would start, so after I ate my evening meal I returned to the *Praetorium* to see what the plan was.

"We can't build a ramp because the sides of the hill are so steep that we'd have to dig out a significant portion of the slope to make it gradual enough to push a tower up to the wall," Crassus told us.

Although I had suspected as much, I was still unsure what approach would be best, since engineering is not my strong point.

"So we're going to undermine the walls. We're going to begin at two points, on opposite sides. Whichever makes the best progress after the first few days is the side we're going to concentrate on."

There was something about this that bothered me, yet before I could ask, Macrinus beat me to it.

"With a hill that high, won't it require us to tunnel a vertical shaft for a good distance?"

Rather than look upset with the question, Crassus beamed at Macrinus like he were a prized pupil reciting a passage correctly.

"That is a challenge, Macrinus, but Paperius has come up with what I think is a good solution."

He motioned to his engineering officer to take up the explanation. Paperius stood, looking self-conscious about being the focus of attention.

"We're going to dig our tunnel at an angle. It won't be equal to the slope of the hill, but it will be close, so that the vertical tunnel won't be much more than a man's height. That way when we make the cavity under the wall, the combustible materials can simply be handed up and won't have to be hauled up a ladder."

There were a number of details to discuss, taking the rest of the night before everyone was satisfied. Retiring for the night, my cot never felt so welcome, and it was not until I actually lay down that all the aches and pains finally hit me.

Perversely, I took this to be a good sign that I was almost healed, despite some bleeding from my side that matted my tunic to me. Even with the discomfort, I was asleep before I could form a conscious thought.

Siegework began immediately, starting the next morning with the emplacement of the artillery, positioned on two sides of the fort to cover the work of the men selected for digging. In accordance with the common practice, the mining working party was not rotated; tunneling through rock and shoring up the created passageway requires special skills, so only experienced men were used for these tasks. Carrying the spoil from the shaft was assigned on a rotating basis, however, while other men continued chopping down trees and dressing the timber for use as supports and such. The Bastarnae could do nothing except stand on their ramparts watching helplessly, like so many others had, while an army of Rome worked steadily and methodically, bent on their destruction. There were no cries of defiance, no shows of anything other than a sort of resignation on the part of the defenders, and the men soon began ignoring their onlookers as they worked. Under torture, Timonax revealed that the fortress had been one of the primary residences of Deldo, which accounted for its relatively large size and that, as Crassus had suspected, there was not just one, but three hidden springs supplying water to the garrison and people trapped inside. Timonax also provided information that Deldo had prepared the place for a protracted siege, with several stone buildings holding grain and other supplies, but he did not know how full they were at that moment. Once Crassus was convinced that he had gotten every piece of information from Timonax that he could, he ordered him and the other envoys executed. While I understood his decision, and in fact recognized that keeping them alive could prove to be a bigger mistake than killing them, there was still something about the whole affair that unsettled me. In effect, Crassus was taking the gamble that he would completely subdue the Bastarnae, when we did not really know that much about them. It was possible, in fact it was probable that most of the remaining Bastarnae were penned up in that fortress, yet there was still the question of the missing cavalry and what they were doing. Silva and our cavalry had only that morning been sent in search of them, but it might be days before he found them and could report back. That was nagging at me, because the only reason I could think of that would make the Bastarnae cavalry leave the immediate vicinity of the rest of their army, and more importantly their families, was that they were going for help.

Similarly to the siege of Naissus, there was not much for me to do except circulate among the men, watching them work. It was easier this time, the men having become used to my presence, and I was learning more about them. Perhaps it sounds strange, or even impossible that one could learn to separate any individuals out of a group of men as homogenous as an army, but I can assure that it is not only possible, it is absolutely essential for a leader to do so. I could not hope to know every man's name, but using a trick I learned from Gaius Crastinus, I learned the name of at least one man in every Century, making sure to use it when others were within earshot. This gave that man a sense of importance, enhancing his standing among his comrades, and giving them something to chatter about around the fire at night. In return, I got information about the state of the Legion, its morale, along with any pressing problems as far as supply or other areas where I could actually help. Once the men accepted me, they were more forthcoming, but I still kept a distance from them and was never too familiar. None of these Legions were mine in the way the 10th had been, so I did not have the excuse of dropping by the fire of an old friend who had been with me since our first days as *tiros*.

The men were working well, but the beginning of the mines took extra time because the Bastarnae were not content just to watch, requiring us to use mantlets and *plutei* to protect those selected for digging from archers, which they had hidden from us behind the parapet. They had held their fire for most of the morning, waiting until we thought they were either unwilling or unable to stop us from working, then fired several volleys of arrows that struck more than a dozen men. Fortunately, none of them were killed, although they would be out of action for varying amounts of time. Once the surprise was sprung on us, we set up artillery and put the mantlets and *plutei* in place, the work then progressing without incident. The going was tough, the miners quickly discovering that under a layer of about a foot of dirt there was nothing but hard rock under the surface. Although not completely unexpected, the toughness of the rock meant that Paperius had to revise his estimate of when the tunnel would be completed. For the next several days, progress was slow but steady with both tunnels. With the men hard at work, I took to riding around the countryside, usually with Scribonius and Balbus and the rest of the Evocati, ostensibly to serve as an early warning for any sign of approaching relief. The reality was that we were bored; without Legions, Cohorts, or Centuries to run, there was nothing challenging or motivating us. This was nothing new, having seen it happen to members of the Evocati before us, except most of them turned to drink as a way to pass the time. Scribonius and I were determined the same fate would not befall us; Balbus, on the other hand, was not as opposed to the idea of drinking himself insensible every day, but the pressure the two of us put on him kept him from doing so. He grumbled about it quite a bit, meaning that a good part of the time on those rides we had to endure listening to Balbus complain about what he was missing. Regardless, we accepted it as the price we had to pay to keep him from going down that path. The countryside was rolling, with thick stands of trees in between hills that were not particularly high, but generally had steep and rocky slopes. We tried to stay out of the valleys, because they are obvious ambush sites, yet while we came across the occasional village, with the people hiding at our approach, there was no real sign of enemy forces. There was also little sign of food to forage, but we did come back with the occasional pig or flock of goats, the people wailing at the prospect of a hard winter as they watched us ride away with the food that would sustain them. Otherwise, our forays were uneventful, until about a week after we began the siege when the weather turned, keeping us in camp. For several days straight, it rained for the better part of each day, filling the tunnels with water that had to be constantly bailed out, slowing the work even more. It seemed that every day Paperius was revising the schedule outward and it became apparent that if things continued in this manner, Crassus would be faced with a choice of whether to withdraw the army to march back to Pannonia for the winter, or spend it camped at the base of this stronghold. If he chose the latter, he would have to send for supplies. A train sufficiently large enough to support an army of this size, through the wild country that we had marched through, would provide a very tempting target for the neighboring tribes. The men clearly sensed this, so without any need for the *vitus* they stepped up their efforts, volunteering to work longer shifts. I suppose it could be argued that they were scared that they would be stuck here for the winter, but whatever their reasoning, it was much appreciated by Crassus. To show that appreciation, he held a formation where he announced that out of his own funds, he would pay the men a bonus of 300 sesterces for the capture of this fortress before winter. This quite naturally spurred them to greater efforts, rising earlier and working later, yet it seemed as if the gods were conspiring with the elements to keep them from accomplishing their goal.

Another week passed with horrible weather, reminding me of that dreadful campaign in Gaul, the only time that Caesar was forced to turn back because of the elements. The memory of that ordeal caused Scribonius, Balbus, and me to speculate about what would happen if the tents began to give way like they had back then. The only difference was that it was not as cold, but being wet and miserable is only marginally better than being cold, wet, and miserable. It was at the end of the second week that a courier arrived from Silva, and the way that he came pounding up the churned mud that had become the Via Praetoria told us that something important was taking place. Diocles was loitering around the *Praetorium*; now that he no longer had the same level of duties that he had as the chief clerk of the Legion he had more free time, which I had him spend cultivating relationships with the current set of clerks in the *Praetorium*. It helped that he was, and is, very friendly and easy to get along with, becoming a natural confidante and unofficial advisor to the younger clerks as he basked in the reflected glow of my position in the army. That day, he came to tell me about the courier, his urgency obvious when he entered my quarters. Balbus was taking a nap, so Scribonius and I hurried to find out what was happening. My stomach churned thinking of the reasons Silva could send an urgent message back to Crassus, and none of them were good.

"Do you think they found a relief column?" Scribonius voiced my worst fear.

"I hope not, but I can't imagine why else he would send someone in this weather," I replied as we paused to try and wipe the mud from our feet, an almost impossible task.

We entered to find Crassus and the Tribunes gathered around the mud-spattered courier, who was clearly exhausted. Crassus was reading from the wax tablet that the courier had brought and I examined his face carefully, looking for clues about what the message contained. He was frowning, but not in a way that would suggest to me that the news was especially grim; it was more a thoughtful look that creased his face. Seeing me approach, Crassus walked to meet me, followed by the Tribunes, reminding me of a mother duck trailed by her ducklings. Waving the tablet, he handed it to me without a word. It took me a moment to decipher the scrawl that I recognized as Silva's, but once I did, I felt what was probably a frown remarkably similar to Crassus pull the corners of my mouth down. I looked to Crassus, not sure what to make of the message, yet he seemed as puzzled as I was.

"Why would the Getae be marching in our direction?"

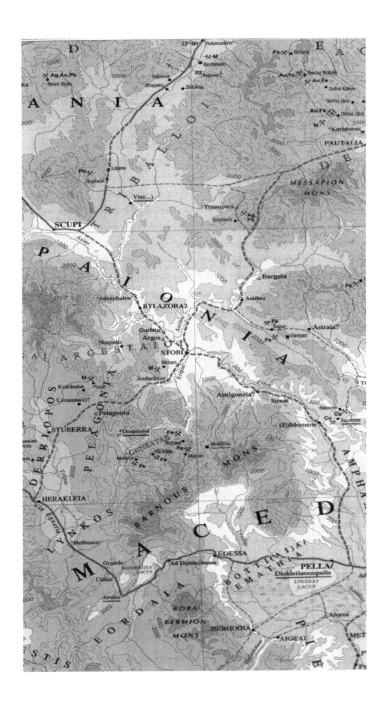

228

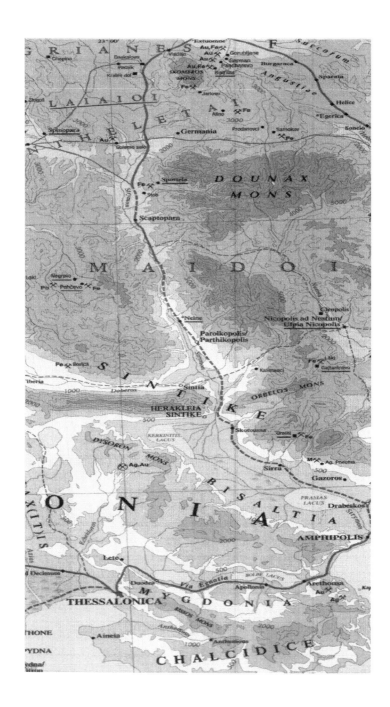

229

Chapter 5- The Getae

News as potentially important and damaging as this is impossible to keep secret, so the talk around the tents that night consisted of little else. With no way at that point to know the intentions of the Getae, the speculation was rampant, and it was not confined to the rankers. We stayed up late into the night, Scribonius, Balbus, and I, talking over the possible meanings, with nothing we came up with boding well for us. Our biggest fear was that they were answering a Bastarnae call for help; only slightly less troubling was Balbus' suggestion that they were acting on their own, taking advantage of the Bastarnae weakness to seize their land. The Getae occupy the lands to the northeast of the lower branch of the Cedrus, all the way to the Euxine Sea. We Romans had fought the Getae before, first during the Mithradatic Wars, where Marcus Terentius Lucullus had led an army against them as punishment for their alliance with Mithridates. This happened shortly after I had been born, and it was several years later that an allied force of Bastarnae, Getae, and Scythians defeated Antonius Hybrida at the Battle of Histria, led by Burebista, who briefly ruled both the Getae and Dacians. Knowing all that, it did not take much imagination to guess that whatever they were doing, it spelled no good for us, and it was with this gloomy thought that we finally retired for the night. The next morning, I was summoned to the *Praetorium*, where Crassus was waiting. Skipping the usual pleasantries, he came right to the point.

"You and I are going to find out what these Getae are up to," he said. Seeing my alarmed look, he hastily added, "Not alone, of course. We're going to take the Evocati and meet up with Silva. I'm going to parley with the Getae and see what it is they want."

Seeing how Silva had given the estimate of the Getae numbers at 10,000, with 8,000 foot and the remainder cavalry, I was not sure what less than a hundred men, even when added to Silva's 500, were going to accomplish in the way of deterring the Getae from swallowing us up. But Crassus was clearly set on this course, so all I could do was salute and go to let the Evocati know that we were heading on what looked like a suicide mission. We rode out of the camp not much later, the Evocati, Crassus, and grudgingly, Tribune Claudius. Seeing my raised eyebrow as the Tribune came trotting up to join us, Crassus quietly explained.

"He can do less damage with us than if we leave him here. Unfortunately, he's the ranking Tribune, and I don't trust him not to do something stupid like he did at the ambush."

I made no attempt to hide my surprise, since I had not mentioned a word of our incident to Crassus, but he just smiled and tapped a finger to the side of his nose, giving me a wink. It had not started raining, though the skies were low and threatening and we had gone less than five miles when they opened up, dumping what felt like buckets of water on us. Pulling out our *sagum* we continued, the courier who had brought the message as our guide. Despite the weather, Crassus set a fast pace, making it shortly before dark when we arrived at Silva's camp. It was my first time in all of my years sharing a camp with a cavalry patrol, and I have to say that I was more than a little surprised at how much of a rougher camp they made than the Legions. Their tents were little better than half-shelters, with open sides that did nothing to keep the rain out if it were anything but vertical. They did not fortify in the same manner as the Legions, the tradeoff being that more men were on watch, counting on their mobility to get away in the event of a surprise attack. All told, it was a rather dreary place, and my respect for the cavalry went up a notch once I saw what life on the march away from the army was like for them. Silva met us at his *Praetorium*, which was the only proper tent in the whole camp, but it was much smaller than even a Centurion's tent. That meant that only a few of us could crowd into it, leaving the others outside in their misery to find whatever shelter they could. Meanwhile, Silva gave his full report to Crassus and me.

"The Getae are about five miles east of here, and they're heading directly for the stronghold. They're led by their king Roles, and it appears that they're coming to help the Bastarnae.

We captured one of their couriers trying to slip past us, and he told us about a treaty of friendship between the two."

"So we've brought down on our heads all of the Bastarnae and the Getae together." Crassus made no attempt to hide his worry, rubbing his head while he paced.

Silva had another piece of information, however.

"Based on what we learned from the prisoner, sir, I don't think that's necessarily true. According to the prisoner, the Bastarnae that we're engaged with are just a branch of the tribe that's chosen to go its own way. Apparently, their chief Deldo made an attempt to seize power of their tribal council, but was blocked in some way. That's why they were heading south, to find new lands farther away so they didn't have to worry about reprisals from the other branches of the Bastarnae."

"That means that it's very unlikely that any other Bastarnae will come to their aid." Crassus was visibly relieved, but it was short-lived.

"Why would the Getae be coming to help a disgraced branch of the Bastarnae?" I asked.

That sobered everyone, and finally Crassus said, "That's a good question. So tomorrow, we're going to go ask this King Roles that very thing."

Under skies the color of sling bullets, we approached the Getae under a flag of truce. Riding in the disorganized mass typical of the barbarian tribes, the Getae vanguard saw where we had positioned ourselves on the crest of a small hill and were waiting for them. Churning to a halt at the sight of us, a small group of riders detached themselves from the mob to trot out to meet us. Silva and I, along with a dozen troopers, descended the hill, meeting the Getae at the base, since it is not customary for the leader of each delegation to be present at the first meeting, or at least so I was told. Surely enough, the Getae selected to be spokesman was not Roles, but a sub-chief named Gundioc, who seemed surprised when I addressed him in Greek.

"I bring greetings from Marcus Licinius Crassus, Proconsular Legate of the Army of Pannonia of the Senate and People of Rome," I began, but he was clearly not impressed.

"I know who your general is, Roman." His tone was brusque, angering me a bit before I realized that this was his likely aim.

"Good." I forced myself to be genial. "Then your king will know that it is in the best interests of his people to have a parley with him before something happens that cannot be undone."

"Like the destruction of your army?" He smiled as he said it, like it was a joke, yet there was no mistaking that he believed this was in the realm of possibility.

"The number of nations that have tried to defeat Rome is long," I replied coolly. "But we still rule most of the known world."

"Not this part of the world," he retorted. "Besides, I believe the Parthians were successful in defeating Rome."

"That is true," I conceded, realizing that the situation was slipping from my grasp. "But you are not Parthian. And if you are so sure that you can destroy us, then surely you can do it tomorrow as easily as today. It won't hurt to talk, will it?"

The Getae threw back his head to roar with laughter, making Ocelus start from the sound.

"I like you, Roman. It will be a shame to kill you," he said, wiping his eyes. Turning serious, he replied, "I will speak to our king. You can either return to your people on the hill, or wait here. It makes no difference to me."

"We'll wait," I said, and we did, watching him return to the Getae.

The rain started again, forcing us to pull out our *sagum* and put them on, worrying me slightly, since it is almost impossible to fight while wearing one. I did not think there was treachery afoot, but there was no way to tell until it happened. Fortunately, the delay was not long, Gundioc returning with the news that the king Roles would meet with Marcus Crassus. The next matter was deciding where the meeting was to be held, engendering more trips back and forth before it was determined that the hill on which Crassus and the rest now sat would be suitable, but only after we vacated it. It was also agreed that each force would be on the opposite sides of the hill where they could watch the two men talk yet still be in a position to come to their aid if either side had treachery in mind. Finally, it was decided that it would only be Crassus and Roles on the hill, while the rest of us would wait. With everything settled, I rode back up the hill, told Crassus what we had agreed before joining the rest as we rode down the opposite side while Crassus waited for Roles.

I have seen many parleys like the one that took place on that hill. However, never have I seen the results swing so dramatically in our favor than I did that day. Crassus and Roles talked for almost two watches; at times it was clearly heated, at other times things seemed to be jovial. It was growing dark when Crassus and Roles suddenly clasped hands, then kissed each other on both cheeks before remounting their horses. Crassus trotted down the hill and when he drew closer, we could see a wide smile creasing his face. When he reached us, without saying anything, he signaled for us to leave the area at a trot. I fell in beside him, intensely curious but unwilling to be the first to speak. Finally, I could stand it no longer.

"Well?" I demanded. "You look like the cat who got into the cream."

He laughed, clearly pleased that he had forced me to ask.

"They were indeed coming to help the Bastarnae. The Getae have had a treaty put in place by Roles' grandfather to offer mutual assistance if they're attacked. But I instantly saw that Roles' heart wasn't in it, so I changed the subject and we talked of other matters."

"Other matters?" I could not think of what else could possibly interest either man when they faced the prospect of fighting each other. "What other matters?"

"Oh, how much he admires Rome, and has always wanted to visit it."

He shot me a sidelong glance, gauging me to see if I could guess where this was headed. I thought I did.

"So you dangled a free trip to Rome in front of him and he snapped at it?"

I shook my head; that seemed to be too good to be true, and an awfully cheap price to turn the Getae home.

"It's a little more complicated than that," he admitted, and I thought, here it comes, but I was not prepared for what was coming. "The Getae are coming back with us to the fortress, just like they promised they would by treaty. But they're now working for us."

I looked at him in astonishment.

"What did that cost us?"

He gave a shrug, as if it were no matter.

"The Getae will be named Friend and Ally of Rome." He threw this out offhandedly, making it sound like conferring such status was of no moment, or consequence.

Now I stared at him in open disbelief.

"Doesn't that have to be approved by the Senate?" I asked cautiously, despite knowing very well that this was the case, although it is no longer.

"Formally perhaps, but I have Proconsular authority," he replied, his tone now stiff.

He knows that he's sticking his neck out, I thought, so I let the matter drop to move to something else.

"You said the Getae are working for us. What does that mean exactly?"

He hesitated for a moment, then said, "That hasn't been worked out in detail yet, but we're meeting tomorrow to work everything out."

We returned to the makeshift camp, where for once I was thankful that my rank allowed me to share space in Silva's *Praetorium* out of the rain, even if it did not make me popular with Scribonius and Balbus. They spent the night huddled together under one *sagum* while wrapped up in another, and were in a very foul mood the next morning. The weather finally broke shortly after dawn, but the ground of the camp was a sea of mud, and the trees continued to drip water. We returned to the hill, where Roles and Crassus met again to work out the details of what form the aid the Getae would give us would take. Fortunately, this did not take nearly as long, the two men once again clasping hands and embracing around mid-morning.

When Crassus rejoined us, he cried, "We've found our Ulysses!"

On the way back, Crassus explained what Roles had agreed to do for us.

"They're going to the fortress, which the Bastarnae are expecting. But once they're allowed in, they're going to seize control of the gate and signal us when they do."

On the surface that sounded fine, but it had one huge and fatal flaw as far as I could see, and I asked Crassus, "And what about us? Are we just supposed to stand by and watch the Getae march up and not do anything about it? That will arouse suspicion immediately."

"You're right," he acknowledged, "which is why we're withdrawing."

"Withdrawing?"

"Once we get close to the fortress, we're going to go to the gallop, like Cerberus himself is chasing us. We're going to go into camp and we're going to break everything down as far as the camp goes, but we're going to abandon all of our tools and the heavy gear, making it seem like we're in a panic to leave. Shortly after we reach the camp, Roles is sending a rider to the fortress to let the Bastarnae know that the Getae are coming shortly. That should explain why we're in such a hurry to leave. After all, between the Getae and the Bastarnae there, we'll be outnumbered."

"Not by much," I pointed out, still not convinced that the Bastarnae would be fooled.

"That's true. Which is why the Getae courier is also going to let it slip that there's another Bastarnae column approaching but is still two or three days away."

Again, on the surface this sounded good, except I remembered what Crassus had related about the strained relations between this branch of the Bastarnae and the rest of the tribe, which I mentioned now.

"That's true," he admitted. "But these people are desperate, and desperate people will believe anything if it means they'll survive. That's what I'm counting on."

It seemed a flimsy thing to rest one's hopes on, except that things had been going Crassus' way, so I decided to wait and see what happened. We drew up just out of sight of the fortress to let the horses rest before we began our part of the plan.

"Remember," Crassus called to all of the gathered Evocati. "The men can't know this is just a ruse. They need to believe that we have to pack up and get out of here as quickly as possible to avoid alerting the Bastarnae that something is going on."

With that last warning, he spurred his horse, beginning the run to our camp. We galloped up and over the hill that led down into the valley surrounding the fortress, whipping our mounts as if we were being hotly pursued. Ocelus' hooves churned up the muddy ground, making sucking sounds that were clearly audible above the shrieking wind, and I gave up trying to dodge the globs that came from the heels of Crassus' mount. I was just happy that I was near the front, but by the time we came pounding up to the camp, skidding to a halt and spraying muddy water everywhere just outside the ramparts of the camp, I was fairly covered in muck. Despite knowing our identities, the duty Centurion still went through the formality of challenging, then asking for the watchword, which Crassus provided without irritation. Charging into the camp and pounding up the Via Praetoria, I dismissed the Evocati to attend to their own packing, while Crassus and I continued to the *Praetorium*. The *bucina* sounded the assembly for all senior Centurions moments later, who did not dawdle, the word of our hurried entrance being too much to keep secret. As soon as all the Primi Pili and Pili Priores arrived and assembled in the forum, Crassus wasted no time.

"A large force of Getae are headed this way, and will be here no later than midday tomorrow. They're coming in

237

response to a plea for help by the Bastarnae," he announced breathlessly, his tone urgent but composed. He waited a moment for the buzz of talk to die down before continuing. "Between their forces and those that are in the fortress, the numbers don't favor us, particularly if, as we believe, other branches of the Bastarnae are coming to help as the Getae are. While we haven't seen any sign of any Bastarnae, it would be foolish to presume that they're not coming. That's why we're breaking camp. I want the army ready to march immediately."

Exactly as Crassus had predicted earlier, this caused an uproar, the Centurions all beginning to talk at once, shouting questions to Crassus.

"What about the artillery?"

"Are we taking the heavy gear?"

"Are we just abandoning the tunnels?"

Crassus held his hands up for silence, but it took several moments before the Primi Pili got control.

"We'll take the artillery, but everything else must be left behind," he told them. "Now I need you to go attend to your duties. I know I can depend on you to get the men ready."

Without waiting for any more questions, he turned on his heel, returning to the *Praetorium*, while I went to my own tent. Diocles had already been told and was working with the other slaves to break everything down and pack up. Scribonius, Balbus, and I did little more than stand watching the camp being broken down quickly and efficiently. The word that the Getae were coming had instantly circulated through the camp, meaning that the Centurions did not need to use the *vitus* to hurry the men along. It may not have been the fastest I ever saw an army break camp, but it was certainly among the fastest, so there was still a fair amount of daylight left when we began the march. Due to the weather, it was impossible to fire the towers and other wooden structures that had been built, which actually was a good thing, since Crassus had no real intention of destroying anything, knowing that we would be returning. He was absolutely convinced that Roles was being true with him, despite my strong reservations, having had enough experience with barbarian treachery to know that

238

nothing was certain until it happened the way it had been promised. However, I did not voice my concerns, preferring to wait and see if he was right in his judgment of Roles. I looked back to see the Bastarnae lining the ramparts, and while we weren't close enough to see their expressions, I could easily imagine their elation at seeing us march away. Only time would tell if they were fooled in the manner Crassus had hoped.

Once safely out of sight, Crassus called a halt to hold another meeting of the senior Centurions to let them know what was really going on. Their reaction seemed to be equal parts irritation at the subterfuge and relief for the reason behind it. Since it was almost dark, Crassus had to make a decision about what to do as far as camp, and he ordered that the men would have to endure a night in the open while we waited for Roles to make his appearance. The men were allowed to settle down in place, making themselves as comfortable as possible, wrapping up in their *sagum* to ward off the chill. Once it got dark, Silva was sent with a small detachment back to watch for Roles, while the rest of the army waited. Fortunately, the rain had stopped, our luck holding for the entire night, making it only slightly less miserable.

When dawn came, the skies were still gray and low, but it remained dry. The men chewed on cold breakfasts, eating what bread or lumps of bacon they had left over from the evening meal. Sitting on their packs, they passed the time talking quietly, the topic exclusively on the news of the subterfuge of which we were waiting to see the results, the moments dragging by. The sun finally made an appearance, causing the soaked ground to emit steam, compounding the misery since it felt like one was in the baths, except fully clothed. We all found ourselves glancing at the sun much more frequently than normal, yet still no word came from Silva. Tempers grew short, men beginning to snap at each other when one asked a question or made a complaint about the waiting, while even Crassus started showing his nerves by incessantly drumming his fingers on the front of his saddle.

"I really wish he'd stop doing that," Balbus muttered. "It's driving me crazy."

"Just like your incessant humming does to me," Scribonius said sourly.

Before a quarrel broke out, I slipped Ocelus between the two.

"Enough," I said. "None of this is helping."

It was shortly before midday when someone cried out that they heard the sound of hoof beats, causing us all to listen intently, but after a moment, there were a number of curses thrown at the man who had shouted the warning, sure that he was hearing things. Just a moment later, he was proven right when a rider came galloping over the crest of the hill, flinging mud in all directions as he did not spare his horse. Thankfully remembering to pull to a stop short of where we were gathered to avoid showering us with muddy water, the man trotted up, his face flushed from the excitement of his ride.

"The Getae have arrived, but the Bastarnae are refusing them entry! The Getae king is talking to the Bastarnae now!"

Obviously dismayed at this development, Crassus managed to maintain his composure.

"Very well. Go back and keep me apprised of what's happening."

The rider was not even out of sight when he was passed by yet another courier, heading back toward us. He was not as mindful as his counterpart and when he pulled his mount to a stop, mud was flung in every direction, sending a round of curses the man's way. The rider, a youngster about Gaius' age, blushed furiously and seemed to have forgotten what he had been sent for as he apologized profusely to all of us.

"Never mind that," Crassus snapped. "What news?"

"Oh," the boy gulped, his mouth opening and closing while he tried desperately to remember what he had been sent for. "Oh yes, sir," he said finally. "The Getae king convinced the Bastarnae to let them in. They're entering the fortress right now!"

Crassus wasted no time, turning to shout orders to the Centurions. We had decided not to use the *bucina* to signal, not

240

wanting the sound carrying to alert the Bastarnae that we were still in the area, making for a bit of scrambling getting the men on their feet, ready to march. Once formed up, Crassus wasted no time, immediately taking the lead while motioning for the Evocati to fall in with him, whereupon we began the short march back to the fortress. Ocelus clearly sensed the nervousness, not only in the air but from his rider, skipping nervously along, his ears twitching and head tossing. I was preparing myself for the possibility that this was a trap, one that seemed to grow to more of a certainty in my mind with every passing step. By the time we crested the last hill and the fortress was in view, I was convinced that we would be met with a hail of missiles, and I began mentally planning the best way to escape as we passed the remains of the camp. The towers were still intact, along with the ditches, although the stakes of the rampart had been pulled up and were with us. Silva came galloping up from his position on the far side where he had been watching the gate, a broad grin on his face, making me feel somewhat better. I had come to regard Silva as one of the best cavalry commanders I had ever served with, and seeing him convinced that all was well made me feel somewhat better.

"The Getae hold the gate and are fighting their way deeper into the fortress. Roles sent a courier to inform you that he's upheld his end of the bargain."

Crassus drew his sword, waving it over his head, the signal to his *cornicen* to sound the advance, then without waiting, began trotting in the direction of the gate.

"I hope this isn't some sort of trap," Scribonius commented, but when I turned Ocelus to follow Crassus, he did the same, with a resigned shrug.

Fortunately, there was no trickery. When we approached the gate, Roles was waiting there, his sword sheathed, a broad grin on his face. There were still a number of Bastarnae bodies heaped around the gate, and when I looked upward, I could see more dead slumped over the parapet, arrows protruding from their backs.

"Marcus Crassus, I present to you this fortress, as part of our agreement." Roles' Greek was excellent, despite having a peculiar accent that I could not place.

He bowed to Crassus, who returned the bow with a nod of his own, then asked Roles, "Is the entire fortress taken?"

Roles shrugged as if it were not important.

"Not yet," he admitted. "But it will be, soon."

I had been listening to the sounds coming from inside the walls and while it was impossible to tell who was winning, what was apparent was that the fighting was fierce.

Crassus obviously sensed the same thing, because he turned to Roles, saying politely, "It sounds like your men are handling things well. I would like to offer one of my Legions to assist in helping to provide security."

Roles' brow furrowed, clearly not liking this offer.

"As you say, Marcus Crassus, my men are handling things. There is no need for any assistance, but I thank you for your kindness."

"If you would allow my men to secure the part of the fortress you've already taken and take care of stragglers, that would free more of your men to continue the fight," Crassus pointed out, which was perfectly reasonable and it was impossible for Roles to argue that.

"All right," he replied grudgingly, giving a wave of his hand to indicate that he no longer cared.

Crassus turned to give a quiet order to Cornelius.

"Bring the 8th up and into the fort."

Cornelius wheeled and trotted off. A few moments later, the men of the 8th came pounding up with Cornelius and Macrianus at their head. Roles stepped aside to let our men through, and they went charging past the gate, with Macrianus pointing in either direction from the entrance. I suspected that Crassus had other plans for the 8th than just securing the perimeter, and he motioned to me to follow him while he rode inside the gate with Roles at his side. Curious about what was going to happen, I followed closely behind. Despite being unable to hear what Crassus said to Roles, I saw the Getae king stiffen in his saddle, but he refused to look at

Crassus as we entered the fort, picking our way past the sprawled bodies of the Bastarnae defenders. Ocelus shied at the scent of blood hanging thick in the air, but I managed to control him as we got our first look inside the walls. This fortress was a town in everything but name, with several dozen buildings, most of them stoutly built of native stone, heavy logs, or a combination of both. The layout was anything but organized; at a glance one could tell that these structures were added haphazardly, creating dead ends and blind alleys, making the place a nightmare to take. I could see bunches of Getae rushing about, with no organization and seemingly more intent on looting those buildings nearest the gate. That was all Crassus needed to see and he leaned over, giving Macrianus a quiet order, whereupon the Primus Pilus began directing his Cohorts forward. I gave Roles a sidelong glance and I saw his jaw set, but to my surprise, he did not object. I supposed that he saw as plainly as we did that if we were to rely on his men to defeat the Bastarnae, we would be waiting quite a while. Catching a glimpse of the Seventh, I saw Gaius with his Century moving quickly up what appeared to be a blind alley and I tried to keep my concern from showing, because I could feel Scribonius watching me from his spot just behind. Crassus began chatting with Roles and slowly the Getae king relaxed, even giving a chuckle at something Crassus said. After a moment, I heard the distinctive sounds of a Roman Legion fighting; the *cornu* calls, the blasts of whistles sounding a relief, along with the shouting in my native tongue that told me that the 8th had engaged with the Bastarnae. With nothing to do but wait, I occupied myself by walking Ocelus along the inside of the wall to watch our men push deeper into the fortress until they made a turn that took them out of sight. From all appearances, the 8th was having little problem, and it was not long before Cornelius sent back word that most of the fortress had been seized, with one last pocket of Bastarnae, including their women and children, surrounded and trapped inside two buildings.

"Let's go take a look," Crassus suggested.

I went with him and Roles, following Cornelius through a seeming maze of small passageways that passed for streets. Nothing was paved, and the rains of the last several days had turned each street and alley into a river of mud. Partially submerged in this mess were the bodies of the Bastarnae who had been cut down, then had the added indignity of being trampled into the mud by the feet of Macrianus' Legionaries continuing their advance. Not all of the Bastarnae were dead, and when one of them moved, seemingly rising from the muddy street like some *numen*, it startled all of our horses. Ocelus reared; I barely managed to grab a handful of mane before I would have been thrown down to join the unfortunate Bastarnae. The horses plunged and bucked, each of us struggling to control our mounts with varying degrees of success, while the Bastarnae who caused all the commotion writhed and moaned. I heard a sodden splashing sound, and turned to see one of the Evocatus struggling to pull himself up out of the mud, where he had landed on top of a Bastarnae body. The impact apparently brought the defeated Bastarnae back to life and, like his comrade, he suddenly jerked, raising one mud-covered arm up out of the filth as if trying to pull the Evocatus back down to the underworld. Giving a frightened shout, the Evocatus leapt to his feet, his entire backside covered in mud, pulling his sword as he did so. I returned my attention back to keeping my own seat and not joining him, so I did not see him thrust his blade into the body of the Bastarnae, but I heard the shriek as the man's life ended. Several moments passed before our animals were calmed enough to continue. Passing the original Bastarnae who had caused the commotion, Balbus leaned over from his saddle, stabbing the man in the chest, even as he held his arms up in the air, clearly beseeching our mercy.

"That's for scaring our horses," Balbus spat, wiping his mud-and-blood encrusted sword clean on an edge of his tunic.

We reached the place where the Bastarnae were making their last stand to find the Getae mixed with our own men, with the Centurions trying to get the men in some sort of formation surrounding the two buildings. This was clearly

244

difficult because the Getae seemed to insist on choosing a Legionary for his particular new best friend, offering our men skins or jugs of plundered wine. Naturally, our men did not want to be rude, except that it made getting them in hand extremely difficult and it was only after some liberal use of the *vitus* that saw the men settle down and the Getae separated. Roles directed his sub-chiefs to call the men of their various bands together, and it was in this manner that matters became less confused, or at least clear enough to allow Crassus to take stock of the situation. While it was true that the Bastarnae were in two separate buildings, they were separate in name only, because a completely enclosed walkway bridged the two buildings. These buildings were clearly built for defense, while I surmised that they had been chosen for the purpose of a last stand because that is essentially what they had been designed for. From one of the Bastarnae captives we learned that these buildings were a combination armory, warehouse, and headquarters. Made of rock and built at least two levels high, it was almost windowless, although there were arrow slits cut into the rock at regularly spaced intervals. Through those slits, the occasional arrow would come flying whenever someone came too close or exposed themselves in some way. It was clear that the Bastarnae were conserving ammunition, since we were well within range, but it also told me that whoever was commanding them was wise enough to know that we would quickly form testudo should they attempt any volley fire. Those windows that were present were all shuttered, as would be expected, but occasionally we could see one crack open, a face peering out for a moment before shutting it again. It would be an extremely hard building to fire, the only flammable portion of the building the roof, which was made of wooden planks. The problem was that the continuous rain had soaked the wood, meaning it would take a great deal of effort to get it to burn. There was a set of double doors, almost as wide as the gate into the fortress itself, set into one end of the larger building, which I assumed to be the armory and warehouse. That was obviously the most logical way in, should Crassus not want to waste time, but it would be a bloody assault. Despite the streets, such as they were, being wide enough to allow the scorpions, I doubted that the *ballistae* would be able to be used, meaning that a battering ram had to be devised. Crassus examined the buildings for several moments before shaking his head, clearly coming to the same conclusion that I had. Turning to Roles, he and the Getae king had a quiet conference before Crassus turned to summon his command group.

Once we had gathered, Crassus said, "The king has graciously offered his men for the assault of the buildings, and I'm inclined to give the Getae the honor of finishing this."

I for one did not know just how much of an honor it would be, but I supposed if he wanted to lose a lot of men, that was his business, so I had no objection.

"However, Roles has one condition." Crassus' words intruded into my thoughts, and the tone of his voice put me on guard. "He believes that since his men are bearing the brunt of the assault, they should reap the rewards."

This was fair enough, although Legionaries don't particularly care about fairness, their Centurions no exception, and I could see that this was not something they appreciated, even while none of them made any overt objection. Hearing silence and taking it for assent, Crassus continued, this time his voice more hesitant.

"And he believes that the proceeds from the sale of any slaves should also go to the Getae."

This was too much for the Centurions to take. They immediately spoke up then, their voices competing with each other as they gave their objections. I had to keep a straight face, since I found it amusing that the Centurions were willing to remain silent over the looting of the fortress, which most benefited the men, yet were not so willing about the sale of slaves, which would be their major source of income from this campaign. Hearing the outcry, Crassus turned to Roles, giving what I assumed was a helpless shrug, as if to say "It's out of my hands," and it appeared to work, because Roles looked nervously over at the angry Centurions.

Muttering something to Crassus, he jerked his horse about, cantering off to talk to his own people, leaving Crassus to tell the Centurions, "The king has graciously withdrawn his request about the slaves."

Giving me a wink, he ordered Macrianus to march the men of the 8th out of the fortress to join the rest of the army still gathered outside.

"We'll stay and observe the Getae taking the buildings," Crassus told the Evocati and Tribunes, so we dismounted to find anything suitable to take a seat and watch the action, the wagering beginning almost immediately.

As I had feared, it was a bloody affair, made needlessly more so because the Getae really had no idea of the best way to storm a fortified position of this nature. Roles seemed content to send his men in carrying axes, with little protection from the fire from the adjoining building, so that one Getae after another either fell or staggered away with the feathered shaft of at least one arrow protruding from some part of their body. His idea of achieving some sort of tactical surprise seemed based on the idea of sending men not just to the double doors, but to a number of the shuttered windows, and predictably, these were breached first. Just as predictably, men trying to clamber through a relatively narrow passageway, coming from the bright light of day into the gloom of a darkened building, made for very tempting targets, the cries of victory quickly becoming shouts of fear and panic when men were cut down as fast as they could climb through. For our part, we just sat watching the Getae getting slaughtered, and I kept my eye on Crassus, waiting to see him get impatient and send for one of the Legions. However, he kept his own eye on Roles, who did not seem in the least perturbed at the sight of so many of his men being cut down, and therefore said nothing.

Finally, after what seemed like a full day, the Getae finally broke down the door, then climbing over the pile of their comrades' bodies, went storming into the building. We could hear the screaming begin, the sounds of men gone mad with bloodlust taking out their rage and frustration on anyone they found in their way. The slaughter continued into the night, with the Getae fighting through both buildings while the comrades who could not fit inside continued their pillaging of the other parts of the fortress. Men were staggering drunk, many of them carrying screaming women over their shoulders, laughing and boasting to their friends about what they were going to do with their prize. In short, it was almost exactly the same sight as one expected to see when a Roman Legion sacked a town, proving that fighting men everywhere are essentially the same.

I had long since grown bored of watching the spectacle, obtaining leave from Crassus to go out of the fortress and return to the camp, which had been resurrected on the same spot. My tent was waiting, as was Diocles, with a jug of wine and loaf of bread, and Scribonius, Balbus and I shared it, along with some cheese and bacon, chatting about what we had seen. We were still chatting when a runner came from the *Praetorium*, demanding my presence immediately. Scribonius gave me a quizzical look, and I just shrugged.

"He probably wants to discuss how we're going to handle the prisoners," I told him, then left to meet with Crassus.

I found him in his office, pacing back and forth, clearly spitting angry. Without waiting, he launched into a tirade that left me rocking on my heels as I listened.

"Do you know what that faithless bastard Roles did?" Before I could answer, he continued, "I'll tell you what he did. He put everyone in that fortress to the sword! There will be no slaves for sale because he killed them all! Can you believe that?"

In fact, I could absolutely believe it, but I knew that at that moment Marcus Crassus did not want me saying anything other than, "No, sir. I can't believe it," and that is exactly what I said.

He did not acknowledge me; I am not sure he even heard as he continued to stalk back and forth like the caged lions I had seen in Cleopatra's zoo in Alexandria.

"He's put me in a damnably awkward spot. Do you think the Centurions are going to care about the fact that he killed the prisoners so there's no money for them? No," he raved, still answering his own questions. "No, they won't. They'll blame me for not watching and making sure that he didn't do anything so underhanded."

That much was true and I could see why it concerned him, but I also did not believe that they would be as angry with him as he thought. It helped that he was liked by men of all ranks in the army, while the more levelheaded of the Centurions would realize that there was no real way he could have controlled Roles. What was important to me was what he was going to do to Roles about it, and that is what I asked him.

"Nothing," he said bitterly. Seeing that I was about to object, he held up a placating hand. "Pullus, there's really nothing I can do. I didn't specifically forbid him from killing the prisoners, and that's my fault as much as his."

"He should have known better," I protested.

"Yes, he should have," he agreed. "But I imagine that his inability to promise his men that they would profit from the slaves was as unpopular as mine would have been. So to relieve himself of the problem, he killed them all. I'm not sure I wouldn't have done the same in his position."

When put that way, it was hard to argue, but I still did not like it any better than he did.

"So you're not going to punish him in some way?"

He shook his head.

"Regretfully, no. I can't justify revoking our agreement, and even with Proconsular authority, given that he's going to Rome to meet Caesar, if I fine him monetarily, he'll just complain, and that will cause me more trouble than it's worth."

With that settled, all that was left was to tell the Centurions, which as I suspected, was the reason Crassus had called on me.

"I'll break the news to them, but I think you should be present."

"I understand," I agreed, and I did.

If he was going to face angry Centurions, he did not want to do it by himself, while having someone like Claudius there would just make matters worse. I was the only real choice, but that does not mean I relished the chore. Crassus had his *bucinator* sound the assembly for all the Centurions, then we walked outside to the forum to wait for them to assemble. It did not help matters that the rain resumed so that the Centurions came slogging up in a bad frame of mind to begin with. When Crassus informed them of what Roles had done, there were the predictable howls of outrage from some of them, with a few even loudly calling for Roles' head. However, the majority seemed to understand, or at least they indicated that they did, and if they did not, they were unwilling to voice that in front of the others. With the matter settled, Crassus took the opportunity to announce his immediate plans for the army.

"We're marching back to Siscia, but we're not heading the most direct way." Waiting for the whispers to subside, he continued with more details. "Our business with the Moesians isn't entirely finished, and I plan on chastising them severely for their attempt to attack us."

I do not believe that this announcement went over the way Crassus had hoped, but I was not surprised at all when I saw Centurions exchanging glances, muttering and shaking their heads. These men did not care about punishing the Moesians any more than they had already been punished; we were nearing the end of the campaign season, and they merely wanted to go home. Nearly all had families, however unofficial they may have been, and something as nebulous as teaching the Moesians a lesson did not appeal to them in the slightest. Crassus shot me a look of alarm, but this was not the place for me to explain why they were reacting in this manner, so my only reply was a slight shake of my head. Saying nothing for a moment, Crassus appeared to be gathering his thoughts, but I was sure he was thinking furiously, trying to think of the reason the men would be showing such discontent. Finally, he gave a broad smile, the kind designed to be seen by onlookers even in the last row.

"Of course, I don't expect you men to go unrewarded. I know I made you a promise concerning the sale of slaves, but because of what happened today, that's not possible, at least with the Bastarnae. But I don't think you're particular about who we capture, are you?"

This got men's heads moving in the right direction, along with the beginnings of smiles, but the men were not quite there yet. Seeing this, Crassus expanded on his promise.

"So whoever we capture in Moesia, the proceeds from their sale will go to you, down to the last sesterce. I vow this before Jupiter Optimus Maximus."

Now he had them, this last announcement met with lusty cheers. To show their appreciation, they hailed him as *imperator* three times, the traditional way that the Legions showed their appreciation for their general. And in doing this, I believe they sealed the fate of Marcus Licinius Crassus.

Camp was broken the next morning, the army marching away from the still-smoking ruins of the Bastarnae fortress. It was good that we were leaving, since one could already start to smell the stink from all the bodies; I do not know the exact numbers, but it was several thousand. We left the Getae behind, most of them still in a drunken stupor from their celebrations of the day before. Roles and Crassus made a great show of friendship before we left, but the Centurions were still unhappy with Roles, even with Crassus' promise, choosing to stand stone-faced as the two clasped arms, then embraced in the manner of the Getae. Our business with the Getae and the Bastarnae concluded, we began the march heading due south, retracing the path we had taken to get there. As soon as I could, I pulled Scribonius aside, both of us riding a short distance away from the column so that we could talk privately.

"Did you hear about what happened yesterday?" I began, deliberately not mentioning the particular incident I had in mind.

"You mean the Centurions hailing Crassus as *imperator*?" Scribonius asked, confirming my suspicions.

"Yes, that's what I mean."

"Hard to keep something like that secret," he replied. Shooting me a sidelong glance, he asked me quietly, "What exactly are you asking me, Titus?"

"I'm asking what you think," I said, irritated because he clearly enjoyed making it difficult for me.

"I think that Marcus Crassus is in a lot of trouble." Scribonius had turned serious, and I felt my heart sink.

Despite the fact that I agreed, having someone as intelligent as Scribonius, who was so much wiser in the politics of Rome than I was, confirm my feelings was not a happy thought.

Trying to find the bright side, I offered, "It wasn't the whole army, though. Doesn't it have to be the whole army acclaiming a man *imperator* for him to be able to claim the wreath?"

"Normally yes," Scribonius said, but his tone was cautious. "It all depends on how it's reported to Caesar. Who else was there?"

I thought for a moment, but I could not remember seeing anyone other than the Centurions. Then I recalled seeing someone walking from his tent, and while he was a fair distance away, I supposed it was possible that he had heard, but I did not think that there would be any threat from this source.

"I did see Cornelius, but he was just passing by," I said offhandedly.

My gaze was averted from Scribonius, so it was only after there was a long pause that I sensed something was not right. I turned to see him staring at me with a look of foreboding.

"I heard about it from Cornelius," he said, which I did not see as a problem, but Scribonius was not through. "And Claudius was standing there when he told me."

It felt like my blood had turned to ice. Claudius had no love for Crassus before I arrived; after Crassus had sided with me at the first meeting between Claudius and me, the little worm hated Crassus almost as much as he hated me. He had been overheard making several caustic comments about

Marcus Crassus, which Crassus had refused to do anything about.

"He's too well-connected," Crassus had explained to me. "His father is one of Caesar's men, which is how he got the post to begin with. As long as he doesn't say anything treasonous, I'm going to ignore him."

I had little doubt that by the time word reached Octavian, what had happened the day before would be distorted in a way that would only harm Crassus, but I did not know what I could do about it, so I asked Scribonius. He frowned, and this was one of those times I was glad to see that look on his face.

"I don't know," he said finally, dashing my hopes that my smart friend had some idea that would save Marcus Crassus from his own success. Shaking his head, he continued, "One thing I do know." He turned to give me a severe look. "You need to keep your nose out of it. Haven't you gotten enough patricians mad at you for a career?"

He was right, and I knew it, but I could not resist the idea of paying him back a bit.

Grinning at him, I replied, "I'm getting bored. Besides, if it all goes wrong, I'm just going to say it was all your idea."

"*If* it goes wrong?" he scoffed. "When have any of your schemes gone right?"

Marching south, we crossed back over the Ister River, except instead of curving to the west back towards Pannonia, we continued south, deeper into Moesia. We followed a track that ran along a river that branched off the Ister, now called the Augusta (Ogosta) , with that river to our left, the spine of the line of hills that eventually ran all the way back to Naissus to our right. It was good ambush country; the hills provided cover, while the river pinned us down, making the men exceptionally alert while we traversed this stretch of country. Fortunately, the Moesians did not attempt to use the country to their advantage, but it was still a nervous couple of days. Reaching the spot where a pass through the hills would take us back to Naissus if we headed west, or heading east would take us deeper into Moesia, Crassus halted us for a day while the command group discussed what we would do.

"If we head a few miles farther south, we'll reach the Nisava. We can follow that to the east to make it through the mountains that separate the two parts of Moesia," Crassus explained, pointing to the spot on the map.

I saw the Primi Pili exchange glances, their faces grim, giving minute shakes of the head to each other. It was clear that they did not like the idea, and I agreed with them. It was late summer by this point, time to think about heading back to Pannonia. Crassus seemed adamant, however, either missing or ignoring the dubious reactions around the table.

"And what is our goal if we head east?" Natalis, Primus Pilus of the 13th asked Crassus.

The Legate frowned as he tried to frame his answer. "Our goal, Natalis, is to show these Moesians the folly of attacking Rome."

"We destroyed Naissus," Aelianus, the Primus Pilus of the 15th pointed out. "Isn't that lesson enough?"

Crassus shook his head.

"I don't believe that it is. That was the direct result of one Moesian nobleman, but Runo isn't the only troublemaker among these people." Giving an elaborate shrug, he finished, "It's a matter of going ahead and finishing the job now, or having to march back here next season."

He was probably right, but it was no certainty that the Moesians had not yet learned a lesson, and I could see that doubt in each of the Primi Pili's eyes. Crassus clearly was not swaying his senior Centurions, and he recognized it.

"Perhaps we can accomplish what we need to without going deeply into the interior. We'll march to the Nisava, and we'll follow it for a week. If we run into any settlements, or significant numbers of Moesian warriors that we can engage and defeat, then we need go no farther."

It was not much of a promise, yet it was also clear that this was as far as Crassus was willing to bend, so the Primi Pili accepted his word, a bit grudgingly perhaps. With the next several days decided, we resumed the march the next morning, the men enjoying the break but ready to keep going. From my perspective, it seemed that it was the Centurions who had more of a problem with Crassus' intentions than the rankers did. I supposed that they were just thinking of their men. While the terrain was extremely rugged, staying next to the river minimized the amount of undulation we had to endure. It also put us in a position to find what villages and towns there were in the area, since the only inhabitable spots were along the river. When we came across a settlement, no matter what size, we laid waste to it, burning everything while taking what food we could find, along with anything else that was not essentially nailed down. There is a maxim among the Legions; anything that is not nailed down is theirs, and anything that can be pried loose is not nailed down. There was precious little food and after the first two or three times, somehow the word spread, meaning that every village we came across, no matter how small, was already deserted and stripped bare. If we managed to capture a Moesian civilian, they would be tortured to reveal the location of their stores of food, knowing from experience that they never carried the food away, but buried it somewhere nearby. Even doing this, our supply of grain was growing lower every day, seemingly dropping at the same rate as the days were growing shorter. There was a chill in the air when we arose every morning, though the abysmal weather had at least turned and the days were mostly sunny. One day short of reaching the Nisava, our scouts reported that they had come across the trail of a large group of men, estimating their numbers at about ten thousand. They did not see them, just the trail of their passing, yet what was troubling was that they were headed in a direction that would put them athwart our line of march at some point. With only ten thousand men, this group did not pose a significant threat, but it had to be assumed that they were just part of a larger group that was gathering, since this was the manner in which barbarian tribes operated.

Crassus was undeterred, and when we reached the Nisava, we made the turn to the east, with the river now on our right. Every march has a rhythm, and we had found the rhythm of this one. This is when men become complacent, no matter how hard the Centurions work to keep the men alert, and the Centurions are just as susceptible to the same problem. It extends all the way up the chain of command, so I was not immune and neither was Crassus; a particularly interesting or animated conversation starts between two friends, usually some sort of argument. Most of the time it is good-natured, sometimes it is not. Other times it will be a particularly entertaining story, usually about some off-duty exploit or something amusing that happened in a battle. In the beginning, there are only two or three participants, but soon enough everyone within earshot is either avidly listening or participating. These types of things are happening up and down the column, in every Legion, Cohort, and Century. That is why we post outriders and in some circumstances where contact is imminent, have Century and sometimes Cohort-sized flanking patrols in order to avoid being surprised. But they are part of the army, and even knowing that their duty is to be vigilant, it is hard to remain that way when day after day passes in the same fashion. I would be lying if I said that I had never let my mind and attention wander those times when I was a *tiro* and *gregarius* or was part of a flanking patrol, making it just a matter of luck that nothing bad ever happened during those times. All that said, men have a duty, and while I have some sympathy, there is no excuse for what happened.

The Moesians timed their attack perfectly, letting the vanguard and the leading Legion pass by before the first hint of their presence was announced by an alarmed shout. They had chosen a spot where the level ground along the river and the flank of the ridge that paralleled it was at its narrowest, with a strip of dense forest that started just a few hundred paces from the riverbank. We were marching in our normal section front, meaning that each rank was eight men across, with an arm's length between each man. The Centurions and Optios were in their usual spots to the side, one at the front and one at the rear of each Century, though as was common practice, many of them were clustered together in small knots, talking while we marched. Technically, this was against the regulations, but it is one of the most ignored in the army. Honestly, it would not have made any difference. No, the fault lay entirely with the Century of the 13th that had been placed on the flank of the hill, perhaps a hundred feet above the tree level to watch for just such an attack. We had just passed a ravine running perpendicular to our line of march that led deeper into the hills, which I imagine is where they had approached and were lying in wait. Somehow, the flank security Century completely missed seeing what turned out to be approximately two thousand Moesian horsemen. The alarm was raised not by the Century, who should have sounded the *cornu* call immediately, but one of the Evocati who had pulled off to the side to relieve himself. He glanced up just in time to see the first Moesians bursting from the treeline, javelins at the ready, already at a full gallop. Not taking the time to tuck himself in, he wheeled his horse while giving the alarm, but he was too late to save himself and fell, the javelins that pierced his back sticking out of his chest. Scribonius, Balbus, and I had been discussing our plans for what we would do when we returned to Pannonia, with Scribonius pressuring us both to go to Rome with him. The other Evocati were engaged in similar conversations, along with Crassus, the Tribunes, and every member of the command staff. Suddenly, I was staring wide-eyed at the sight of a mass of Moesian cavalry, my attention captured by the cry of the Evocatus who paid for alerting us with his life, something that I turned just in time to see happen. Ocelus, without waiting for any jerk of the reins, turned suddenly, going from the walk to the gallop in the blink of an eye, accelerating so suddenly I was almost thrown. Somehow, he knew not to head for the river, not because he was afraid of the water; he had forded many rivers with me by that point, and clearly enjoyed the water. However, if he had done so, I would have made an easy target. Unfortunately, some Evocati opted to try to make it to safety in that direction. Acting as a giant wedge, the Moesians split the column in two, then in an obviously prearranged movement, peeled into separate formations, one attacking to the left, the other to the right. Their commander had seemingly thought of everything; since the contingent to the right was attacking men facing them, he had put roughly two-thirds of his force in that group, while the one attacking to the left was hitting the command group and vanguard from the rear. I honestly do not know why Ocelus turned to head upriver, toward the head of the column, but in doing so, he saved my life and probably his. It was not because turning downriver would have run us directly into the Moesians attacking the rest of the column from the front, because he made his decision before they split up. Perhaps it was just luck, but I still believe that somehow he knew that our only chance lay in trying to escape by heading upriver towards the relative safety of the vanguard Legion. Whatever the case, he turned and was already several lengths farther upriver when the smaller Moesian force made their move in our direction. The scene was massive confusion, with men going in seemingly every direction in their haste to escape to safety. While most followed Ocelus' lead to head in our direction, a fair number simply made the wrong choice and I suddenly found myself on a collision course with a Tribune who was furiously whipping his horse. He only had eyes for the oncoming Moesians, his head turned to the right, obviously having no idea he was headed straight for me. It was Claudius, and as we galloped toward each other, the terror on his face was clearly visible.

"Claudius, you idiot!" I roared this at the top of my lungs, taking the risk of letting go of the reins with one hand to wave to him in a frantic attempt to get his attention. "You're going the wrong way! Turn around!"

He paid no attention, but his horse, seeing me wave at him, began to slow, forcing the Tribune to turn his head around to see why his mount had done so. Seeing me, his face registered surprise and confusion as his horse continued to go from a frantic gallop to a trot. I do not know why I did what I did next, but I did the same thing, pulling hard on Ocelus' reins, who clearly did not want to obey, only reluctantly pulling up. Reaching out, I grabbed the bridle of Claudius' mount, startling the Tribune, who opened his mouth while beginning to pull the reins in an attempt to wrest control of his horse from me.

"Come with me if you want to live," I snarled at him, using every bit of my commanding presence and glowering at him.

I admit that I was somewhat surprised when he meekly obeyed, dropping the reins, allowing me to yank his horse's head around. When the animal turned about, I slapped it on the rump while at the same time gave Ocelus a hard kick in the ribs. In a few blinks of an eye, we were back at the gallop, yet that pause cost us valuable time. I turned to see that Scribonius, who had hesitated just a fraction of a moment before following me, having been several lengths behind, had now caught up. A javelin whizzed by just in front of Ocelus' nose, missing him by less than the width of a hand. Still, he never broke stride. It was as if now that we were back at the gallop he was not going to stop for any reason until we were both safe.

"Where's Balbus?" I shouted back to Scribonius, but I could not hear his answer before I became fully consumed with trying to avoid being skewered by Moesians as they continued their onslaught.

I caught a glimpse of Crassus, Cornelius next to him but pulling away as he tried to make it to the rearmost ranks of the last Cohort of the vanguard Legion, which had just turned around to face the threat. The Moesians were shouting their battle cries, which carried above the sound of the wind in my ears while Ocelus ate up the ground in a blur. Out of the corner of my eye, I saw perhaps 50 Moesians, apparently having seen Marcus Crassus, angling their pursuit in an attempt to cut him off before he reached the Legion. Shouting a bitter curse, I wish I could say that I was concerned for the safety of my commander, but the path they were taking in their attempt to get to Crassus was going to cut me, Scribonius, and even Claudius off. Risking a glance behind me, my heart sank at the sight of only a dozen men who had chosen to go this way. It would not be enough to cut our way through this group of Moesians, meaning our only hope was that Crassus made it close enough to the Legions that they could drive the enemy off with their own javelins. Looking ahead, I could see that it was going to be desperately close, while also seeing that with the speed Ocelus was carrying, we would be among the Moesians very quickly. To that point, they had been completely focused on Crassus, and I had not seen one head turn our way. However, there were still a large number of them that were now effectively behind us as well, having reached the river, and I could hear the cries of men when they either struck a blow, or were stricken in return. I could not worry about any of the Evocati who had been caught, no matter who they were, because my small group was in enough danger themselves. Claudius still seemed to be out of his head with fear, as I glanced over to see him staring straight ahead at the Moesians with an expression I had seen all too often among men who have let their fear take control over them. I had begun to slow Ocelus again and this time he did not resist, perhaps sensing it was wise to do so. Claudius kept going at full speed and I called to him, trying to get him to slow as well, but he was oblivious. Scribonius pulled alongside me, also shouting at Claudius, who was now two or three lengths ahead of us, but the Tribune gave no sign of hearing.

"He's out of his mind with fear," Scribonius said grimly, and I nodded.

Turning around to see that there were less than ten of us left, it appeared the Moesians behind us had evidently turned their attentions elsewhere, although it was impossible to tell clearly because of the dust churned up by the horses. Seeing that there was no immediate threat to the rear, I turned my attention back to see just in time as Crassus leapt his mount over the kneeling men of the last Cohort of the vanguard, who immediately stood to fling their javelins at the Moesians. Horses and men were pierced two and three times, yet the Pilus Prior of the Cohort had given the order to loose too early, so that only the first dozen of the Moesians who were closest were hit. That left more than 40 Moesians, who were now turning away from the Legionaries, knowing that their quest to kill our Legate had failed. There were still targets, and one of them was Claudius.

We had slowed to a canter, but the gap was still narrowing too quickly, so I hefted my shield, preparing myself to try my best to ward off the shower of missiles that I was sure would be coming our way. Much like the Numidian cavalry, most of these men carried sheaves of javelins in leather containers attached to their saddles. Some of them carried long spears and a few swords, but they did not worry me as much as the javelineers. More than for myself I was worried about Ocelus, because even at the canter, if he was hit and stumbled I would be hitting the ground extremely hard, making an easy target for one of the spearmen. That was how they went after Claudius. He was now many lengths ahead and had completely isolated himself, but was still too far from the protection of the Legions. Seeing a number of blurred lines streaking across my field of vision, I saw two javelins hit Claudius' horse, one in the neck and one in the front shoulder, just forward of Claudius' leg. The wound to the neck was most likely not fatal, nor was the one in the shoulder, but it was a disabling one and the horse stumbled, going to its knees and throwing Claudius over its head to the ground. The Tribune had not been expecting it and hit the ground awkwardly, tumbling with his limbs splayed in every direction before coming to a stop, lying still, telling me he had been knocked unconscious. Immediately, I saw one of the Moesians with a spear head for Claudius, who was facedown and unmoving, the mounted spearman lowering his weapon for the easy kill. Again, without any thought, I kicked Ocelus, who did not hesitate, moving from the canter back to the gallop.

"Titus, no! Leave him, he's a dead man," I heard Scribonius shout, and I knew he was right.

And I also knew that it would be the smart thing to do to allow this Moesian to finish Claudius, ending the threat to Crassus and to me. But there is something in me that will not allow a Roman, even a man I despised as much as Claudius, to be killed by an enemy if I could help it. The thought that he might be grateful never occurred to me; in fact, if I had been forced to think about it, I would have made the guess that he would have hated me even more, perhaps to the point where he actively tried to destroy me. None of that was in my mind as I was galloping Ocelus to place us in between Claudius' inert body and the charging Moesian. I only had one thought, to kill this Moesian bastard. It was only made possible because Ocelus was simply one of the fastest horses I had ever seen, closing the gap with a speed that was almost unbelievable and was rapid enough that the Moesian clearly miscalculated. He had looked over at me, seen me approaching, and had given me an insolent grin, lowering his spear and still heading for Claudius, sure that I would not arrive in time. His surprise was evident on his face when Ocelus proved him wrong, his mouth opening in shock when I turned Ocelus at the last possible moment to draw alongside the Moesian. By force of habit, I had reached to my side, drawing my Spanish sword and not the *spatha* on my saddle. Still, we were close enough for my Gallic blade to do its work, despite the awkward angle, forced to reach across my body as I was. The Moesian desperately tried to use the shaft of his spear to knock my blade aside, but my thrust was too strong. He did manage to deflect the point upward just a bit so that it punched right under his ribcage to drive up into his liver and lungs. He did not shout, I suppose because his lungs were punctured and he had no air with which to do so, letting out more of a gasp, frothy blood appearing on his lips. Giving him a shove to free my blade, he toppled from the saddle and I pulled Ocelus up just a couple of paces away from Claudius. Scribonius reached my side, his *spatha* drawn and shield up, still watching the Moesians, who for the moment had become disorganized and were milling about.

"You're an idiot," he shouted at me.

Ignoring him, I slid off Ocelus' back to reach down and grab Claudius by the neck of his cuirass. He gave a moan, his eyes fluttering open, weakly trying to swat my hand off of him.

Looking up and trying to focus, he muttered, "What are you doing?"

"Saving your patrician ass," I told him while dragging him to his feet, and reaching for the saddle. The Moesians now saw three men, one on a horse and the other two dismounted. With a shout, they began turning their horses to head for us.

"Titus, you better hurry," Scribonius warned.

"I'm trying," I snapped. Realizing that I had to let go of Claudius, I asked him, "Can you stand?"

Despite his obvious fear, he nodded. Leaping aboard Ocelus, I reached down, again grabbing Claudius by the neck of his cuirass. Using all of my strength, I lifted Claudius to place him across the front of my saddle, kicking Ocelus at the same time. Claudius gave a grunt of pain as the saddle punched him in the stomach, and I felt Ocelus gather himself before he leapt forward again.

"Come on," I shouted to Scribonius, who needed no urging, turning his horse and going to the gallop immediately.

The Moesians were now within javelin range and I heard one whistle just behind my head, seeing several more slash through the air in front of me and to the side. Somehow, none of them struck Ocelus, while I managed to block two with my shield, where they stuck, making holding it awkward. Ocelus was laboring now, but we were almost to safety, Claudius still hanging head down, one hand clinging to my leg so tightly that it hurt. Suddenly, I heard a cry of pain. Turning, I saw Scribonius reeling in the saddle, and I veered closer to him to see how badly he was hurt. His face was white, his lips a bloodless line, yet he grimly held on to the reins, leaving me feeling completely helpless. I could not reach out to steady him without letting go of the reins, because my right hand was holding Claudius on the horse, but my friend looked dangerously close to falling. Looking across Scribonius, I saw a Moesian, this one armed with a spear, whipping his horse, desperately trying to get close enough to stab Scribonius, who was barely conscious. The Moesian had his spear parallel to the ground, heading at an oblique angle, the point aimed for a spot just above the rim of Scribonius' shield, which he was barely holding up.

"Sextus, raise your shield!" I screamed at Scribonius at the top of my lungs, but he gave no sign that he heard me.

Seeing him start to topple from the saddle, in desperation I let go of the reins and, with the shield still strapped to me, reached out to grab Scribonius by the arm. Squeezing Ocelus with my thighs with every bit of strength I could muster, I watched helplessly as the Moesian closed the remaining distance to pull within striking distance of Scribonius. The thought flashed through my mind that it might have been better to let him fall, but I could not see where he was wounded, and it was just as likely that hitting the ground would have shoved the javelin in even further and killed him, if it was lodged in his upper body. There was nothing I could do; I literally had my hands full. As it was, I was barely clinging to the back of my horse, who was still running for all he was worth. Everything had slowed down and I could clearly see the Moesian's grin of triumph as he pulled his arm back to drive the spear home into the body of my best friend. I was so focused on the man's face that I did not see the javelin that hit him full in the chest, throwing him backward from the saddle. From my viewpoint, one moment he was there, then in less time than it takes to blink, he was gone. I turned my head back to the front just in time to see the Century of Legionaries that the Pilus Prior had sent in front of his main line scattering out of the way, men diving to either side as we thundered by. We had made it to safety.

Grabbing the bridle of Scribonius' mount, I pulled both horses to a stop, unceremoniously dumping Claudius to the ground. Leaping off of Ocelus, I still kept hold of Scribonius, who was slumped over. The Pilus Prior of the Century now between us and the Moesians, thinking quickly, had his men form a modified testudo, keeping his men in the ranks, with the front line kneeling with their shields in front of them. The second rank stood, holding their shields in front of their kneeling comrades while the third did the same for the second and so on, protecting themselves and everyone immediately behind the Century. I could hear the clattering of Moesian javelins striking the shields of the Century, but I was paying more attention to helping Scribonius off the horse. He was unconscious, which I suppose was a blessing, yet it was scaring me immensely to feel the dead weight of his body as I dragged him from the saddle. Protruding from his side, low on his rib cage just a matter of less than a hand span away from his spine, was the shaft of a javelin. His side was soaked in blood. Laying him gently on the ground, I bent over, listening intently for any sound of life. My heart felt like it was about to stop, seizing in my chest when at first I could hear or see no sign that Scribonius was still alive before he took a shallow breath and I saw his chest rise and fall. Relief washed through me, but it was short-lived as I tried to think what needed to be done. The bleeding had slowed to a trickle, so I knew that the chances of him bleeding to death were slight, as long as the javelin remained where it was. But what kind of damage was it doing to his insides? I wondered. I was in an agony of indecision, kneeling by my friend's side, oblivious to the sounds of the fighting that were beginning to wear down because our men had gotten organized and started inflicting casualties on the Moesians. Scribonius' face was deathly pale, his eyes closed, mouth open in his struggle to breathe. On impulse, I took off my neckerchief to use as a bandage, reaching for the shaft of the javelin to yank it free.

"Don't do that! You'll kill him!" I heard a voice shout and turned to see Crassus striding up, leading his horse.

"He can't breathe," I told him, hearing the desperation I was feeling in my voice. "I'm afraid that the javelin is doing something to his lungs. I need to get it out of there."

Crassus knelt next to me, putting a hand on my shoulder.

"If you do that, he'll bleed to death, and you'll probably rip something loose inside him," he said gently.

"Where's Philipos?" I asked him.

I had not seen the Greek once in all the confusion. Crassus shook his head before rising to look about, searching for sign of the physician.

"I haven't seen him, and I don't see him now."

"General, will you go find him?" I made no attempt to hide the fact that I was begging him, and for once, I was not even ashamed that I was doing so.

Crassus hesitated and I could see that he was trying to find a way to refuse me gracefully. I realized that I was asking a great deal of my commanding general, especially at that moment, but I did not care. I was being selfish, because Crassus needed to be the commanding general at that moment, rallying the men and getting things organized, except in that moment I convinced myself that after all I had given the army, and to Crassus in particular by ridding him of Prixus, that he owed me and I was about to remind him of that when I was saved, from the most unlikely source imaginable.

"I'll go find Philipos."

Crassus and I turned in surprise to see Tribune Claudius, standing upright. Weaving a bit, but upright. The look of terror was gone, replaced by a look that I had never seen on his face before, something resolute, if a bit embarrassed. Seeing our faces, he flushed but did not flinch.

"It's the least I can do for the Prefect. He saved my life."

I stood and walked to Ocelus, thrusting the reins towards Claudius. Claudius took them hesitantly, Ocelus clearly not liking the idea of a strange man riding him. Grabbing the bridle, I pulled his head down so we were eye to eye.

"You will let him ride you, do you hear me?"

He tossed his head in answer, though I had no idea if he was listening. However, I tried to seem confident when I boosted Claudius into the saddle. Ocelus arched his back, which was a sign that he was going to buck, then immediately settled down. Without wasting another moment, Claudius turned and Ocelus bounded away, back toward the bulk of the army. The Moesian attack was breaking off, yet there were still clusters of them gathering together after they had finished off one of the Evocati, or the odd Legionary that had gotten cut off. Claudius had to navigate past these hazards, and I alternated between watching him and keeping an eye on

Scribonius. Crassus stood there awkwardly for a moment, then cleared his throat.

"Pullus, I have to go get this mess organized. If I see Philipos before Claudius, I'll send him immediately."

I did not answer, only nodding my head and keeping my eyes on Scribonius, who despite my fears, continued to breathe. I sensed Crassus leaving, hearing him start his horse in the direction that Claudius had gone. There were men lying all over the field, some moving but many not and I scanned the area, looking for Balbus, but saw no sign of him. The attack had been devastating, perhaps not in the total number of casualties, however, in one stroke the Moesians had disrupted the army and judging from what I saw it would take at least two days to recover from the damage done. Scribonius let out a low moan, and I squeezed his hand to let him know that I was there. Only now, years later, can I admit how frightened I was, in some ways more scared than when I had maintained my vigil over Miriam. Scribonius had been part of my life since I was 16 years old, and I am not ashamed to say that I loved him as much as any person in my life, thinking of him like a brother and comrade in arms. I could not imagine he, or Balbus, for that matter, not being part of my life. These were my thoughts while I waited helplessly for help to come, oblivious to everything going on around me.

Hearing the pounding of hooves, I looked up to see Claudius returning, and my heart sank before he pulled aside. I saw immediately behind him Philipos, bouncing in the saddle, clearly unaccustomed to the fast pace of his horse. Climbing down from his mount, he walked stiffly over, but I was not concerned with his discomfort.

"He needs help," was all I could think to say.

"I can see that, Prefect," Philipos replied, kneeling down and putting his head to Scribonius' chest to listen carefully.

After a moment, he took my friend's wrist, feeling for his pulse before gently laying it down. His face was grim as he looked up at me.

"His breathing is ragged, but there is no blood in his lungs. His pulse is very weak, but it is surprisingly steady." He stood, reaching out to grip me by the shoulder. "We have to remove the javelin, but I must warn you, that doing so must be done very, very carefully to avoid inflicting any more damage." He hesitated, and I braced myself for what was coming. "But no matter how carefully we do it, it still may kill him."

"We don't have any choice though, do we?"

In reply, he only shook his head. I took a deep breath.

"What do you need me to do?"

"I am going to withdraw it by grasping it where it entered his body. I need you to hold the end, but it is very important that you follow the direction in which I pull it out. You cannot move the shaft in any direction, it must be drawn straight out," he finished, his tone urgent. "Do you understand?"

I swallowed hard, but nodded that I understood. We squatted down; I positioned myself so I could grasp the end of the javelin while Philipos took hold of the shaft right where it disappeared into Scribonius' body. Looking at me to see if I was ready, the Greek took a deep breath, nodded his head, then began to pull on the shaft. I could feel it vibrating when Scribonius spasmed in pain, emitting a groan, his eyes opening briefly, looking straight up at the sky. With one smooth motion, Philipos pulled the javelin free, releasing a gout of blood from Scribonius' side, the point of the javelin red and slick with gore. Tossing it aside, Philipos did not do anything for a moment, watching the blood pouring from Scribonius' wound while I looked on in growing alarm. Finally, I could take it no longer.

"What are you doing?" I shouted at Philipos. "Do you want him to bleed to death?"

Philipos made no reply, just holding a hand up while continuing to stare at the wound, and I was about to throw him aside when I saw the flood slow to a trickle. Only then did Philipos take my neckerchief, placing it on the wound. Taking a roll of narrow linen from the bag around his shoulder, he motioned to me.

"Hold this tightly against his side. Even if he moans in pain, you must keep the pressure on the wound."

Nodding that I understood, I used my other hand to help Philipos raise Scribonius gently off the ground into a semi-seated position, while Philipos wrapped the roll of linen bandage around his body several times. While he was doing so, I asked him why he had let Scribonius continue to bleed.

"The blood had filled his chest cavity and was pressing on his lungs, making it difficult for him to breathe," he explained. "I had to allow the blood to drain to give his lungs enough space to do their job."

I looked down at Scribonius' face, still deathly pale, but I could see that he was clearly breathing easier. Seeing that the physician had obviously been right, I apologized to him for my harsh words, which he shrugged off.

"Don't thank me yet." He turned to look me directly in the eye. "Your friend has been very seriously wounded. His lungs were not punctured, though I don't know how the javelin missed, but I do not know what other damage has been done to his insides. It's amazing that he is still alive, which is a good sign, but he has a long way to go. I've done all I can for him right now. I am going to send orderlies to attend to him, but he can't be moved very far or he will certainly die."

With that, he left to go attend to other men of the command group and Evocati, while I watched him leave, still clutching Scribonius' hand. I sensed movement out of the corner of my eye, and I looked to see that Claudius was still standing there, clearly unsure of what to do.

"Thank you," I said quietly. "You didn't have to put yourself at risk to save him, but you did, and I'll never forget it."

He looked embarrassed, but I could tell my thanks pleased him.

"I must thank you as well," he replied formally, still a little stiff. "I may or may not have helped to save your friend, but you undoubtedly saved my life. I am in your debt."

"I'd never let one of these bastards kill another Roman as long as I could stop it," I told him, thinking to add, "no matter what our differences."

He gave me a brief nod, then began to look around at the shambles that was just beginning to be cleared up.

"Tribune, I'm sure that Crassus needs all of the help he can get clearing this mess up," I told Claudius gently.

I did not want to rupture the fragile peace between us, yet I knew that what I was saying was true. He did not seem to take offense, which pleasantly surprised me, but also seemed at a loss as he looked around.

"You're right, Prefect. But I'm not sure what to do, and besides, I don't have a horse." He gave me a smile then. "Unless, of course, you want to lend me your animal."

"No, I'm going to need him." I smiled back. "But you can take Scribonius' horse."

I stood and walked over to where Scribonius' mount was standing next to Ocelus, leading him to the Tribune and handed him the reins. I gave him a boost into the saddle, then he turned to follow in the direction Crassus had gone.

Before he did, he said softly, "I hope your friend survives, Prefect. He seems like a good man."

"He is," I said firmly, "and he will. Because I won't let him die."

Fortunately, Crassus made the decision to make camp where we were on the banks of the river. It was not an ideal location, yet the surprise attack by the Moesians had inflicted enough damage that time was needed to sort things out. As Philipos had promised, two *medici* arrived and, with my help, gently placed Scribonius on a litter, carrying him to the spot on which the hospital tent was to be erected, where he was laid next to the dozens of seriously wounded. Seeing that there was nothing else I could do for the moment, I extracted a promise from one of the *medici* that he would not leave Scribonius' side, then went looking for Balbus and the rest of the Evocati. I saw immediately that the brunt of the losses were in fact borne by the Evocati, command staff and the leading Cohort of the second Legion in the column that day, the 15th. Particularly hard hit had been the noncombatant clerks that marched on foot with the command group, their bodies having already been heaped in a pile. The contingent of cavalry that marched drag had come up and along with the 14th had posted themselves as security, the Cohorts arranged facing the strip of woods. However, there was no sign of the Moesians, save their dead and wounded, and there were precious few of those. I found Novatus, dead on the field, a gaping wound in his side, his eyes staring up at the sun but not seeing it, and I was beginning to think that would be how I found Balbus. I reflected on how horrible a day it would be if I lost both of my closest friends, all because of what was little better than a raid. Walking Ocelus, I took an inventory of the losses to the Evocati; there were 21 men dead on the field, but no Balbus. Hearing a shout from the direction of one of the Cohorts guarding the site, I turned to see a group of horsemen emerge from the woods, coming out of the ravine that bisected the ridge.

"What in Hades is this?" I muttered, I suppose to Ocelus, since there was nobody else around.

Thinking they were Moesians, I quickly realized my mistake when I saw that the Cohort nearest the group did not sound any kind of alarm. Curious, I headed Ocelus in their direction, squinting to try to make out the identity of the 20 or so horsemen. Finally, they drew close enough and I cannot describe the relief that flooded through me when I saw at their head Balbus, his scarred face more beautiful than the sweetest Vestal to me at that moment. He had a bloody bandage tied around one thigh, yet otherwise seemed unhurt, while the men with him, all Evocati, were in much the same condition. Some sported bandages made from their neckerchiefs, one man having it wrapped about his head, looking like one of the Egyptian tribes that live in the desert, but none were seriously wounded. Seeing me, Balbus broke into a canter, and we pulled alongside each other, clasping arms.

"It's good to see you alive, you bastard," I told him, too affected emotionally to say more.

"Same to you," he grinned back.

"Where have you been?"

Balbus spat on the ground.

"We went after those cocksuckers."

I looked at him in astonishment.

"Just the 20 of you?"

He gave a laugh, but it was tinged with bitterness.

"I didn't say it was smart. Besides, they were already withdrawing. We just made sure that they kept going."

"Did you catch any of them?"

"No." He was clearly disappointed, jerking his head over his shoulder. "But those worthless bastards in the 13th finally woke up and pulled their heads out of their asses. They managed to ambush them as they were withdrawing and took a few down with javelins. They had a strong position on the slope of the hill, so the Moesians didn't stop."

That made it clear to me that this was nothing more than a raid, and the Moesian commander had no intention of trying to engage in a battle of any scope.

"How did a force that size manage to slip past our flanking patrol?" I asked Balbus.

"That's a question I'd like to know the answer to as much as you," he grimaced. I realized that I had been putting off telling him about Scribonius, but he forced me to tell him when he looked around, and asked casually, "Where's Scribonius?"

I opened my mouth, yet the words would not come, and he looked at me in alarm.

"What happened? Titus, tell me!"

"He was hit with a javelin," I finally managed to say.

"Where?"

"In the chest," I replied.

He shook his head like it would dispel the news I was giving him.

Seeing my face, he asked quietly, "How bad?"

"It's bad. The good news is that it didn't puncture his lung. Other than that . . ." I could only shrug.

"Where is he now?"

272

I pointed in the direction of where the hospital tent was even then being erected. All around us, men were digging the ditch that would form the perimeter of the camp, working with an urgency that did not need to come from the Centurions. They knew we had been hurt, and they knew that there were comrades whose lives hung in the balance and depended on how quickly they could be settled and treatment for their wounds could begin. It had been a bad day for Crassus' army, and I wondered how he would react to this setback, whether or not it would convince him that it was time to turn around, or make him more determined than ever to crush the Moesians. I found it hard to think about at that moment, so when Balbus turned his horse without another word to head in the direction I had indicated, I turned to follow him. The truth was that I would be useless for anything the next few days.

Scribonius survived the night, which Philipos assured us was a good sign, while also warning us not to read too much into it.

"If his wound does not corrupt, he may survive, but only time will tell. I am surprised that he has lived this long."

"I know he doesn't look it, but Scribonius is one tough bird," Balbus said, and I looked at him in some surprise.

"I think that's the first time you've ever said anything nice about him," I said to him.

"That's not true," he protested, sounding defensive.

"Oh really? Name the last time."

After a moment, he could only shrug.

"I know I said something nice about him at some point," he grumbled.

"He will need all the help you can give him," Philipos told the both of us, but I was mystified about what he meant and when I glanced to Balbus, I could see he felt the same.

"What can we do?" I asked Philipos. "We're not physicians, and he's just lying there right now."

"There is a lot you can do. Do not underestimate the power your presence has on him while he is, as you say, lying there."

"But he's unconscious," Balbus protested. "He can't possibly hear us."

"Do not be so sure," Philipos replied, glancing down at Scribonius' inert form. "Over the years, I have seen that men who had many visitors who talked to their friend, despite the fact that they were unconscious, seem to have a higher rate of recovery than men who do not." With a shrug, he added, "Again, it is just something I have noticed. Besides, it cannot hurt."

So it began that either Balbus or I spent every moment at Scribonius' side, even when we resumed the march and he was consigned to bouncing in the wagon. Crassus gave us an extra two days in camp, ostensibly to handle the matter of disciplining the Sextus Hastatus Posterior of the 13th Legion for his lapse that allowed the Moesian attack. Balbus took over for me at Scribonius' bedside, since I had to attend the tribunal that was held. The senior Tribune Claudius, as the name implies, was actually the presiding officer, with the other five Tribunes making up the panel. Legate and Prefect were there as observers, although any Tribune who was not completely out of his mind, or so well connected that he could go against the wishes of the Legate in a matter would do exactly what the Legate wanted. Tribunals were generally held in the *Praetorium*, but Crassus decided that an example should be made of the Hastatus Posterior, a sorry specimen named Quintus Plautus, because of the impact of the Moesian attack. Consequently, he had chosen to have it held in the forum, in front of all the Centurions and Optios of the army.

Plautus was escorted by his Pilus Prior and Natalis, the Primus Pilus, both men stone-faced when they led him to stand in front of the assembled tribunal. One Tribune had been elected as the prosecution, and one as the defense, and the unlucky Centurion drew Cornelius as his defender. Cornelius had many good qualities, but public speaking and the ability to make an argument were not among them. To be honest, it would not have made any difference. Perhaps Cicero could have swayed the Tribunes, but Crassus had already made it known that Plautus had to pay a severe price for his carelessness. I had been one of those who had pressed the Legate to impose a stiff punishment, arguing that an example needed to be set to ensure there was not a repeat. Only now, years later, can I see clearly that as much of a motivating factor for me was my grief about what had happened to Scribonius, and to a lesser extent Novatus and the other Evocati who had paid with their lives because Plautus had let his mind wander. The trial was short, with Crassus following my recommendation; Plautus was stripped of his rank, busted all the way back down to *Gregarius*, and he was given ten lashes, though without the scourge. The Optio, who according to the men of the Century, had actually tried to do what he could to keep the men alert, received a lighter sentence of a stiff fine, and like the rest of the Century, was put on barley bread and water for 30 days. As a final penalty, the men of the Sixth Century of the Sixth Cohort of the 13th Legion were put on punishment detail, cleaning out the stables and filling in the *cac* trenches for a month. I told Scribonius of the punishment, sitting next to his bed that night, while the army made preparations to continue the march.

As I had surmised, the attack by the Moesians had fired Crassus' determination to inflict even more punishment on them. Meanwhile, the Primi Pili recognized that their chances of talking him into turning around ended that day. When the army began to march the next morning, Scribonius was loaded into my wagon, which I had emptied of my baggage, the Primi Pili and even Tribune Claudius making room in theirs for my gear. I did not want him to have to share a wagon with other wounded, even of Centurion rank, of which there were three. Instead of placing him on a hard board, I had the leather *immunes* create a sling of the type that I had seen sailors use aboard ships that reduced the jolting he would receive. I sat in the back of the wagon with him, Ocelus tied to the wagon, and

I continued talking, despite the fact that both Balbus and I had grown hoarse. It was a good thing that we had more than 30 years of memories to relive, which was mainly what we talked about, but Scribonius never made any kind of coherent response. Every once in a while he would moan softly, and one time he began flapping his hands weakly, like he was trying to beat something away from his body. Otherwise, he remained silent and still, swaying in his sling with the wagon rocking over the rough ground. It was perhaps the second day of the march, when I had run out of matters to talk about, that I began to talk to Scribonius of other things, matters that had weighed on my heart but had never talked about. It felt good to unburden myself, and despite knowing I was taking the coward's way out by talking to an unconscious man, I could not stop myself. Philipos came several times a day to check on Scribonius, but all he would say was that every moment that Scribonius lived helped his chances. Balbus would come to relieve me, whereupon I would spend some time with Crassus, who did not press me on official business. Claudius was also a frequent visitor, surprising Balbus greatly the first time, until I explained to him what had transpired.

"Well, at least something good came out of this," was his only comment.

While Claudius and I were not friends, and would never be friends, there was no longer the tension between us, which was a relief. I planned on talking to him at some point about the incident with the Centurions hailing Crassus *imperator* to try to make sure that he did nothing to damage Crassus with Octavian, but judged that the time was not right. Some of the wounded men died, some recovered, and it took time for the *Praetorium* to begin functioning again because of the death of so many of the clerks. I sent Diocles to help out, along with the Primi Pili's clerks, and soon enough the paperwork was flowing again, and the army recovered from the attack.

"Where am I?"

Somehow, I had managed to fall into a light doze and I was sure that the words I heard were part of the dream, until it was repeated. That forced my eyes open and I looked over from my spot on the bench that had been placed in the wagon to see Scribonius staring up at the ceiling, wearing his familiar frown. Normally, I did not like seeing that plastered on his face, but at that moment it was one of the most beautiful things I had ever seen. Of course, I could not let him know that.

"It's about time you decided to wake up." I tried to sound gruff, except my voice was too hoarse with emotion to carry it off.

I rose to the half-crouch that I had to adopt to fit inside the wagon, crossing to Scribonius' sling. The whites of his eyes were a horrible yellow color, his face was sunken in, the skin on his cheekbones was pulled taut, but he was alert.

"You're in a wagon," I told him.

"I gathered that," he said dryly, his voice hoarse from the days he had been unconscious. "But why am I in a wagon?"

"You don't remember?"

He gave a minute shake of the head, his eyes searching my face.

"The last thing I remember was the attack," he whispered. He frowned again before giving me an accusing look. "Then I remember chasing after some big idiot who decided to try and rescue a worthless Tribune that had caused him nothing but grief. Does that remind you of anyone?"

"About that," I began, but he cut me off.

"So it wasn't a dream!" His tone was accusatory, and he fixed me with what I am sure he thought was a fierce glare.

"No, it wasn't a dream," I admitted.

"You almost got me killed," he said indignantly.

I had imagined this scene many times; Scribonius regaining consciousness, and all the things I would say to him. However, this was not going at all the way I had thought it would. I held my hands up in a placating gesture.

"Sextus, that wasn't my intent, to get you killed."

"I should hope not," he retorted.

As quickly as it had come, his ire dissipated, his head dropping back onto the pillow. His face had become even paler, and I was afraid that he was going to lapse back into unconsciousness. I watched anxiously, but his eyes remained open, although they fluttered as if he were trying to fight off sleep.

"You were badly injured," I began, feeling the need to tell him exactly what his condition was, since I would have wanted someone to do for me.

"Really? I wouldn't have guessed that," he replied, except this time there was a sleepy smile on his face.

I went on to describe the extent of his injuries, what Philipos had said, and what he had prescribed to help his recovery. I was somewhat embarrassed to admit that we had been talking to him while he was unconscious, but Scribonius got a strange look on his face.

"I remember," he said slowly, then paused for a moment. "You were talking about Miriam. And Gisela."

My blood froze; I was mortified that he had actually heard the things I had said.

Seeing my face, he added hastily, "I really don't remember anything other than their names."

I knew he was lying, but it was one of those fictions that I was willing to believe for the rest of our days.

"Anyway, the fact that you're still alive is a good sign. Your wound was clean and has stayed that way. Philipos says the pus is draining clear, which is normal for this stage. All in all, things are looking good, but you're still not completely safe."

"Good to know," he said, then yawned.

I told him that he should try to stay awake long enough for me to get Philipos, and he promised he would, and I left to go find the physician. When we returned, he had passed out again, but Philipos examined him, listening to his heart and breathing.

"He is getting better. His pulse is stronger, and his breathing is good. It's time to try and get some food into him. Start with weak broth and see how he tolerates that."

With these instructions, he left me to sit staring at my friend, wondering just how much he had heard of all my confessions.

Chapter 6-Ambush

We were following the Nisava upstream, meaning that we were traveling uphill, making the going slower than Crassus liked. Hills turned into mountains, rising steeply from the valley floor up which we were traveling. We ran into the occasional village or small town, along with isolated farms, all of which were put to the torch, and the granaries emptied, but the foraging was becoming more difficult with each passing day. The weather was changing from the combination of the season growing late and the increased elevation, the nights becoming bitterly cold. Still, Crassus seemed intent on continuing and, to that point, the men, while clearly not liking it, were marching without more than the usual complaint. I was not sure that it would last much longer before there was open discontent, and not just with the rankers. As Philipos had instructed, Scribonius had started taking nourishment in the form of broth, sometimes with a scrap of meat thrown in. He grumbled about not getting any bread, but both Balbus and I stuck to what we had been instructed to do, ignoring his complaints for the most part. The color was slowly returning to his face, but his eyes still had their yellow cast to them, which Philipos said was due to some sort of imbalance in his bile. Personally, I do not believe that the Greek had any real idea what had caused this condition, but I did not say anything. I was just happy to see my friend slowly regaining his strength. Our scouts had cut the trail of what they believed was a second Moesian band, a bit smaller than the first. However, troublingly, they appeared to be headed on a course that would intersect with the first band at some point ahead of us. Despite the fact that these two groups combined would still not be enough to defeat us, we had to assume that there were other bands coming from other directions that would join with the two that we knew about. Reaching the point where the Nisava turned almost due north and up into the mountains where its headwaters lay, we were able to cross with little difficulty, since at that spot it is no more than a swiftly flowing stream with a rocky bottom. More importantly, it marked the spot where Crassus had told the Primi Pili that we would turn around, except when we crossed at about midday, continuing east without pause, I knew that he had made up his mind. Despite the Primi Pili not saying anything outright against continuing, it was clear that they did not like it, and I saw all four marching together, talking a short distance from the column. Therefore, that night when they came to my tent, I was not surprised.

"We're going to talk to Crassus," announced Macrinus, who had been elected spokesman of the group, I suppose because of our connection through Gaius and the fact that we had a good relationship.

"What about?"

I knew perfectly well what they wanted to discuss, but I saw no point in making it easy for them. To his credit, Macrinus was not thrown off.

"About his promise to only go as far as the headwaters of the Nisava before turning for home."

Actually, what Crassus had said was that we would follow the Nisava for a week, and we had exceeded that, but that was because we had paused for three days after the attack.

"If I remember correctly, he made that conditional on finding significant numbers of Moesians to engage, or a settlement of substantial size that we could take," I pointed out. "Not to mention that we haven't been able to capture nearly enough prisoners to make up for the ones Roles killed."

Macrinus glanced over at the other Primi Pili, and I saw each of them give a slight nod, then he turned back to me.

"We don't care about the prisoners anymore," he said flatly. "We talked it over with our Centurions, and they all agree that as much as we'd like the extra money, we want to return to Pannonia more."

I studied the faces of the four men, and saw that they were grimly determined.

Sighing, I told them, "I'll go with you. But don't be surprised if he doesn't listen," I warned them. "He seems dead set on chastising these people in a big way."

"We'll never know unless we try," was Macrinus' response, which was true enough.

I put on my uniform, minus my helmet, and we marched to the *Praetorium*.

On the way, I reminded them, "I'm going along as a witness, and if he asks my opinion, I'll tell him that I believe it's time to turn back. But if he doesn't ask me, I'm not going to venture my opinion."

The others looked disappointed, but my mind was made up on the matter. Although I understood the desire of the men to head for home, this campaign had not been that severe in terms of hardship. I suppose that the memory of Parthia always stuck with me, because I tended to compare every campaign after that against what we had been forced to endure during that nightmare. That is probably unfair, yet I cannot help feeling that way. We arrived at the *Praetorium*, and since Crassus had given standing orders that if I, or any of the Primi Pili requested an audience they be ushered in immediately, we were taken right into his office. The Legate was seated behind his desk, and did not seem surprised in the least to see us, but his gaze lingered on me for an extra moment.

"To what do I owe this honor?" he asked in a light tone, looking from one man to the other.

As often happens, once actually in front of the general commanding the army, there seemed to be some confusion among the Primi Pili, then I saw Natalis give Macrinus a nudge from behind. Shooting Natalis an irritated look, Macrinus cleared his throat to begin speaking.

"Sir, we're coming to you to respectfully request that you honor your promise to turn back at the headwaters of the Nisava," Macrinus said carefully.

Inwardly, I winced; I had tried to let him know that Crassus had not actually promised anything, but Macrinus seemed intent on ascribing to Crassus at least the intent of making a promise, even if his words did not meet that standard. Worse, Macrinus was starting by going on the attack, essentially challenging Crassus' honor, and the Primus Pilus' words had the predictable effect on the Legate.

"I don't recall making any such promise," Crassus flared, his lips a thin line. "What I said was that we'd follow the Nisava for only a week, provided," he leaned forward to emphasize what he clearly saw to be the central point, "that we come across a significant number of Moesians that we could teach a lesson, and we haven't. Other than the force that attacked us and escaped, that is."

"We've taken and sacked three towns," Macrinus pointed out, and I felt I could almost mouth the words as Crassus said them when he responded.

"You call that collection of huts and hovels towns?" he scoffed. "They hardly qualify as being anything worthy of this army claiming a victory over, wouldn't you agree?"

I suppressed a smile; Crassus had just scored a major point. In every Legionary's record goes an account of every engagement worthy of mention that he is involved in, including towns and cities taken. Crassus was right in that none of the settlements we had razed would qualify as worthy of mention, even for the most vainglorious of Legates, and as extremely ambitious as Crassus was, he was not excessively grasping for credit. He wanted to earn his accolades rightfully and in that, I could not blame him, because it had been much the same for me during my career, albeit on a smaller scale. The two parties looked across Crassus' desk at each other, neither willing to budge. I knew that for there to be any hope that this meeting ended amicably, I would have to go back on what I had told the Primi Pili earlier, and speak before spoken to. I cleared my own throat, which sounded extremely loud in the silence, and Crassus looked over at me with a peeved expression.

"Yes, Prefect? I suppose you're on their side?"

"I'm on the side of doing what's best for Rome," I said stiffly, a little irritated at his presumption. I could not resist adding, "And for this army as well."

I meant this as a warning to Crassus of what my role was, but his face gave away nothing.

"So? What is it you'd like to say?"

"Actually, I'd like to ask you a question, if I may, sir." He looked surprised, but nodded for me to continue. "Can you provide specifics for what you're trying to accomplish? With all due respect, saying something like we're looking for 'significant numbers' is a bit.....nebulous, don't you think, sir?"

I was using my very best Ranker When Addressing A Senior Officer tone; respectful, even a bit deferential, but it still pinned Crassus down, and he knew it. So did the others, all turning to look at the Legate expectantly, while he ignored them to glower at me.

"Why, Prefect, I am impressed," he did not bother to hide the sarcasm from his tone, "with your vocabulary. I'd never have thought I'd hear the word 'nebulous' come out of your mouth."

"I am full of surprises, sir," I replied cheerfully, and I could see the others suppress smiles.

"Indeed you are, Prefect," he said ruefully.

Sitting back, he folded his hands on the desk, seemingly studying them intently. Finally, he looked up.

"Very well, I concede your point. I want one engagement, with a force of at least 10,000 Moesians, which would qualify to be included in the record of the campaign. Or, if we can't come to grips with a force of that size, I want to capture a town of at least 5,000 defenders and 10,000 inhabitants." He crossed his arms, looking at each of us. "There," he finished. "Is that specific enough for you?"

For a moment, I was afraid that Macrinus and the others would ask for a moment to discuss matters, and that would have been the worst thing they could have done. Everything Crassus had done to that point had been lawful, and well within the traditional role of a Legate commanding the army, particularly a Legate with the Proconsular power with which Crassus had been vested. Whether or not he was participating in a venture that would be of such a scope that it would mark him as a possible rival to Octavian was a larger question. Most importantly, it was nothing that any of the Primi Pili, or me for that matter, should have been concerned with. If they had asked to confer outside of Crassus' presence that would smack of mutiny, and could be seen as a direct threat to Crassus' authority. Fortunately, at least Macrinus seemed to understand this, because he snapped to *intente*, gave a perfect salute, then assured Crassus that it was indeed.

"Then, is there anything else?"

Macrinus shook his head, but then Natalis blurted out, "How much longer are we going to keep looking for a fight that matches your criteria?"

I could hear Crassus' intake of breath at the question. I must say that he had been neatly caught out and he clearly knew it. His face reflected his unhappiness at being pinned down even further, yet he seemed to consider the question carefully before answering.

"Another month," he finally replied.

Now it was the turn of the Primi Pili to have their breath taken away.

"A month?" Macrinus was clearly struggling to maintain his composure.

The others were not so circumspect, at least with their facial expressions, each of them clearly dismayed.

"A month would put us at the Ides of October," Macrinus said carefully. "Then we'd be marching well into winter, especially once the weather turns. I know that it only snows on the peaks here, but that means that we'll be marching in mud. We'll be lucky to make half the distance we're making now. Which would mean that we might not arrive back in Pannonia until after the end of the year. The men would have perhaps two months to recover, and the Legions to refit before we had to turn around and march back."

Macrinus was right, but Crassus was prepared. I do not know if he had thought of this before, or he was making it up as he went, but his manner was so assured it was impossible to tell.

"That's why we're not returning to Pannonia," he said smoothly. That was the first I had heard this, along with the Primi Pili. "We're going to march south, through Thrace, which is friendly to us, and down into Greece. We'll winter there, although I haven't decided exactly where, but I can assure you that it will be somewhere that can support an army during winter quarters and provide plenty of diversion for your leisure time."

He favored all of us with a brilliant smile and despite my shock and anger, I grudgingly had to admire the man. In the blink of an eye, he had turned the tables on the Primi Pili, and I suppose on me as well, given that most of the members of my household were in Siscia. The collective jaws of the Primi Pili dropped, then they exchanged bleak glances, all of them knowing that they had been outmaneuvered.

Lying in my cot that night, reviewing what had taken place, I believe that Crassus had brilliantly exploited a regulation that, as I have mentioned numerous times, is one of the most flaunted in the army. When he had announced that we would be wintering in Greece, he had put the Primi Pili in a losing position, and he knew it. Unspoken between the two parties in this discussion was the real reason that the Primi Pili, and more importantly the men, wanted to return back to Pannonia and that was for the sake of their families. Families that are expressly forbidden by army regulations, as we all knew. Despite it being true that a fair number of unofficial wives accompanied us on every campaign, the larger number of the women tailing along were camp followers, whores by another name, who plied their trade on the march just like, if in a different way, a Legionary. Mothers and their children are usually left behind, since it is harder for them to keep up with us on the march. That is not to say that there were no children, but most of them were babes in arms, born on the march and carried by their mothers. However, there were not many of those. Going by the strict letter of regulations it should not have mattered to any man in the army where they spent the winter, since they should have had no attachments that would

286

make a difference. The reality was far different, but the Primi Pili knew that they could not use that as a reason to return to Pannonia. While they generally liked and admired Crassus, I could not imagine any of them being willing to take the risk of exposing themselves to a tribunal should Crassus choose to enforce the regulations the way they are written. In short, the Primi Pili, and by extension all the men with families back in Pannonia, were well and truly fucked. They stayed up late into the night arguing about what to do, except I refused their request that I attend, telling them in no uncertain terms that I was done with the whole business. As far as I was concerned, the affair was over, having been decided in Crassus' favor, and after a sleepless night, the Primi Pili finally came to the same conclusion. Now each of them had to find a way to tell their Legions that not only was there another month of marching looking for a fight, but once done, they would be spending their winter far away from their loved ones. I did not envy their predicament, and this was one time that I did not miss being in charge of a Legion in the slightest. When I told Scribonius of all that had taken place, he was grim.

"That's going to hurt Crassus more in the long run than the men," he said, in between spoonfuls of broth.

"How so?"

He paused while he considered his answer. He was looking better every day, yet he was painfully thin, and still haggard. Several days' growth of beard partially hid his sallow complexion; in truth, he looked more like a barbarian than a Roman at that moment.

"Because he's overextending himself," Scribonius finally said. "Octavian is all about the customs and traditions of Rome, at least on the surface. And he's just as adamant about the unwritten rules as those on the bronze tablets. Crassus has just handed Octavian an excuse to take him down a notch. He can say that Crassus flouted one of the longest-standing traditions of the army, even if it is an unofficial one." I sat listening, and when he was finished, I realized that what he was describing was very likely exactly what would happen. I shook my head sadly, evidently causing Scribonius to ask me,

"Titus, why do you care what happens to Crassus? After all the trouble men like Crassus have caused you during your career, I would think you'd be happy to see another one fall."

"Crassus is different," I began, to which he snorted in derision. Ignoring him, I pressed on. "He reminds me of his father. You remember how loved Publius was in Gaul, don't you?"

Scribonius' eyes took on a faraway look, traveling across the years back to when we were young and in the ranks.

"Yes, I do," he admitted. "But don't let your nostalgia for those days cloud your judgment."

"I don't think I am," I replied. "Although I'll admit that it's possible." Thinking about it some more, I finished with, "Whether he's just like every other patrician or not, there's one thing about him that I'm sure of, and that is that he's capable. And Rome needs as many capable men as it can get."

As I expected, the rankers did not take the news that we would be continuing on and spending the winter in Greece well at all. Despite the fact they were not openly mutinous, or even disobedient, they expressed their discontent in the myriad ways that men in the ranks have. Moving a step more slowly than normal when doing some task; getting to their feet after a break on the march an extra heartbeat later than they have in the past; low, muttered conversation on the march instead of the spirited banter, all of these are weapons in the arsenal of the ranker to let their Centurions know they are unhappy. Moments like these are the real test of a Centurion, and in those days, I saw the cream rise to the top. Unfortunately, I saw the dregs as well. I had learned long ago, from the likes of Gaius Crastinus and Pulcher what not to do, which was trying to beat the men into a better frame of mind. Unfortunately, there were a fair number of Centurions throughout the army, in every Legion, who took that approach, beating men with the *vitus* because they were in a sullen mood. That was bad enough, but what made it worse was when those Centurions acted surprised when morale did not improve. I will say that I only saw two or three Centurions in the 8th who acted in this manner. The worst by far was the 13th, which already had morale problems because of the shame that Plautus' Century had brought on the Legion.

Natalis seemed at a loss on how to handle the problems in his Legion and I began spending time with him in an attempt to help him straighten matters out. After a bit of time with the man, I began to suspect that Natalis was one of those Primi Pili that was more of a political appointment than a man who had risen to the post on his merits. In some respects, every Primus Pilus is a political appointment; I am not blind to the fact that the same could be said about me with some justification, although I would put my record in battle against any man's in the army, having the scars and decorations to back it up. In fact, I had been informed by Crassus just a few days before that he was awarding me a Grass Crown for saving Claudius, making my second such award. The first one I won was for saving Scribonius, many years before, and I was happy that my friend seemed to be on the way to recovery now. He was still too weak to stand, yet he could now sit for short periods before the pain became too much to bear. Most of the less seriously wounded men had recovered enough to rejoin the ranks, while others succumbed to their injuries. The bouncing and jolting of the wagons probably had as much to do with killing these men as their initial injuries, but it could not be helped. If it had been possible, all the seriously wounded men, including Scribonius, would have been sent back to winter camp, or to some city that was safe for Legionaries to stay. However, we were too far from Pannonia, the situation too uncertain to risk sending several wagons with perhaps a Century escort through what was essentially enemy territory.

We were now at a spot just north of the Thracian border, in between two chains of mountains, the southernmost forming part of what was a natural barrier into Thrace, while the northernmost curved from an east-west axis slightly northward, creating a broad valley through which a river (Hebros) ran. We turned north to follow this new river deeper into Moesia. The land began to flatten out, becoming more fertile, and it was not long before we began seeing more and more signs of habitation, beginning with small farms and villages. It was now the early part of the harvesting season, so parties were sent out to reap whatever crops were being grown. This served two purposes, helping to fill our own supply wagons while depriving the Moesians of food. Crassus believed, as did I based on experience, that the Moesians could not long remain passive, because of the threat not just from us but from their own people, who would become desperate at the prospect of starvation. If a leader cannot protect his own people, he is not likely to remain their leader for long, and as we moved northward, leaving columns of inky black smoke rising in the air, our scouts reported increased signs of enemy activity. Finally, just over a week after Crassus announced the extension of the campaign for another month, we got our first real glimpse of a large force of Moesians. We had been shadowed by outriders constantly since we had been attacked, but this was the first time we saw signs of anything larger. As was usual in these cases, it was in the form of a large cloud of dust, the rains that had plagued us earlier having ceased and left the ground extremely dry. Immediately, all the grumbling and sullen behavior was swept away, the men becoming excited at the prospect of battle. They were eager to avenge the embarrassment of the attack, along with holding the hope that if we could force the Moesians into battle and soundly defeat them, Crassus would be satisfied and we could end the campaign. The cloud was moving across our front, from east to west, causing Crassus to issue immediate orders to change our own course, putting us on a path that would intersect with the Moesians. We were headed to battle.

One disadvantage of being the pursuer, particularly in a strange land, is that the pursued is likely heading for a spot of their own choosing, where the ground will favor them. I was keenly aware of this, as were the Primi Pili, and to his credit, Crassus took our counsel seriously. I suppose that very prominent in his mind was the memory of what had happened when his grandfather had refused to heed the

290

advice of the native nobles attached to his command, leading to one of the greatest disasters ever to befall a Roman army. To avoid being lured into a trap, Crassus ordered us into an *agmentum quadratum*, with the baggage train in the middle, in the same manner that Antonius had used during our time in Parthia. This slowed our progress, but it put the men more at ease knowing that we were prepared for an ambush. With the army in a more secure posture, we closed the distance to the last point we had seen sign of the enemy. The dust cloud had disappeared, telling us that on the other side of a high and rugged line of hills waited the Moesians, probably in numbers that they felt were sufficient to offer us battle. Whether or not they stopped of their own volition, or the circumstances of our ravaging the land forced them to do so might make all the difference. Men fighting willingly are likely to fight harder than men who have been compelled to, but I suspected that these Moesians would put up a good fight, if for the only reason that they were fighting to keep from starving this winter. Our supply situation had improved thanks to the bounty of the early harvest, yet it was still not completely solved, especially if we found ourselves in this land into winter. We needed to settle this to Crassus' satisfaction, and every man in the army knew it. The mood of the men was one of quiet determination; they seemed to have left their discontent behind, accepting their lot, and were looking forward to fighting the Moesians again to exact vengeance. However, the first challenge was finding a passage through the hills that had a track wide enough and with a grade that could be ascended by the wagons. This turned out to be more difficult than anticipated, and we had to make a wide detour of several miles farther north before we found one. Even then, the men of the Legions had to help push the wagons up and over the final part of the grade, matters not helped by the extremely rough nature of the track itself. Several wagons suffered broken wheels, creating even more of a delay, prompting Crassus to briefly consider leaving the baggage train behind, thereby allowing us to march more quickly to close with the Moesians. The idea was barely out of his mouth when Diocles came rushing to get me from where I had been supervising the handling of Scribonius' wagon, much to the discomfort of the poor bastards who had been assigned to it. I was shouting at them to be careful and not rock it back and forth so much, knowing how painful it must be for Scribonius, despite the fact he had not uttered a peep in protest. Diocles quickly told me what Crassus was thinking, so excusing myself with a warning to the men, I rode Ocelus at a canter to where the command group was gathered. I did not wait for Crassus to bring it up, or even to offer a greeting. Saluting, I immediately asked, "Is it true that you are thinking of leaving the baggage train behind?"

He looked startled, but said that he was indeed thinking that very thing. Drawing him aside, I tried to keep my voice low.

"General, I am just going to tell you now without waiting for you to ask. That is a very, very bad idea."

"Well, thank you for telling me something I already know, Pullus." His tone was mildly reproving, but he was smiling as he said it. "It was just something that I was thinking about, and I almost immediately came to the same conclusion. Your man, Diocles, isn't it? Yes, he should have waited a bit longer and he would have heard me say as much."

Slightly chagrined, I still wanted to get what I thought was an important point across, befitting my duties as the most senior man from the ranks.

"Please don't blame Diocles for coming to tell me," I began. "One thing that can get a Legate, and a Primus Pilus for that matter, in a lot of trouble is the habit of thinking out loud."

Crassus raised an eyebrow, but said nothing, which I took as a sign to continue.

"The fate of every man in this army is in your hands, sir. And that means that they hang on every word that comes out of your mouth. I know I do not have to tell you that the walls of the *Praetorium* themselves have ears, and so does every tree and bush when we're out here on the march. It's not that the men are nosy, at least most of them. It's just that if they have the chance to find out beforehand what's waiting up ahead for them, well, you can hardly blame them for taking it."

Crassus appeared thoughtful, then nodded his head slowly and said, "That is a good point, Prefect. I will keep that in mind."

Snapping back to the matter at hand, he informed me, "But we're not leaving the baggage train behind. I don't want to be thought of as another Marcus Antonius."

Since that was precisely the thought that had gone through my head when Diocles had informed me of what Crassus was thinking, I saw then that he had gotten the point. By the time the baggage train cleared the top of the ridge, the last one just leaving the lower slope, it was late enough in the day that a decision had to be made about making camp. We were now on the same side of the mountains as the Moesians, according to our last reports, but were almost seven miles away. That presented Crassus with three choices, and he called a meeting to discuss the options before us.

"I'm inclined to camp here," he told the Primi Pili and me. Pointing to a rivulet cascading down the slope of the hill we had just descended, he continued, "This is sufficient for camp tonight, and we don't know exactly what water is available ahead. I know that means a longer march to battle tomorrow."

"It also means we'd have to bring the *medici* and the hospital tent closer," Macrinus pointed out. "We can't expect to carry men all the way back to camp, if we want as many to survive as possible."

"And we don't know what the Moesians will do when we show up," Aelianus put in. "They might be content to allow us to give the men a chance to rest after the march there, but I wouldn't count on that. So we have to consider the possibility that we'll go into battle without any rest."

I remained silent, believing that the Primi Pili were doing an adequate job of pointing out the shortcomings of Crassus' plan. Personally, I was in favor of pushing on at least three miles; four would be better. That was far enough away that we could not be surprised, yet short enough that the men could march directly into battle without being winded. However,

293

Crassus' concern about the water was valid, so after a moment when I saw that nobody was mentioning it, I felt compelled to bring up a question.

"If we keep marching, but don't find water, how much are in stores right now?"

There was some hesitation when the Primi Pili looked at each other, waiting for someone else to speak, causing me to lose patience.

"Are you telling me that none of you know how many barrels of water each of you have on hand?"

"I know," Macrinus answered instantly, giving the others an apologetic look. "The 8th has an average of four full barrels per Cohort. The First has nine barrels."

"We're about the same," Aelianus said, the others finally mumbling that they were roughly the same as well.

The moment I got the answers, I knew why they had been hesitant. On a normal day of marching, in temperate weather of the kind we were experiencing, the consumption of water per Legionary, for drinking, cooking, and the like, was roughly one barrel of water per Century per day. That meant at any given moment, a Cohort should have on hand six barrels, except for the First Cohort, which requires twelve. This amount was to be kept in reserve at all times, for the very reason that we were facing now. If we had to make a dry camp, the men would have enough water for a normal day, but being short, Crassus was almost forced to stop, if only to refill the barrels. Despite it making sense tactically to push on, now it was a risk, because if we marched the remaining miles with no sight of water, the men would go into battle with dry throats.

"How did this happen?" I snapped. "Each of you is too experienced to make that kind of mistake. It's the kind of thing that I'd expect an Optio or a Centurion in the Tenth to make, not the Primi Pili of the Legions!"

Crassus sat on his horse, looking bemused, the original topic seemingly forgotten. I was extremely angry, as much at myself as at the Primi Pili, because I had not thought to remind them to check the water supply.

"What about the animals?" I asked unhappily. "What's the water supply for them?"

"It's better, but not by that much," Macrinus admitted.

"Not for us," Natalis responded, which did not surprise me.

I turned to Crassus, and said, "There's the essence of the decision, General. We either take the gamble that there's water somewhere ahead, so that our march into battle is shorter, or we do as you were inclined in the first place and camp here."

Crassus thought for a moment, then called for his *bucinator*.

"Sound the call to make camp."

With the prospect of a tiring march to battle the next morning, the men were even more pensive than one would expect before a fight. They had taken the measure of the Moesians, meaning there was a familiarity with the enemy that is oddly comforting to a fighting man. Of all the things about battle that men fear, next to being killed of course, is the fear of that which has never been seen before. The Bastarnae were an example; before we actually faced them across the field, the men of the Legions talked of little else than the supposedly invincible falx-wielding Bastarnae warrior. Once we faced and defeated them, they were no longer an object of fear and suspicion. To that point, few if any men in this army had gone straight into battle from the march, and it was easy to see that they were worried about it. That night before we faced the Moesians marked the first night that Scribonius actually sat by the fire. When he had recovered to the point that he could be moved from the wagon to my tent every night after camp was made, we would keep the flaps open so that he could at least see Balbus, Diocles, and sometimes Gaius and me sitting by the fire talking. There is something comforting about a fire at night, especially for old campaigners like we were, and I knew that he missed it. That night, Balbus and I were sitting discussing the next day, and how the army might perform, when I saw Diocles leap to his feet out of the corner of my eye. Turning, I saw Scribonius walking unsteadily toward us, his face suffused with the orange glow of the fire, which he stared at with the same longing of a man for a woman when he has not had one in a long time. I rose to help him, but he gave me a warning shake of the head, telling me in unspoken words that he wanted to do this himself. Balbus looked up, but if he was surprised, he did not show it.

"Well, look who finally decided that we were good enough to be in his presence," Balbus said by way of greeting.

"I just figured that Titus was probably tired of hearing about whores and drunken brawls and was ready to talk about other topics," Scribonius shot back.

Despite the sharp talk, I knew that they were both pleased, Balbus to see Scribonius up and about, and Scribonius because Balbus was not fussing over him the way I did.

"Other topics?" Balbus rubbed his chin. "What other topics are there?"

Scribonius did not stay long, but it was nice to have him back at the fire, so that for a short while, things were back to normal. I had been keeping Scribonius apprised of everything taking place, both as a courtesy and because I valued his counsel, since he always had insight into things that I often missed.

"You think Crassus made a mistake by not getting closer, don't you?" Scribonius' question came out of nowhere while he sat staring into the fire.

"I think either way he goes, he's fucked," I said after thinking about it for a moment. "Because of our water situation, he was forced to choose between the men being tired, or possibly being thirsty going into battle."

"Neither is a good thing," Scribonius acknowledged. "But what's he going to do about the wounded?"

"Macrinus asked the same question, and it was never really answered," I told him.

He gave a frown, and I could see that he was troubled.

"I hope that you'll bring it up tomorrow," Scribonius said.

"Since when are you so worried about the wounded?" Balbus cut in.

Scribonius looked at him with a lifted eyebrow.

"I wonder why," he replied dryly. "If Philipos hadn't been right there, and we hadn't made camp right there on the spot, I'd be dead. Maybe that has something to do with it."

Over the years, I had observed that Scribonius' attitude was not at all unusual. Men who had been seriously wounded tended to think more about that, and the possibility of it happening to others, than men who had not. Whatever the reason, he had reminded me of something that I needed to bring up with Crassus. Once Scribonius had returned to the tent, I left to go to the *Praetorium*. On my way, I stopped outside the circle of light of a few fires, standing in between the tents to listen to the men talk about the next day. After a bit, I had heard enough and I continued on to talk to Crassus.

"The men are worried about tomorrow," I told him.

"Men are always worried before battle," Crassus replied dismissively.

"Not like this." I shook my head. "They're worried about the normal things, but it's more than that. They're particularly worried about the idea of a hard march into battle, and what's going to happen to the wounded."

"I thought we already went over that." Crassus was clearly peeved.

"I suggest that we break camp early tomorrow morning, bring the baggage closer, leave behind a Cohort from each Legion to guard it, and set up the hospital tent, at the very least."

Crassus pursed his lips in thought, and for a moment, it looked like he would refuse.

"Very well," he said finally. "I'll send for the Primi Pili to give the orders."

Feeling somewhat better, I returned to my tent to make my own preparations for the coming day. I had long since lost count of how many times I had done this, but the feeling was always the same. There was a tightness in my stomach, while my mind raced through all the things that needed to be done, although it was a much shorter list now overall, compared to my days as Primus Pilus. I took my Gallic blade and the *spatha* to the armory *immunes* to put an edge on both blades, using my rank to take head of the line privileges. With that done, I went to see Ocelus, who seemed to sense my tension and was highly spirited, pawing at the dirt as he nosed through my tunic for his treat. Having done all that I could think of, I returned to my tent to try to get some sleep, wondering what the next day would bring.

We broke camp a third of a watch before dawn, earlier than normal, the men working quickly and efficiently to pack everything up. The sun was barely peeking over the horizon when the army formed up to begin heading in a westerly direction. Silva's men ranged ahead, alert for any sign of ambush, but there was no sign of the enemy. Approximately four miles from our original camp, we found a cascading stream crossing our path that was adequate to supply water, and despite being a bit short of how far we wanted to go, Crassus decided not to risk pushing on and not finding another source of water. The baggage train was left behind, along with a Cohort from each Legion, as I had suggested, the rest of the army pushing ahead. There was a very low ridge branching off of the line of mountains to our left that was just high enough to block our view of the ground on the other side. Silva's troopers were within sight, climbing the ridge before suddenly pulling up short. A moment later, I saw a rider come galloping back, and I knew this meant that the enemy had been sighted. The messenger pulled up in front of Crassus, and I did not hear what he said because I was too far away, so I trotted Ocelus up as Crassus and the Tribunes were talking.

"They've spotted the Moesians," Crassus told me, which I expected. What I did not expect was what he said next. "And they've sent a delegation out under flag of truce. They want to talk."

Crassus marched the army to the top of the ridge, arraying them on a front of three Legions, leaving the fourth hidden behind the hill. Across a broad valley, about a mile away, stood the Moesian host, spread out on their own hill, a bit higher and steeper than ours.

298

"They chose good ground," Crassus commented as we took a moment to survey the potential battlefield.

"It makes you wonder why they want to talk," I replied, my eyes on the small knot of horsemen standing out alone roughly halfway between the two armies.

"There's only one way to find out."

Crassus turned and signaled to Claudius, telling him to take a dozen of Silva's troopers with him to make the initial contact with the waiting Moesians. Saluting, the Tribune waited for Silva to select the men to go with him, then without a word turned to trot down to meet the Moesians.

"There's been quite the change in the Tribune," Crassus said idly, his eyes on the retreating man's back.

"Yes, there has," I agreed. "And really, he's not a bad sort, once he got that stick out of his ass."

I do not know who was more surprised at these words coming out of my mouth, and I felt Crassus' eyes on me before he burst out laughing.

"I hadn't thought of it in those terms," he said, still amused. "But I suppose that's as good a way of putting it as any."

Returning our attention to the scene before us, we saw Claudius reach the Moesians, and I found myself clenching Ocelus' reins, waiting for some kind of trick. When nothing untoward happened, I relaxed as the Tribune and the Moesians talked. My attention was drawn to one man in particular, a heavyset man with a dark beard that had startling streaks of white that were visible even from this distance. By his position a bit in front of the others, I deduced that this must be the leader of the Moesian army that, like ours, was standing on their hillside waiting. The conference between Claudius and the Moesians did not take long, Claudius returning at the trot.

"They request a meeting with you to discuss a possible peaceful settlement," Claudius told Crassus. The Legate lifted an eyebrow, exchanging a glance with me.

"Well, well," he said softly. "This is unexpected."

For a moment, I thought he was going to refuse the meeting, then he gave a shrug. "I suppose it can't hurt to hear what they have to say." Turning to me, he said briskly, "Prefect, I'm leaving you here in command of the army. If the Moesians have some sort of trick to play, you know what to do."

"Destroy them," I replied.

"Exactly."

Beckoning Claudius to follow, Crassus descended the hill with the same troopers as an escort. I sat on Ocelus, who was getting bored, tossing his head, communicating his desire to go for a run.

"Maybe later," I told him, patting his neck.

Hearing the sound of hoofbeats, I turned to see Balbus coming to sit beside me while we waited. I was happy for his company, and we sat in silence, watching the Legate approach the Moesians. Although I did not think there would be any treachery, I was also not taking my eyes off the scene below in the event I was wrong. The heavyset man did all the talking for the Moesians, it quickly becoming apparent that this would be as protracted a negotiation as the one with Roles had been. After a short while, the Primi Pili allowed the men to sit in place, and it was barely a few heartbeats after that the dice were broken out, and the gambling began. I finally dismounted from Ocelus to let him graze and get the load off his back, while Balbus did the same, lying down to take a nap.

"If you wouldn't drink so much, you wouldn't be tired all the time," I chided him.

He opened one eye to squint up at me.

"And I would be as boring and as little fun as you," he retorted, shutting his eye and was soon snoring.

The sun continued to climb, except there was a cool breeze, making it very pleasant, and I found that I was fighting the urge to nod off myself. Finally, there was a movement when Crassus and the heavyset man clasped hands before returning to their respective parties. Crassus remounted his horse, the party immediately turning to trot back towards us, while I watched carefully to make sure that the Moesians did not try anything. However, they were content to return to their own army, and I waited for Crassus to find out what was going on.

"That was a profitable discussion," Crassus said as he dismounted, a wide smile on his face.

"Oh? How so?" I asked.

"We just made two thousand talents of silver, and fifty royal and noble hostages," he said, not a little smugly.

I could feel my jaw drop, and I heard Balbus, who had gotten to his feet at the sound of the approaching horses, gasp in astonishment.

"They're going to pay that to keep from fighting?"

Crassus nodded, then added, "A bit more than that. I agreed that we'll leave Moesia immediately, and will suspend all hostilities against any Moesian tribe for this season and next."

This seemed too good to be true, and he could see my dubious expression.

"They're going to pay us a thousand talents by sundown today, and the rest will be delivered next year, once we fulfill our end of the bargain. The hostages will be with the money."

While that was good news, I still could not see the reason behind making this agreement from the Moesian perspective.

"Why would the Moesians give us that much money?"

"I don't know exactly," Crassus admitted. "I suspect that there's some internal dissension that their leader, that's the man with the streaked beard, is trying to deal with. His name is Arrianos, and he claims to be the high king of all the Moesian tribes."

He gave a shrug, turning his gaze back to where the man Arrianos and his party had just rejoined their own army.

"You never know with these natives. But what I do know is that this should make the men happy. As soon as we take delivery of the money and hostages, we're turning south and heading for Greece."

On the surface, that sounded completely reasonable, but I was not so sure.

"Don't underestimate the greed of the Legions," was the way I put my concerns to Crassus.

Giving me a sharp look, he asked cautiously, "What do you mean?"

Drawing him a short distance away from the others, I laid out what I thought the likely reaction of the men to be at this news.

"As much as the men want to go home, since they're not going back to Siscia, they want the opportunity for loot. One reason they fight is for the chance at making money off of what they can take from an enemy. There's also the matter of the slaves you promised the Centurions," I went on.

While I was not absolutely sure that Crassus had no plans to share this bounty with the men, I assumed it to be the case based on what I had seen previously with men of the upper classes getting their hands on that much money. My judgment seemed to be confirmed when he made a face that clearly indicated his displeasure at the idea.

Except that he said, "I was already planning on paying each man a bonus of three hundred sesterces per man for the ranks and a thousand for all second-grade and lower Centurions. The first grades were to receive fifteen hundred, and the Primi Pili two thousand."

I did some quick mental calculations in my head, which I was able to do thanks to Scribonius teaching me many years before.

"That's well more than one thousand talents. In fact, I think that would be a bit more than two thousand, wouldn't it?"

"I haven't really thought about it," he said carelessly, reminding me that he was so wealthy that two thousand talents was a sum so inconsequential that he did not bother to notice whether the sums he had come up with exceeded the total.

"Well," I replied, somewhat ashamed that I had so readily assumed that he would keep the money for himself, "that changes things quite a bit. I think the men will be very happy with this news."

"I hope so."

Crassus dismounted and called his *bucinator* to sound the call for the Primi Pili to assemble. Immediately upon their arrival, he announced the latest developments. The Primi Pili took the news that there was to be no fight with mixed reactions; Macrinus clearly wanted to fight, while Natalis looked the most relieved. The more I had seen of Natalis, the more certain I became that he was not fit to lead a Legion, and I began turning over in my mind the best way to make sure he was removed. However, they all turned more cheerful when Crassus announced the bounty that he would be paying to the men. As soon as he was finished, the Primi Pili were dismissed to alert their Legions. It was easy to tell when each Legion was told, since the men raised a rousing cheer at the news, shouting praise to their general and generally rejoicing, though whether it was for the money or for the end of the campaign it was hard to tell. Unfortunately for the men, and for everyone else, we could not leave the hill until the money had been delivered, and Crassus was unwilling to risk sending part of the army back to make camp as long as the Moesians were still arrayed across from us. They did not leave, so we were forced to stay put, the day dragging by slowly. Finally, three wagons appeared over the crest of the far hill, accompanied by what I assumed to be the hostages, except there were far more than fifty. I quickly remembered that, similar to the situation in Gaul, these highborn hostages were all bringing at least one and usually more retainers or slaves to attend to their needs. I remembered how much of a headache keeping track of all the Gauls had been, along with the amount of mischief they had caused, and I hoped that these Moesians did not prove to be as much trouble. I went down with Crassus and several clerks from the *Praetorium*, along with a Cohort guard, sitting and watching the Legate inspect the contents of the wagons, dictating to a scribe as he counted. There was no way to tell if each ingot of silver was the same weight, although I supposed that the Moesians would not be willing to take the risk of coming up short. Crassus announced that from his initial count, it appeared that the entire amount

303

was there, but that we would make sure that night. The wagons were sent back to the army, while the clerks recorded the names and tribe of each of the hostages, along with any other information that Crassus deemed pertinent, before we joined the rest of the army. The hostages seemed to be in anything but a sullen mood, chattering excitedly in a mishmash of their tribal tongues and Greek. From what I gathered, most of them were under the impression that they would be sent to Rome, and were looking forward to it immensely. I remained silent, not sure that any of them would get anywhere near Rome.

We began the march south the next morning, after the clerks stayed up half the night conducting a thorough and complete count of the bullion. All of the men were in high spirits, their initial disappointment at not heading back to Siscia allayed by the news of the bonuses, which would be paid once we settled in wherever our winter quarters happened to be in Greece. With Moesia settled and the Bastarnae vanquished, Crassus justifiably felt good about all that had been accomplished. He had been sending regular dispatches back to Rome, but there had been no response, which we interpreted in two different ways. Crassus took the silence as approval for all that he was doing; I took it as an ominous sign, one that Scribonius and I had talked at length about. I was heeding his advice, keeping my mouth shut and not getting involved in any intrigues, despite my feelings for Crassus. I had come to regard him as one of the most likeable of the upper classes I had met. I did not hold him in the same regard that I had Caesar, and I did not fear him the way I feared Octavian, but I respected both equally, for completely different reasons. Where Octavian was, and is cold and aloof, Crassus was personable and approachable. Octavian might have been more competent, and at organization he is unparalleled, but Crassus was no slouch himself. I think the biggest difference between the two was in the way that Crassus carried the weight of his ancestry and position among the Roman elite. By virtue of his birth, and more importantly his wealth, he had every right to be a snob, yet he was anything but, having a common touch that I had only seen before in Caesar, and to a lesser extent, Antonius, except as I would learn with Antonius it was more of a sham than genuine. I never got that feeling from Crassus; if it was an act, it was a good one that I never saw slip. I suppose that is why I worried as much as I did that he had overstepped and would pay a steep price. As pressing as these thoughts were, the daily monotony of the march and the need to alleviate the boredom of plodding mile after mile soon pushed them to the back of my mind. Most worrying was the gradual change in weather; just our second day of the march to Greece saw a hard frost on the ground when we awoke, the chill lasting through the better part of the day. Looming ahead of us was the line of mountains that we had to cross to get into Thrace, snow already well down their flanks.

On the fourth day of the march, we reached the foot of the mountains to begin the climb up, following a narrow river valley that cut through the range. The lower slopes leading down to the river consisted of striated rock, alternating between shades of red and white that is quite striking. These are the kinds of things one notices to pass the time, but the narrowness of the valley acted as a funnel for the wind, so it was not long before men who had them broke out their socks and *bracae* to cover the legs, while everyone began wearing their *sagum*. I pulled my fur-lined *sagum* out of my baggage, as did Scribonius, who was now strong enough to spend the whole day in the saddle. He still retired immediately after our evening meal to the tent, but his strength was coming back little by little every day. However, there seemed to be something missing from him, some spark that I had seen extinguished in other men who had almost died. It had not happened to me, and I spent a great deal of time thinking about why this was the case. Scribonius was every bit as brave as I was, and while he may not have been as skilled with the sword as I was, I was convinced that it was only because he did not practice as much as I did. He was also not as large and physically strong as I was, yet that was something that he could not help, and neither could I; both of us had been born with our condition and really had nothing to do with what the gods had given us. The conclusion that I reached was that what Scribonius lacked was the gift of fury, that feeling of rage that came over me in battle that fueled a savage desire in me to destroy any who stood in my way. Thinking it through, I attributed this feeling of anger that I had, always seething just beneath the surface like a volcano that is waiting to erupt, to the circumstances of my childhood, along with the relationship of hatred and fear between my father and me. When Scribonius had finally opened up about his background, his life of privilege and opportunity that came with being the son of a wealthy equestrian in Rome, the one thing that he had communicated was the love he had felt from his father, along with the regard and respect Scribonius held for his *paterfamilias*. While it had helped make Scribonius the good man that he is, it also meant that he would never be as single-minded as I was when the time came to pick up the sword to slay the enemy. Finally, I believe that in the heart of every successful warrior is the secret belief that they cannot be defeated, that there is no man who can strike them down. It is a myth, a fantasy that we convince ourselves is true in order to give us the ability to wade into a fight without fear. We all expect to be wounded, and in fact we bear these scars with immense pride, but there is a difference between the wound that is part of a victory over a foe, and one where you are the one that is struck down. For those fortunate few of us who receive a wound that proves mortal to others, it can rob us of that secret belief that we are invincible, and that is what appeared to have happened to Scribonius. I honestly do not know why even after my near death at Munda, that belief never left me, yet it had not. Balbus noticed this as well, and we had more than one whispered conversation about our friend, but we both knew that only time would tell if the old Scribonius would come back.

It was in the middle of our second day in the mountains that the blizzard struck, out of nowhere, completely surprising the army. Even wrapped up as we were, the cold sliced through the layers of clothing that we wore, in bare moments the visibility dropping next to zero. I was instantly reminded of Parthia, except the one blessing was that we did not have a dropoff of several hundred feet to send men plunging to their deaths. Still, the footing was treacherous for man and beast. Even Ocelus, normally so surefooted, slipped several times before I finally dismounted to begin leading him. The wind was howling so loudly that it made normal conversation impossible, keeping communications to a bare minimum of shouted orders while we trudged along, struggling forward. Time seemed to stop, our world now reduced to just the few feet we could see in front of us, while the most important thing was putting one foot in front of the other. I kept a careful eye on Scribonius, and after I saw him stagger a few times, I made him get back on his horse, which I led alongside Ocelus. As the day progressed, the storm showed no signs of abating, and the *exploratores*, those men designated to range ahead of the army to find a place to camp made their way back to report that the spot they had chosen was still more than ten miles distant. It was now perilously close to dusk, meaning that even if the storm had miraculously cleared, there was no way that we would make it to the site before nightfall. Moving forward in the dark and in a blizzard was simply out of the question, prompting Crassus to make the decision that we would continue on until it was no longer light enough to see, whereupon we would have to settle in the best we could to wait out the storm.

When we did stop, there was simply not enough room to spread out and pitch more than the hospital tent, but with the army now spread out on the trail over several miles, with the baggage train at the rear of three Legions, there was no way to even do that. This meant that the few men still seriously wounded enough to remain in the hospital, along with the sick, had to endure a night out in the cold. Even with a fur-lined *sagum* and wearing my extra pair of fur-lined socks on my hands as mittens, it was bitterly cold, forcing Balbus, Scribonius, Diocles and me to huddle together, shivering the night away. I do not believe any of us got much sleep, while I worried the most about Scribonius, although he seemed to bear up well and without complaint. The storm raged through the night, covering men in a blanket of snow, actually serving to make things a bit warmer once we were encased in the stuff like a cocoon. It finally abated shortly before dawn, and by the time the sun rose, all traces of the storm had been scrubbed from the sky, the day dawning bright, clear, and bitterly cold. Inevitably, some of the sick and wounded succumbed, not responding when a *medici* came to check on them, and it was not long before we learned that it was not only these men that were lost. In some cases, men who had been on sentry duty had lost their bearings and could not be found, never to be seen again. Other cases involved men who had not been deemed ill enough to be placed on the sick list, but had obviously been weakened enough that the night in the bitter storm had been too much for them.

"I hope this doesn't turn into another Parthia." Scribonius finally voiced what was on my mind and I was sure was on Balbus' as well.

We had just started the day's march, and I only had to look at my friends to see the fatigue that I knew was weighing down on every man's shoulders after the hard night. Only Ocelus and the other horses did not seem the worse for wear, although my animal did seem to appreciate the fact that I had placed my other *sagum* over him to help cut the cold. He was exceptionally frisky, hopping a few times when I mounted him, blowing huge clouds of vapor while he tossed his head, his hooves churning up the snow.

"I'm glad you had a good night," I told him sourly, and I swear that he laughed at me.

The deep snow that had fallen on the ground presented a problem for the leading elements of the army, and it was only a short while before Crassus ordered Silva and the Evocati up front to let the horses break through the snow for the vanguard Legion. It was incredibly slow going, even with the horses doing most of the work, and we had to rotate the leading rank to keep from exhausting the animals. It was up to their chest, although by the time the five hundred troopers of Silva's command and the remaining Evocati passed through it was packed down enough that the men had little difficulty. By the time the wagons rolled through, I imagined that the snow was packed firmly enough that they would not have trouble. I was wrong, because it was not long before the word came to stop in order to keep the army from getting too spread out on this torturous track.

By the time we reached the spot that the *exploratores* had selected for the camp we were supposed to make the day before, it was well past midday, making it an easy decision to stop. The only problem was that the snow had to be cleared out, at least along the perimeter of the camp, to allow the ditch to be dug and the rampart created, extending the amount of time it took to get the camp set up. Compounding matters was pitching the tents on snow, not only because it was not as firm as the ground, making them hard to stake down, but sleeping on snow is not exactly a pleasant experience. Even using our cots, the interior of our tents were only marginally warmer than outside. Until, that is, the combination of our body heat and the lamps began to melt the snow, meaning that by morning we were essentially wading in ankle deep water. Fortunately, as Camp Prefect, I did not have to worry about that, since like the *Praetorium* I had a wooden floor that insulated me from such unpleasantness. The other men, including the Evocati, did not have that luxury, and as a result, I got to listen to the complaints the entire next day when we continued the march. I believe it was at our morning meal when Balbus made an offhand comment that I had cause to remember several times on that march.

"I hope that these last couple of days aren't an omen of what's to come," was how he put it as we ate our morning bread and piece of cold bacon.

In fact, while I had given up believing in omens and portents, I must admit that his words would come back to my mind several times.

After another two days of similar struggle, we finally crossed the mountain barrier into Thrace. It was only then that Crassus gave the order for the men to sling shields and did not send out flanking patrols. Given what happened, I suppose it is easy to fault him; indeed, this was one of the reasons used as the pretext for what happened to him later, but honestly, I can find nothing in his decision that was objectionable. After all, Rome had a treaty with Thrace, and it was because of that treaty that we originally marched to chastise the Bastarnae, making it hard to condemn him for relaxing his guard. Certainly, some fault lies with Silva and his cavalry; the whole purpose of cavalry when on the march is to act as the eyes of the Legate, in order to prevent being surprised. However, I also know that when a commander of any value is set on it, particularly when in their own territory, hiding an army of a relatively small size is not that hard. Perhaps I am saying this because being second in command, I could have said something, but truthfully I was not expecting trouble any more than Crassus was. That is why when it happened, the surprise was devastatingly effective. We were skirting a heavily wooded area, the men talking and singing marching songs when a hail of missiles came flying out of the thick underbrush. The vanguard and the command group had already passed by the woods, our only warning of an attack coming when we were alerted by the alarmed shouts of men struck by a missile. Crassus reacted immediately, jerking his horse around without hesitation to gallop back towards the rear.

"We better go with him," Balbus grumbled, although I noticed he did not hesitate to follow Crassus, beating me by several heartbeats.

Before I went, I told Scribonius sternly, "Stay here. You're not recovered enough for this."

"So now you're a doctor?" he retorted, and I was secretly pleased to feel his presence behind me.

The rest of the Evocati followed along, and on our approach to the woods, which were on the right of our original direction of march, we could see a mass of barbarian

310

warriors surging out of the shelter of the forest, following up their initial barrage of missiles, which had caught the men completely unprepared. The Legion being attacked was the 15th, and drawing close enough we could see that the attack was localized to a front of three or four Cohorts, and they were beginning to fight back. Crassus had arrived on the scene, and it was obviously his presence that sprang the second part of the trap. Bursting from the cover of the woods was a second force, this one mounted, heading directly for Marcus Crassus, who had outrun us and the rest of his cavalry escort, still somewhere behind us. In the moment it takes for Diocles to write this, Crassus was surrounded and fighting for his life, desperately parrying thrusts that seemed to be coming from every direction. Balbus, still a few lengths ahead of me, did not hesitate, drawing his *spatha* and kicking his horse to go slamming into a well-armored warrior who made the fatal mistake of turning his back on us in his haste to try to dispatch Crassus. I saw Balbus' arm draw back to drive his *spatha* into the unprotected side of the warrior before I was occupied with my own battle, with Ocelus propelling me into the midst of three warriors flanking Crassus. My horse, with a scream of what I can only describe as rage, stretched out, grabbing the neck of one of the enemy horses with his big yellow teeth. The other beast screeched in agony, blood running down its neck, and in its desperate attempt to twist from the grasp of Ocelus, moved so violently that its rider lurched to the side, flailing his blade desperately for balance, giving me the opening I needed. Plunging my own sword deep into his side, I twisted it free, turning to find another target even before the other man fell. Ocelus had released his grip on the other horse, which galloped off, weaving through the dense mass of warriors.

Picking out another warrior pressing Crassus, I barely registered the threat from my left until it was too late, and because I had not had time to unstrap the shield from my horse, I was completely unprotected from that side. Sensing the movement out of the corner of my eye, I turned just in time to see another warrior, teeth bared in a triumphant grin, drawing his arm back to thrust his long cavalry spear into my side. Everything slowed down as I began to try and twist my unarmored body, yet I knew I was too late, my only hope lying in moving just enough that the thrust did not kill me outright. My eyes were focused on the man's face, seeing the savage look that a man has when he is about to strike his foe down, a look that I had had on my own face more than I could count. Just then, I saw a blur of movement in the form of a long blade slicing through the air, the point of the sword taking the man in his right armpit, plunging deeply into the man's side. Instantly, his expression changed to one of shocked surprised, and I turned to see Scribonius, his own face set and determined as he withdrew the blade.

"Good thing I didn't listen to you," he shouted over the noise of the fighting, while the man who had been about to kill me slumped over and fell to the ground.

There was no time to thank Scribonius properly, instead just giving him a nod before I turned my attention back to my original target. It was only then that I noticed that the man I had selected was wielding a Thracian sword, except at that moment it did not register anything more significant than telling me the best way to attack the man. He was slashing at Crassus, who was bleeding from a cut to his upper arm, but seemed otherwise unhurt. By this time, enough of the Evocati and the cavalry bodyguard assigned to Crassus had arrived to tip the balance of the fighting in our favor, but the men we were facing seemed oblivious to that change. Attacking the warrior pressing Crassus, I made a thrust that he blocked with his shield, jarring my arm up to the shoulder. Crassus was too busy fighting with another warrior to take advantage of my own attack, leaving me engaged with this man, who was much younger than I was but very skilled. There was something that I had noticed, it only being later when I had time to reflect on it, that the last several men I had faced in battle seemed to have become more skilled than I remembered. When I mentioned this to Scribonius, his reaction was to burst out laughing before he reminded me that it was more likely that I was getting old than I had suddenly run into men who were a cut above all the other opponents I had faced. He was right, but at that moment, all I was concerned about was avoiding my opponent's answering thrust, just managing to do so, although the tip of his sword tore into my tunic. I was ruing that I had rushed after Crassus so impetuously and not unstrapped my shield, along with the lack of armor, though none of us was wearing any. That did not help me in facing this man, and for the space of several heartbeats, our blades clashed together repeatedly, first one, then the other seeking an opening while the other parried. I could feel the fatigue creeping into my arm, making it hard to hold the sword at the proper height and angle to meet an attack, hearing my breath rasping in my ears. In contrast, my foe seemed to be hardly exerting himself; I was fading quickly and he could clearly see it. This led him to be overconfident, or at least so I believe, because he made a mistake, giving me the opening I needed. It is equally possible that he was distracted by the flurry of movement when one of his comrades, in a desperate attempt to unhorse Crassus, launched himself from his saddle at the Legate. Whatever the cause, he had just made another lunging thrust, moving his upper body to add force to the attack, which I had managed to parry by allowing his blade to slide up my own. This is a dangerous tactic because despite it being deflected, you are allowing the point of your opponent's sword to come at you, but I was desperate. This resulted in his overextending his body, making him lean dangerously away from his horse. Since my left hand was free, I reached out, using the advantage of my longer reach to grab him by the collar, pulling him violently toward me. I did not even have to move the point of my sword, essentially pulling him onto my blade. I felt the sudden resistance when the tip pierced through his chain mail before sliding into his body, his blood running down the groove of my blade. It was not a mortal blow; my blade was tipped up and in my attempt to parry his thrust, I had tilted the blade so that it was perpendicular instead of parallel to the ground. It sliced into the front of his chest, feeling like it scraped along his ribcage without penetrating it. I could just see the point push his chain mail up slightly below his collarbone before I recovered to slide the blade out. My foe grunted in pain but did not cry out, and in fact tried a backhand slash which, if it had any power behind it, could have shattered my cheekbone, perhaps even slicing all the way through. As it was, I could feel the white-hot pain of his blade cutting me down to the bone before it slid away while the warrior, his right arm now falling to his side, jerked his horse away and without hesitation turned to gallop away. I made no attempt to pursue, mainly because I could feel the warmth of my blood flooding down my face. When I reached up, tentatively touching my cheek, I could feel the flesh hanging down like a flap.

Fortunately, the fight was rapidly wearing down, the attackers realizing that the initiative had been lost, making them now more concerned with disengaging to escape than trying to inflict any more casualties. That did not mean that they still did not try to engage in targets of opportunity, and even as they were withdrawing, some of them took one last parting shot at one of us. Crassus had survived, with only the damage the wound on his arm and a cut on his forehead, and he was already snapping out orders to the men around him. I could see a short distance away that the infantry attack had also stopped with the enemy warriors, who I still had not bothered to try to identify, withdrawing in good order. Meanwhile, the men of the 15th, who had managed at least to unsling their shields, were flinging their javelins as an incentive to send them on their way. In that glance, I saw many bodies lying on the ground, some belonging to the barbarians, but more belonging to us. I also turned about to find Scribonius, who was wiping his blade clean, watching the backs of the departing barbarian cavalry. I had not seen Balbus, and once I saw that it was safe to do so I looked around, seeing him off his horse, bent over the body of one of the barbarians.

"That figures," I said to Ocelus. "The battle's not over and he's busy looting a body."

It was at that moment, out of the corner of my eye I saw one of the barbarians turn in his saddle. Apparently seeing

Balbus with his hands ripping at the clothes of one of his comrades, perhaps even a close friend or relative, he let out a howl of rage. Pulling his arm back, he flung his spear at Balbus' back. Before my mind could form a thought, I heard a shout that echoed above even the last sounds of fighting.

"Noooooooooooooooooooooo!"

My cry made Balbus start, and he was just beginning to turn when the spear caught him in the back just behind the right shoulder, slicing through his body so the point emerged just below his left ribcage under his arm. He stood there for a moment, completely still; in that instant our eyes met, and I could see a slightly puzzled look on his face before he slowly toppled over.

When I reached his side, he was lying on his back, staring up at the sky, blinking rapidly, I suppose, as the reality of his situation was setting in. His lips were frothed with blood, a sign that his lungs had been pierced, and I could barely feel my legs when I jumped to the ground to kneel by his side. Looking over at me, he tried to smile, but it was a gruesome sight, his lifeblood coating his teeth to dribble out of his mouth. I felt the tears welling up in my eyes, yet I did not even try to hide them as I took Balbus' hand.

"I think this might be bad," he wheezed, even at the last trying to make a joke, but I could only answer with a choked sob. With his waning strength, he squeezed my hand, forcing me to look him in the eye.

"Don't grieve for me," he ordered, an order that I would never be able to obey.

I was vaguely aware of someone else appearing on the opposite side of Balbus, and I looked up to see Scribonius, his face mirroring my own with the sorrow that he was feeling. Balbus glanced over and, seeing Scribonius, gave a weak grunt.

"I got tired of seeing everyone fawning all over you, so I decided to show you how it's done." He gave another grin, but it was more of a grimace as a spasm of pain shot through his body.

"You always were able to outdo me," Scribonius replied, his own body shaking from sobbing.

"Don't you forget it," Balbus said, and I could see that he was weakening rapidly.

His life was now measured in breaths, which were becoming more labored with each passing moment. I knew from observation that what was happening was that his lungs were filling with blood, and he was drowning in his own fluids.

"I never did want to get old," he whispered. "Now I don't have to. My only regret is that I never got to make someone's ball sac into a coin purse."

"Don't worry, that's what I was planning on doing with yours," Scribonius said through his tears, causing Balbus to give a gurgling laugh, forcing blood to come spewing up and out of his mouth, making him choke.

With that, he died while Scribonius and I each held a hand of our oldest friend, feeling it grow cold in our own. I was completely oblivious to the world around me, refusing to let go of his hand, as if I could somehow transfer my own lifeforce into his body, but I watched his eyes taking on that faraway look, glazing over as his *animus* fled. Finally, I looked over to Scribonius, who was sitting on his heels, weeping as unashamedly as I was, then we leaned over and fell onto each other, over the body of our friend. I have no idea how long we sat there in this way before I became aware of someone standing over us, and I looked up to see Crassus, his arm now bound. His face reflected what I believe was genuine sorrow at the sight before him. He also had a job to do, which I could read in his face as well, and I nodded to him to say what he needed to say.

"First," he said awkwardly, "I'm profoundly sorry about Balbus. He was a great Legionary and Centurion of Rome, and I swear to you that he will be honored in a manner worthy of his status."

"Thank you," I answered for both Scribonius, who was still too affected to do anything but stare down at Balbus' body, and me.

Crassus started to say something else, but before he could, he was interrupted by someone calling his name. We both turned to look to see a Centurion, accompanied by two Legionaries, between whom they were dragging a barbarian warrior. I recognized the man as belonging to the 15th, but at the moment I could not place what Cohort he belonged to. Saluting Crassus, he beckoned to the Legionaries, who half-carried the man forward so that Crassus could get a good look at him. His head was hanging down, and the Centurion reached over to grab a handful of hair, savagely yanking the man's head back. With no choice but to face Crassus, he looked at the Legate with what I was sure he thought was defiance, except that his fear was all too plainly written on his face.

"Sir, this man is Thracian," the Centurion announced. "Triballi, to be exact."

"Thracian!" Crassus was clearly astonished, and I suppose I would have been if I had not been half out of my mind with grief.

"What are the Thracians doing attacking us? Especially the Triballi? We don't have a treaty with them, but we chased the Bastarnae away before they could lay waste to their lands," Crassus fumed, glaring at the Thracian prisoner.

"They're Thracian, sir, just like that bastard Spartacus who caused us so much trouble all those years ago," the Centurion ventured.

Crassus ignored him, speaking instead to the captive.

"Is this true?" he asked the man in Greek. "Are you Triballi?"

The captive did not answer for a moment, clearly trying to decide whether he would be betraying anything by replying. Finally, he just nodded his head, his eyes staying on Crassus' face. Cursing bitterly, Crassus looked down at me, clearly angry at having this confirmed. I was not looking at Crassus, instead focusing on the Thracian, who was still being held between the two Legionaries. Now that the attention was no longer on him, or so he thought, I saw him look down at Balbus, whose eyes were still open, staring at a sky he could

317

no longer see, and I swear that I saw the hint of a smirk cross his face at the sight of my dead friend. I am not sure what happened, because my next memory is standing with my Spanish sword in my hand, despite having no recollection in drawing it from the scabbard on my side, the blade dripping blood, with the Thracian lying at my feet. His intestines were in a greasy puddle next to him, while the two Legionaries were standing like they had become rooted to the spot, their mouths hanging open. Crassus looked no less astonished as he stared at me, while I slowly came back to my senses.

"What was that for?" the Legate gasped.

"He smiled at Balbus lying there," was all I could think to say.

Hearing that, Crassus' face changed, and he gave a shrug.

"Then he deserved what he got. I was going to have him executed anyway. But, Prefect," while his tone was gentle, there was no mistaking the fact that he was giving me a command and not a request. "Next time, please warn me before you do something like that."

"I'm running out of friends," I said bitterly. "I doubt that there will be a next time at this rate."

I instantly saw that I had embarrassed him as he shot a glance at Scribonius, who was oblivious, still kneeling at Balbus' body with his head bowed. Crassus excused himself, saying that he had to see to the 15th and the other men. Before he left, he told me that he would send Philipos to attend to the wound on my cheek, which I had completely forgotten about. Then he rode away, leaving me and Scribonius alone with our friend.

Because we had been marching in our tunics and without wearing our armor, the casualties were much higher than they should have been. The 15th alone suffered almost one hundred men dead, with nearly three times as many wounded, the majority of the wounded being hit by the initial missile barrage. Of the Evocati, besides Balbus we lost another eleven dead, but because we had been involved with their cavalry, we did not have nearly as many wounded. Counting me, there were four men who could still ride, while five were litter cases, one of which would die before the next sunrise. Philipos stitched my cheek back together, leaving me with a crescent shaped scar to match the one on my left cheek.

"It's a good thing that you are so charming," the Greek commented as he worked. "Because I think that with your face looking like this the chances of winning the favors of a woman are very slim now."

I knew he was trying to make me feel better, but I was in no mood for humor. I managed to refrain from saying something biting in reply, choosing instead to remain silent. He quickly took the hint, finishing his work in silence himself. Crassus had chosen to make camp at a spot less than a mile from the scene of the attack, and the men were hard at work, the shock of the attack having worn off, and the urgency of their situation making them perform their tasks with vigor. The *Praetorium*, which is always the first thing erected so that all distances for the dimensions of the camp are measured from that spot, was swarming with activity already, Crassus having called an immediate briefing. I had been excused to get my cheek attended to, but the moment Philipos was through, I left to go to the briefing. I was extremely worried about Scribonius, who had still not uttered a word since Balbus' death, and it had been the better part of a day, yet I could not spare him the time. Entering the *Praetorium*, I saw that all the Primi Pili and the Tribunes were gathered around Crassus, and they turned to stare at me. At first I believed that it was because of the new scar on my cheek, but when I got close enough I could see the sympathetic looks and I realized that they had all heard about Balbus. I was in no mood for talk of Balbus, so before anyone could speak, I asked Crassus what I had missed.

"Not much," he replied. "I just gave the order that we march in full armor and unslung shields until I say otherwise. We're going to march in *agmentum quadratum* as well."

Those were sensible precautions, but I wanted to know what we were going to about punishing the Thracians for what they had done. I waited to listen to hear from Crassus what he had in mind; I was clearly not the only one who wanted to know, since it was Macrinus who finally asked the question. Crassus hesitated for a long moment, clearly not happy that he had been put on the spot.

Finally, he said carefully, "If we're attacked again, we'll pursue and destroy our attackers. But otherwise, we're going to continue to march to Greece."

This was met by an uproar that in my mind was entirely predictable and justified. I knew that my judgment was clouded by my need to avenge the death of my friend, but I also believed that the Thracians needed to be punished severely for this attack. After all, I reasoned, we had done much more to the Bastarnae for much less. They had not attacked us; they had only come wandering into territory that was not theirs. It was clear that the Primi Pili felt the same way, and Crassus listened patiently to all they had to say. I had yet to voice my opinion, and when the others subsided, Crassus turned to me.

"I agree with the Primi Pili," I said flatly. "I think we need to punish the Thracians. However," I was willing to concede this much to Crassus, "I think that we should focus our attention only on the Triballi."

Crassus pursed his lips as he considered this, or at least pretended to, but I suspected that his mind was made up and nothing we said was going to change it.

Finally, he shook his head and replied, "It's already too late. The season's over and we need to get to Greece. We can come back to Thrace next season and destroy the Triballi for what they've done. After all," he pointed out, "we promised the Moesians that we wouldn't return, as long as they give us the second half of the payment. We made no such promises to the Thracians."

This decision was extremely unpopular; not only with the Primi Pili, but with the entire army once they learned of it. However, the next morning, the men packed up and we continued the march. The night before we left, we consigned our dead comrades to the flames, Scribonius taking charge of Balbus' ashes.

"He didn't have any family, at least any that he cared about," he explained. "So he might as well stay with me."

And he did, and still does. Scribonius told me not long ago in a letter that he would have Balbus interred in his own family tomb once Scribonius himself leaves this world. Despite how much they picked at each other, they truly loved and cared for each other, and there is no greater proof than that. Crassus gave a funeral oration for Balbus worthy of his status and renown, for he was as well known throughout the Legions in his own right as I was. My only regret in this matter is that I was so overcome with grief that I do not remember what the Legate said, nor did I have Diocles transcribe his words, because my slave was as devastated as Scribonius and I. Balbus' was not the only funeral, the smoke seeming to fill the sky with men sending their comrades on their way in Charon's Boat. Unsurprisingly, the mood throughout the camp was somber, even for those Legions who had not lost any men; any loss of comrades is felt by all the men to a certain extent, particularly under these circumstances. There was anger at the treachery of the Thracians, yet it was muted by the fact that we were not going to exact vengeance.

When we broke camp to resume the march the next morning, it was the first time since I had been with this army that the men seemed to actually hope that the Triballi, or any Thracians for that matter, would try another attack. There was no sight of them, the only signs the buzzards hanging in the sky above the relatively few Thracian bodies we had left in the open for the carrion birds and animals. Otherwise, the countryside was empty, with even the animals having begun to settle down for the winter. Our only companion was the wind, now blowing from the north, meaning that at least it was at our backs. Its keening moan was a suitable match for my mood, and I was thankful that Scribonius was in a similar frame of mind, so we could ride in silence without it being uncomfortable. As ordered, the army marched in *quadratum*, slowing our progress considerably, but nobody was complaining, and the Centurions had no trouble keeping the men alert. I knew that this would last at most a week, before the monotony began to wear men down again, although only time would tell if the Thracians tried to take advantage of any lapse when it came. We did stop occasionally when we came across the unfortunate farm or small village, leaving behind nothing but smoking ruin and strewn bodies in our path. While Crassus did not waver from his orders that we would not retaliate by hunting for any armed band of Thracians, or a large city, the nearest being Serdica, he did not try to stop the men from exacting some measure of revenge.

I passed the time thinking of all that I had lost during my time in the army, and for the first time in my life, I felt ready for things to end, not just my time in the army, which I had experienced before, but this whole pathetic drama. Just like it is impossible for one to remember a time when they actually felt good when they have some illness or injury, it was impossible for me to remember at that moment the periods of happiness I had experienced. I became even more withdrawn, unwilling to talk to Scribonius, Diocles, or even Gaius, who I will say did his best to penetrate my wall of indifference. I was oblivious to even the worsening weather; the trees had already changed colors and were now bare, the skies constantly leaden gray, matching my mood perfectly. Once we were out of the mountains, we did not have snow, but a portion of every day it rained, and without the sun, it did not take long for everything to become sodden. Nothing ever really dried out, including the men's boots, which were so caked with mud that they spent a significant part of their free time every evening trying to clean them off. It was not long before they started falling apart, and very quickly, the quartermaster ran out of extra pairs. Men had to wrap their feet in rags to protect them once their boots rotted away, but they were expected to keep up on the march, and given what had happened, they did not need any extra urging to do so. Illness began to become an issue, the constant wet and cold beginning to wear men down, and soon the wagons were full of the sick to go with the wounded from the attack. The sounds of coughing became the dominant sound as this miserable march continued. Crassus did his best to keep spirits up, yet it was a losing battle. When we reached the headwaters of the Struma River, Crassus held a briefing where he announced our destination, at long last.

"We're headed for Thessalonica," he told us. "It's a large city, and most importantly has a good port. That way we can receive the supplies we need to refit to come back here and properly handle the Thracians."

It was this last part that the Primi Pili really cared about. Thessalonica was a secondary concern, although I suspected that the men would care more about that than going after the Thracians, with the possible exception of the men of the 15th. This announcement seemed to do the trick with the men in getting them more motivated and moving with a bit of energy in their step. When there is no clear destination, it is easy for men to start believing that they will be marching until the day they die, trudging along with nothing to look forward to. With a clear goal, one like Thessalonica at that, men began to actually believe that they would live to see the end of this campaign, and talk soon turned to what was known of the fleshpots and wineshops of where we would be spending the remainder of the winter. I did not care one way or another if we spent our winter in Thessalonica, Siscia, or inside the gates of Hades, for that matter. The only real plan I had was to drown myself in as much wine as I could down, and to see if I could stay drunk the whole winter, which is precisely what I did.

We rolled into Thessalonica on the Kalends of December, long after the end of the campaign season. The men were ragged, tired and we had lost a fair number in every Legion due to illness, along with a number of the wounded who succumbed to the rigors of the journey. Even though I had been attending to my duties as Prefect, such as they were at this point, I will be the first to admit that I did so in a perfunctory manner. Fortunately, Crassus did not find fault with the manner in which I did so, or he was too wise to make an objection, since it would have been bad for both of us. Scribonius, while melancholy, had recovered better from Balbus' death than I had, and I actually saw him laugh a time or two. I did not begrudge him this in any way; in fact, I wish I had been able to do the same, but I could just not find it in myself to take joy in anything.

One advantage that Thessalonica had was a winter camp, already constructed and maintained by a staff of retired veterans, and it did not take long to get settled in. Crassus immediately secured the men from all but the most pressing duties, and it was a sign of their fatigue that very few left camp to hit the whorehouses, at least for the first few days. As soon as I was able, I secured a supply of wine, sending Diocles into the city to negotiate for the delivery and for the first time in some time, I was not particular about the quality. I attended to my duties during the day, but at the earliest opportunity, I retired to my quarters to begin what would become a night of drinking until I was insensible. I told myself that what I was doing was my own way of saluting Balbus, who always drank more than Scribonius and I combined. However, I was not fooling myself, nor was I fooling anyone else. I became accustomed to waking with a sour stomach and an aching head, but I still forced myself to torture my body with my daily exercises. Unfortunately, with every passing day it became harder and harder to find a reason to do so. Diocles tried on several occasions to water my wine, but I always caught him; only after threatening to beat him did he finally desist and let me be. Scribonius stopped coming to my quarters, causing me to drink even more, but I was too proud to go and apologize for the way I was acting. Crassus turned a blind eye to my obvious decline, though I believe that he also had other matters on his mind, since he was preparing to leave for Rome to celebrate his triumph. At least, so he believed at that point, and I never heard even the whisper of a rumor that he had received any hint from Octavian that he had fallen out of favor. In fact, according to friends of Diocles who worked in the *Praetorium*, the dispatches from Rome were full of glowing praise for all that Crassus had done. Crassus had announced that he would take the 8th Legion with him to march in his triumph, which was another reason for my depression, because it meant that Gaius would be separated from me for the first time since he had started his career in the army. Naturally, in the same way I was with Scribonius, I refused to let Gaius know that I felt any distress that he was leaving. In fact, I was quite surly with him on those occasions when he came to see me. One evening in particular stands out in my mind, and I am still ashamed of how I acted.

I could see the moment he showed his face that he had something momentous to tell me, his being the kind of face where every emotion is plainly written on it. Judging from his expression, I was sure that it was good news, which I suppose made things worse, since I was in no mood for anyone to have any kind of joy in their lives.

"Uncle, I have some news," he said, politely ignoring my slovenly appearance and my rudeness at not greeting him when he arrived, except to give a bare wave to a chair. He was clearly waiting for me to ask, but my only response to take another swallow of wine. Finally, he decided to plunge ahead, the smile still plastered to his face, irritating me more with every passing heartbeat.

"Primus Pilus Macrinus has just informed me that the next opening in the Centurionate that becomes available in the 8th is mine. I'm going to be a Centurion soon!"

Secretly, I was as thrilled at this news as he was, yet I was wallowing so deeply in my own misery that I refused to give him even the slightest sign of how I really felt. Instead, I stared at him as if he were out of his mind.

"Why in Hades would you want that?" I demanded, watching his jaw drop as he gaped at me in astonishment. He said nothing for several moments, clearly thunderstruck, before he managed to stammer, "I thought you'd be happy for me."

"Why?" I asked sourly. "Why would I be happy to see you give everything you have to give, for men who don't appreciate it?"

"How can you say that?" he gasped, rocking back in his chair.

"How can I say that?" I echoed, giving him a mocking laugh that I could see lacerated him to the core. "How can I not say that? I'm merely speaking the truth, and you should know it before you make the same mistake I did."

"Uncle, you're one of the most respected and famous men in all of the Legions." The poor boy looked near tears. "You're a wealthy man. You've told me yourself on many occasions that you have more than you ever dreamed of when you were a boy. You're the highest ranking man from the ranks that it's possible to be, so how can you say such things?"

He was absolutely right, but I had no inclination to think about these things, at least at that moment.

"Oh, I have money. But what else do I have? Everything I've ever loved and cared about has been taken from me. I've watched more friends die than I can count."

I was almost shouting now, feeling a lump forming in my throat, along with the hot prickling of tears, making me even angrier.

"I've been used as a piece in patrician's games, and I've almost lost my life because of it. I've watched them use men like me, making us kill each other to further their own ends, all the while telling us that it was for the good of Rome. But they lied, because it was always to further their ambition. That, boy, is what it means to be a Centurion of Rome."

"Even Caesar?" Gaius asked, his face revealing nothing. "Was Caesar doing it to further his own ambition at the expense of Rome?"

Oh, he knew that was the way to get me. I glared at him, and I must confess I almost struck him.

"Caesar was ambitious," I said finally. "But his ambition was aligned with what was best for Rome, so in that he was different."

"Ah," Gaius replied, his tone neutral. I saw him swallow hard, the struggle he was feeling clear to see on his face while he tried to frame his thoughts. When he spoke, he was very careful with his words.

"Uncle, I hear what you're saying, and I understand, as much as it's possible for me to do, given my position. But just because all these terrible things happened to you, doesn't mean it will happen to me."

"Then you're a fool if you believe that boy," I said scornfully, before draining another cup of wine to wet my throat before continuing. "And that's precisely why it will happen to you, because you're not me. If it happened to Titus Pullus, it will happen to you."

Gaius said nothing, just regarded me evenly for a long period, making me feel very small.

"Are you still planning on marrying Iras?" I asked abruptly, surprising him with the change of topic.

He nodded, replying, "Yes, Uncle. I am."

"Another stupid idea," I snorted. "You haven't learned anything from watching me?"

"You loved Miriam a great deal, Uncle," Gaius said quietly.

"Yes, I did, and look where it got me." I slammed my hand down on the table, making Gaius jump a little, but I was once again trying to fight back the tears and needed the distraction of hitting something.

"Iras is young and healthy," Gaius insisted. "There's no reason to think that what happened with Miriam will happen to her."

Seeing that yelling wasnot getting me anywhere, I leaned forward to gaze directly into my nephew's eyes.

"If you don't hear anything else I've said, hear this." My voice throbbed with the intensity of the emotion I was feeling. "You might have a career in the army that is rewarding in every way. And you might have a long, happy married life with Iras and have many children, and you'll both grow old together."

I jabbed my finger at him to emphasize this last point.

"But you can't have both. The gods will not allow it. You're many things, Gaius, but you weren't born to this the way I was. As hard as you work, you'll never achieve what I have, because you're not hard enough. But that very lack is what will make you a good, even a great *paterfamilias*. So you have to choose one, or the other. But if you follow my path, you will never be where I am now; you just don't have it in you. And that's not a bad thing."

I sat back, spent. Until I articulated what I had just said to Gaius, I had never given it a great deal of thought, but now that it was said, I realized that I was speaking the truth, at least as I saw it. Now, I waited to see how Gaius would take it. I expected him to be hurt, except he was not. Studying his face, I got the sneaking suspicion that he was looking at me with pity.

"Uncle, when's the last time I said I wanted to be like you?" Gaius asked me quietly. "Not since I was a boy. I realized long ago that I'm not the same as you when it comes to the Legions. But that doesn't mean that I don't love the army in my own way, and that I can't be proud of what I have, and will accomplish. Yes, I may die, but we all die. And I understood and accepted the risk long ago. I just want to be Gaius Porcinus, and I'd like you to be proud of me, even though I will never be like you."

All I had to say to make everything right between us was to be honest, to tell him how deeply proud I am of the man he was, and is to this day. But I could not, or more accurately, would not. Instead, I said harshly, "The only way I'll be proud of you is if you listen to what I say and finish your enlistment, then go back to the farm with Iras. You'll still inherit everything I have, because I gave you my word."

Now it was Gaius' turn to get angry, and he abruptly stood up, glaring down at me.

"I'm sorry you feel that way, Uncle," Gaius said stiffly. "But if I'm not worthy of you being proud of me the way I am, then I have no desire for your money, or your name."

"Then get out," I roared at him, slamming the table again, this time so hard it knocked my cup over, spilling wine across the table.

"Don't worry, I am," he shouted back, and turned to stalk out before I could say another word.

That night, I got the drunkest I had ever been; in the morning, the pain was still just as raw as it had been when I watched his retreating back.

This was the manner in which the next weeks passed, at least as much of it as I remembered. Crassus left for Rome, meaning that I was in command, and I did manage to curtail my drinking enough so that it did not affect my duties. At least, that is what I told myself, while everyone who was in a position to tell me differently was too afraid to speak up. I was never drunk on duty, but I was almost always hung over, making even the smallest problems that had to be dealt with more difficult. Before he left, Crassus tried to have a talk with me, and I listened politely enough before immediately forgetting it the moment I left his office. I became a virtual recluse, much in the same way that Antonius had when he returned from Actium, albeit on a more modest scale, since I did not build my own house. Off duty, my only contact with the outside world was Diocles, our only discourse my growled commands for more wine, or occasionally food to be brought. I had finally stopped my daily exercises, meaning the inevitable happened, and I watched in dismay as my waist grew thicker, the body of which I was so proud quickly losing its definition. Ocelus was suffering from a lack of exercise as well, because I had given up going on my daily rides, preferring to spend that time drinking instead. The 8th was in its final preparations to embark for Rome, scheduled to leave as soon as the weather broke, which would be soon, it now being late Februarius. I still had not spoken to Gaius, and while I longed to make things right, something in me refused to budge. One night, I was brooding about this, and as a result, I drank even more than had become normal for me. I had been finding that it was taking more and more wine to achieve the desired state of drunkenness, so I really have no idea how many cups I had consumed that night, nor do I remember how I made it to bed. My next conscious memory was being awakened in the worst possible manner, when someone poured a pitcher of cold water on me. One moment, I was passed out, blessed with no dreams, for a short time at peace with myself and the world; the next, I was gasping for breath at the shock of the water soaking me while I opened my eyes, trying to understand what was happening. Before I could gather my wits, another shock was waiting for me, when a pair of strong hands grabbed the edge of my cot, tipping me onto the floor. Adding to the jolting pain of hitting the hard wooden floor was the indignity of landing in a pool of foul-smelling liquid face first, the sour odor making my stomach lurch. Evidently, I had vomited at some point in the night, a not uncommon occurrence. Now the results of my night of drinking were soaking my face and the upper part of my tunic. I was just shaking my head in attempt to clear it when what I assumed was the same pair of hands that had dumped me to the floor now grabbed the back of my tunic then, albeit with a great deal of difficulty from the sounds of his grunting, hauled me to a semi-upright position. This gave me my first opportunity to see the face of my attacker, and despite my vision still being bleary, the room dimly lit by a single lamp, it was a face with which I was very familiar. Sextus Scribonius stared down at me, his face a mask of disgust and contempt. That look more than anything he could have said cut me to my very soul. At least, so I believed until he spoke.

"Diocles told me you were this bad, but I refused to believe it until I saw for myself." His tone was scornful, his lip curled in a sneer that I could not recall ever being on his face before.

"What do you want?" I was now on my knees, feeling sullen, stubborn, and ashamed all at the same time, glaring at Scribonius.

"I don't want anything. I just came to see how far the great Titus Pullus has fallen." He shook his head, then added quietly, "I never thought I would see you like this."

"Well, now that you have, you can leave."

"No," he said simply, going to take the chair from my desk and dragging it so that he could sit across from me.

Taking a seat, he studied me for several moments, making me feel extremely uncomfortable. My head felt like Vulcan had moved his shop inside it, my stomach was roiling from the stench of the stale vomit still soaking me, and now I was being examined like a man deciding whether it was time to send the horse to the butcher's or not. When he spoke again, there was no mistaking the sadness in his voice.

"You refused to let me die, so how can I not do the same? Titus, do you realize how much it hurts me to see you like this? Or Diocles? Or Gaius?"

It felt like I had been stabbed in the heart by his words. Even with the shame, I also felt the anger starting to burn. I had been so taken by surprise by Scribonius' attack that I had not had time to get angry, but now I was feeling it growing inside me.

"What should it matter how I choose to live my life?" I retorted. "All of my adult life, you've been feeding off of me. First it was Vibius, now it's you, and Diocles and Gaius. All of you, expecting me to be your champion, your leader, your protector. Well, I'm tired of it! No more!"

I imagine that if I had uttered these words to anyone other than Scribonius, they may have gotten up and walked away, but he was having none of it.

"Oh, spare me your self-pity," he snapped. "You're the one who set himself up as all the things you just described. How often have I heard you boast about what it means to be Titus Pullus? How many times have I had to listen to you describe how you killed this man, or that one?"

He jabbed his finger at me while he spoke, plainly angry, perhaps as angry as I had ever seen him.

"You chose the path you're on, and now you complain because the burden is heavy? Why now? What makes this time any different from all the rest?"

"You know why," I shouted. "You of all people know better than anyone else why I've had enough!"

Scribonius' face softened, suddenly all the anger seeming to rush out of his body, and he sagged back in his chair. For the first time, I could see every one of his more than fifty years showing.

"I miss him too, Titus." His voice was barely audible as he hung his head, looking at the floor. "Maybe more than you. Whenever you were off doing what it is that Titus Pullus does, it was always Balbus and me together who were left behind. While you were consorting with the generals, and playing dangerous games with the patricians, it was Balbus and I who were there to pick up the pieces."

I had never thought of it in this light, and that only made me more ashamed. I finally blurted out what had been gnawing at me since I saw our friend die.

"I watched it happen, and I couldn't stop it," I said, feeling the bitterness rising up in my throat, threatening to choke me. "What good is it being Titus Pullus, hero of the Legions, a legend in the army, if I can't even save my own friend?"I spat a glob of bile onto the floor, trying to clear my throat of that feeling of failure before I continued.

"That's why I'm tired of being Titus Pullus, Sextus. I'm just sick of it all, and if I could stay drunk for the rest of my days to stop from feeling this way, then that's what I would do."

Scribonius gave me a smile, but it was one filled with sadness.

"Titus, the only man expecting you to do all of those things is you. Nobody blames you for what happened to Balbus. It was his time, and nothing you could have done would have stopped it from happening. Even if you had managed to warn him in time, somebody or something else would have killed him. The only difference would have been the way it happened."

"You really believe that?" I asked, feeling the first tinge of something that was different from the unending despair that had dogged my every waking moment.

"I do, very much," he replied firmly. "And none of us, not me, not Diocles, not Gaius ever considered for a moment that he died because of something you did or didn't do. You take too much on yourself, Titus. You always have, but that was a choice you made for yourself a long time ago. And it's not like you to whine about it, and frankly, I'm tired of it, and so is everyone else. So consider this your final warning, from your oldest friend. Unless you change this path that you're on, our friendship is over, and I'll never speak to you again and purchase my remaining time out of the Evocati and go home."

I had remained on my knees, which had begun to hurt, but suddenly the pain was forgotten as I regarded Scribonius, trying to determine if he was bluffing. It did not take me long to recognize that he was not; I had seen that set of his jaw before, telling me now that he was determined to follow through on this course. Even if I had been inclined to say or do something that would force him to carry out his threat, what he said next clinched it for me.

"The real tragedy in all this, Titus, is that two friendships might die because of Balbus. Do you think he would want that, for either of us?"

I shook my head slowly, feeling the anger ebbing away, my mind thinking through what the rest of my life would be like without the friendship of Scribonius.

"No, he wouldn't," I admitted, then offered my surrender. "Very well, Sextus. I'll do as you say. I'm through getting drunk every night, if that's what it takes to get you to stay."

"That's not all," he interrupted.

"What else?" I asked, knowing I sounded peevish, but I felt like I had given him what he wanted and he was now stretching the boundaries of the territory he had just gained by my acquiescence.

"You need to apologize to Gaius, and you need to do it now, before the 8th ships to Rome."

"Apologize? What for?" I demanded.

"For the things you said to him the last time you two were together," he replied.

"How did you know about that?"

I suspected I knew, and it was confirmed when he said, "Diocles told me."Seeing my eyes narrowing while I felt the anger coming back, he hurried on. "Don't blame him. He's as concerned about you in his own way as I am, and I asked him to let me know if you did anything exceptionally stupid, which of course you did."

"Why, thank you," I snapped. "It's good to know that no part of my life is safe from your prying."

"Somebody has to save you from yourself." Scribonius was unruffled by my irritation, while I was secretly relieved.

I had been agonizing over how to approach Gaius to make amends without sacrificing my *dignitas*. Now I could pretend that I was doing so only because Scribonius essentially ordered me to do so in order to salvage our friendship. It's a thin porridge I know, but a starving man cannot be choosy.

"All right," I said finally. I was almost afraid to ask, but I did anyway."Anything else?"

My heart sank as he nodded, rising from the chair.

"Yes, take a bath. You stink."

I did take a bath, but not before I went to see Gaius. Diocles, quite understandably given all that had transpired, had disappeared, forcing me to clean and dress myself up the best I could before I left my quarters, donning my full uniform for the first time in weeks. The men of the 8th had transferred down to the docks to begin the process of boarding, their equipment and baggage already stowed in the cargo holds of the transports they would be using. It was too early for the Etesian winds, meaning their progress would be slow, and not without risk. Despite it being past time for the winter storms, it was still early enough that a late season gale could blow up. It was not unheard of, in fact happening fairly often, which was in my mind as I watched the men filing up the wharves. The standards for each Century and Cohort were on display, telling men where to gather, while Macrinus' chief clerk called out the order in which they were to board. At first, I was afraid that the Seventh had already loaded, but I finally found them on the farthest wharf, most of them sitting on their personal packs, talking or playing dice. I spotted Gaius standing, talking to Vettus, his back turned to me. As customary, since I was in uniform, men climbed to their feet, coming to *intente* when I passed, with me waving them back to what they were doing in an attempt to keep from making a fuss that would alert Gaius. I do not know why, but I had this irrational fear that if he saw me coming, he would turn to flee in order to avoid having to talk to me. For all intents and purposes, I was sneaking up on him. However, Gaius could not help but notice men leaping to their feet, and he turned to face me. I saw his body stiffen, yet his face betrayed none of his thoughts at my approach, both he and Vettus snapping to *intente* while rendering salutes worthy of a formation on the forum. I returned it, then stood there for a moment, unsure how to broach the subject that had brought me there. I did know I had no intention of blurting it out in front of others.

Finally, I said awkwardly, "Come with me."

Inwardly I winced at my tone; I had not meant to sound so harsh, but it was too late to go back. Besides, I reasoned to myself, if it sounds like an order, he is much more likely to obey. I sensed that he was following me while I looked about for a spot that offered a bit of privacy. Finally, I spotted an alley on the other side of the street that ran the length of the wharves, in between two warehouses. Beckoning to him, I strode to the alley, turning to wait for him to reach me. He was a few paces behind, his face set, still revealing none of his thoughts, yet his tone was polite enough.

"Yes, Prefect?"

My heart sank at the use of my title, instead of his usual "Uncle," recognizing that he was still angry with me.

"Gaius," I hesitated, searching desperately for the right words. "I just wanted to, er, apologize for what happened between us the last time you came to visit."

I had been hoping that this would suffice, but he gave no sign of softening.

"Thank you," he said politely. "Of course I accept your apology."

I felt desperation at that moment, a feeling that I was singularly unaccustomed to, the beginning of a realization that it was entirely possible that I had damaged my relationship with Gaius beyond repair.

"Then why are you still angry with me?" I blurted out, startling me as much as it did him.

"I'm not angry with you," he said uncomfortably.

I waved his denial off.

"I've known you long enough to know when you're not telling the truth," I countered. "And I can see that you're just saying that."

"That's not true," he protested, for the first time showing some emotion. "I'm just very surprised. I never thought that I'd see you standing here, apologizing to me."

"Neither did I," I admitted, giving him a rueful grin. "But you can thank a very stubborn friend of mine for making me realize how badly I've been behaving lately."

"Scribonius." It was half-question, half-guess, which I confirmed with a nod. He gave a short laugh.

"If anyone could get through to you, it would be him," he said.

For a moment, we stood there, neither seeming to know what to say next. Finally, I decided that since I had come this far, in both senses of the word, I should continue.

"I didn't want you leaving for Rome, and not see you for the gods know how long, without you knowing that I'm truly sorry for what I said."

"No." He shook his head. "What you said was the truth, no matter how hard it may have been to hear. You're right, Uncle. I don't have whatever it is that you have in you, and I've known that for some time. I'm sorry if you're disappointed in me."

"Gaius." I placed both hands on his shoulders so he would look me in the eye. "I couldn't be prouder of you than I am. And it's because you're *not* like me. Forget the things I said the last time. I was drunk, and I was trying to hurt you. I don't want you to do anything other than your duty to the best of your abilities, and that's more than enough for me."

I saw his eyes fill with tears, and felt the beginning of the same in mine, something neither of us wanted to be seen by his men, so I gave him a clap on the shoulder.

"So we're all right then? I can go back to my quarters and you can go to Rome in peace?"

"Yes," he agreed. "We're all right."

I felt it was safe to embrace him then. We hugged and I kissed him on both cheeks, the way an uncle to a nephew would.

"Have fun in Rome," I told him.

"I will," he grinned. "I'm looking forward to marching in a triumph. I've heard that it's about the most fun a Legionary can have."

I was about to say something about not getting his hopes up, then bit my tongue. I had repaired things with my nephew, and I did not want sour words from me ringing in his ears when he shipped off to Rome. Instead, I wished him an uneventful voyage, promising that I would see him as soon as he came back. I still refused to wish him the favor of the gods, but he did not seem disappointed. I walked with him back to his men, who had just been ordered to begin boarding, then stood there to watch them board the ship. Giving him a final wave, I turned to go back to my quarters, feeling better for the first time in months.

I did not get drunk that night, the next, nor any night after that for a very long time. Instead, I went to the baths to try to sweat as much wine out of me as possible in one sitting, and I did feel better afterward. When I returned to my quarters, Diocles was still making himself scarce, and I assumed that he was with Egina somewhere in the city. I vaguely remembered him mentioning that he had found a place where Egina and another servant's woman were sharing space to live, but I had been too drunk to pay enough attention to know where it was. I will say that a part of me found it somewhat humiliating to think that I owed someone who was ostensibly my slave an apology for my behavior, yet Diocles had long before become much more than that to me. While at that point I did not consider him a friend on the same level as Scribonius, it was more due to the longevity of my friendship, and the fact that we were essentially counterparts, than any closeness of feeling. In fact, there were things that I confided to Diocles that Scribonius did not know, although I cannot recall that the reverse was true. By virtue of his position for so many years as

337

the 10th's chief clerk, Diocles knew all the secrets of the Legion, probably more than I did. I could not really fault Diocles for being missing, given that I had been essentially impossible to live with, let alone serve for a good while. Still, it was technically a violation of our agreement that he was not there to attend to my needs, yet somehow I managed to put myself to bed that night. The next morning, he was there, and I began the morning in the same manner I had for many weeks, at least as far as he was concerned, by growling his name the moment I heard him stirring in the front office. I could hear him heave a sigh, then the door opened and he appeared with what had become my breakfast, a piece of bread and a jug of wine. Seeing the jug, a feeling of shame washed over me at the thought of how far I had let myself go, but I remained in my cot, looking at Diocles with what I hoped was the bleary-eyed look he had become accustomed to.

"Where were you last night?" I demanded, and I will confess that my irritation was not completely an act.

I had wanted to set things right with Diocles the night before to get it out of the way. To his credit, he did not flinch or attempt to make excuses.

"I was with Egina," he told me. He set the tray down then, without waiting, filled my cup with wine.

"I don't recall giving you leave last night," I told him.

He did not say anything at first, looking down at the tray, before turning to look me in the eye.

"Would you remember if you did?"

Instead of answering his question directly, I pointed to the cup.

"Pour that out," I commanded. The look of surprise on his face was sweetly satisfying. "And fill it with water. I'm done with wine until I tell you otherwise."

Diocles made no attempt to stifle his smile; if he obeyed all of my commands with the same alacrity that he showed then, he would have been worth his weight in gold, and I would have sold him to someone. Fortunately for both of us, I did not and do not need the money. I waited for him to return with another pitcher, this one with water, taking a breath before getting to what I wanted to say.

"I've been behaving badly, Diocles. And unfortunately, you've borne the brunt of that behavior."

The little Greek man, just beginning to show signs of gray at the temples of his curly dark hair, inclined his head in acknowledgment of what I had said.

"That's my duty, Master," was his reply, which was true enough, except we both knew that there were more masters who would have never considered the feelings of both slave and servant than would have thought to render an apology, but I was determined to be different. In the past, whenever I found myself taking Diocles, or any of my household slaves for granted, I would remind myself of Phocas and Gaia, both slaves according to the law, yet who were my parents in everything but name. These past weeks I had forgotten them, along with everything else good in my life, and it had taken Scribonius dumping water on me, then throwing me to the floor to remind me.

"I know it's your duty," I said, feeling a bit impatient, but I could not really blame him if he did not want to make this easy for me.

"But that's no excuse for the way I've treated you. I've never treated you that way before now, and for that, I want to apologize, and to tell you that I've recovered from whatever it was that was eating at me."

"Self-pity," he responded matter-of-factly, which did not make me feel better, I can assure you.

Everyone around me seemed to know what had been bothering me, but I had been too absorbed in my own misery to realize it.

"Whatever its cause," I said, a little stiffly perhaps, "I can assure you that it's gone now, and I'm back to being my old self."

"Master, I can't tell you how good it is to hear you say that." Diocles seemed to be genuinely relieved, and happy, judging by his smile. "So, are you going to resume your daily exercises?"

"Yes," I said firmly. "But first, there's one more thing I must do to make amends."

When I finished my breakfast, I turned to that last chore, going to see Ocelus, who was clearly happy to see me, immediately sticking his soft nose into my tunic while I stroked his neck. For some reason, I found it much easier to apologize to my horse than to the people I had wronged. We went for a good, long ride, finishing up with a gallop that left me breathless and happy, for the first time since Balbus had died. I would experience bouts of sadness, happening at odd moments, usually catching me by surprise, but that was the last time I suffered from a prolonged depression to this day. Unfortunately, there would still be cause for sadness in my life, and it was not long in coming.

Somewhat to my surprise, Tribune Claudius had remained behind with the army, while Cornelius and most of the other Tribunes had, as is the custom, returned to Rome. While part of the reforms of Octavian called for the Tribunes to serve a longer term than just a campaign season, there was nothing in the rules about them returning home. Many Legionaries did the same as well, going back to Italia, which was possible to do, then still return in time for the next season. Those men still in the army from Hispania were not so lucky; it was simply too far a trip for them to make with any assurance that they would return in time to start a new campaign season. There had been a great change in young Claudius, very much for the better, since his brush with death. I had seen such things happen many times before, usually with younger men, and while at first I had been skeptical, the change seemed to be genuine and heartfelt. Our relationship had improved dramatically; speaking indelicately, it was as if the stick had been removed from his ass, just like I had remarked to Crassus. That is not to say that he was no longer a snob, but it was not as obvious, while he seemed to have a deeper appreciation for the men of the ranks than before. Most importantly, at least for his own career, he and Crassus had reached some sort of understanding as well. That is why I was

340

surprised when he did not accompany Crassus back to Rome, but I had been so absorbed in my own misery that I had not bothered to ask Claudius about it. Finally, perhaps a week after I stopped drinking, I found myself in the *Praetorium*, with just Claudius, who had stopped by for some reason. Crassus' private office was now mine to use in his absence, so I called him into it to find out. After exchanging pleasantries, I asked him why he had not gone to Rome with Crassus.

He hesitated before answering, finally saying, "He asked me to accompany him, and I was going to, but….." His voice trailed off, and he looked away, clearly torn about what to say.

I had a suspicion I knew what he was going to answer, and decided to finish for him.

"But someone told you it wouldn't be a good idea."

He looked a bit surprised, but nodded unhappily.

"My father," he said at last. "He wrote me and basically forbade me from accompanying the Legate back to Rome. He said that doing so would threaten my future."

"Did you tell Crassus about this?"

He hesitated before giving a nod.

"Even though my father swore me to secrecy. I just felt I owed him that much."

"What did Crassus say?"

"He laughed it off." He shrugged. "Said that he appreciated my loyalty to him, but that I was worried about nothing."

Something in the way he said that bothered me, so I asked him, "Didn't you tell him that it was your father who warned you?"

A look of what I took to be guilt crossed his face.

"No," he admitted. "I was already betraying my father's trust by telling Crassus. I suppose I was being a coward."

"Not really," I told him, except I did think it was a bit cowardly, but I could remember what it felt like to fear your father. "You were in a tough spot. I probably would have done the same."

He seemed genuinely relieved to hear me say as much, but my mind was occupied with what Claudius' father had told his son, sure that the Tribune was leaving something out.

"Tribune, if you don't mind my prying, what exactly did your father say?"

His face took on a guarded expression, and for a moment, I thought he would not answer.

"He said that Caesar was very unhappy with Crassus' performance, both with the Bastarnae and the Moesians," he said finally, if a bit grudgingly.

While this confirmed what Scribonius and I had been speculating for some time, it was nonetheless chilling to hear it confirmed.

"Did he mention specifics?"

"He did," Claudius replied, but said nothing more. I waited; finally seeing that I was not going to be put off, he heaved a sigh before continuing. "Specifically, the Legate's plans for a triumph, and for his dedication of Deldo's armor as *spolia opima*. You are aware, aren't you, that the *spolia opima* has only been claimed three times in our history?"

"I'm as well versed in Rome's history as any man," I said stiffly, while in truth I could not remember who, other than Romulus, was the first to make such a claim.

"Then you know that only Romulus, Aulus Cornelius Cossus, and Marcus Claudius Marcellus have done so, and Marcellus, who's one of my ancestors by the way," he added with obvious pride, "was the last and that happened two hundred years ago. The fact that Crassus was making such a claim apparently infuriated Caesar."

He paused for a moment. When he spoke again, his voice dropped to almost a whisper, despite us being the only two in the room.

"But that's not what's going to do him in," he said. If he was pretending to be saddened, he was doing a good job of it. "It's the fact that he was hailed as *imperator* three times. My father says that Caesar simply can't let that be known, since it would make Crassus a challenger for his position as *Princeps Senatus*."

342

"*Princeps Senatus*?" This was the first time that I heard this title applied to Octavian, although it would become his first official title conferred by the Senate.

"Yes, that's how Caesar is being referred to now," Claudius confirmed. "My father says that Caesar is in the last phase of consolidating his power, and matters are very delicate right now. Crassus poses a threat, especially since the army has declared him *imperator*."

"But it wasn't the army," I objected. "It was only the Centurionate, and not the whole army."

"That's not how it was reported back to Caesar," Claudius said, confirming another prediction that Scribonius had made.

I regarded the Tribune for several moments, trying to decide the best way to frame what was an obvious question. Finally, I took the same approach I always did, charging straight ahead.

"Tribune, please forgive me for asking this, but are you the one who informed on Crassus about this matter?"

For a moment, I thought the Tribune would lose his head and strike me, or attempt to do so, but then he got hold of himself.

"No, I did not," he said stiffly. "And I resent the implication that I did, Prefect."

"Forgive me, Tribune," I said gently. "But you must admit that until recently, your relationship with the Legate has been . . . strained, to say the least. And if I remember correctly, you once swore that you would get even with the both of us for insults done to you."

His body stiffened for a moment, but he slowly relaxed, letting out a long breath.

"You're right," he conceded, trying to smile as he said it, except I could see that he was still rankled. "But that was before . . ." He did not finish, nor did he need to, and I nodded in understanding.

"Again, forgive me, Tribune. I was just making sure."

"You do believe me, don't you?" His face was anxious, and I could see that it was important to him.

"Yes, I do."

"Good." His relief showed in his face, but I could only think about what was facing Crassus.

"Did your father tell you what's going to happen?"

Claudius shook his head.

"Not specifically, but I can guess."

"And?"

"Marcus Crassus is going to disappear from public life. At least that's what I think will happen."

"But how?" I was truly curious how Octavian would affect someone as well known and wealthy as Crassus to do what Claudius was suggesting.

"Oh, I would imagine that Caesar will be very persuasive," he said evasively. "Probably there will be a triumph. The campaign out here is too well known by now for even Caesar to ignore. But I'm as sure as I can be that there will be no *spolia opima*, and shortly after the Triumph, there will be some public announcement that Crassus was seriously ill, probably as a result of the rigors of the campaign, and that he'll retire. For a short time, anyway, or so the announcement will go. But then Caesar will count on people forgetting, and Marcus Crassus will spend the rest of his life in exile. Comfortable exile," he added hastily, perhaps seeing my expression. "But exile nonetheless."

I considered what the Tribune had said for several moments, before I finally voiced my thoughts.

"But what if Crassus refuses?"

I was sure I knew the answer, but I wanted to have it confirmed.

"If he refuses, I'd imagine that the business of the ambush by the Thracians, when your friend Balbus was killed, would be used to convince him otherwise." Claudius looked away when he said this, as if ashamed that it would occur to him.

I knew he was more than likely correct; it was exactly the sort of leverage that Octavian would use, and by the time he was through, Crassus' reputation would be ruined.

"It hardly seems fair," I said. "Crassus was only doing the best job he knew how to do."

"Forgive me, Prefect, but we both know that is horse*cac*." Claudius' rebuke was mild, but clear. "Marcus Crassus was extremely ambitious. That's no fault; in fact it's a trait that I have. Where he erred was in being too good at being a general, and in the army loving him too much."

It was this last point that I believe was what ultimately doomed Marcus Crassus. It turned out that Claudius was right, in every particular. Marcus Crassus was awarded a triumph, but denied the honor of *spolia opima*. Shortly after his triumph, it was announced in the Senate, supposedly with great sorrow by Caesar himself, that Marcus Crassus had taken ill. The official diagnosis was "exhaustion," presumably brought on by the rigors of the campaign where he had distinguished himself. His physicians had decreed that the only way to save his life was a regimen of total rest and isolation, and he retired to one of his villas on the isle of Capri, with his only company his staff of slaves, and the goats who roamed the island. If you were to ask the average Roman pleb today who Marcus Licinius Crassus was, very few of them would even think to name the grandson instead of the father. Such is the fickleness of the Roman people, a trait that Octavian knows perhaps better than any man alive. But there are some of us who still remember the grandson, and miss him.

Chapter 7- The 13th

That April, in what is now known as the second year of the reign of the man they call Augustus, at that point still known as Caesar, I celebrated my fiftieth birthday. Since my oath to Scribonius, I had returned to my daily exercises with a vengeance, yet the weight that I had put on so easily was extremely loath to leave me. Despite finally getting close to my former weight, I had lost the definition of which I had been so proud, and I never regained it. It is in these small ways that the gods take pleasure in tormenting us, or at least so I believe. My fitness also returned, though again, I did not have the same vitality that I had enjoyed before, and for one of the few times in my life I actually became ill with a cold that lingered for weeks. Add to that the loss of another tooth, and I was feeling every one of those fifty years. Still, when I looked at other men my age or even younger, I was in good shape; it was just not what I had been so accustomed to for most of my life. For the first time, I got a hint of what it was like for other men, and I suppose I should have been thankful that, outside of being wounded several times, I had enjoyed such robust health for my entire life to that point. However, I took it as just another sign that I was being punished by the gods, except this time I refused to fall prey to self-pity, preferring instead to just work harder at maintaining what fitness I had.

As soon as the weather permitted, we received orders from Rome to march back to Siscia to our permanent base, where the 8th had already been sent after their triumph in Rome. No Legate was sent to command, putting me in charge of moving the army, and my first decision was to take the more circuitous route through Greece, in order to avoid the possibility of clashes with the Thracians or Moesians. I also decided that we would hug the Dalmatian coast, since it would be easier to be resupplied by sea while on the march, despite some rugged mountains that still have to be traversed because they run right up to the edge of the water in some places. The enormity of the task turned out to be a blessing, since it kept me so busy that I had no time to fall back on bad habits, if I had been so inclined. For the first time since I had been made Prefect, I actually felt useful. I was also reminded of how much I hated paperwork, not to mention the amount of it that is needed to get an army of three Legions, cavalry, and auxiliaries ready to move with the gear and equipment they would need for the march, which is staggering. Ingots of iron had to be melted down to make the blades for turfcutters and spades, while countless ash and oak trees were felled to make the handles for these implements. Shiploads of hides had to be procured to make the leather goods that the men would need; boots and one spare pair per man, since it was not only a long march, but a rugged one.

Diocles was pressed back into service, with my naming him chief clerk of the army, which was not a popular move, at least among the other clerks who felt that they were more senior. That was undeniably true, but what none of the others had that Diocles did was my trust and faith in his abilities. I cannot say that he was entirely happy that I did him such honor; like me, and Scribonius, there was a part of each of us that enjoyed the freedom and leisure our respective posts brought to our lives, but he made no complaints, aloud at least. I even pulled Scribonius into the mess, mainly to be an advisor on certain matters, particularly one concerning Natalis, the Primus Pilus of the 13th. As I have mentioned, I long had doubts about his fitness for the post, those doubts being confirmed during our time in Moesia. Unfortunately, his performance during winter quarters was no better than when we were on campaign, meaning that of the three Legions, the 13th was by far the most unprepared to march. Much of that rested on my shoulders; as the ranking officer, I should have intervened much sooner than I did, but I had been too absorbed in my own problems to do so. Now I, and the rest of the army, was suffering from my inaction, unable to march until the 13th was ready. While the army quartermaster is responsible for supplying each Legion with the raw materials they need to operate, the requisitions for all of which I had to sign for, it is up to each Legion's various *immunes* to turn these raw materials into the goods and equipment they would need, which was where the 13th had fallen behind. The 13th had an extremely high rate of men going absent, not deserting, but going missing for a short period of time, and this was something I had talked to Natalis about on more than one occasion. His remedy, as he told me, was flogging; consequently, the 13th also led the army in men on the punishment list. I specifically forbade him to flog a man without my express permission, something that Natalis did not like at all. Not surprisingly, things only marginally improved, and it was only after Scribonius actually sat down to compare the lists of men absent and those receiving punishment that he found a cause of the problem. And in finding it, he also gave me what I needed to remove Natalis.

"There are a lot more men who have gone absent than are being punished." Scribonius sat at a clerk's desk in the private office of the *Praetorium* that I was currently occupying.

He had been poring over the lists for the better part of the day, making notes in wax tablets while he worked. Bleary-eyed, looking like he desperately needed some rest, he nevertheless continued working, ignoring my friendly advice to take a break. When Scribonius was working out a problem, he was like a dog with a bone, worrying at it constantly until he got it figured out. In this case, he finally called me over to share with me what he had found. On his tablet, he had tallied up the number of men that had been reported absent in one column, while in another the number of men punished. As Scribonius had said, the two numbers were vastly different, almost at a ratio of two to one. When I saw this, I made an assumption that Scribonius had missed something, which I pointed out.

"Did you just count the number of men flogged? The Centurions probably meted out other punishments besides flogging."

The look Scribonius gave me can only be described as scathing.

"Why, thank you, Titus. I never would have thought of that myself," he said scornfully. He pointed to a pile of tablets."These are the lists of non-martial punishment," he explained. "And the numbers you see in the second column take those into account. So it's all types of punishment that's in the number of the second column."

I was about to ask him if he was sure that he had gone through every report from the 13th, but then thought better of it, judging that it was highly unlikely that he had missed anything.

"So why are all of these men, reported absent in the Legion diary, going unpunished?" I asked, more thinking out loud than anything.

Scribonius gave me a long, searching look, and again I was reminded how well we knew each other, because he communicated to me the answer without saying a word.

"Another payoff racket," I muttered, to which Scribonius simply nodded.

His frown deepened, then he said, "But I will say this. I've never seen one that involves a whole Legion. A Cohort yes, but a whole Legion?"

He gave me a meaningful look, and again we conversed without a word being spoken. This was not the first, or second time I had run into such a scheme, but Scribonius was right. The first time was when I was the Secundus Pilus Prior of the 10th, and it was just the Century under Longus. Then, when I had been Primus Pilus, it had been a Cohort, and again Scribonius was right; I had never seen, or even heard a rumor of a racket that extended through a whole Legion. The reason was simple enough. For a scheme of this nature to work, the vast majority of the Centurions have to be involved, or if not involved, at least paid off to look the other way. With a Century, it was an easy matter, since only the Optio is the other participant, with perhaps a Sergeant or two. Even with a Cohort, it only took the participation of at most five other Centurions and Optios. But for a Legion, that would mean that sixty Centurions, and sixty Optios had to either be participants or at least know what was going on. The fact that none of them had come forward, despite the evidence that this had been going on for some time, was a good indication that somehow Natalis had managed to either persuade or coerce all of the Centurions and Optios of the Legion to go along with him. Nothing I had seen of Natalis to that point convinced me that he was made of hard enough metal to scare his men, meaning it had to be persuasion of some sort. I rubbed my face, trying to think things through, but after several moments, nothing came to me. Turning to Scribonius, I asked if he had any suggestions, yet for once, my smart friend was at as much of a loss as I was.

"We can't pull what you did with Cornuficius in Alexandria and just kidnap a Primus Pilus, for a number of reasons," he said. "And we don't have a Vellusius in the ranks to find out what's going on. We don't have a relationship with any of the Centurions. Most of them think you sit at the right hand of Mars himself, and aren't likely to confide in you."

He shook his head, his expression bleak.

"But we can't let this go," I protested. "The 13th is the worst Legion in this army, and it's not likely to improve with Natalis in charge."

"Then what do you suggest?" Scribonius retorted, but I still had no idea.

We sat in glum silence for quite a while, then Diocles knocked, and I bade him enter. Seeing our expressions, he asked what was wrong. Scribonius glanced at me, and I gave a minute nod, so he called Diocles over, showing Diocles his figures while explaining the problem. My Greek slave instantly understood, except his expression was one of surprise when he looked up at me.

"I thought you knew about this," he told me, and I felt my jaw drop.

"Why, by Pluto's cock, would you think I knew about it?" I demanded.

"Because everyone in the army knows about it," he replied, still looking surprised. Scribonius seemed equally astounded as I felt at this news.

"How did we miss this?" I asked, again more out loud than seeking an answer, though Scribonius had one nonetheless.

"We don't have the connection with these men that we used to have with the 10th, and Antonius' army," Scribonius explained. "Like I said earlier, no Vellusius or any of the other old Legionaries we knew. And while Gaius is likely to know, he's not here to tell us."

"How long has this been going on?" I asked Diocles.

"Legion-wide, not that long," he replied. "Perhaps the last six months, while we were in Moesia. Something happened while we were on campaign, but I don't know exactly what. I just know that Patroclus told me that the punishment list of the 13th shot up about a month before the end of the campaign."

"What changed?" I wondered, completely perplexed.

Again, it was Diocles who provided the answer, even if this time it was unwittingly.

"The only thing I can think of is when their Pilus Posterior died," Diocles commented. "Remember? He didn't die in battle, or of a wound. He had some sort of rupture as I remember."

Once Diocles mentioned it, I did indeed recall, yet at the time it was just one of those things that sometimes happened. While it was somewhat unusual for a Centurion of the first grade to succumb to a sudden illness, it was certainly not unheard of, and at the time, I had just put it down to one of those unfortunate happenings that are part of any campaign. Men die without being touched by an enemy sword or missile, and in extreme circumstances, such as when a plague strikes, illness can ravage a Legion and an army worse than any enemy. Now I tried to recall the man's name, and whatever I could remember about him as a Centurion.

"Wasn't his name Plancus?" I asked Diocles, who responded with a nod.

"Lucius Plancus, as I recall," Diocles said.

I tried to remember more about the man, cursing the fact that when Crassus had returned to Rome, he had taken all of the Legion diaries, along with the mountain of paperwork generated by his time as Legate, to be stored in the archives. From the moment he had assumed supreme power, Octavian had been a stickler for proper record keeping, so Crassus had insisted that all necessary documentation be completed, as per regulations. Of course, that did not help save him from his ignoble fate of exile, making me wonder if Crassus ever regretted executing Octavian's orders so faithfully, but that is just an old man rambling. At that moment in the *Praetorium*, I was struggling to recall what I had heard about Plancus. I vaguely remembered his features; almost as tall as I was, but of a wiry, lean musculature, with a long, thin face that ended somewhat incongruously with a strong jaw, giving him a look of resolute determination even in repose. He had an aquiline nose, with piercing dark eyes, but what I remembered most about him was an air of tough competence, one of the few positive observations I had about the 13th. I recognized that perhaps I was coloring the picture in my head after the fact in a manner that fit with the growing suspicion I was harboring, but I did not think so.

Suddenly, I was struck by a memory, and I turned to ask Scribonius, "Do you remember one day having a conversation with this Plancus?"

I went on to describe him as I remembered him, and Scribonius snapped his fingers.

"Yes," he exclaimed. "Now I do. What I remember most is what he said at the end of our conversation."

In fact, this was exactly what I had remembered as well, because it was one of those things that, only after the fact does it carry any significance. At the time, it just seemed to be the kind of morbidly dark humor that many men exhibit while on campaign, particularly at moments like the one when this conversation took place. In order to pass the time, I had taken to spending part of the day either riding alongside or walking with the men of the Legions, alternating my time between them. That day I had talked Scribonius into going along with me, so as luck, or fate would have it, we were walking with the men of the First Cohort of the 13th Legion. That is when we

352

had spent some time talking to Plancus, out of earshot of Natalis, who was off somewhere else. I had asked Plancus about himself, and he had given us a bit of information about his background, not much of which I remembered, other than he had just celebrated the birth of his first son.

"My woman has given me four daughters," he had said, obviously proud, "and I had just about given up hope."

"Did you get to spend much time with him?" Scribonius asked.

Plancus shook his head regretfully.

"He was born the night before we left," he replied sadly. "I only got to hold him for a short while before I had to leave."

That explained why his woman was not with the army; while Legates, Tribunes, and Primi Pili looked the other way with the camp followers, the line was drawn at mothers with newborns, or heavily pregnant women whose due date would fall sometime during the march. Regardless of this prohibition, there was always a woman or two, and their men, who took the risk, so there were inevitably babes born outside of a Roman army camp, but this was not the case with Plancus. He had left his woman and child behind in Siscia, and clearly missed them.

When we parted, Scribonius said to Plancus, "You'll be back to see your boy before you know it."

"Only if I live through this campaign," was his reply.

It was the sort of thing that men say to each other all the time, and is of no great moment. Except of course, when the man who says it actually does die, as in the case with Plancus. What also made it slightly unusual was that this type of dark comment was usually uttered by rankers, or men on their first campaign who have yet to be blooded and are absorbed with thoughts of the unknown. For a Centurion as senior as Plancus to voice such a thought indicated a reason for his worry, at least in retrospect.

"What did he know?" I wondered. "Was he worried that something might happen to him, aside from the normal danger of battle?"

"Remember that he died of a rupture," Diocles pointed out, but I quickly dismissed that.

"Without seeing the Legion diary, we don't know for sure." I searched my thoughts, some of the pieces slowly coming back to me the more I thought about it. "What I remember is that Natalis announced his death at our morning briefing. You're right, Diocles, I remember now, that Natalis did indeed say that he had suddenly become ill overnight, but died before he could be rushed to the hospital tent."

I wished Philipos had not gone with Crassus, sure that he could have shed some more light on what had happened to Plancus, even if he had not examined him personally.

"So everything you know about his death you know from Natalis," Scribonius concluded.

This discussion had been singularly unsatisfying, creating more questions than it answered, while the problem still remained about what to do about Natalis. And there was still an army to get prepared to march.

Until I decided what to do about Natalis, I swore Scribonius and Diocles to secrecy, telling Diocles to ask discreetly for any scrap of information through his network of clerks and slaves. After all that he had done to help solve what had happened in the deaths of the men at the hands of Celer and his cousin, I trusted his abilities completely. Meanwhile, I began increasing the frequency of my interactions with not only Natalis, but all of the 13th, ostensibly to put pressure on them to step up their efforts to prepare. If I could establish some sort of communication with either one of the younger Centurions or even one of the old veterans from the ranks, I thought it might be possible that I would learn about what was going on. As hard as it was for me to believe, I had to assume that all or most of the Centurions either were actively involved in payoffs, or were being paid to look the other way.

We were less than a week away from the date I had set for our departure back to Siscia, requiring the men of the 13th in particular to put in very long watches to get ready. I tried to be everywhere at once, meaning that I was putting in long

354

watches myself, but I never neglected two important tasks every day: my daily exercises and taking Ocelus for a ride. Scribonius would accompany me on my rides, where we would discuss what had been learned, either by my talking to the men, or from Diocles, which was precious little. Not surprisingly, the one thing I had learned was that morale was terrible in the 13th because it was a Legion ruled by fear and fear alone. I did not get the sense that men respected their Centurions, with one glaring exception, which was Plancus, whose fear of not surviving the campaign had come true. Despite the fact he had been dead for months, his name was still spoken with a respect bordering on reverence, not just by men of the First Cohort, but the entire Legion. My sense was that until his death, there had essentially been two Legions within the 13th, one run by Natalis, and one by Plancus, something that Diocles was able to confirm through his own sources. This explained why Plancus met an untimely end, yet not how, nor did it give me any ideas on what to do about it. Poisoning was the obvious method, yet that was more of a woman's weapon, but it was certainly not unknown for a man to use it to eliminate a rival. The real question was how to get to the truth; perhaps it sounds odd, but it was moments like these that I missed Balbus the most, since he had the iron in his soul to help me do what had to be done. One day when we were out riding, I broached the subject with Scribonius about the best way to go about getting to the bottom of the matter, albeit in an indirect manner.

"I wish Balbus were here. He'd say we should just snatch Natalis and put the tongs to him until he talked," was how I began the conversation.

It was the first time I had uttered my friend's name aloud, and while it still caused a pang of grief, it had lessened over the months.

Scribonius laughed and said, "That's true. And he'd talk about the whole ball sac thing again."

We both chuckled at the memory of our friend's fascination with this gruesome idea, before Scribonius turned serious.

"While I agree that would be effective, I've never been one to get information by torture when other means would do just as well."

"Such as?" I asked.

"Such as using your brain instead of your muscle. All it takes is a little time and patience."

"How much time?"

"I'm many things, Titus, but I'm not an augur. I don't know how long it will take. It will take as much time as is needed. It's not like we're marching on campaign," he pointed out.

That was true, but while I had learned the value of patience over the years, it still did not come naturally.

"Well, you just talked yourself into being responsible for this investigation," I told him.

He did not seem that surprised, so I imagine he had already assumed that.

"I don't have anything else to do," was his only reply, but I could already see his mind working on how he was going to go about conducting this particular task.

Two days before our scheduled departure date, Diocles, Scribonius, and I met to discuss where matters stood. Scribonius had been consulting what records we did have, taking copious notes that he refused to share with me when I asked.

"You put me in charge of this, so let me do it my way," he told me.

That evening when we met, he did share the manner in which he was approaching his task.

"As much as we complain about paperwork, we all know that any attempt to manipulate our system leaves some sort of trail. What I'm most interested in is what's missing, not what's there. My hope is that if I can see where those pieces are missing from the whole picture, a pattern will emerge."

That sounded like pure Scribonius, and I knew that if anyone could make a whole cloth out of threads that were not there, it would be he, but I was looking for more substantial information, so I turned to Diocles.

"I suppose my approach is similar to Master Scribonius', but I'm doing it with what people tell me and not what's written down," he explained. "I agree that what's not there, or more accurately, what people are not saying is just as informative as what they say."

"That's wonderful." I tried to hide my impatience; as usual I could not. "But perhaps you could tell me exactly what you've learned from what people haven't told you."

"I was getting to that," Diocles replied defensively. He took a deep breath before plunging ahead."The most important thing I learned came from one of the junior clerks of the Legion."

"Which one?" I interrupted. Somewhat to my surprise, he shook his head.

"I'm sorry, Master, but I promised the man that I wouldn't divulge his identity. He's one of five of the junior clerks, and that's all I can say."

"We'll have to know his identity if it comes to a Tribunal," I countered, my own words instantly telling me why Diocles was so loath to divulge the man's identity, and why the clerk was equally reluctant to be known.

While clerks are a mix of slaves and freedmen, if he was a slave, then the only way his testimony could be used was if he were tortured. Even a freedman was not necessarily safe if the matter was important enough, and it was not a stretch of the imagination for a freedman to think that any matter involving a Primus Pilus of a Legion would be considered sufficiently important to be put to torture. I could see that Diocles was refusing to budge, so I waved at him to continue with his report.

"This clerk told me that it's commonly known throughout the 13th Legion that Primus Pilus Natalis has a very powerful sponsor in Rome."

Despite this being something I suspected, hearing it confirmed, even partially, was not a pleasant feeling.

"Octavian?" Scribonius guessed, but Diocles shook his head.

"Not Caesar, but almost as powerful."

"Surely not Agrippa." I could not fathom that the best general of Rome currently living would see anything worthy in Natalis to act as his patron, and I was relieved when Diocles again shook his head.

"Maecenas," Scribonius breathed, Diocles giving a perfunctory nod of his head. He hesitated for a moment, telling me that there was more than just the identity of Natalis' patron to talk about. Finally, he said, in barely more than a whisper, "The man I talked to wouldn't give specifics, but he made very broad hints that Natalis and Maecenas had a...special relationship."

Scribonius' eyebrow shot toward the top of his head, mine not far behind as we exchanged a glance. I had only seen Gaius Maecenas a few times, but it only took one look at him to know exactly what his preference was concerning his sexual appetite. The rest of what I knew about him was almost completely rumor and innuendo, but one of those rumors is that he liked to indulge a taste for men in uniform. Reading between the lines, it appeared that Natalis was one of those sweaty, grimy Legionaries that graced Maecenas' bed.

"But does that mean that Natalis is protected by Maecenas?" Scribonius asked. "Just because he's buggering Maecenas doesn't mean that he's also a client of the man. In fact, I would argue just the opposite. Maecenas is a lot of things, but stupid isn't one of them. I doubt that he'd take the risk of letting Natalis have that kind of leverage over him."

"My informant went to great pains to tell me that Natalis has never openly said that. But neither has he denied it, and this man claims that Natalis was confronted about it by another Centurion while we were in Moesia."

"Plancus," I muttered, which Diocles confirmed with a nod, but he was not through.

"It goes further," he explained. "Supposedly, this man overheard Plancus tell Natalis that he had proof that whatever relationship Natalis had with Maecenas, it didn't extend to any kind of business relationship, and that if Natalis didn't quit whatever this business was, he would expose him."

I could not help letting out a whistle, because this information all but confirmed that Natalis was guilty of something that he did not want exposed, and it followed that he would be willing to kill to keep his secret safe. However, I did not see how we could pursue this matter legally without exposing Diocles' source to the light of day, and subjecting him to the harsh treatment that would result from it. I looked at Scribonius, who seemed lost in thought, girding myself to tell Diocles that he would have to go back on his word. Before I could, Scribonius spoke up.

"Most of the Centurions must be convinced that Natalis is being protected by Maecenas."

"It would seem that way," I admitted.

"But Plancus said that he had proof that this wasn't the case, and that Natalis was using Maecenas' name falsely."

Again, I agreed, not seeing where Scribonius was heading.

"What we know of Plancus was that he was no fool," he continued. "So I think it's safe to assume that in fact Maecenas and Natalis have no relationship, at least as far as client and patron, or Plancus wouldn't have confronted Natalis. I think that means we operate from the same viewpoint."

"That makes sense," I replied. "But it doesn't bring us any closer to cleaning up the 13th."

"Yes it does." Scribonius smiled at me, clearly pleased with himself.

"How?"

"Relieve him of his command, effective immediately," Scribonius said, and I must confess that I had not seen that coming.

"I can't do that," I gasped out my first reaction, though as usual, Scribonius had thought things through and was already ready for my reaction.

"Why not? Show me in the regulations where it says that you can't do that very thing."

Scribonius had me, and he knew it. I suppose I should have thought of it myself. The position of Camp Prefect was still new, and while Agrippa had been thorough in the explanation of my duties, at that point there was not much written down. This had proven to be both a blessing and a curse; it led to conflicts like the one I had with Tribune Claudius when I first reported to this army, yet it also gave me the freedom to do things that I could not if I had been Primus Pilus. Scribonius had gone straight to the heart of the matter, proposing at least a partial solution by understanding that what the regulations did not say was equally important compared to what they did.

"I suppose I could then," I said slowly, trying to think things through. "But then what? Who would I put in his place? If I just move everyone up a slot and promote from within, I'm just as likely to put someone in that spot who at the very least knew what was going on and looked the other way as not. If Plancus was the only one who had the courage to confront Natalis, then I have a bunch of sheep as candidates to take over the 13th."

"You're getting ahead of yourself," Scribonius said calmly. "If you relieve Natalis, it will do two things. First, you'll demonstrate that Natalis isn't connected to Maecenas in any way that would prove useful in getting his job back. Like I said earlier, I think it's safe to assume that whatever proof Plancus had was sufficiently strong enough that he felt confident in confronting Natalis. In essence, you're calling his bluff. Second, it will force the other Centurions of the 13th to declare themselves in one way or another. The cream will rise to the top without a Primus Pilus, and you'll see for yourself who the real leaders are and who aren't."

I absorbed all that Scribonius had said, and I could see there was much sense in it. However, it was all well and good to discuss this matter in the comfort and security of the *Praetorium*; even though I agreed that it was highly unlikely Natalis was attached to Maecenas in a dangerous way, I was still cautious. I believe I had good reason, given my experiences with men like Maecenas. They were dangerous adversaries to have, which I had learned the hard way, meaning that now I was somewhat timid about the idea of taking the risk, however small it may have been, of running afoul of Maecenas.

"I'll think about it," I finally said, and I could see that Scribonius was not pleased.

"You better hurry and make a decision, because if you decide to go through with it and relieve him, it should be before we start the march and not after."

"Let's say I do it," I told Scribonius. "It's one thing to relieve him; it's another thing entirely to make sure he stays that way. I can see your point about not wanting to do it on the march. We don't want him lurking about, and at this point, I don't have enough to banish him from the presence of the army. Here I can put him on a ship and send him wherever I please, but it will be extremely damaging to me if I relieve him, only to have him come popping back up because I couldn't find something that would stick to him that is serious enough."

"Leave that to me," Scribonius said firmly. "I'll take care of that part of it."

It was hard to get any sleep that night, since I lay tossing and turning, trying to decide what to do. I continually reminded myself that the Titus Pullus of even ten years before would have not hesitated for a moment. In the next instant, I would chide myself for that thought, telling my imaginary adversary in my head that I had simply learned the hard way the value of prudence. Back and forth, I went all night, until I finally got up to sit at my desk, trying to think. At last, I reached a decision, and that feeling of relief that comes when you have set a course allowed me to get a bit more sleep. The next morning, before speaking to either Scribonius or Diocles about the Natalis matter, I left for the *Praetorium* while sending a runner to request that Claudius come to meet with me. I had decided to hedge my bet, and that was with Claudius. It also meant that my act of relieving Natalis would be delayed until after we arrived in Siscia, yet that could not be helped, given what I was going to ask Claudius to do. He arrived not long after, and if he was upset at being summoned, he hid it well. While we were certainly not friends; someone of Claudius' status could never be a true friend to a member of the lower classes like me, we were friendly and had established the type of bond that comes from one man saving the other's life. In some way, we would be tied together for the rest of our lives, so I think we both internally decided to make the best of it.

"Yes, Prefect? You asked for me?" His salute was rendered perfectly, without insolence, nor given grudgingly like it had been in the past.

"Yes, Tribune, I did. Please, have a seat."

It was early for wine; instead, I offered him water, telling one of the early clerks to bring us some bread and honey to break our fast. While we waited, we chatted about the coming march, and what I expected of him concerning his duties. Once we were served, I decided to plunge ahead.

"The reason I asked you here is about a rather delicate matter," I began, predictably piquing his interest. Indicating for me to continue, he sat watching me intently while I continued.

"A situation has come to my attention concerning the 13th Legion. There is major misconduct and abuse of the position of Primus Pilus going on that I must take action on. Before I do, however, I need to gather more information, and that's where you come in."

He looked confused, but said nothing, causing my heart to sink.

"The men of the 13th, and a number of Centurions, though I don't know exactly how many, have been given the very strong impression that Primus Pilus Natalis is being protected and is in effect working for someone very close to Caesar. He's been using that....impression, shall we say, to extort money from the men of his Legion. What I need to find out, before I make any move, is if by some chance Primus Pilus Natalis is telling the truth, which I seriously doubt. This is something that you have an ability to find out, through your father, and that's what I'm asking of you. Will you please write to your father to determine if Primus Pilus Natalis is indeed a client of Gaius Maecenas?"

I sat back, waiting for Claudius to answer, who in turn was staring back at me with a puzzled expression, saying nothing for several moments. Does he not understand what I am asking? I wondered. I opened my mouth to repeat myself, but he held up a hand.

"Forgive me, Prefect, but I must confess that I'm confused. I had thought that my father's letter spelled matters out very clearly."

It felt as if my blood froze in my body.

"Letter?"

My mind raced in an attempt to understand what the Tribune was telling me. After a moment, it fell into place. "You mean the letter that was sent to you on behalf of Pilus Posterior Plancus?"

He looked relieved that I now understood him and he nodded.

"Exactly. That letter. I received it shortly before we left Siscia, but I didn't get around to reading it before I gave it to Pilus Posterior Plancus until we had been on the march for a while."

"Humor me, Tribune. What did the letter say?"

"That your suspicions are correct. The Primus Pilus has been using Gaius Maecenas' name in a fraudulent manner. They have an acquaintance, that's true, but Natalis isn't a client of Maecenas, nor do they have any other kind of relationship."

Now that this had been confirmed, I had to decide exactly how to proceed, except I was not quite through with the Tribune, sure there was something missing from his story.

"Tribune, what exactly happened after that?"

"What do you mean?"

"You delivered the letter to Plancus?"

"Yes."

"How long after you delivered the letter to Plancus did he die?"

He thought for a moment, then replied, "Perhaps two weeks later."

"And you didn't think that was suspicious?" I asked, for this is what was bothering me the most.

"Prefect, my task was to make sure that Pilus Posterior Plancus received the letter. What happened after that was really no concern of mine. Besides, Plancus came to me about a week after I gave him the letter and told me that everything had been settled."

"What?"

I was astonished, feeling almost dizzy from the twists and turns this matter was taking.

Claudius gave a small frown as he remembered the events.

"I will admit it was strange," he said. "At least the circumstances of his visit."

I could not stop from heaving a sigh, thinking what could be any stranger than what I had already learned?

"And what was it about the circumstances that were unusual?"

"The fact that he came shortly after I had retired, when the tent was dark. I supposed that it was all part of some ruse on his part to keep from being detected. Whatever the reason, he stood outside my quarters, said that he didn't want to disturb me, then told me that he and his Primus Pilus had come to an understanding."

He gave a shrug, looking away, clearly not wanting to look me in the eye as he continued.

"I just figured that he had used the letter as leverage to get involved in whatever Natalis had going."

"It was a matter for the rankers," I offered, and he flashed me a guilty look, but nodded his head. His frown deepened as apparently something else occurred to him.

"I do remember one thing, though."

"What's that?"

"While it sounded like Plancus, his voice was . . . different. I just put it down to him having a cold. Then, when he died, I assumed that it was from his illness."

"He wasn't ill when he died," I told Claudius, who did not look altogether surprised that he had been fooled. "It was very sudden, supposedly of a rupture."

He looked distinctly uncomfortable now, but I was not through.

"Tribune, didn't you think it odd that Pilus Posterior Plancus should suddenly die when there was some sort of dispute going on between him and his Primus Pilus?"

It was clear that he had been expecting the question, and equally clear that he did not like it.

"Truthfully speaking, Prefect, I never gave it much thought," he said stiffly. Seeing my expression, he softened a bit. "I suppose I was preoccupied with my own troubles at that point and was not paying much attention to anything else. If you remember, that was before . . ." His voice trailed off, but he did not need to finish.

That was before he had been sure he was going to die and had been saved, completely turning his ordered world upside down. I had no desire to rub the Tribune's nose in it, another sign that I had mellowed with age, and I spoke in a more conciliatory tone.

"That's perfectly understandable, Tribune, and please understand that I don't hold you at fault in any way." I was struck by a sudden idea, making me decide to apply just a bit of pressure.

"However," I continued, and his expression quickly became guarded again. "We are still in a bad spot. A spot that probably should have been addressed some time ago."

I drummed my fingers on the desk as if thinking before asking the question that had come to me.

"Tribune, can I ask a favor of you? To help clean this mess up?"

"Perhaps," he said cautiously, not sure what he had gotten into.

I explained what I had in mind, and as he listened, I saw him relax a bit. When I had finished, he simply said, "Yes, I can do that."

We worked out the details. After seeing him out, I returned to the larger task of making last-minute preparations for the 13th to march without a Primus Pilus.

Later that day, I met again with Scribonius and Diocles, and the most pressing question on my mind was for Scribonius.

"You said you'dd have what I needed in time to relieve Natalis before we left. I plan on making my move in the morning. Will you be ready?"

I had to suppress a smile at the sight of my friend, with his dark circles under his eyes and ink-stained fingers, looking like one of the clerks. He was clearly in a sour mood, seemingly about to make a sharp retort before simply nodding his head.

Turning to Diocles, I told him, "If things go according to my plan, your friend's testimony won't be needed, but I want him detained anyway, just in the event that things don't go well."

Diocles was unhappy, but I was adamant that my order be carried out, and I knew that he would comply despite his feelings. I knew I could trust these two implicitly, and there was only one other person involved. While I was not completely sure about Claudius, he had nothing to gain by warning Natalis, and I do not know what Natalis could have done if he had been warned, other than to disappear. That would have actually made my life much easier, but I did not want this to have a hint of impropriety, or be personal in any way. As far as I was concerned, in my functions as Camp Prefect and de facto commander of the army, I had become aware of activity that was strictly against not only army regulations, but Roman law. I was acting in the best interests of Rome by relieving Natalis. Because of this new information, my original motivation for removing Natalis because he was not a good Primus Pilus had become secondary. I went to bed that night strangely calm, perhaps because I knew that I had done all I could do, and that Scribonius would not fail me. The only question in my mind was Claudius, but there was nothing I could do about it. I fell asleep quickly, waking the next morning ready for what was coming and wondering if Natalis had any idea that his world was about to cave in on him. While I dressed, the thought came that I was about to end a man's career, perhaps causing Natalis to do something desperate, making it prudent to have some of the Evocati there as guards, but I quickly dismissed the idea. The thought of needing to be protected from anyone stuck in my throat; the only time I had done so was when Cleopatra was trying to kill Miriam and me, and I judged her to be far more dangerous than Natalis could ever be. I did strap on my Gallic sword, just in case, then headed to the *Praetorium*, where everything would take place according to the plan. Diocles accompanied me, with Scribonius meeting us there, along with the materials he had prepared, which I took time to examine before the next phase of the plan. Claudius also arrived, moving to the spot I designated, and Diocles and Scribonius left the office; Diocles to summon Natalis, Scribonius to make himself scarce, although I knew that he would be nearby somewhere. With nothing left to do but wait, I found that I had a similar feeling that I experienced before the start of a battle, where everything seemed to be exaggerated; colors were brighter, the sound of my breathing was louder in my ears than normal. I clenched and unclenched my hand, a habit that I had developed over the years, flexing my fingers in the event that I needed to use my sword. It seemed like a full watch before I heard the outer door open, and I took a deep breath to calm myself, turning my face into the official mask I used when I was destroying a man's career. The inner door opened, with Diocles entering first.

"Primus Pilus Natalis is here, Prefect," he said formally.

"Very well," I answered. "I will be with him in a moment."

While I wanted Natalis to get here to the *Praetorium* unaware that there was a trap waiting, once he was here I wanted him unsettled, so I used the old trick of making a man await a fate that was uncertain. I took the time to check Scribonius' paperwork again, making a couple notes on a tablet to refer to when I was talking to Natalis. Once I determined that enough time had elapsed, I called Diocles to bring Natalis in. The Primus Pilus of the 13th marched in, *vitus* under his arm in the proper position, coming to *intente* precisely centered on my desk, rendering a perfect salute, which I did not return. Instead, I stared at him, my face composed into a frown, borrowing the *numen* from my long-departed Primus Pilus Gaius Crastinus, the invisible spirit that seemed to always wave a hot, smelly turd under his nose. Now it was under mine as I looked him up and down while he held the salute. Finally realizing that I was not going to return it, he dropped his arm uncertainly while staying at *intente*.

"Primus Pilus Natalis reporting as ordered, Prefect."

His tone betrayed his confusion, but he kept his eyes on a spot above my head, just as we had all been taught. Finally, I began speaking, making sure that my tone betrayed not the slightest hint of compassion or warmth, easy to do considering how I felt about the man.

"Primus Pilus Natalis, I am officially informing you that you are being relieved of your command of the 13th Legion, effective immediately."

Natalis' eyes shot open wide, as if I had run him through, taking a staggering step back.

"For what cause?" he managed to gasp.

"For gross abuse of your position as Primus Pilus in the extortion of the men of the 13th Legion. While the rate of men going absent is extremely high; not only is it the highest in the Army of Pannonia, but the highest I have ever seen, the number of men actually punished is very, very small. You and a number of your Centurions are involved," this was a guess on my part, but I was absolutely sure that I was right, "and you have been enriching yourselves off the backs of your men. There is no greater abuse of trust than what is being perpetrated here, and for that reason, I am relieving you, pending a Tribunal that will determine your punishment."

All color had escaped from his face, and for a moment I was sure that he would faint dead away, tottering on his feet, his mouth working open and shut while he tried to frame a response.

"This . . . this is absolutely untrue," he finally managed. "I don't know what you're talking about, Prefect. I swear it on Jupiter's Stone."

"Well then, Primus Pilus," I said reasonably. "If you are innocent, then it's even worse, because this extortion scheme is most certainly going on right under your nose. Either way, that is cause for immediate relief of your position."

He had fallen neatly into that trap, and I could see his mind working furiously about what to say next.

"What proof do you have of these charges?" he asked finally. I fought the urge to smile.

The report that Scribonius had compiled was damning in its detail. I proceeded to unroll the scroll on which he had written his findings, using vellum, both of us knowing it would have an impact just from its appearance. It is only on official documents of great import that vellum is used, and I could see Natalis' eyes drawn to it, beads of perspiration popping out on his forehead as I began to read from the document. Incidents of absence were meticulously recorded, then crosschecked against actual punishments, yet Scribonius did not stop there. Somehow, he had managed to obtain the records of the Legion bank account, enabling him to provide the actual deductions taken from men's accounts very close to the dates where they had been reported absent. What had become clear was that Natalis and his cronies had established a variable scale, where longer absences that merited harsher punishment cost more for men to buy themselves out of trouble. As I recounted the details of this corruption, there was something that continued to bother me, which I did not mention at that moment, but I will explain here. Natalis had not taken any precautions to cover his tracks; all it took was a cursory examination, like Diocles and Scribonius had done, to spot a troubling pattern. Whereas it made sense that he operated more or less in the open from the perspective of the rankers, reinforcing their belief that he was protected by someone close to Octavian, I could not see that it made any sense to do so when he clearly had no such protection. At that moment, I summarized Scribonius' report, just providing enough detail to let Natalis know that he was well and truly fucked. Once I had finished, I looked at him with a lifted eyebrow, knowing that something was coming and suspecting what it was.

"Prefect, I have only the utmost respect for you, so I believe that I should warn you that you are dealing in matters that you have no business meddling in."

There it is, I thought. The beginning of the threats, but I pretended not to know what he was going to say.

"Oh? Why is that, Primus Pilus?"

"Believe me, I do not mean this as a threat," he lied, "but I think it's only fair that you know that I have a special relationship with someone very close to Caesar, and that whatever I do, and I'm not saying that I've done anything wrong, I do under the protection of this man."

He tried to sound ominous, and I pretended that I was concerned.

"Would you care to elaborate?" I asked, as if I was actually interested.

I do not believe he was expecting that, and he stammered a bit, saying, "Well, as I said, I am a . . . friend of someone who's as close to Caesar as any man. While these things you're accusing me of aren't true, even if they were, anything I'm doing I do with the full knowledge and approval of this person."

"And who might that person be?" I asked pleasantly. "Prefect, I'm sure you understand that this is a delicate situation," Natalis said evasively. "And I would prefer not to actually name this man, but I swear to you on my honor as a Centurion of Rome that he is very important and very highly placed."

"I can hardly be expected to be quaking in fear if I don't know who I should be afraid of," I replied.

Again, he had been outmaneuvered and he knew it. He could see that I was not going to back off with such a vague threat, and I was giving him no choice but to up the stakes. I saw his chest rise from taking a deep breath, and I could just imagine what was going through his mind as he tried to decide what to do. However, his career was at stake, and he realized that saying nothing would have no chance of success at scaring me off.

"Gaius Maecenas is the man that I'm referring to, Prefect. I assume you're familiar with him and his relationship with Caesar," he said, trying to sound calm and unruffled.

"Yes, I believe I have heard of him," I said dryly. I rubbed my chin, pretending that I was thinking about what to do next.

"Perhaps I was a bit hasty," I said. I know I was being cruel, but I looked at Natalis the same that I would at one of the leeches that infest the swamp. He was sucking the blood from his men, and creatures like that are not deserving of any pity. I saw a look of hope flit across his face, nodding his head in clear approval of my wavering.

"It's understandable, Prefect." I could almost feel the oil oozing out of him. "I admit that it does look suspicious, but I assure you that there is nothing going on that . . ."

I waved at him, interrupting him. "Yes, yes. I know, you're doing whatever it is that you're not doing under the protection of Gaius Maecenas. I don't suppose you have any proof of this relationship, do you?" I asked suddenly, catching him off guard like I had hoped.

"Proof? Er, I'm not sure what kind of proof you're looking for, Prefect."

"Oh, something that would provide positive proof of this special relationship. Perhaps a token with Maecenas' seal." I snapped my fingers, pretending something had just occurred to me. "Or a letter from Maecenas to you. That's what would be best, at least for you. Yes, that's it. A letter. Do you have something like that?"

"A letter?" he asked cautiously.

"Yes. A letter like the one that was sent to Pilus Posterior Plancus before his death, where a man of impeccable standing and objectivity approached Gaius Maecenas himself to ask about this supposed relationship and was told by Maecenas himself that no such relationship existed." My voice had turned hard now.

I stared directly at Natalis, giving him a look that I had used on other men who had been in similar trouble, some of whom had ended up dead. Just as quickly as Natalis thought he had regained his footing, he found himself on shifting ground again, a clear look of panic flashing through his eyes, and he licked his lips, something I have learned is a sure sign that a man is under pressure. But I must give him credit; he recovered quickly, a look that struck me as sly coming over his face.

"I don't know what you're talking about, Prefect," he replied. "Perhaps if you could show me this letter you're talking about?" he asked innocently, but I could see the corners of his mouth twitch.

"No, I can't," I admitted. "The letter has been lost somehow. And of course, Pilus Posterior Plancus is dead as well, so he can't verify that he received the letter."

"Yes, his death was a great blow to the 13th." Natalis tried to look mournful, yet was singularly unsuccessful. "So, if there is no letter, then there's no way to prove this claim, is there?"

"No," I said again, drawing it out some more. I said nothing for several moments, both of us staring at each other for a long while.

"But, I have something almost as good," I continued, enjoying the moment.

I turned to where Claudius had been waiting behind the wooden screen that was used to give the clerks some privacy, calling to him. He stepped from behind the screen, but my eyes at that moment were fastened on Natalis, and it was a supremely satisfying moment to see the look of shock and dismay.

"You know the Tribune, of course. As I'm equally sure that you know that the man I mentioned who approached Maecenas was the Tribune's own father. Tribune," I turned to Claudius, "would you please describe the contents of that letter?"

"Yes, Prefect," Claudius answered.

He went on to give the details of what was contained in the letter, and I do not know if he embellished it, but he was extremely thorough. I kept my eyes on Natalis, who I thought for a moment would collapse upon seeing his last hope vanish. But there was something else in his eyes as he stared at Claudius, completely oblivious to my examination, something that I could not immediately place. When Claudius was finished, I spoke up.

"Citizen Natalis, do you have anything to say?" Before he could say anything, I held up my hand to finish. "If you do, you should know that the evidence is overwhelming, and that your fate is decided."

"You can't do this," he protested, his voice desperate. "You don't have the authority to relieve me!"

"I am the *de facto* commander of this army, and I was appointed by Caesar to fill this post. I assure you that I have the authority and the right to do exactly what I am doing."

I stood now, and I was not subtle about putting my hand on the hilt of my sword, finishing the official part of my duties by saying, "You are hereby dismissed with dishonor from the Legions of Rome. You are not entitled to a pension, nor any lands that may have been assigned to you as part of your retirement. You will not be allowed to take your savings from your Legion bank account, as they are hereby confiscated to compensate for the damages done by your actions. You are to be escorted out of camp by the provosts, and I have arranged passage for you on the first ship out of Thessalonica. If you show your face around the army, you will be executed on sight. Do you understand me?"

Natalis was shaking all over, all color gone from his face, yet when he spoke, there was just as much rage as fear in his voice.

"This is an outrage! This is not justice!" he shouted at me. "Nothing I've done is worthy of this harsh a punishment! And even if I did do what you charge me with, it's not something that hasn't been done before by countless Primi Pili!

"Not in my Legion," I said coldly. "And not in this army."

"Prefect, I will not accept this punishment! I demand a Tribunal, as is my right under Roman law and custom! I still maintain you do not have the right to do this, and I will appeal to the highest authority in Rome . . ."

"I could have you crucified!" I roared at the top of my lungs.

I could almost feel the walls shake, and to my satisfaction, Natalis reeled a step backward. Even Claudius looked shaken, and I was not yelling at him.

"You are the worst Primus Pilus I have seen in all the time I have been in the Legions." I lowered my voice, but only a fraction. "The 13th is the worst Legion in the Army of Pannonia, and I'd be willing to wager that it's the worst in the entire Roman army. And while there's no way to absolutely prove it, I know that you're responsible for the death of Pilus Posterior Plancus. Consider yourself lucky that you don't join him in the afterlife so that he can take his vengeance on you there. Know this, Natalis," I pressed, seeing the kill and going for it. "If you go forward with your demand for a Tribunal, I will do everything in my power, fair and unfair, to see that you *are* crucified, and that your legs not be broken."

Natalis held his hands out in my direction in a beseeching manner, yet there was no mercy to be had from me. Seeing this, he turned to glare at Claudius, the hatred so palpable that it seemed to make his face glow. Then he spoke, making matters instantly more complicated.

"You!" he hissed. "You're just going to stand there and let this happen? We had a deal!"

I turned just in time to catch Claudius' reaction, the look on his face making my heart start hammering as I realized that I had missed something.

"I don't know what you're talking about," Claudius said stiffly. "You're just trying to bring anyone down with you that you can."

"You know exactly what I'm talking about," Natalis shrieked, and it looked very much like he was going to try to strike the Tribune, prompting me to draw my sword.

The rasp of it when the blade left the scabbard was very loud in the room, bringing Natalis back to his senses, but he still glared at Claudius.

Finally, he turned to me, saying in a shaking voice, "Very well, I waive my right to a Tribunal and accept the punishment. Prefect, since, as you say, my fate is sealed, I want to tell you everything about what has been going on. Which that man there," he pointed at Claudius, "knew about and was a part of."

"You lie," Claudius shouted, his fists balled up in fury, shaking one at Natalis.

My mind was reeling as I tried to determine the best course of action.

"I am not lying, and you know it, you faithless cocksucker," Natalis shouted, whereupon Claudius began hurling insults.

The noise from both men was making it impossible to think, and finally I had to intervene.

"Enough!" I bellowed, gratified that at least both men immediately ceased their shouting.

I sighed deeply, rubbing my face while I continued to think. Finally, I called Diocles, who had been waiting outside, no doubt listening to every word by the expression on his face when he entered.

"Call the provosts to escort Citizen Natalis to his quarters and keep him confined there until I call for him again."

I turned to Natalis.

"I assume that your baggage is already packed for the march, but it will be searched to make sure that you're not taking any of the money that's to be confiscated. However, on reflection, I have decided that you will be allowed to take the sum of one thousand sesterces with you to help you start on a new life, far away from the Legions of Rome."

Natalis opened his mouth, but apparently thought better of it, instead simply giving a curt nod before turning to follow Diocles out of the office, where two provosts were waiting. The moment he left, I sheathed my sword, turning to Claudius, who was standing looking at me uncertainly.

"I think we need to talk, Tribune," I said quietly, motioning him to take a seat. I took my own, prepared to hear the rest of the story.

"I was angry, and I wasn't thinking straight," Claudius told me as soon as we began talking. "Like I told you, it was in that time before, well you know. Before," he said meaningfully. The words seemed to come pouring out of the Tribune, and I got the feeling that this had been a burden on him that he wanted lifted from his soul.

"So when Plancus came to me and told me of his suspicions, and asked for my help, I agreed to do so, but not for the right reasons."

At that point, he asked for some water, saying his throat was dry, and I had Diocles bring a pitcher. He drank a full cup before continuing, but his voice was still hoarse from some emotion. Claudius had been looking away from me. Now he turned to look me directly in the eye, his gaze not wavering as he continued, and given what he said, I had to respect him for doing so.

"I decided that I'd use this dispute between Plancus and Natalis to exact vengeance on you and Marcus Crassus. That's why there are two letters, not one."

This was indeed a day for surprises, and not good ones. I sat back, trying to remain impassive while Crassus continued.

"I had my father, actually my father's chief scribe who takes dictation from my father and has done so for so long that people assume that a document supposedly written by my father is actually written by Apollodorus, write a letter. That's the scribe's name," he added unnecessarily. "I offered Apollodorus a very attractive sum, along with the promise of manumission immediately upon my father's death to write these two letters. One is the letter that you know about, where my father supposedly states that Gaius Maecenas and Natalis have no relationship, and that's the one I gave Plancus. However, behind Plancus' back, I made a deal with Natalis where I told him that once this came to light and Plancus denounced him publicly, that I would produce the second letter, which told a very different story. I left it up to Natalis to make sure that the first letter disappeared somehow."

"So you knew that Natalis was going to kill Plancus?" I asked, not seeing any way that Claudius could have not realized that Plancus' life was in danger.

"No, that I did not know," Claudius said adamantly. "Because I thought that Natalis was smarter than he turned out to be. What I thought would happen was that he would figure out a way to get the letter, and then when Plancus tried to denounce Natalis, Natalis would produce this second letter saying the exact opposite of what Plancus was claiming, and that would be enough to ruin Plancus, or at least so he thought since he did not know the true contents of the second letter. Natalis and Plancus hated each other, and I learned that there was bad blood between the both of them that went back a long way. It wasn't until after Plancus died that I realized how deeply it ran. Natalis wasn't content to just ruin Plancus' career, he wanted him dead."

What Claudius was saying made sense, and I could easily see the Tribune involved in such a thing, at least the Tribune that I knew before I saved his life. But there was still something I did not quite understand, and I asked him, "So how was this going to hurt me and Crassus exactly? I mean, other than being embarrassing to us that all of this was going on without our knowledge?"

Now Claudius looked away, clearly uncomfortable, not answering for several moments. Finally, instead of speaking, he reached inside his tunic, producing a scroll that he leaned forward to place on my desk.

"Read that, and I think you'll understand," he said quietly, our eyes meeting briefly before he turned them downward.

Unrolling the scroll, I squinted at the script, which was written in the old style, without the dots over the ends of the words that Caesar used, making it difficult to follow. Pulling the lamp closer, I began plodding through, feeling my chest tighten while I read the words. It began in the same manner of the first letter that Claudius had described, which I now

377

realized he had known word for word because he had been the original author, while this Apollodorus had simply transcribed his words. Where it differed from the first letter was that it stated in no uncertain terms that while Gaius Maecenas and Natalis did not have any kind of business relationship, there was in fact such an arrangement, but it was between Marcus Crassus, me and Natalis, where we were supposedly sharing in the profits from the scheme that Natalis was operating. It was precisely worded, and very detailed, even going into the percentages that Crassus and I were receiving from Natalis in exchange for looking the other way. The supposed author of the letter claimed that he learned of the scheme by bribing one of Crassus' slaves back in Rome, who was keeping the accounts in a ledger safely tucked away far from the army. Reading further, I realized that this was all too plausible, and would be easily believed, especially by men who had no love for either Marcus Crassus or me. When I was finished, I sat back in astonishment, looking at the unhappy Tribune long and hard. I was awash in waves of conflicting emotions; part of me wanted to run Claudius through for even thinking of trying to destroy Crassus and me, while another part of me respected his courage for sitting in front of me to make such a confession. I found myself rubbing my face again, for the second time in a short period trying to decide what to do. There was one last piece that I did not understand after reading this through, and I decided before I made any decision I should at least fully understand the whole story.

"One thing I don't quite understand is how this helps Natalis," I said to Claudius, holding the letter up. "It says nothing about this relationship with Maecenas that he's been using to keep his men in line and paying up. In fact, he'd be as destroyed as Crassus and I."

"That's because he didn't know what the letter really said," Claudius explained. "He never saw it; he just relied on what I told him it said. That's why he said we had a deal. What he didn't know was that he was just as fucked as you and Crassus would have been."

"Why destroy Natalis along with us?" I asked curiously. "Had he done something to you as well?"

"No, not really," he shrugged, suddenly finding his fingernails worthy of study. "I suppose I could say that part of me despised him for what he was doing to his men, but that would be a lie. The fact is, I didn't care enough about Natalis to worry about what happened to him."

He looked up at me, and I was surprised to see the glint of tears in his eyes.

"The truth is, Prefect, I am not a good man, in any sense of the word. Being exposed to men like you and Marcus Crassus made me ashamed of what I was, and am. But I vowed to Jupiter Optimus Maximus and to my ancestral gods after you saved me that I would try to be a better man. That's why I never used that letter, and I'm asking you now to destroy it in my presence, so that I'm never tempted in a moment of anger and weakness to try and use it to harm you or anyone."

Well, well, I thought. Perhaps the gods are listening after all. I studied Claudius' face carefully, but I could see no hint of guile in his eyes, only the sincere desire to make amends and to do what he said in trying to be a better man. Without saying a word, I pulled the lamp closer, lifting the scroll just above the flame. It took a moment to catch, then we both watched it burn down to the wooden rolls, destroying the evidence that Claudius would have used to destroy me. Once it was finished, the Tribune looked at me, and I saw him swallow hard before he spoke.

"I imagine that you want to place me under arrest now," he said, his voice flat and emotionless. "I waive my right to a Tribunal, and will accept any punishment you deem is appropriate for my treachery."

At that moment, I was proud of Tribune Claudius, but I would not let my face show any emotion.

"Tribune, I'm going to ask you, on your honor as an officer of Rome, to confine yourself to your quarters while I decide what to do. Will you give me your word that you won't try to leave the camp for any reason?"

"Yes, Prefect, I swear to you on my honor I will stay in my quarters."

With that, I dismissed Claudius, who walked out on wobbly legs, but with his back straight and head up. The moment he left, I called for Diocles.

"Go get Scribonius," I said grimly. "We have a lot to talk about."

"So, what do I do?" I asked the two of them, after I had explained everything, leaving nothing out. Diocles did not hesitate.

"He has to be punished for trying to betray you," he said instantly. "He should be sent packing immediately, with a letter of censure written in your own hand to be put in his permanent record."

A letter of censure, for a military Tribune, written by his commanding officer, was the punishment just short of a full Tribunal, and in many ways was more damning than an actual trial. With a Tribunal there was always a chance, however slight, of an acquittal, either on the merits or because the accused Tribune was wealthy enough to find the price for the members of the panel. A letter of censure, however, was essentially a finding of fault in the Tribune's conduct or performance of his duties, but gave the accused no chance of refuting the charges. Despite the fact it did not call for any punishment in itself, a man with a letter of censure in his record was essentially finished in public life, his journey on the *cursus honorum* done before it really got started. This was what Diocles proposing, and he was adamant that I take this course.

Scribonius had been listening, a frown plastered on his face, telling me that he did not agree. Once Diocles was finished, I turned to Scribonius.

"Well?"

"I say you do nothing," he said after a pause.

"Nothing?" Diocles exclaimed, looking at Scribonius as if horns had suddenly sprouted from his forehead. "How can you say that? He tried to destroy Master Titus! That can't go unpunished! I thought you of all people would see that," he finished crossly.

I must admit that I was amused at the fire my little Greek was showing, and touched as well that he would show such a fierce devotion. It was not the normal way in which slaves talked to men like Scribonius, but my friend remained placid, listening to Diocles with a similarly indulgent expression.

"What I see, my little pederast, is that for the first time since Gaius Julius Caesar was alive, Titus Pullus has a chance at having a true friend in a high place."

I turned to Scribonius, surprised at his words. Seeing me about to speak, he held up his hand.

"Hear me out, Titus. First, let me ask you this. Do you believe that this change we have both seen in the Tribune is heartfelt and genuine?"

I considered for a moment, then nodded.

"Yes, I do."

"So do I," Scribonius agreed. I heard Diocles give a snort, but he said nothing. Ignoring our lone dissenter, Scribonius continued.

"And I think that he is genuinely remorseful about the part he played in this plot. And I also think he'll be eternally in your debt, more than he already is, if you do nothing about this. Think about it this way; you'll have saved not only his life, but his career. How much more of a hold could you have over a man, especially one as ambitious and well-connected as Claudius?"

I looked over to Diocles to see how he would rebut this, and while he opened his mouth, after a moment he shut it, shaking his head as he did so.

"He's right," he muttered. "I didn't think about it that way."

"Of course you didn't," Scribonius said with a smile, "because you're a Greek. You people don't understand things like honor and repaying a debt."

"I know that the next time someone wants help translating a passage from one of his books, he's on his own," Diocles shot back.

"I'll try to get by," Scribonius said dryly, before turning his attention back to me.

"So, what will it be, Prefect?"

After what Scribonius had said, I did not see how I could go any other way.

"It looks like I have a new friend," I said with a grin. "And hopefully one that will prove profitable."

With that decided, Diocles asked, "What about Natalis? Aren't you worried that he will be telling everyone who will listen that he was double-crossed by Claudius?"

I considered for a moment.

"He won't have any proof. It will just be the ramblings of a disgraced Centurion."

"But keep in mind that while you're gaining a friend, you also have a new enemy for life. Natalis doesn't impress me much, but he will be desperate," Scribonius warned. "And desperate men will do all sorts of stupid things."

That was sound advice; I promised that I would keep my eyes open, and when I escorted Natalis down to the wharves to take ship, I would be on my guard. Then, I turned to Diocles.

"Go fetch the Tribune. We have some matters to discuss."

Diocles returned with Claudius, wearing a wary expression on his face as he rendered a salute. I told Diocles to leave us, but not before he brought some wine. I wanted this to end in a convivial fashion, but first I wanted to make an impression on the Tribune. While Diocles went to fetch the wine, Falernian from my private stock meaning he had to go to my quarters, I took the time to eye Claudius coldly for several moments. Finally, I spoke, making Claudius start a little at the sound of my voice.

"Tribune, I've given this much thought," I began. "And I have to say that I'm not surprised that you planned to try and destroy me. After all, you did make a vow to do that very thing, didn't you?"

Claudius gulped hard, but nodded in answer.

"But I also believe that under certain circumstances, men can change. And I believe that you are one of those lucky few men who were given the opportunity to change into a better man, and a better Roman."

I leaned forward to pin him with my eyes, wanting to make sure I emphasized my next words.

"And I also believe that you have taken that opportunity, and that the change I have seen in you is genuine."

His body sagged in relief as I continued.

"I think that I'd be doing Rome a great disservice in taking any action against you, and the truth is that I bear you no malice for what you thought you wanted to do before this new opportunity presented itself. Besides," I grinned, "I burned the evidence so there's not much I can do about it anyway even if I wanted to."

Tears came to his eyes again, and I looked away to avoid making him feel shamed by his weakness.

"Thank you, Prefect." Claudius' voice was husky with emotion. "I swear to you that you will not regret this."

"I hope not," I said lightly.

Nevertheless, that was a real fear. As much as I did believe that Claudius had changed, I also had been scarred enough by the perfidy and capricious nature of patricians to know that I was still making a gamble.

"I won't let you down," he said earnestly. "And know that when my time in the army is done, and I return to Rome and the *cursus honorum*, you'll always have a friend that you can rely on, for anything."

"Thank you Tribune, I appreciate that."

"No, Prefect. I'm the one who's appreciative, and not just for this."

He smiled, standing to offer his hand, which I took, and he said, "Although I hate to admit it, I've learned a great deal from you, and from my time in the army. I'll never forget it."

"See that you don't." I said it in a joking manner, but I was actually serious. "We men of the ranks need all the friends in high places we can get."

With that, there was a knock on the door, Diocles returning bearing the wine, with a timing so perfect that I suspected he had been listening at the door, but I did not begrudge him that. If he were disappointed by my decision not to punish Claudius, he did not show it in any way. Claudius and I spent the next few moments chatting about the coming march. Finally, as soon as it was decent, I excused myself.

"Forgive me, Tribune, but I have one last piece of business to attend to," I told him, and he nodded, his face grim.

"Good luck, Prefect. And watch your back," he warned me, unknowingly echoing Scribonius' words. "Natalis is desperate and there's no telling what he might try."

"Thank you," I replied, touching the hilt of my sword. "But I think I'll be safe enough."

As little as I feared Natalis, I still took two provosts with me to escort him to the docks, along with Scribonius. The men of the 13th had learned of Natalis' dismissal, thanks to a few carefully placed words by Diocles on my behalf, and they were lining the Legion streets to watch their disgraced Primus Pilus. Despite not showing it, I was watching the faces of the men carefully, particularly the Centurions, which is why I had brought Scribonius with me. I believed that by giving the men the chance to see Natalis in this manner, I would get a good handle on how they viewed his dismissal. More importantly, I hoped that the relatively short notice would catch them by surprise, particularly the Centurions, making their reactions at the sight of him being marched out of the camp under escort more honest and would give me an idea of which Centurions were involved in Natalis' scheme. It was certainly not a thorough or entirely accurate method, but I believed that it would at least give me a starting point in weeding out those Centurions who needed to go. I was determined to rebuild the 13th, turning it into a better Legion than it was now, and that started with the Centurions. There was nothing wrong with the men; in all of my years in the army, I had only seen on one or two occasions a *dilectus* that was composed of mostly worthless men, and I knew that even those could have been turned into marginally competent Legionaries if they had been pushed hard enough. Nothing I had seen of the men of the 13th suggested that they themselves were the problem; they were just poorly led.

Now, marching Natalis out of the camp, along with his personal slaves and baggage down the 13th's main street, I saw that most of the men were trying unsuccessfully to hide their joy at the sight before them. I also noticed that there were a fair number of Centurions missing, at least if they were not attempting to blend in with their men. Despite the men being clad only in their tunics, I did not know of a Centurion who did not carry his *vitus* with him at all times. However, even if they did not, it was highly unlikely that the men would crowd around their Centurion the way they would a comrade. Even in a tightly packed crowd, a Centurion is always given a little extra space, and these were the things that I used to judge that a large number of Centurions were missing. This was not a good sign; if they had hated Natalis, or at the very least not agreed with what he had been doing, I was sure they would have been there to see his downfall. For his part, Natalis walked with his eyes straight ahead, refusing to acknowledge the few men who called out to him, probably because most of them were not saying charitable things to him as he passed. I suppose I should have called for silence, but I decided to give the men this small measure of revenge on the man who had been squeezing them and taking their hard-earned money. Marching down the street, more and more men began yelling things at Natalis, and seeing that I did nothing to stop them, their words became steadily more hostile.

"It's about time!"

"Hey, Natalis, who are you going to bend over and fuck now?"

"Goodbye, Primus Pilus! I'm glad to see the back of you!"

The apple had rotted, and when it was thrown and hit Natalis, it splattered into hundreds of tiny chunks, covering his upper chest and face. Luckily for whoever threw it, his aim was good and did not hit me, or I would have flogged the lot of them. However, that was where I had to draw the line, and I pointed at the area from which the fruit had come.

"Find out who did that and put him up on charges," I snapped to one of the provosts, whereupon he immediately turned to push his way into the men, each of them stepping aside with sullen expressions.

"The next man who throws something will be flogged," I commanded, and we had no more incidents the rest of the way out of camp.

Like I expected, none of the men were willing to point out who had thrown the apple, the provost returning to my side before we reached the gates. News of the sort like the dismissal of a Primus Pilus is big not just within the Legion, but the entire army, meaning the rest of the way out of the camp saw a similar gathering lining each street. Natalis' humiliation was witnessed by the entire army, and I could see the struggle in his face while he tried to maintain his composure. His slaves looked similarly discomfited, and I must say that I felt a pang of sympathy for them. As Diocles will tell you, gentle reader, just like there is a structure of rank in the army where every man knows his place, the same is true for slaves, albeit unwritten. There is a hierarchy, both among slaves and freedmen, and being the slave of a Primus Pilus of a Legion carries a prestige with it, not to mention a more comfortable life, at least when compared to other slaves attached to the army. A Primus Pilus lives well, in every sense of the word, and unless the Primus Pilus is otherwise inclined, which I had never seen, his slaves live well also. Natalis' slaves' fortunes had plummeted along with their master's, through no fault of their own, making their expressions suitably glum as they led the mules and small wagon with all of Natalis' possessions. The baggage had been thoroughly searched, and Natalis' sword had been taken at my order, which I was going to return to him by way of the ship's captain once they were at sea. The only ship I had been able to find that was leaving on the following tide was bound for Thapsus, carrying olive oil and other cargo, and it had cost a fair sum to book passage, but I wanted Natalis far away.

Where he finally ended up, I did not care, provided it was nowhere near the 13th Legion. We walked out of the main gate, and I was beginning to regret my decision to walk and not ride Ocelus, except I knew that if Natalis made a break for it in the narrow streets of Thessalonica, I would be better off on foot. Natalis himself had not said a word to that point, but once we exited the camp, he turned to me. He sounded like he had resigned himself to his fate, only making me more cautious.

"I wasn't lying about Claudius," he said.

I do not know why, but I felt I owed him at least the truth.

"I know you weren't," I told him.

Natalis looked at me with a mixture of surprise and bitterness. "But I suppose nothing will happen to him."

"What happens to Claudius is none of your affair," I told him coldly, slightly nettled by his presumption that Claudius would go unpunished, even if it were true.

"Men like him are never punished," he said bitterly.

"Not always," I said. "Antonius got punished pretty severely."

"Him." Natalis was scornful, surprising me somewhat. Maybe he had a redeeming quality in him after all, I thought. "He was the biggest thief of them all."

"And he's dead now. That's justice, isn't it?"

"If you want to call it that. But how long did it take?"

That much was true, and we were silent for a bit while we continued walking.

"You're keeping the money for yourself, aren't you?" he asked suddenly.

"No." I was more surprised than angry, because it had not occurred to me.

He gave a snort of disbelief.

"Pullus, you may fool some people, but you don't fool me. You were a Primus Pilus. I know you made a tidy sum off your men. Maybe not the way I did, but in some way."

I felt a cold lump of anger forming in me, my loathing for Natalis growing stronger and erasing any thought I had about his judgment of Antonius showing any kind of integrity.

387

"And you don't fool me either, Natalis. You're more crooked than a warped *vitus*, and you think everyone does what you do because that's the only way you can live with yourself. You're a piece of dog *cac*, and how you got to be Primus Pilus is beyond me."

"I got there the same way you did," he snarled, all attempts at winning me over or eliciting sympathy clearly gone. "I paid for the privilege."

I almost stopped short, staring at him in disbelief. I was not so much of an innocent that I did not know that men purchased a position in the Centurionate from unscrupulous Legates, but I had never heard of it happening with the position of Primus Pilus.

"Unlike you, Natalis, I didn't have to pay a single brass *obol* for my promotion," I said, not without some pride. "I was appointed to that post by Gaius Julius Caesar himself."

"Oh, you paid," he sneered. "Maybe not money like I did, but you paid all the same. Nothing in this life is free, Pullus."

That was true enough, and if I were to be fair, Natalis was right. Caesar had not made any money off of me, at least directly, yet he had a price for the position nonetheless, which was to be his man to death. It just turned out that his death came first, but it was a price I gladly paid, and would do it over again in the amount of time it takes to blink. Still, I was in no mood to be fair to Natalis.

"Like I said, Natalis, I'm as unlike you as it's possible for a man to be. I earned my post by the point of my sword, and there are heaps of bodies that are nothing but bleached bones in every corner of this Republic and beyond to attest to that."

"Oh, I know you're good with a sword." Natalis was dismissive. "But that doesn't mean that much now."

I knew I should not ask, but I was overcome with curiosity, so I did anyway.

"Who exactly did you purchase this post of Primus Pilus from? I would love to know what Legate was crooked enough to do that."

Natalis did not answer right away, giving me a sidelong glance, a strange expression on his face.

"You really don't know?" he asked finally.

I opened my mouth to answer him and assure him that I did not, but something stopped me. Perhaps it was the way his eyes were darting about as we walked, looking at the civilians standing watching us go by, clearly curious about what was happening since it was obviously out of the ordinary. Looking back, I believe that there was something so familiar in the way he was looking over his shoulder that it both warned and informed me at the same time. Without saying it, I knew exactly who he had bought his post from, and he was right and smart not to say anything out loud.

"Once you're out to sea, the captain will restore to you your sword," I deliberately changed the subject. However, now that I realized who he was referring to, I decided to give him a form of advice, albeit grim. "And if I were you, I would seriously consider using it to end your life."

We had reached the wharf where the ship was docked, and I saw the ship's master, a burly bearded man in a sun-bleached tunic standing on the quarterdeck roaring out orders. We stopped then, and I looked down at Natalis, his expression as bleak as his future. There were still one or two lingering questions in my mind, and I decided that it would not hurt to ask.

"So how long did you run this scheme? And how did you keep Crassus from spotting it? It wasn't hard to see once you took a look at the absentee report and punishment list."

I did not think he would answer, but then he gave a shrug like it no longer mattered, and that was certainly true.

"I bribed the clerks in the *Praetorium* to submit different numbers to the Legate," he said indifferently, telling me that the *Praetorium* needed to be cleaned out as well. Then he added, "Of course, that was before your precious Tribune found out about it. Then I had to cut him in as well, but you already knew that, didn't you?"

It was more of a statement than a question, and it was good that he was not paying particular attention to me, because I am sure the surprise showed on my face.

"Of course," I said hastily, lying through my teeth. "He confessed everything."

"Oh, is that why he's not being punished?" Natalis asked bitterly. "Or is there more to it than that?"

He turned to give me a shrewd look, and I admit that it felt uncomfortable.

"Yes," he said softly. "I see now. You're too good to dirty your hands with money, so I suppose you might be telling the truth about not squeezing your men. It's influence that is your money. You aren't doing anything to Claudius so he'll owe you in the future. It's good to have someone who owes you in high places."

He gave a bitter laugh, with no trace of humor in it.

"I could use one of those right now."

"Yes, you could. But you don't have one," I said evenly. The urge to twist the knife suddenly struck me, brought on by his accuracy in deducing why Claudius was escaping unscathed from this whole mess. "And one other thing you should know. That letter you were counting on so much?"

"What about it?" His expression was wary, and I thought grimly that he looked as tired of nasty surprises as I felt.

"It didn't say what you thought it did. Essentially, it said the same thing as the first letter did, that there was no special relationship between you and Gaius Maecenas. You were fucked either way."

I did not divulge the contents of the other part of it where Crassus and I had been implicated. I saw no need for Natalis to know that particular secret.

"That figures."

His mouth twisted into a grimace, and he spat into the water between the dock and the ship.

"Fucking patrician scum. They always talk about us lower classes and how treacherous and untrustworthy we are, but they're even worse than us. At least we don't pretend to be anything but what we are."

There was much truth in what Natalis was saying, and I would not waste breath disputing something with which I essentially agreed. Besides, I had one last thing on my mind.

390

"Other than the obvious reason, why did you kill Plancus? Like Claudius told me earlier, if you had been smart, you would have just destroyed the letter and then when he denounced you, you'd have that other letter from Claudius' father."

"That didn't say what I thought it did," he pointed out.

"Yes, but you didn't know that at the time."

"True," he said grudgingly. "I'm not saying that I killed Plancus, understand?"

He looked up at me, the sly look back on his face, and I sighed, cursing my own curiosity and need to know.

"Natalis, I'm dismissing you from the Legion, and the truth is I want to be done with the whole mess. As long as you don't run the 13th, that's really all I care about. What happened with Plancus can't be undone, and I didn't know the man, so I have no interest or reason to exact vengeance. You're about to get on a ship for a faraway port, and if you're smart you'll either do as I say and fall on your sword, or you'll stay in Africa and just disappear. Otherwise, you could burst into flames on this very spot and I wouldn't piss on you to put you out."

Hatred seemed to radiate from Natalis' very body, giving me just a glimpse of the true nature of the man, his lips curling back for a moment before he caught himself. He had leaned forward, like he was preparing to spring at me, but he could easily see that I was prepared, my hand on the hilt of my sword and watching his face intently. Exhaling a long breath, he regained his composure, then gave a shrug.

"Plancus was a lot like you," he said finally, squinting out to sea, refusing to look at me while he spoke. "He thought his *cac* didn't stink, and that he was better than everyone else."

"You mean he thought he was better than you," I cut in, which he did not deny.

"He thought he should be running the Legion, and that I wasn't doing a good enough job, something that he never hesitated to point out," he said bitterly.

I suspected that it was more a case that Plancus by his very competence was setting an example of what a Centurion should be. In contrast, Natalis was sadly lacking, and he did not like being made to look what he was: incompetent. I decided to bite my tongue and just let Natalis continue to talk while his slaves continued to load his baggage aboard the ship.

"But he found out differently, didn't he?" he said abruptly, for it was not really a question. "He's dead, and I'm alive."

That told me that he had no real intention of falling on his sword, not surprising me in the least. Men like Natalis will do anything to stay alive, no matter the cost to themselves or others.

"I swore I'd piss on his corpse, and that's exactly what I did," he said vehemently, spitting into the water again.

I looked at him in disgust, sorely tempted to take my sword and run him through, but that would have created more problems for me, so I did nothing. Seeing that his baggage was loaded and his slaves aboard, I gestured to the gangplank.

"I don't ever want to see you again, Natalis. If I do, I'll kill you myself," I warned him.

He glared at me but said nothing, abruptly turning and walking onto the ship. He did not look back again, but the provosts and I watched the ship shove off, moving slowly and weaving between the other ships in the harbor. Once I saw that the ship was clearly underway, I turned with the provosts, heading back to camp. I had one last task to begin to set the 13th Legion right again before we could begin the march. I also had much to think about concerning Tribune Claudius, because I believed Natalis.

We were in the *Praetorium*, which had been stripped of everything that would go with us, leaving the bare bones of the headquarters for the next army to occupy it. Scribonius was there, along with Diocles, both anxious to hear that we had seen the last of Natalis.

"What about the 13th now?" Diocles asked. "Who's going to be the Primus Pilus?"

"Funny that you should bring that up," I grinned. "Because I think I've found the perfect candidate."

Scribonius and Diocles glanced at each other, their curiosity aroused as I went on.

"He's very experienced, battle-tested, and is a great leader, with a good head on his shoulders. Most importantly, I trust him with my life."

I enjoyed watching their mystified looks gradually changing. Diocles turned and looked at Scribonius, whose eyes grew wide in what appeared to be horror.

"Me?" he gasped. "Are you out of your mind?"

"Probably," I laughed. "But you're still the new Primus Pilus of the 13th Legion."

"But I can't," he protested. "I'm an Evocatus, not on active duty. You can't make me Primus Pilus."

"Yes I can," I countered. "You're the one who told me that I could, remember? Show me any regulation that forbids a Camp Prefect from naming an Evocatus as Primus Pilus."

Scribonius' face turned red, his shock giving way to anger, but I still waited a bit before I let him off the hook.

"That doesn't mean that you can just decide that I'm going to be Primus Pilus, just because you want to," he objected. "It's not . . . right."

"That is the worst argument I think I've ever heard you make." I laughed again. "But you can relax. I'm not planning on you becoming the permanent Primus Pilus. It's just for the march to Siscia. At the end of it, I want you to give me your opinion on the Centurions of the First Cohort, or even the Second Cohort, regarding their fitness to be Primus Pilus. I also want you to observe the Centurions so we can get some idea which ones are the bad apples that need to be culled out."

Scribonius considered what I said, grumbling, "You could have said that in the beginning."

"It wouldn't have been as much fun that way." I grinned. The moment passed, then I turned serious.

"There's one other thing," I told them. "Natalis told me something before he got on the ship that is troubling, to say the least."

"Which is?"

I went on to explain what I had learned about Claudius, how the Tribune had demanded to be cut in on the money being made off the men of the 13th once he had discovered what was happening. When I had finished, I asked the pair what I should do. Diocles was looking very smug, clearly believing his judgment of the Tribune had been confirmed.

"You already know what I think," he said, shooting Scribonius a look that clearly communicated "I told you so." Scribonius was unruffled, silently thinking it over before he spoke.

"Do nothing," he said finally, barely getting it out of his mouth before Diocles squawked in protest, and I was struck by the thought that this was familiar territory.

"What? He lied! You can't trust him, Master! What more proof do you need?"

In fact, I had been leaning in the direction that Diocles wanted, but Scribonius' answer intrigued me.

"What do you mean?" I asked Scribonius.

"If you punish the Tribune, you'll lose that friend in a high place that I think you of all people will need at some point."

"But he lied about his involvement in Natalis' scheme," I felt compelled to point out.

"Did he?" Scribonius asked, eyebrow raised, looking at me. "Did you ever ask him directly what his involvement was in this scheme?"

I thought hard about my talk with Claudius, and I realized that in my excitement about learning of the existence of a second letter, I had not even bothered to ask if he was involved.

"No," I was forced to admit. "I didn't. But he should have told me."

"If you were in his place, would you?" he asked gently.

Reluctantly, I shook my head, and I recognized that my friend was once again right.

"Fine," I sighed. "His secret stays safe with us."

I gave Diocles a stern look.

"Is that understood?"

He was clearly not happy, but he nodded his acceptance of my command. I did not worry about Scribonius.

"Now that that's settled, we need to get some sleep. We have a big day tomorrow. Especially you, Primus Pilus." I grinned at Scribonius, who gave me a vulgar sign in return.

I had decided that I would wait until the last possible moment to announce to the 13th that Scribonius was their Primus Pilus. That way, I reasoned, those Centurions who had been in league with Natalis would have no time to organize any kind of protest or resistance to the move. The next morning dawned with clear skies and a gentle breeze blowing, perfect weather for marching, the men of the 14th and 15th in fine fettle, ready to begin heading back to Siscia. Matters were different with the 13th, standing around uncertainly, talking in small groups and looking more like a mob of barbarians than a Roman Legion. Their Centurions were as flustered as the men, explaining why the rankers were being allowed to wander around. As Scribonius and I approached, I saw his eyes taking in the sight, his jaw setting in what I knew was his determined look. We had drawn the proper uniform for Scribonius from stores, and I must say that he looked better wearing the transverse crest.

"How does it feel to be carrying the *vitus* again?" I asked as we approached the 13th.

"Not bad," he admitted, nodding in the direction of the men. "But it looks like I have my work cut out for me."

"That's why I picked you," I told him. "Besides, I always wanted you to be a Primus Pilus like me."

He gave a short laugh.

"That makes one of us. I just want to get this mob to Siscia in one piece."

"You know that I'll back you up on anything you decide," I assured him.

"I know. Let's just hope I don't need the help."

One of the Centurions finally turned from their huddled conversation to see us approaching, then faced the men and bawled out the order to fall into formation and come to *intente*. Just like I suspected they would, the men responded in a half-hearted manner, moving just quickly enough to avoid being struck with the *vitus*, the Centurions operating in much the same manner.

"This is worse than I thought," Scribonius muttered, and I had to agree.

The 13th was a veteran Legion, at least in terms of time served and campaigns, but they looked like a mob barely out of their time as *Tirones*. The confusion was somewhat understandable, since there was no Primus Pilus to make sure that everyone in the Legion was doing their jobs, yet I expected more from the Centurions and they were not showing me much. We stopped in front of the Legion, now assembled in parade formation, on a front of Cohorts, with each Century lined behind the First of each.

"Report," I barked out.

There was no movement, and I glared at the Pilus Posterior of the First, standing in the second row, trying to look inconspicuous.

"Pluto's cock, he's thick," I muttered to Scribonius. Finally, the hapless man took the hint. He left his spot, marching towards us, the expression on his face showing that he was hoping that the earth would somehow swallow him up before he reached us.

"Pilus Posterior Aulus Festus, reporting as ordered, Prefect."

He was fit-looking, a good size, but there was something about him, a weakness of the chin, or the way his eyes shifted about that gave me a suspicion that he was one of those that would be a problem. It made sense; he was Plancus' replacement, which meant that Natalis had selected him, and I seriously doubted that he would have put another Plancus in place. We waited for this Festus to continue with the prescribed ritual for reporting that the Legion was all present or accounted for and ready to march, but he stood there, his eyes still looking everywhere but at us.

"Aren't you forgetting something?" I finally growled at him, despite having to suppress a laugh because he looked very much like a deer that I had flushed from hiding by accident once, surprising us both.

For a fleeting moment, I thought that he might turn to flee for his life, yet somehow he remained in his spot. He opened his mouth, but no sound came out, and I was about to roar at him when Scribonius spoke in a gentle tone.

"Pilus Posterior Festus, I believe you heard your Primus Pilus say the words many times, didn't you?"

Festus gulped, yet somehow managed to nod.

"And you remember what those words were, don't you? After all, you heard them every day we were on the march."

His eyes roamed upward, as if peering into his skull to find the prescribed reply. Finally, his face lit up and he said, "The 13th Legion is all present and accounted for and is ready to march at your command, Prefect."

"At last," I cried, applauding him, yet mocking him at the same time. "Festus speaks!"

I sensed as much as saw Scribonius give me a furious sidelong glance, and he said, "Well done, Festus. I knew you could come through."

Festus was beaming with pleasure, and despite my irritation, I found myself smiling back. He seemed to be hopelessly out of his element, but perhaps he was not a bad sort, and maybe Scribonius could actually turn him into something.

"Very well, Festus. Your report is received and acknowledged. Now resume your post. I have something to say to the men," I told him.

Festus saluted, then hurried back to his spot next to the Second of the First, while Scribonius and I stood silently, surveying the men before I began speaking.

"Men of the 13th Legion," I bellowed, pausing to allow my words to be carried back to the last row of Centuries. I had not called them "comrades," or even "Legionaries," because as far as I was concerned, they had done nothing to earn either approbation.

"As you all know by now, your former Primus Pilus has been dismissed with dishonor from the 13th Legion, for crimes against the men he was entrusted with by Rome. That means you. What I can tell you is that Natalis will no longer prey on you, will no longer be sucking the blood from you as he had been."

Not surprisingly, the men gave a loud cheer over that news, but I was not through and I knew that some of them, wearing the transverse crests mostly, were not going to like what came next.

"But he did not act alone," I bellowed even louder, pleased to see the men in the front ranks jump a little. "There are men in the ranks of the 13th Legion who wear the transverse crest and carry the *vitus* who are not worthy of that office. While I do not know the identities of those men, I tell you today that starting on this day forward, every man, every Optio, and every Centurion is going to have to prove that they are worthy of their rank, whatever it may be. I cannot go back and change the past, but what I can do is ensure that from this point forward, the 13th Legion will be held to the same high standards and expectations that are demanded of a Legion of Rome. To that end, I have appointed Sextus Scribonius, formerly the Secundus Pilus Prior of the 10th Equestris, of *Caesar's* 10th," I emphasized, "and currently a member of the Evocati, as the interim Primus Pilus, for the duration of this march to Siscia."

I paused again, knowing that there would be a stirring at this news, and I was right, pausing to let the men mutter to each other.

"During the march, he will be evaluating every one of the Centurions and Optios, as will I. I am going to be giving the 13th my particular attention." I smiled broadly, except it was not a nice smile. "Every man's job in this Legion is in danger of being lost, down to the last *immunes* and the man holding it being demoted . . . or worse. Only after we have returned to Siscia will each Centurion be told of his fate; whether he will stay in his post, or be sent back to the ranks. Or promoted," I added meaningfully, because I did not want to have only a stick and not a carrot. I closed with, "And know this. Primus Pilus Scribonius' word is law. Any man who tries to test him will rue the day he was ever born, I promise you that."

I turned to Scribonius, saying in a loud voice. "Primus Pilus, the 13th Legion is yours to command."

Scribonius gave me a perfect salute, which I returned before he turned to give his own address to the men of the 13th. I was not surprised when he was brief and to the point, without any of the menace that I salted my talk with, since that was not Scribonius' style.

"Today marks a new beginning for the 13th Legion." Despite speaking loudly enough for his words to be relayed, they still had a quiet quality to them, especially when compared to my bluster.

"As the Prefect said, the past cannot be changed, but as far as I am concerned, it is forgotten. I do not care what you did in the past; all I care is what you do now. Each one of you has a chance to prove that you are worthy of whatever position you hold within the Legion, or to show that you are worthy of advancement. The decision to do so is yours to take."

With that, he turned to salute me again, , announcing that the Legion was present, accounted for, and ready to march. With that, we could start the march to Siscia.

As eventful as the few days preceding our march had been, the march itself was the exact opposite. We were blessed with fair weather, even for the time of year. Our progress was slow at first, like most early season marches are when there has not been enough physical training, and early on, the 13th suffered the most, with the most stragglers at the end of every day. However, the men began to respond to Scribonius much more quickly than I had thought they would, showing just how starved for good leadership they had been. That is not to say that there were not problems; at the end of each week, Scribonius and I would meet to discuss his observations, and very quickly the Centurions who had been one of Natalis' minions became apparent by their actions, or lack thereof.

When I use the term "minion," I usually do not mean it in the literal sense, but this time is an exception. It turned out that many of Natalis' Centurions shared his same proclivities, creating some tension with the men in those Centurions' centuries.

As Scribonius put it one night, "You'd think that we somehow have a Legion full of Spartans."

There was not much we could do about this, other than make sure that these Centurions did not make unwanted advances to men in the ranks. Day after day, we made our slow progress across Greece, heading for the coast where we would turn north up into Dalmatia. Nearing the coast, we began to experience a change in the weather, with storms sweeping in off the ocean, although they did not last long, yet it was enough to make the ground soft, slowing the baggage train down. Entering Dalmatia, I recognized the possibility that some of the Dalmatian tribes might make mischief. Consequently, I forced the men to march in their armor at all times, with shields uncovered, unless it rained. Predictably, the men complained bitterly, clearly forgetting what had happened months before, but they obeyed, which is what matters. We took a few days to rest and make repairs from the wear and tear of the journey in Lissus, the men allowed to go into the city to enjoy themselves for a night. That turned out to be a mistake, because I was accosted by a delegation of very angry citizens demanding that reparations be made for the damage caused by the Legionaries. At first, I was willing to listen to them, and while I knew that some of these tales were exaggerated, even stripped down to the bare bones, it was apparent that the boys had been very bad indeed. But when they demanded a full talent for all the damages, my willingness to cooperate vanished, and I had them physically thrown from the *Praetorium*. As they left shouting all manner of vile things at me, I told them they should consider themselves lucky that I only gave my men a night, and if they were not careful, I would unleash my army to do with Lissus what they pleased. This shut them up instantly, and moments after they left, I had forgotten all about it.

I was pleased at the progress Scribonius was making. Once again, it reminded me that there is more than one way to effectively lead men and make them better Legionaries. He rarely shouted, and I never saw him use the *vitus*, yet he was firm with the men, never hesitating to enforce the rules. And the men of the 13th responded, along with most of the Centurions, though not all of them were willing. By the end of the first month of the march, we had a good idea of which Centurions and Optios were salvageable and could end up being effective leaders, as well as those who were damaged beyond repair and would have to be moved out of the Legion in some way. Out of the bad bunch, some of them were old enough that they could be safely pensioned off, yet there were a few that had been like me and had achieved the Centurionate in their first enlistment. Fortunately, most of these men were in the lower Cohorts, making the impact of a change in leadership in those Cohorts have a less dramatic effect on the Legion as a whole. If these problems had occurred during my first enlistment or earlier in the years of the Republic, it would have been more haphazard, since the system of introducing men into the Centurionate into the lowest Cohorts was not nearly as formalized. With Octavian, as part of his reforms, he had demanded that this be stringently adhered to, and as the 13th had been one of his Legions, he had ensured that it followed this example. With one glaring exception, of course, which had been Natalis, and I was still exceedingly curious how such an obviously unfit candidate had been made Primus Pilus, especially by such a shrewd judge of character as Octavian.

By the end of that first month, we had reached the southern edge of the Dinaric Alps, which serves as the inland barrier running north, separating the coastal strip from the interior of Dalmatia. We had the choice then of turning north to march over a pass and into the interior, where Siscia would be due north, or continuing up the coast until Siscia was directly to our east before turning to march through lower Pannonia. Although the first route was shorter, it was more

401

rugged, but that is not why I chose the coastal route. The Dinaric Alps were still largely untamed, both the land and the people, and I did not want our baggage train to present a tempting target to some Dalmatian tribe. Therefore, we continued up the coast, prolonging the march, causing some grumbling around the fires at night. My other reason was that I wanted to give Scribonius more time with the 13th, except that was not something I could vocalize to the other Primi Pili. When I talked with Scribonius about it, I told him that it was all about the men and nothing else, but the real reason was that I saw how much Scribonius was enjoying himself, and I wanted to prolong the experience for him. I had always thought he would have made a great Primus Pilus, despite the fact that he insisted he had no desire for the position. I do not think he would admit it, but I believe that once he got the taste of what it was like to run a Legion, he found it very much to his liking, and had some regret that he had not done so. This is not to say that he did not have his share of headaches, that there were not days when I could see the frustration showing in his face and speech, but overall he was having one of the best times of his life. Scribonius also reinforced a lesson that I had learned from my second Second Pilus Prior, who had been killed at Alesia, that one does not have to be an effective leader by bellowing at the top of his lungs and thrashing men with the *vitus* at every opportunity. My first Pilus Prior Favonius, the man who was my once removed predecessor as Primus Pilus, Gaius Crastinus, had been more of this mold, although we learned that his bark was worse than his bite in most ways. That did not mean he could not and did not bite, but he chose his moments to do so, otherwise showing a gruff, somewhat standoffish exterior. I had modeled myself after Gaius Crastinus, who I considered, and still consider to this day, one of the greatest Legionaries that Rome has ever produced, yet that did not mean that I did not occasionally take a softer approach, usually at Scribonius' gentle insistence. Men did their best for Scribonius because they did not want to let him down, not because they knew a beating or berating was coming if they did. That made it gratifying to watch the

13th transform itself into at least the semblance of a tough, competent Legion. I knew that just the weeks we had on the march would not be enough to complete the transformation, creating a problem for me that occupied much of my thoughts as Ocelus and I rode at the head of the army. Should I turn over the 13th to a new Primus Pilus immediately when we arrived in Siscia? Was there even a Legate there to make the selection? We were in another area where the duties of Prefect had not been spelled out clearly; did I, as Prefect, have the authority to select a permanent Primus Pilus? While I was sure that Scribonius would push me to take advantage of this lack of clarity, on this I was not willing to be pushed because of the sensitivity that the upper classes have to having their prerogatives eroded. They would view an upstart like me selecting a Primus Pilus as an affront to their authority, and that was trouble I did not need. But how could I prevent another disaster like Natalis being thrust upon a Legion? If that were to happen twice to the 13th, the effect would be devastating, and I was sure that they would be finished as a fighting Legion, suitable only for garrison duty away from any possible combat. This has always been the challenge faced by career Legionaries when there was not a Caesar in command, or an Agrippa for that matter, men who knew what was needed in a good Primus Pilus. Despite the fact that all Legates are essentially political appointees, as in all offices in a system like ours the abilities of each officeholder vary widely. Some patricians and upper-class plebians went about their mandatory exercises and training on the Campus Martius with a great deal of dedication, earnestly wanting to learn the profession of arms. Others showed scant interest; early on, we had heard that Octavian was one of these, preferring instead to have his nose buried in some scroll written by a dead Greek. However, Octavian was an exception as far as his military abilities went, because he was a competent commander despite his lack of interest. I believe it is a sign of his overall brilliance that he can still prove to be capable on the field of battle even when his heart is not in it. But for every Octavian, there is an incompetent, puffed-up, self-important toad who views the post of Primus Pilus as a candied plum to give to one of those lickspittle Centurions who start fawning over the man from the moment he shows up. These Legates are the most dangerous, not just to the Legion or Legions they command, but to anyone who thwarts them in their designs and schemes. All these things were part of my thinking on our nearing Siscia, the men becoming more excited with each passing day at the thought of being reunited with their families. Since I had no family to come home to, I could devote my time to examining every possibility that I could come up with concerning the 13th and what to do about it. If there was a Legate waiting for us, I would have to make a quick determination what sort he was. If he was in the same class as a Caesar, or Agrippa, then I could rest easy knowing that he would select a Primus Pilus based on what was best for Rome. On the other hand, if he was not, I had to do whatever I could to limit the damage he could do by presenting him with a set of candidates that would do their job competently at the very least and who had outstanding records. When presented alongside his personal choice, my hope was that their achievements and records would contrast so sharply with his political appointee that a blind man could see what the Legate was trying to do and, in order to avoid scrutiny, would opt for one of the more qualified candidates. If that failed, I would try to bribe the Legate to put a better candidate in the spot. That was my plan, but I would only know what to do when we arrived in Siscia and I got a sense of how things stood.

Siscia had grown while we were gone, yet it still had the raw, new look of a frontier town in a recently conquered land. Despite the absence of most of the army, the fact that it would be serving as the home base for most of the Army of Pannonia meant that men and women looking to make a quick and easy sesterce were already in place, waiting for the men to come marching through the gates. The growth of the town was not a surprise; what was a bit of a shock was the presence of the 8th Legion, returned from Rome after Crassus' triumph, the Legate himself being in the process of his fall from grace. It was a good surprise, at least as far as I was concerned, because it meant that a certain Optio, or perhaps even a Centurion would be there, and once I realized that Gaius was in Siscia I became as excited as the men. We came marching into the town, the camp being located on the other side from our approach, to see the citizens and off-duty men of the 8th lining the streets, making it a bit like a small triumph when they greeted us with cheers and accolades. I was riding Ocelus, and for the occasion I had put the 13th in the vanguard position, the first time they had been allowed that privilege the whole march. I rode next to Scribonius who, in what had become his custom, was marching with his men as Primus Pilus instead of riding his horse as Evocatus. He had not ridden once on this march, and this may not sound like a big thing, but Scribonius was no longer a young man; also, his brush with death had weakened him a great deal, and the men loved him for making the effort. He was no longer on the verge of collapse at the end of every day's march, but he had lost weight from his already spare frame. Still, he was in as good a mood as I was, each of us grinning at the other while little boys scampered beside the Legions, some of them calling to their fathers in the ranks. Women were waving and calling to their lovers, or future customers, some of them showing their wares to an appreciative audience.

"It's not Rome, but it's not bad," Scribonius called to me over the noise of the crowd.

I agreed, my eyes scanning the crowd for the familiar faces of my nephew, or even Agis or Iras. We marched through the town, since it was still not very big. Approaching the gates of the camp, we saw yet another crowd gathered around the entrance. This group was composed mostly of the men of the 8th, but there was a sprinkling of civilians and women gathered on either side as we entered. Just before we reached the gate, over the other cries of men calling to friends in the ranks, I heard a familiar voice.

"Uncle! Uncle Titus!"

I turned to see the tall, lean figure of my nephew, dressed in just his tunic and belt, but carrying a *vitus*, a broad smile on

405

his handsome face as he waved to get my attention. I felt a lump form in my throat at the sight of him, thinking of how we had parted when he boarded ship for Rome, happy to see that he was clearly pleased to greet me. He had obviously received his promotion to Centurion that Macrinus had promised, making me even prouder. I got a bit of a shock, however, when my eyes naturally moved away from him, drawn to the next person in line. It was Iras, yet that was not the shock. What caught my eye was the clear bulge in her belly; Iras was visibly pregnant, not terribly far along, but enough to notice. I looked back at Gaius with a raised eyebrow, to which he responded with a deep blush. Calling to Scribonius, I pointed at the young couple, and he burst out laughing at the sight.

"Looks like she hooked him good now," he commented.

"He didn't waste any time," I agreed, my eyes torn away from the young couple only reluctantly, once we reached the gates, where the duty Centurion was waiting.

He saluted, going through the formality of challenging us upon our approach, then recognized me as Prefect before waving us through. We had arrived in Siscia, and were home.

While the men got settled into their quarters, I made for the *Praetorium*, where there was a red pennant flying, a signal that we did indeed have a Legate, and he was in residence. I did not relish the idea of meeting this new Legate, but knew it had to be done and done quickly. Dismounting Ocelus, I entered the *Praetorium* to find it buzzing with activity, with clerks scurrying about while Tribunes sat or stood about trying to look important and busy. In other words, it was a normal day, yet I paused at the doorway nonetheless, trying to determine the underlying mood. I had learned that commanding officers by their very natures set a tone within a *Praetorium*, and if one is observant, it is possible to get an idea of what can be expected concerning the relationship with the Legate. Are the men working hard, yet seem to be worried while they go about their tasks, looking over their shoulders? Are conversations muted, short snatches of whispered comments, but the eyes dart about, looking for possible eavesdroppers? Do they look tired even when it's early in the morning? These are the things that I had learned to look for, and standing there, I was cautiously pleased to see that these signs of tension seemed to be missing from the working men, and took to be a good sign. Only after I walked fully into the outer office did anyone stop to take notice of my presence, while the first man to approach me with a broad smile on his face was the Tribune Cornelius. I was happy to see that he had decided to stay with the army for at least another season. After we exchanged salutes, I clasped his arm as we exchanged greetings.

"How are things?" I asked him, to which he made a face.

"Eventful," he replied, looking me in the eye with what I took to be a warning.

Intrigued, I wanted to ask more, but he gave a warning shake of his head.

"And we have a new Legate?"

He nodded; I could see by his expression that his concern did not seem to be a result of our new general. However, he said nothing more, and I swallowed my irritation, reminding myself that Cornelius was not the most intellectually gifted man I knew.

"Are you going to tell me who it is, or do I have to guess?"

He looked chagrined, replying quickly, "Ah, yes. Sorry about that. Our new Legate is Gaius Norbanus Flaccus. Do you know him?"

"Only by reputation," I replied, keeping to myself that the reputation was not particularly covered in glory.

He and Saxa had commanded a blocking force against Marcus Brutus and Gaius Cassius, charged with holding a pass to block their line of march before the Battle of Philippi, yet had failed to do so, being betrayed by a local with knowledge of a goat track who led Brutus and his army around them.

"Well, he certainly seems to know a lot about you," Cornelius replied.

He did not make it sound like it was a good thing.

"Is he in his office?"

Cornelius nodded, adding, "He's chewing on one of the other Tribunes right now, though."

He gave me the smile of a man who is just happy that misfortune is falling on someone else's shoulders, then excused himself. I decided to wait until the victim of Norbanus' wrath emerged from his office. A few moments later, he did, looking rather shaken. I crossed the outer office to knock on the door, waiting until I heard a muffled voice bark permission to enter. Opening the door, I stepped into the office and marched up to the desk, my eyes above the seated man, using the outer portion of my vision to take him in. He was about the same age that I was, with iron-gray hair cut very short in the military fashion, except that it was expensively barbered and oiled. He had a huge hooked nose, making him look a bit like a bird of prey, particularly the way he was hunched over, looking up at me through a pair of shaggy eyebrows. Completing the picture was a mouth that looked like a gash cut in his face, carved into a perpetual frown.

"Camp Prefect Titus Pullus, reporting that the 13th, 14th, and 15th Legion have arrived from their winter quarters in Thessalonica, sir," I told Norbanus.

He returned my salute but stayed seated, looking me up and down, still frowning.

"About time," he grunted, but said nothing else.

I remained standing, knowing the game that was being played, yet it still irritated me. My eyes remained fixed on the wall above his head while he pretended to read something. Finally, he put it down, leaned back in his chair to regard me silently, my anger growing by the moment.

"Caesar has told me much about you," he said finally.

"Good, I hope."

He gave a short bark that I took to be a laugh.

"Some of it," he granted. "But he also said that you are headstrong and sometimes forget your place, and that you have ambitions to raise your station. Is that true?"

I shrugged, not seeing any point in denying something he already knew.

"Caesar has promised that if I serve for ten years as Prefect I'll be elevated to equestrian status under his sponsorship."

"Yes, yes, he told me that. But you're not there yet, so you need to keep that in mind and don't get ideas above your station."

"I'll try to keep that in mind, sir." I had to make an effort to keep my tone neutral.

"Good," he grunted, moving on to other matters. We spent the rest of the time discussing the state of the bulk of the army before I broached the subject of the 13th and the need for a new Primus Pilus. That certainly got his attention, and he asked, "Why? Did the other one die?"

"No," I replied, trying to keep my tone even, acting like what I was telling him was nothing of great import, but my heart started beating faster nonetheless.

Scribonius and I had discussed this moment at length, both of us knowing that if there were to be any repercussions against me for overstepping my authority, it would start at this moment.

"He was relieved for cause and dismissed with dishonor from the Legion for extortion against his men."

Norbanus peered at me from beneath his eyebrows, which I was beginning to learn moved up and down quite a bit in an indication of his mood. Now they were positively bobbing as he digested what I had said.

"Who relieved him?" he demanded. "Crassus told me nothing about this when I met with him before I left Rome."

"I did," I said, watching his face suddenly flush, his jaw dropping while his eyebrows began doing a dance.

"You? You?" he repeated. "By whose authority did you do such a thing? That is the duty of the Legate and the Legate alone."

"That was true in the past," I replied, using the argument that Scribonius and I had rehearsed. "But that was before the position of Camp Prefect. As I'm sure you know, Caesar created this rank to serve as second in command of the army, and since Marcus Crassus had already departed for Rome when the full extent of Natalis' predations on the men was discovered, I had no other choice but to relieve him."

"No doubt," he retorted sarcastically. "Probably you waited until Crassus was gone before you settled some old score with Natalis. I know how you men in the ranks operate."

"General, I assure you I didn't know Natalis before this posting," I said stiffly. "And the evidence against him is overwhelming. I can have the report and documentation sent to you so that you can examine everything yourself. You'll see that there is no question of his guilt."

"Be that as it may," he shot back, clearly impatient with me. "You still overstepped your authority."

"Perhaps you can show me in the regulations exactly where the Camp Prefect is prohibited from doing such a thing?" I asked, trying to sound innocent.

For a moment, I thought his eyebrows were suddenly fleeing in an attempt to join the hair on his head. Clearly flummoxed, his mouth opened and closed a couple of times before he finally spoke.

"Well, I don't believe such a regulation has been written yet," he said grudgingly. "So I suppose that going by the letter of the regulations, you were acting within your rights. But," he poked a finger at me, "you're violating the spirit of the regulations, and well you know it. Still, I don't suppose it would hurt for me to examine this evidence."

I nodded my appreciation of the wisdom of his decision, but he was not through.

"However," he glared at me as he spoke, I suppose thinking he looked quite fierce, but it took more than a Norbanus to scare me. "If I find that the evidence is not quite compelling, you and I are going to have some trouble. Do I make myself clear?"

"Absolutely, sir."

"I can see why Augustus warned me about you," he said, almost to himself.

"Augustus?" I had not heard that term before. He looked at me sharply, then seemed to realize that we had been in the hinterlands of Greece for the last few months.

"Oh yes, I suppose you wouldn't have heard. The Senate, in recognition and appreciation for all that Caesar has done, has awarded him the title of Augustus. That's how he's to be known in all official documents, monuments, and so forth from now on."

"I see," was all I could think to say, for while I would refer to him publicly by whatever name or title he deemed appropriate, to my inner self he would always be Octavian.

Even now, in these words that Diocles has been laboriously scribbling while I talk, I will continue to refer to him in the manner in which I first met him, with all the bravery of a man who is no longer important enough for it to matter.

"It was the least the Senate could do," Norbanus went on, interrupting my thoughts. "Especially after he relinquished all of his power back to the Senate and people."

I was sure that I had not heard correctly, and he evidently saw my surprise. He gave another of his barks.

"Yes, I suppose if you didn't know of Augustus, you wouldn't know about that either. Well, I don't have time to tell you of all that has occurred in Rome. I suggest you find someone to let you in on all that's happened. That is all."

I saluted, and walked out the door, my head spinning with all that Norbanus had just told me. I had to find someone who knew what was going on, as quickly as I could.

"Yes, he is now Augustus. And yes, he called a meeting of the Senate where he relinquished all authority and returned it back to the Senate and people of Rome," Cornelius confirmed after coming to my quarters at my request. I sat sipping my wine while he talked, my mind racing, trying to determine what was really going on. I may not have known Octavian that well, but I knew him well enough to understand that there was more to what was going on than just a simple transfer of power. It was the year of his seventh Consulship

411

and Agrippa was his colleague again. Octavian was now thirty-six, while I was about to turn fifty-one, and he had spent every year since his nineteenth trying to first gain, then consolidate his power and control over Rome. Now, he was just giving it up? I could not see that happening, and I shook my head at Cornelius.

"I'm not buying it," I said flatly. "There has to be more to it than that. I just don't see him giving up everything he's worked for almost half his life."

Cornelius' face gave away none of his thoughts, his tone very careful as he continued.

"He still retains a great deal of *autoritas*. After he made his announcement to the Senate, there was a great uproar by the assembly, as I'm sure you can imagine."

I very well could, sure that the sleek, well-fed members of the Senate had the same thoughts running through their head that ran through mine. Octavian represented security and most importantly stability; his stepping down would seem to threaten that, which was not good for anybody.

"The members of the Senate prevailed upon Octavian to accept the Praetorship of the provinces of Hispania, Gaul, and Syria, for a period of ten years. With Proconsular authority, of course," Cornelius added, unnecessarily in my opinion, since I could not imagine that Octavian would take a Praetor's post without having the ability to select Legates to rule on his behalf.

Simply put, he could not be in three places at once. Cornelius went on to describe some of the other honors that the Senate conferred on Octavian. The doorway of his villa on the Palatine was decorated with laurel and oak in recognition of his *ob cives servatos*, the saving of the lives of Roman citizens, presumably by his actions in salvaging the Republic from the chaos of civil war. It was on this occasion that he was also given the *cognomen* Augustus, despite insisting that he continued to be referred to as *Princeps*. Finally, a golden shield, in the shape of a shield of the Legions, was erected in the Senate house, this monument in recognition of his valor, such as it was. Octavian is no coward, but martial ardor is not high on the list of his qualities. His courage is not primarily physical, yet I cannot say that he is not courageous; for a boy of nineteen years old to lay claim to all that Caesar had left him, in the face of men as formidable as Marcus Antonius, takes a tremendous amount of courage, along with a hard lump of iron in the soul. I thanked Cornelius for taking the time to inform me of these interesting developments, then sent him on his way. There was only one thing left to do, trying to determine what this all meant, and there was only one man I would trust to be able to tell me exactly.

"I admit that it's puzzling, but I don't think that Octavian has really changed things that much," Scribonius said, sitting in the same spot that Cornelius had been a short time before.

We were sipping wine, Scribonius still carrying the *vitus* as acting Primus Pilus of the 13th but finished with his day's duties. Before we started discussing this latest development from Rome, we had gone over one last time the list of candidates from the Centurions of the 13th for the new Primus Pilus that we would present to Norbanus, despite having no assurance that Norbanus would take our recommendations. There was also the business of getting rid of the dead wood from the Centurionate and the Optionate of the 13th, but somewhat to my surprise, that list was fairly short, or so Scribonius insisted. Putting that aside for the moment, I listened while Scribonius thought through all that I had told him. After his initial statement, he sat staring reflectively into his cup, his frown firmly in place. Finally, his face came alight, and he looked at me with a smile that told me he thought he had unraveled the mystery of Octavian's decision.

"There's an army in each of these provinces, correct?"

I thought for a moment, then nodded. Under his reorganization, Octavian had fixed the sites for garrisons all about the Republic, and it was true that each of these provinces had a garrison in it.

"True, but that's not the entire army," I pointed out. "There are more armies that he doesn't have control over."

"Yes and no," Scribonius replied. "He doesn't have physical control perhaps, but do you doubt that any of the Legates in command are not Octavian's men? Like Norbanus," he pointed out. "He's Octavian's to the death, as are the other Legates, I'll wager. So what has he given up, really? Besides, there are twenty Legions under the control of one man, while even if the Legates in the provinces not under his control decide to make mischief, they'd be heavily outnumbered. Whoever controls the bulk of the army controls Rome."

"True," I granted, seeing the truth in what Scribonius was saying the instant it came out of his mouth.

"And you can bet that the Senate knows it as well. Oh, some ambitious men may hold secret meetings and mutter about taking some sort of action to seize power, but it won't go any farther than that."

I hoped he was right, though I was not so sure. I should have had more faith in Octavian's ability to know what was going on in men's minds and taking steps to stop any threat to his power before it really had a chance to get started. Marcus Crassus was a prime example of what would happen to a man who overstepped as far as Octavian was concerned.

"So for all his protests to the contrary, Octavian hasn't given up a thing, and I feel sorry for any man who forgets that. Now we'll see what he does next, whether he actually leaves Rome and lets things settle down, or if he stays put and keeps an eye on the Senate," my friend concluded.

"What do you think he'll do?" I asked.

"If I were him, I would make myself scarce." Scribonius did not hesitate. "If he stays around, it will show even the thickest Senator what a sham his stepping down is. No, he almost has to leave Rome to make his plan work."

"Yes, I can see that," I said slowly, continuing to digest the conversation. I had a sudden thought because for the first time, what Octavian was doing made some sort of sense to me.

"He's not doing anything that hasn't been done before," I said. "So he can safely say that he's upholding the traditions of Rome as it was. And by giving up, or seeming to give up his power, he protects himself from the charge that he's trying to finish what his adopted father started by taking Rome back to being ruled by a king."

Scribonius was clearly pleased that I had worked this out for myself.

"Exactly, but the reality is that he gives up nothing. He still has Proconsular power, and he's still the senior Consul for the year. Most importantly, he keeps the power of the army to himself. Make no mistake, Titus. Octavian is a king in everything but name."

Despite the fact that we were alone, I still found myself glancing over my shoulder. Accusing a man of aspirations to be a king is an extremely dangerous thing in Roman society; one only had to look at what happened to Caesar to understand that.

"So what does that mean for us?" I asked suddenly.

Scribonius considered for a moment.

"I don't think it changes much." He shrugged. "We'll still march where we're told, kill who we're supposed to, and Rome will go on. And that's what's important, isn't it?"

"That it is," I agreed, lifting my cup in a toast to that sentiment. "Octavian needs the army more than ever because it ensures his status, so he's unlikely to do more to us than he already has, at least in the short term. Farther down the road, who knows?"

Now that I had an idea of what was happening, I felt better and was ready to enjoy our return to Siscia, so I summoned Diocles.

"I know it's short notice, but I want to have a dinner tonight with Gaius and Iras."

I expected that Diocles would not be happy that I was putting this on him, but he just gave me a smile.

"I expected that, and we're already making preparations and I sent Agis to invite the young couple. They'll be here shortly after sundown."

I barely had time to get to the baths for a good cleaning, scraping, and changing into a clean tunic before my guests arrived, and I must say that I was looking forward to seeing

415

my nephew. Scribonius was of course invited, and I even allowed Agis to sit at the table as well, telling Diocles to bring Egina, who had been waiting for him in Siscia while we had been on the march, or at least so I thought.

"She ran off with a wine merchant from Pamphylia, or at least so I was told," Diocles said, though he did not seem all that upset about it. I did not pry, but I admit I was curious about the story.

When I entered the dining area to count the table, I saw that there was one extra setting, and when I looked over at Diocles with a questioning glance, he said nothing, but I knew immediately who it was for, and I felt tears stinging my eyes, understanding that it was for Balbus. I shook the depression off, refusing to allow myself to go back to that place I had been in the time after Balbus' death. When Scribonius arrived, also cleaned up, and saw the empty place, he had the same reaction. We looked at each other, sharing our sadness without saying a word. Our momentary bout of self-pity was interrupted by the sound of knocking at the door, and I heard Diocles open it, followed by the sounds of enthusiastic greetings. Despite my sadness, I felt a smile creasing my face, turning to the entrance just in time to see Gaius enter the room, followed by Iras, looking radiant in a yellow gown, her face suffused with that glow that seems to come to women with being pregnant. Seeing her looking so happy caused yet another pang of sorrow from remembering other women in my life who had that same glow, shaking it off as I crossed the room to embrace first Gaius, then Iras.

"You didn't waste any time did you?" I teased him as we embraced.

"I don't want to crush you since you're pregnant," I told her, while she blushed prettily. So did Gaius, who looked on, beaming with a mixture of pride and embarrassment.

"Who's the extra chair for? Are we expecting someone else?" Iras asked.

"It's for Balbus," Scribonius answered quietly. "Since he'll always be with us, he'll always have a place at the table."

When Scribonius was finished, there was a long silence, each of us lost in our own thoughts.

I finally looked up to see Gaius sitting there with a look on his face that I could not identify, yet somehow knew did not bode well. Our eyes met, and he swallowed hard before speaking.

"There's no easy way to say this, Uncle. But I'm afraid I have some bad news."

It felt like my blood froze in my body, and my first thought was that it concerned Gaius' mother, my sister Valeria. My face must have reflected that, because he said hastily, "No, it's not about my mother. She's fine. In fact, she wants to know why you don't write more often." He gave a weak smile before he continued. "But it is about home. It concerns Vibius Domitius. I'm sorry to tell you this Uncle, but Vibius is dead."

Despite my relief that Valeria was in good health, it was a short-lived feeling as I absorbed what Gaius had just said. I sat back, the queerest feeling I have ever experienced flooding my senses. Vibius Domitius, my boyhood friend, our bond first formed when I had rescued him from having his head dipped into a bucket of *cac*, was dead.

"How did it happen?" I heard Scribonius ask.

It took a moment for me to remember that Scribonius and Vibius had been good friends, and had maintained that friendship long after Vibius and I had our falling out.

"My mother wasn't sure of the details, but apparently he had some sort of apoplectic fit at his tavern and just keeled over dead," Gaius explained.

I do not know why, yet I found that funny, and I gave a chuckle, causing some surprised looks around the table.

"Probably someone tried to leave without paying," I said, looking over to Scribonius, who was staring at me with disapproval. "You know how mad he'd get about being cheated."

Scribonius' frown melted and he gave a soft laugh.

"That's true. He would certainly get worked up."

417

"You remember the time he thought Achilles had filched some of his vinegar when we were *tiros*?" I asked Scribonius, my mind transported back to the days when we had been the closest of friends, close comrades in every sense of the term, and sure that nothing would ever change that.

Scribonius threw his head back, laughing again, this one from the belly as he went back with me through the years.

"By the gods, I thought it would take every one of us to hold him down," he said. "All for a bottle of vinegar."

"It's not the vinegar, it's the *principle*," I shouted, mimicking the words that Vibius had continuously shouted while he had struggled to get free to continue going after Spurius Didius, who we had nicknamed Achilles for the time he had stepped on a rusty nail during our first battle, taking himself out of the fight.

Scribonius and I were now roaring with laughter, tears streaming down our face. Despite the others joining in, I think it was more at the sight of the two of us than the humor. With the others listening, Scribonius and I told stories about our old friend, and for the first time in years, I completely forgot the rancor of our falling out, when I had threatened to strike him down for his part in the mutiny against Caesar after Pharsalus. Instead, I remembered only the good times, or the times when we had shared hardship and dangers, and for the first time ever, I related the story of our first visit back home, when I had killed one of Vibius' tormentors from the day he and I first met. Marcus was still a bully, with a gang of other youths that always seem to follow the boy with the biggest mouth. They had been terrorizing Astigi while Vibius and I had been on our first campaign in northern Hispania against the Lusitani and Gallaeci. When we had come home to visit, they had been in their usual spot loitering about the forum, looking for trouble. Unfortunately for them, Marcus and his friend Aulus had chosen to make some sort of slighting comment within our earshot. Vibius and I confronted them, and Marcus made the mistake of trying to draw a dagger, but neither Vibius nor I were raw youths anymore. We had become battle-hardened men, Legionaries of Rome, so in the time it takes to blink an eye, I had pinned Marcus to the wall with a thrust of my sword through the mouth. We escaped getting in trouble, partially because Marcus and his gang were known troublemakers, and it is very hard to punish Legionaries for crimes against civilians, even if they were citizens. However, the man who served as the unofficial provost of Astigi, a veteran himself, made it clear to us that we needed to go back to the army as quickly as possible. The dinner passed in this manner until, seeing that our guests were tiring of hearing old men reminisce, I changed the subject to Gaius' visit to Rome.

"Was it everything you thought it would be?"

Gaius' eyes widened at the memory of all that he had seen and he grew animated talking about his first visit to the city from which all Romans claim their heritage.

"It was more than I ever imagined," he enthused. "I've never seen so many people crammed into one place, from all over the world!"

I smiled indulgently, remembering my own trip to Rome for the first time, where I had much the same reaction. While Gaius described the sights, Scribonius and I exchanged glances with raised eyebrows. Once Gaius paused to take a breath, Scribonius commented, "It sounds like things have changed a bit."

"Oh yes, Caesar, er, I mean, Augustus has commissioned a great number of new public works. Most of them weren't completed when we left, but it's going to be spectacular when he is finished."

"I didn't realize that you were so enamored of Augustus." Scribonius seemed to read my mind, because I had been thinking the same thing, and Gaius' face flushed.

"I'm not," he said defensively. "But you must admit that he's done a lot for Rome. And if you saw all the work going on in the city, you'd be forced to agree."

"I don't doubt that he's doing all the things you say," I put in. "But I'd caution you against putting too much into the reasons why he's doing what he's doing. The upper classes say a lot of things about helping the people of Rome, but at the heart of it, they're only doing what helps them advance their own interests."

"I know that," Gaius replied. "But if their interests result in new baths, or a new hippodrome, or new aqueducts for the people to get water, I don't really care."

"It's hard to argue with that," Scribonius said wryly, giving me a warning look that I should drop the line of questioning.

"Did you attend the games?" I asked, tacitly accepting Scribonius' warning.

"Of course." Gaius grinned. "Every day that I could. I got to see Victor fight. He's the best I've ever seen."

"For a gladiator maybe," I scoffed. I did not then, nor do I now, think highly of gladiators, particularly after my fight with Prixus.

"Still," Gaius insisted, "he's very good and he puts on a good show."

"I suppose," was all I would say, a bit grumpily, I admit. This conversation seemed to be bound to head into dangerous topics, so I decided to steer it to a safe course that could not possibly cause any friction. Pointing to Iras and her growing belly, I asked, "And how did that happen?"

"How do you think?" Iras retorted tartly, causing a laugh around the table. Now it was my turn to feel the heat rising to my face.

"You know what I mean," I shot back. "Like Scribonius said, you didn't waste any time."

Gaius gave an elaborate shrug, trying to show that he was not concerned, but I saw through it immediately.

"She got pregnant as soon as I got back," he said a bit too casually.

I did the mental calculations in my head, and while I am no expert on childbirth, Iras looked much farther along than the three months Gaius had been back from Rome. I said nothing, yet I could see the worry in his eyes as we exchanged a glance. For her part, Iras looked anything but worried at the possible problem with the timing of her pregnancy. However,

420

I knew what a good actress she was, so I did not put much faith in her seeming innocence.

I believe that Iras was as eager to change the subject as I was, because she pointed to my rawhide harness covering the stump of my little finger and asked, "How did that happen?"

Quite frankly, I had forgotten about my finger, having become accustomed to the feeling of the harness, the stump now well healed and toughened. I glanced down at it, and I could feel Scribonius' eyes on me, making me feel acutely uncomfortable. Although he had guessed the real cause of the injuries I had sustained, I had never acknowledged that he was correct in his assumption. I suppose that there were forces at work that night that convinced me that it was time to clear the air between us of this last mystery. Maybe it was learning of Vibius' death, reminding me that our time on this earth is limited, and none of us know when our end will come. Perhaps it was the presence of a new life at the table, reminding me of all that I had lost. Whatever the cause, I proceeded to tell the story of Prixus and how he came to meet his end by my hand in a darkened room. I left nothing out; I started with our first clash, and I talked about how Egina had been the unwitting cause and excuse for our final confrontation. Without thinking about it, and because it seemed a natural part of the story, I told the tale of how I had found Egina sharing Diocles' bed. This part of my tale did serve to lighten the mood, everyone around the table laughing about it, with one notable exception, and I became acutely aware of someone glaring daggers at me from his spot at the far end of the table. It seemed that no matter what topic I selected, it was fraught with hidden dangers, and it did not take me long to announce that I was extremely tired from my journey, which was true enough, even if it was not the real reason for calling an end to the evening. We said our goodbyes, with Scribonius and me agreeing to meet the next day to finalize our plans to present Norbanus with our candidates for Primus Pilus of the 13th. Once everyone had left, I was alone with my thoughts, and I found myself thinking about a short, bandy-legged boy who I had never imagined would be anything but my best friend for the rest of my life.

Somewhat to our surprise, Norbanus accepted our recommendations for Primus Pilus, but as I was to learn, his gruff exterior and biting remarks were more of an act than representative of the real man. Once we worked together longer, my initial impression of Norbanus changed, and I grew to respect him, while I believe he felt the same. After much discussion between Scribonius and me, we decided to select three candidates from inside the 13th Legion, along with one each from the 8th and the 14th, men who had come highly recommended from their own Primi Pili. The Centurion from the 8th came from the First Cohort, and I had seen enough of him in action when it had been just the 8th with Marcus Crassus to approve of Macrinus' judgment that the man was ready for the duty of Primus Pilus. Not surprisingly, Festus was not one of the men from the 13th we considered, although he was not as much of an incompetent or crook as I assumed, knowing that Natalis had handpicked him. He was just not bright enough to run anything more than a Century, and truthfully, he should not have been in the First Cohort to begin with, but his performance was satisfactory enough that we had no real reason to remove him. We had made a number of moves within the Legion, while persuading four of the worst cases that it was time to retire and take their pensions, along with the money they had in their Legion accounts, even though we knew that it was most likely ill gotten. This was not an easy decision to make, since it rubbed both Scribonius and me the wrong way to let men essentially get away with robbery and keep the money, yet neither of us relished the idea of having to go through the spectacle of formally charging these men, because it would subject my removal of Natalis to deeper scrutiny. After our initial meeting, Norbanus had reviewed the case evidence that Scribonius had gathered, and we had a meeting where he abruptly announced that the evidence was indeed overwhelming and that he agreed with my decision to remove Natalis. That was the last mention of it, and I did not want to stir things back up again. Accordingly, we told each of the four men that in exchange for their agreement to retire quietly, we would allow them to take their money with them. Only one of them balked at this, but after a quiet visit to his quarters one night, he decided the next morning to accept our generous offer. In many ways, these men were the easiest to deal with because they were straightforward matters; get rid of them, out of the Legion and out of the army. However, there were three men that Scribonius and I agreed were damaged beyond any hope of redemption who were young enough that they were still on their first enlistment, with more than a year left to serve. If it had been a year or less, there were ways that we could have finessed the situation, keeping them on the rolls for the remainder of their time while removing them from actual physical command. Of course, it was impossible to perpetrate that fiction for more than just a few months before someone higher up was bound to notice, meaning this approach was not viable for us. With these men, there was nothing for it but a Tribunal, presenting the same problem that we had with the older men. Scribonius and I discussed at length our options, until we finally arrived at only one conclusion. These men had to disappear, but on their own. I for one was not willing to shed more blood; there was enough of it on my hands for several men's lifetimes, and I knew Scribonius agreed. The trick would be to convince these men that it was in their best interests to disappear quietly, leaving the Legion before they were publicly punished and humiliated. I decided that it was time to pay a visit to Tribune Claudius.

"I know that when you found out what Natalis was up to, you insisted on being cut in on the money." I went on the attack immediately after Claudius had arrived in my quarters.

He had been smiling when he arrived, a sign of our improved relationship, but it froze on his face as he stared at me. I saw his body stiffen for a moment, but I held him in my gaze for several heartbeats. Finally, his shoulders slumped, all the fight instantly draining from his body. He looked at the floor, the misery plain on his face, yet I had no wish to humiliate the Tribune.

"Please take a seat, Claudius," I said quietly.

A look of surprise flickered across his face, but he sat obediently in the chair that I had indicated.

"I didn't call you here to chastise you or threaten you with punishment in any way," I told Claudius. I heard him exhale in clear relief as I continued.

"I can't change what happened, and frankly I don't think it would serve the army or Rome any good in seeing that you were punished. The scheme wasn't your idea, and your involvement was more a matter of opportunity than design."

Before he had the chance to think he had gotten away completely free, I hardened my voice.

"But we have a huge mess on our hands, and you do owe the men of the 13th. I'm giving you the opportunity to help me clean it up. If you do that, then your secret is safe and will go with me to the afterlife."

Claudius' expression hardened, and I could see that he did not like the implied threat. However, after a moment he took a deep breath then nodded again.

"I agree," he said quietly. "What do you need me to do?"

I outlined the plan that Scribonius and I had come up with. He listened thoughtfully, then said, "When do you want me to do it?"

Once we were finished, I called for Scribonius to tell him that Claudius had agreed. Now all we had to do was wait for Claudius to do his part.

I have said many times, there are no secrets in the army. There are ears everywhere, always listening for any piece of information that will give the men a hint of what lies in store for them. We were counting on this when we told Claudius to have a conversation with Cornelius, who we had already informed of what was happening. They were in the *Praetorium*, the absolute best place to have a secret relayed to the rest of the army, where Claudius was telling Cornelius of an upcoming Tribunal of three Centurions.

424

"There's no doubt of their guilt," he told Cornelius. "So I need your vote of *condemno* to make an example of these men. They've been bleeding their Centuries dry for quite some time. As far as I'm concerned, they deserve to be flogged with the scourge and if they're still alive, crucified afterward."

"I don't know," Cornelius said doubtfully, but he was simply mouthing what we had told him to say. We knew that if Cornelius readily agreed to such a harsh punishment, this would arouse suspicions that there was something contrived going on. Our only concern was if Cornelius could be convincing essentially playing a role. "That sounds excessive to me."

"Do I need to remind you that you owe me, Cornelius?" Claudius asked stiffly, again part of the words we had instructed him to say.

"No, you don't need to," Cornelius said loudly enough for the clerks to hear.

"Good, then I can count on you?" Claudius insisted.

Cornelius assured him that he could, promising the vote of *condemno* on the behalf of another Tribune who by common knowledge was a close friend of Cornelius. Three votes would be enough to ensure the punishment would be carried out. Once the seed was planted, the two Tribunes parted. It was only a matter of three or four days before the Centurions who Claudius had named in his conversation to Cornelius decided to absent themselves during the night, two of them on one night, the other on the next. I was called to the *Praetorium* the day after the third Centurion disappeared to face Norbanus.

"We have a disturbing development in the 13th," he said abruptly, without waiting for any pleasantries to be exchanged. Despite knowing exactly what he was talking about, I played the game.

"Oh? And what is that, General?" I asked, keeping my face neutral.

Norbanus glared up at me through his shaggy eyebrows.

"As if you didn't know," he snorted, but he did not press the issue. Pointing to the tablet before him on his desk, he

425

continued, "We've had three desertions from the 13th Legion in the last two days."

I raised my own eyebrows in mock surprise, trying to make it seem as if I was genuine.

"Really? That is somewhat surprising. I thought Scribonius had done a good job of turning the Legion around."

"Oh, stop with the pretense," Norbanus snapped. "You know very well what I'm talking about. We've had three Centurions desert in the last two days. I can't remember that ever happening before, can you?"

"No," I was forced to admit. "But I can't say that it's altogether surprising. Natalis made some very poor choices in Centurions during his time."

He brushed aside my defense with an impatient wave.

"Be that as it may, do you realize how badly this reflects on me, to have Centurions deserting from the army? What will Augustus think?"

Before I could answer, he continued, his words tumbling from his mouth and it was clear that he was truly concerned about what Octavian thought.

"I'll tell you what he'll think. He'll hear of this and think that I'm such a tyrant that even the Centurions are deserting! I can't have him thinking that, do you understand me?"

There was a desperate quality to his voice that told me that he was truly concerned about this, so I hurried to calm him.

"General, I'm sure that it won't come to that," I spoke to him in the same soothing tone I used when Ocelus was spooked.

"Oh? How can you be so sure?" he demanded.

"Because Rome is far away, and as many things as Augustus has on his mind, I'm sure that three Centurions deserting won't be enough to draw his attention." I paused for a moment. "As long as their desertions are spread out enough in the Legion diary, that is."

Norbanus stared at me for a long moment before he asked, "What do you mean?"

426

"I think you know what I mean." I was not willing to be this coy with Norbanus.

I needed him to agree to this ruse immediately, because he was correct. If I had stopped to think about it, I might have recognized how strange it would seem that we were talking about Octavian and his reaction, despite the fact that he had supposedly relinquished his power to the Senate. However, both Norbanus and I knew the fiction of his announcement to the Senate, making it no surprise that he was concerned.

"I understand that Caesar, I mean, Augustus," I had to make an effort to correct myself, "is extremely involved with the affairs of the army, but not even he can carefully read every single Legion's diary and try to determine whether or not things are as they appear. If the Legion diary records that a Centurion deserted this week, then another one in a couple of weeks and the last in a month, Augustus won't be able to determine whether this is accurate or not."

"So you're suggesting that we lie in an official document?"

Oh, Norbanus was cagey, I must give him that, but I had been playing this game just as long as Norbanus, and I had been taught by some of the best men in the history of Rome. In answer, I gave an elaborate shrug.

"General, it makes no difference to me one way or the other. I'm not in overall command here. I'm simply offering a way whereby you can avoid the scrutiny of Augustus, and we both know that these men deserting are the best thing in the long run for the 13th and the army as a whole."

Norbanus continued to glare at me, yet there was a subtle change in his expression that I was just beginning to learn to read.

He said nothing, fiddling with his stylus for several moments before he said, "Very well. What you say makes sense, as much as it pains me to do something so underhanded. But I suppose it can't be helped."

"Not if you don't want Augustus asking a lot of questions."

"No," he sighed. "We don't want that. It would serve no purpose and alarm Augustus unduly. I know that we're making the right decisions with the army and the 13th, so I'll do as you suggest. But," he pointed a finger at me in warning, "if this turns out to be a mistake, I'll drop you in the *cac* to keep me company, Prefect. I'll tell Augustus that it was your idea to make these fraudulent entries in the diary."

I cannot say I was surprised, but I did not like it. However, I bit my tongue, simply giving a curt nod at his warning. With our business concluded, I left the *Praetorium* to return to my quarters, content that we had finished with our work in setting the 13th right again.

I suppose that with the affairs of the 13th settled, this is as good a place to stop as any, as I have grown very, very tired. There is just one more part to my story, one last chapter of my life that must be told, not just to finish my own tale, but to honor those men who are as much a part of it as I am. It concerns my last campaign, and the greatest threat, not just to my career but to my life that I ever faced, in one full of narrow escapes and brushes with death. But before I can do it justice, I need to pause and refresh myself, and I have an old friend, waiting for me in the stable attached to my villa, ready to try to jump at least one more fence or ditch. Because while I may be old, and not the man I was, I am still Titus Pullus, Legionary of Rome, and I have some life in me yet.

Printed in Great Britain
by Amazon